THE STARS ARE OURS
PART 1 - EMERGENCE
BOOK THREE OF THE CELESTRIAD

Marise Morland

THE STARS ARE OURS
PART 1 - EMERGENCE
BOOK THREE OF THE CELESTRIAD

DOUBLE DRAGON

Also by the author

**The Celestriad Book One – The Songs of
Symerid Three**

The Celestriad Book Two – The Synectic Snare

Prologue

On a warm afternoon in late spring, the city of Alda Mexa basked peacefully in the sun. The Lyricon was all but deserted, many people having decamped to Lake Holpen or the Tyvian Gardens; but on the stage, three small children were performing an impromptu play. Laura and Nefyrra, seated nearby, looked on indulgently as the action proceeded.

The play had been Clemis' idea. Her method of improvisation - since her telepathic abilities were not yet reliable - was to whisper lines to her fellow actors, who would then say them aloud. Nefyrra's son Trevone, placid and obliging, followed these instructions to the letter. Kalyx, half a year older, tended to be less amenable, as befitted the son of First Citizen Tralvar.

Clemis, all blonde hair and dimples, continued her story - or rather, Laura's. Her little dramas were invariably centred around her adoptive mother. Laura wasn't too happy about the fascination her life held for Clemis, but there wasn't a lot she could do about it.

"At least they've quietened down a bit," Nefyrra remarked.

"Thank goodness," answered Laura with a wry grin. The previous act - Idenion rescuing Laura from a murderous Alendis - had consisted of screaming and little else.

"While we're on Earth I shall practice my singing," announced Clemis, in character.

"Mmm...oooh...aaah...eee." She copied Laura's facial exercises perfectly, but her attempt to sing was little more than a croak. She hadn't yet learnt to be embarrassed about the vocal dysfunction which afflicted her entire race.

"While I'm on Earth," said Trevone after a hasty prompt, "I shall talk to the animals and find a girl to take sciesha with."

Nefyrra chuckled; Laura frowned. Was nothing in her past safe from her daughter?

"Now, Kalyx, er, Tralvar," said Clemis importantly, "you're sad because Laura's gone, and you couldn't record her voice." She whispered in his ear and Kalyx looked furious.

"I'm not saying that! My father's experiments don't fail."

"This one did."

"Didn't."

"Did."

"Didn't."

"Did. Laura, you tell him."

"Sorry, little one. I'm keeping out of this."

From the custodian's apartment, far above the terraces but well within range of the Lyricon's acoustics, Tralvar surveyed the proceedings and sighed. "See what I mean, Idenion? Whenever my son and your daughter meet it ends in a sparring match."

"Just like you and Laura of old," Idenion said lightly.

"Ninfi wanted my advice," Tralvar went on. "She says the boy's a poor scholar. Can I help it if he was born with my good looks and her intellect?"

Idenion hid a smile at Tralvar's caustic humour. "Well, Ninfi's certainly to blame for this falling out. Kalyx has absorbed her idealised view of you."

"Then I suppose I'd better enlighten him," Tralvar said. "Screen your perception. I think I can reach him from here but it'll be uncomfortable at close quarters."

"I'll warn Dena and our guest." Idenion retreated from the balcony, leaving Tralvar to direct his thoughts at the distant stage.

+Kalyx! Be quiet and listen to your father+

Awed, Kalyx paused in his tirade and peered upward. +Yes, First Citizen?+

+No need to be so formal. Tralvar will do+

+Yes, Tralvar?+

+That's better. I want you to apologise to Clemis, because she's quite right. My early attempts to record sound were unsuccessful+

"See?" shrilled Clemis triumphantly, hands on hips.

"I don't care," retorted Kalyx. "It's a stupid play anyway. I want to go home."

"Don't sulk, little brother," admonished Nefyrra. "Clemis invited you to join her game, so the least you can do is be polite to her."

"I'll speak the line, Clemis!" piped Trevone, ever the peacemaker.

"Go on then," said Clemis dubiously.

"My experiment has failed!" Trevone announced with a broad smile.

"That's not right," objected Clemis. "You've spoilt it." Her lip began to tremble. "You've both spoilt it."

9

"Oh, don't cry!" said Kalyx irritably, worried that Tralvar would be angry with him. "I'll say whatever you want. Just stop crying, will you?" Then, in a surprisingly resonant stage voice: "My experiments have failed. Why should I try again now Laura has gone and the voices of my people are silent? What is music without song? What shall I do, what shall I do?" And he wept so convincingly that Laura nearly ran across to comfort him.

"She'll come back, Kalyx," said Trevone anxiously.

Tralvar, about to quit the balcony, witnessed the little soliloquy in some surprise. "Well, what do you know?" he murmured. "Ninfi, I think our son's just found his vocation!"

Laura was similarly impressed. It was a remarkable piece of acting from a boy of seven.

"He's only four," Nefyrra pointed out.

"Sorry. I'm still converting their ages into Earth years," Laura confessed. "It's the only way I can keep track of their development. Trevone and Clemis are three and a half, but on Earth that's a pre-school age. It's easier to think of them as six. But on the other hand, I'd rather be twenty-one than thirty-five!"

Clemis stood at centre stage, pouting. She wasn't sure what Kalyx had done, but she did know she was no longer the centre of attention. She was supposed to rush in at this point and present him, or rather Tralvar, with the solution to his problem; a gramograph or graphophone or whatever it was called. But if he was going to show off, she wasn't about to encourage him. The decision was taken out of her hands when a voice behind her suddenly said:

"Hello! What's all this then?"

Kalyx bounded toward the newcomer. "Uncle Lydion!" he yelled delightedly.

Lydion embraced his nephew warmly and ruffled his hair. "I didn't expect to see you here, young man!"

"I'm going to be an actor," Kalyx announced. "I just played Tralvar. You missed it."

"I'm really sorry," said Lydion with sincerity. "How about a repeat performance? You could pretend to be me this time."

Nefyrra glared.

"On second thoughts," he amended, "perhaps you're a bit young for that."

"Lydion!" Clemis, determined not to be left out, tugged at his sleeve.

"Hey, it's my best girl!" Lydion swept Clemis off her feet and whirled her round in mid-air. She shrieked with excitement.

"Lydion, put her down," Laura said crossly. "You'll get her all wound up and she won't want to sleep."

Lydion obeyed with exaggerated care. "Anything to please you, First Singer. And now, might I ask why you and these delightful children are here? Not planning a concert, surely, with half the scolia on a sabbatical?"

"Tralvar's decided to step down as First Citizen," Laura explained.

"Ah. And how does Idenion feel about taking over? Nervous?"

"He's as ready as he'll ever be. He wants to hold the inaugural ceremony here rather than the akron, so the pair of them are upstairs sorting it out. It was Kalyx's day to visit, so Dena brought him too."

"I didn't think they'd be as long as this," said Nefyrra with a glance toward the apartments. "I'm thirsty."

"Then why don't you and Laura go and join the meeting?" Lydion asked. "I'll keep these urchins company for a while. Tell them a story maybe."

The urchins chorused their approval.

"Just don't give them nightmares," Nefyrra warned.

When they reached the mezzanine stairway Laura looked back, perturbed by the unnatural hush. Lydion was seated halfway up the first terrace, his voice inaudible save to his young audience. The children were rapt and silent.

"He's so fond of kids," Laura said softly. "Such a pity he doesn't have any of his own."

"It hasn't been for want of trying," Nefyrra observed coolly. "But yes, it is a shame."

Laura glanced back once more. The sun's rays, increasingly golden as evening approached, burnished the weathered stone and cast a benign haze about the distant group. For a moment she felt an inexplicable sadness.

"They're growing so fast," Nefyrra murmured.

But Laura's mind hadn't been on the children. She was thinking of Lydion - lively, goodnatured

Lydion, lover of women, brought low by his ill-considered romance with the elite-wife Tarlatine. When the Narvellans, a reluctant Tarlatine among them, had left for an unknown destination, Lydion had been inconsolable. Eventually he had bounced back - but not, many suspected, completely. Idenion's Golden Girl sequence of poems, sensitively documenting the sad tale, had become an overnight success. Most households in Alda Mexa had a copy. Asked to comment, Lydion would merely smile and reiterate: "Idenion tells it better than I do. I'll let his words speak for me." Which, since Lydion was a born raconteur, suggested to Laura that a line still had to be drawn under the affair.

"Father! There you are!" Nefyrra stepped out of the elevator into her living quarters, Laura at her heels. "What's been taking you so long?"

"I'm afraid I'm responsible for the delay, Custodian." A middle aged man rose to his feet apologetically.

"Guildmaster Lann! I thought you were in Tivenne."

"Tralvar invited me here to discuss his musical requirements," explained Lann.

"It's an important day," Dena put in. "We need a good musical director - and who better than Melor's successor?"

"There'll be plenty of music, but no poetry," Idenion added cheerfully. "Tralvar will disown me if so much as one rhyming couplet makes an appearance!"

"And it took you three ilden to decide that?" inquired Nefyrra.

"No, just a few astallen," said Tralvar, putting aside some paperwork he had been studying. "You probably don't realise it, Nefyrra, but Lann and I have a lot in common. I'm a scientist with designs on being a scolia master - not that I ever will be - and Lann's a scolia master with a natural aptitude for science."

"I've always wished I could follow both careers," Lann admitted. "When Tralvar sent for me, I took the opportunity to show him some of my work."

"This essay on particle physics is brilliant," enthused Tralvar, waving the sheaf of papers at his daughter. "It could have numerous applications. I'll have to study it in depth."

"What a strange coincidence," Nefyrra said, intrigued. "Three of my leading players have just begged time off to attend a maths symposium."

"And two of my dancers are obsessed with transposal theory," Dena added.

"Why do you think it strange?" asked Laura. "There's always been a strong link between music and mathematics. Not that I've any talent in that direction!"

Nefyrra handed round some iced drinks. "So when exactly is the big day, Idenion?"

"We still haven't decided. There are a few wrinkles to iron out first."

"Such as?"

"Oh, just details," said Idenion evasively. "Tralvar will explain." But Tralvar was once more in conversation with Lann, and Nefyrra's question went unanswered.

Presently the gathering broke up. Laura and Idenion returned to the akron with a tired and fractious Clemis; Tralvar and Dena headed for their villa on Lateral Three, which Tralvar still preferred to the akron itself; Nefyrra gave Trevone his supper, hoping that Jarras would be home in time to read to his son; and Lydion obligingly took Kalyx back to Ninfi's house in the textile quarter.

That evening, Tralvar couldn't relax. He wandered in and out of his study and generally fidgeted about, until Dena said:

"If it's worrying you that much, go and see her."

"What, now?"

"Why not? Clemis will be asleep and Idenion will be in the library."

Still Tralvar hesitated. "What if she says no?"

"Believe me, she won't," Dena assured him quietly.

It was just starting to rain as Tralvar made the short ascent to the akron, but the path took him straight to a side entrance, and within two astallen he was outside the first floor apartment where Laura and Idenion currently lived. He had once occupied these rooms himself, before the Narvellan coup.

As Dena had surmised, Idenion was immersed in his studies. Laura, however, was still in the nursery, soothing her tearful daughter back to sleep. Tralvar quietly sat down and waited, recognising - with a degree of sadness - the lullaby she sang. "Sleep, little one. Sleep, little star." She'd sung it to him once, after he'd nearly died at the hands of the Narvellans.

Eventually, the song having done its work, Laura emerged. She wasn't surprised to see him. "Remind me to give Lydion a clip round the ear," she said with the hint of a smile.

"What's he done this time?"

"Told our kids some horror story about a sea monster. Clemis dreamt it was under the bed."

"Lydion hasn't the sense he was born with," remarked Tralvar. He wasn't smiling.

Laura led the way back to the reception room and poured herself some wine. "Resnay?" she asked.

"Please. You know how Dena rations it."

She handed him a measure of the strong liquor. "And now, why are you here? Something to do with this afternoon?"

"Astute as always, Laura. Idenion asked me to speak to you about his forthcoming appointment. He didn't ask me to do it tonight, but it's too important to put off." He downed the resnay in one swallow, then continued: "Idenion says he can't handle the First Citizenship alone. He wants you to rule with him."

"As his partner in unity. Of course."

"As joint First Citizen, with all the authority vested in the title."

Laura stared. "But I'm not even Celestrian!"

"You'll do."

"But...." Laura twisted her hands together indecisively. "Is there a precedent for this? A husband and wife team in charge?"

16

"The last time was about four hundred years ago."

"Oh, well, that's all right then," said Laura with a nervous laugh. "I'm sorry, I don't mean to sound facetious. But I don't know how to answer you. I really don't."

Tralvar took her troubled hands in a firm, warm grip. "For what it's worth," he said, "I think this is the best decision that Idenion's ever made - which is why I volunteered to speak for him. Will you do it?"

She hesitated, then acquiesced. "I don't have much choice, do I? I always knew he'd need me at his side. Go ahead, make it official. With one proviso."

Tralvar released her with some reluctance. "Which is?"

"My full commitment mustn't start until Clemis is older. First and foremost, I'm a mother. I'm sure you understand."

"Of course." Tralvar's smile was tired but grateful. "I'll have the documents drawn up. We'll need to consult the histories..." Then he paused, startled.

"If Idenion's hiding behind the door, tell him he can come out now," Laura suggested.

"It isn't Idenion," Tralvar said slowly. "It's Jarras. He's on his way up, and he's in a panic."

Almost before he'd finished speaking, Jarras burst into the apartment.

"Shh!" Laura hissed angrily. "You'll wake Clemis."

"Your pardon, Laura, but this is an emergency." Jarras turned breathlessly to Tralvar. "I've a flitter waiting to take you to Communications. Axmiol's on the transposer. He says he doesn't have much time and insists on speaking to you and only you."

"Do any relayists know of this?"

"None: I followed your orders. No relayists, no radio. But Dena knows, of course. I went there first."

Laura looked from one to the other in bewilderment. "Orders? What orders? The Narvellans vowed they'd never contact us again!"

"I never quite believed that." Tralvar suddenly seemed to have aged. "Come with us, Laura. I'd value your presence."

"I can't leave Clemis."

"Idenion can look after her, can't he?"

"Tralvar, we don't have time for this!" Jarras protested.

"He's right," said Laura calmly. "Find out what Axmiol wants, then if you still need my advice, get it later. Though if the Narvellans are in trouble again, I don't see what they expect us to do about it."

"Do you think Axmiol needs our help?" inquired Tralvar as he and Jarras hurried downstairs.

"No," Jarras said reluctantly. "I think he wants to warn us about something."

It wasn't the answer Tralvar wanted. But it was the one he'd expected. It was now completely dark. Just as they landed at the spaceport the rain intensified; subdued thunder rumbled in the distance. The lift crawled toward the top of the communications tower and Tralvar swore at the delay.

"Chaos, this place needs an overhaul! If we've lost that signal - "

"We won't have," Jarras reassured him. "I've got it pegged through all three manifolds."

"Ingenious. I'm glad it was your shift."

"One astal more and it wouldn't have been. I was just about to hand everything over to Treva Control and go home."

"Is no one on duty tonight?" asked Tralvar, faintly scandalised.

"Discords, no! You're out of touch, Tralvar - we haven't done that in years. Treva's the only place to keep a continuous watch." Jarras stepped out of the elevator and went briskly to the transposer panel. "The link's holding. No visuals though. He's a long, long way off."

Tralvar sat down, clearing his throat. "All right, Axmiol, talk to me. What's happening?"

"Tralvar, at last. What took you so long? Now listen very carefully: time's running out and I may not be able to repeat this."

"Time's running out? What do you mean?" began Tralvar. "Where are you?"

"My co-ordinates are on the data stream. Please don't interrupt, First Citizen. I'll tell you everything you need to know." Axmiol sounded defeated, exhausted. Tralvar wondered how long he'd been calling before Jarras picked up the fragile transmission.

"Our landfall wasn't a success," the weary voice continued. "We had several crop failures and numerous deaths from an indigenous disease. By ballot we decided to relocate, and sent out scouting parties to find a more hospitable world. They found three possibles, but after one bad decision I was unwilling to give the casting vote. Sijek and I continued the search, venturing ever further from the existing colony.

"On one such trip we detected a stardrive signature. We immediately assumed it was one of our lost spheres and tracked it to an inhabited planet - the first humanoid civilisation we'd seen. The people were technologically advanced, with interplanetary travel, as evidenced by settlements throughout their solar system. Seeing no further trace of the sphere, we decided to make contact."

Tralvar bit back an angry cry.

"I know, Tralvar. You cautioned us - you told us never to do anything like that - and we didn't listen. My only concern was for our colonists."

"Did you find them?" Tralvar forced himself to be calm.

"No. They were long dead, their sphere dismantled and studied. What we'd seen was a prototype transposal drive without a system of navigation or communication: in short, without working crystals. When we appeared, the order went out to secure our crystals at all costs."

Tralvar listened numbly. This was worse, far worse than he'd imagined.

Axmiol detailed his plight in a few terse sentences. "We're the unwilling guests of the

Eldorian Empire, a military dictatorship. We were duped by a reception committee who really believed their government was offering us shelter and supplies. The double deception soon revealed itself but it was already too late to run. We were seized, ridiculed and imprisoned."

"How did you get out?" Tralvar heard himself ask.

Axmiol gave a dry chuckle. "Have you forgotten the power of the Narvellan mind? These people are nonconversants. Their minds are exposed and vulnerable. But I can only target individuals, and the Eldorians know my limits now."

Jarras gave Tralvar a nudge. "Ask him again what he means about lack of time."

Axmiol overheard. "Quite simply, Jarras, I'm cornered. I'm trapped in my spacecraft, which is underground and surrounded by armed men. A decryption team is working on the locking code. Sijek is still a prisoner.

"My escape was necessary for two reasons: to alert you, and to warn the colony. I've already spoken to Bydlor and told him to choose one of the shortlisted planets, move everyone without delay and torch everything when he leaves. A hasty solution, but it should serve. I carry no co-ordinates for the new worlds."

Tralvar regained some presence of mind. "What armaments do the Eldorians have?"

"Projectile weapons, beam weapons, bombs. No nuclear capability, though it's often talked about. They've just had a civil war, with no real victors. It keeps the arms industry buoyant." A muffled impact sounded in the background. Axmiol hesitated, then went on more rapidly: "The danger to you is more specific than you yet realise. The Eldorians gleaned significant intelligence from the crew of the first sphere. They know about the solar flares and our refugee status, and they've heard stories of a peaceful planet dispensing scientific knowledge. A planet called Celestra.

"They know we obtained our spheres from you and they intend to find you. Celestra's location was expunged from our databases long ago, but that will only delay them, not deter them."

"You cannot allow yourself to be taken alive, Axmiol." Tralvar's voice was clear and cold.

"I can't abandon Sijek."

"For pity's sake, Axmiol, think of us! You know so much about us. If you're recaptured they'll torture Sijek to get information out of *you*!"

"You wish me to take my own life?" Axmiol inquired without rancour.

"You must."

There was an agonised silence. "I won't do it, Tralvar," the Narvellan said at last. "Sijek is my lifebonded. He's terrified and he needs me."

"Then we're all dead," Tralvar declared.

"Before they break in," Axmiol went on as though he hadn't heard, "I'm going to do as much damage as I can, starting with this transposer. That's one piece of technology they shan't have yet. Prepare yourselves! With luck, you'll have years. Tralvar, Jarras, I'm sorry. I'm so very very sorry..."

"He's offline," said Jarras, powering down the array.

22

Tralvar leant his forehead on the console. He was perspiring and shivering at the same time. "Am I never to have any rest?" he muttered.

"I should get you home. You're ill."

"Nothing that a few shots of resnay won't cure." Tralvar straightened up with an effort. "What's the status of our deep space scanners?"

"Alda Mexa, Treva, Kest and Alcine are fully operational. Corayn and Ninka are out of service and we're having some trouble with the automated station on Alda Six."

"Then send someone to repair it. And I want all our bases continuously manned from now on. If anything larger than a pebble enters our solar system I want to hear about it."

"Aren't you forgetting something?" asked Jarras.

"What?"

"You won't be in charge. Laura and Idenion will."

"Oh, chaos!" Tralvar ran his fingers though his greying hair. "I'll have to let the inauguration go ahead or they'll assume I don't trust them."

"And do you?"

"I trust them to do their best, which isn't the same thing. Idenion has all the makings of a good peacetime ruler, but he'll be out of his depth in this situation. And Laura's life revolves around her little girl. I can stay in command long enough to set up the early warning system, but after that..." He shrugged.

"Tell me how I can help," said Jarras impulsively.

"Discords, Jarras, give me time to take this in!" Tralvar pushed himself to his feet. "I need a couple of days to outline some kind of strategy. At the moment, there's nothing constructive either of us can..." Then he paused, inspired. "On second thoughts, there *is* something. Tomorrow we'll go on a little trip to Tivenne. We've matters to discuss with Guildmaster Lann."

"What has the scolia to do with this?" Jarras asked, bewildered.

Tralvar didn't answer. He was gazing from the observation window into the rain-lashed night. "Do you believe in the cosmic balance?" he inquired unexpectedly.

Jarras was taken aback. "I suppose so."

"Our ancestors' directive was that no species should be given transposal if they hadn't found it for themselves. We thought we knew better and gave it to the Narvellans, who allowed it to be stolen. Result: a greedy and corrupt empire will soon have the freedom of the galaxy. It's a chain reaction, Jarras, and we're responsible."

"What can we do?" asked Jarras helplessly.

"Find a way to defeat them. I don't know how, or with what, but we must be ready for them when they get here." He glanced back at the silent transposer unit. "Axmiol thinks we'll have years. For all our sakes, I hope he's right."

24

Chapter One

"Did you have to take off in such a hurry?" grumbled Trevone. "I hadn't been given clearance. Anything could have been in our way."

"Relax," said Clemis lightly. "Obviously nothing was."

"And I knew it, but you're missing the point. There are rules to be followed and you ignored them. The Communications team's going to be quite disgusted with us."

"Why? For being quick off the mark?"

"For disregarding security. People still haven't recovered from that Eldorian scare."

"Then it's about time they did. It's been eight years."

"Tralvar thinks we're still at risk. So does Jarras. And between them they've kept all the monitoring stations on high alert. Any spacecraft behaving eccentrically is likely to set off alarms."

"What, going in *this* direction?" laughed Clemis. "Stop complaining and let's see if your invention really works."

"It will."

"In that case we're going to knock the stars out of previous acceleration records."

"It's not just speed that counts," Trevone pointed out self-importantly. "This new system will give our spheres more manoeuvrability. Those tedious deceleration programmes will be a thing of the past."

"So you'd have me believe," said Clemis. "Come on, let's get started."

"Very well. Activate main thruster array and prepare to commence test procedure. *Don't* start yet, wait till you're told."

"Nobody dictates to me," Clemis declared. "Not even you, Trevone." And before he could protest she had sent the sphere hurtling from the Alda system into deep space.

"Clemis, wait! I haven't laid in a course - "

"Don't worry; I've done it for you." Clemis studied the Drive diagnostics calmly.

"But - "

"I suggest you come and look at this. *Now*, Trevone!"

The young inventor scarcely had time to take one set of readings before the panel display froze and the viewscreen blanked out. There was no sound in the cabin save the faint high keening of the aldacite crystals.

"We *can't* be in transposal already!" breathed Clemis.

"It looks as if we are. I hope you know where we're going, Clemis, because I certainly don't."

"We're going to Myrma," she said a trifle uncertainly.

"Seventeen light years. Just an astal or so in transposal, then. Let's wait and see what happens."

They did. The sphere remained in transposal.

"Normal flight programmes don't work under these conditions," Trevone explained patiently.

"Why didn't you tell me?"

"You didn't give me a chance."

26

"But I thought..." Clemis paused to assess exactly what she *had* thought. "I thought we'd simply reach the transposal point more quickly."

"The usual point?"

"Well, yes. Why not?"

Trevone sighed. "We've attained transposal prematurely. I'm not even going to try and explain how transposal points differ, so you'll just have to accept that they do. This one could lead anywhere. And, of course, the test's been invalidated."

"Oh, Trevone, I'm sorry!" Clemis was genuinely upset. "All I wanted was one little adventure. Just one. When Laura was about my age she met Idenion and they did all sorts of exciting things. My life's rubbish, Trevone. I'm not *good* at anything. I'm not musical, I'm not clever - I can't even dance like my birth-mother. I don't think I'll ever do anything worthwhile."

"You can't possibly know that," Trevone protested.

"And now we're stuck in transposal, thanks to me. How long will it be? A day? An octal?"

"Nothing like that. Trust me, I've an instinct for these things."

Clemis did her best to believe him. "I really am sorry I messed up your experiment."

"My experiment has failed!" Trevone declaimed with a theatrical flourish, trying to make her laugh. "A smile! That's better. Now come and sit by me, have some liman, and we'll just wait it out."

She obeyed, curling up beside him in the huge, padded chair. They fell silent, mentally exchanging youthful confidences and trying to ignore their present concerns.

The waiting was soon over. Three astallen later, the viewscreen suddenly re-lit and the soft singing of the crystals ceased.

"There, what did I tell you?" Trevone tried not to sound relieved. "I'll just define our quadrant and then I'll know exactly where we are." He pored over the logic system so long that Clemis began to grow restive. "Hmm, that's odd."

"What is? Where are we?"

"Well, we've travelled about two hundred light years, but there aren't any named stars close by. In fact, there isn't *anything* close by. The nearest stars are..." He recited a few catalogue numbers, which meant nothing to Clemis. "But the strange thing is, someone's been here ahead of us."

"How do you know?"

"Because when we transpose, we leave a form of marker at the entry and exit points. On infrequently used routes the marker fades, but with popular ones like Myrma it's there all the time."

"You've lost me," said Clemis unapologetically. "Do you mean something like a space buoy?"

"Think small. Think sub-atomic. These things are so tiny that they can only be detected by their influence on our Drive circuits. So here we are, at the forgotten end of nowhere, with clear evidence of a marker. All Drives have a tendency to home in on them - which explains how we found it, but not who left it."

"Aren't there *any* named stars around here?" asked Clemis, already bored with Trevone's lecture. He consulted the monitor again.

"Yes, about ten light years distant. Symerid."

Clemis sat bolt upright. "Symerid? Are you sure?"

"Of course I'm sure. Why?"

"Symerid Three," Clemis informed him loftily, "happens to be Laura's birthplace. Don't tell me you'd forgotten!"

"You always call it Earth. So does she."

"You're very young," said Clemis teasingly, "so I'll excuse your ignorance. Although I'd have thought that the son of Jarras would be better informed."

"Father doesn't talk about his visits to Earth. He was nearly killed the second time."

"You're exaggerating."

"No, I'm not. There's a retrace. Tralvar arranged for me to see it."

Clemis was impressed. "You didn't tell me you had Tralvar's favour."

"Only where my research is concerned. He wanted to demonstrate how much stress could safely be put on the Drive in an emergency. It's strange, though: Jarras and I have been in friendly competition over the Drive improvements, and I'd have expected Tralvar to give *his* work precedence. They've always been so close. Instead, he keeps giving me surreptitious help."

"Maybe he wants you to win."

"Or maybe he knows I'm on the right track." Trevone had gravitated back to the logic system.

"Jarras thinks of it as an engineering project but I think the answer's in the software. Correction: I *know* it is."

"Trevone..." Clemis slid her arms around his neck. "Now that we're so close to Earth, couldn't we have just one tiny peep at it? I promise I'll be good. I won't go near the controls, I swear. I'll just sit here and watch the viewscreen. *Please*?"

"All right," said Trevone absently.

+You mean *yes*?+ Clemis was so surprised that she read him, suspecting he hadn't been listening. But he had.

"Tralvar sanctioned this research and it's him I report to. I know he'd want me to take a closer look at Earth."

"Why?"

"They're emergent, aren't they? And no-one's checked on them for years. Tralvar would be reassured to know they're not rampaging all over their sector of the galaxy."

"*If* they're not," Clemis said wryly.

Trevone returned to the pilot's console. "So, shall we do this?"

"Ready when you are. Er...don't overshoot, will you?"

"That was *your* fault," Trevone said indignantly. "This will be flawless - and quick."

Again, a few brief moments of acceleration preceded their entry into transposal. The viewscreen was extinguished once more; the crystals sighed softly.

"How long this time?" asked Clemis edgily.

30

"We'll be there before you know it," Trevone promised. "Ten light years is nothing. We - "

A klaxon shrilled and they both cried out. The subdued lighting turned crimson and the sphere dropped out of transposal with a lurch that almost threw them from their seats.

"What....was that?" inquired Clemis.

"A failsafe," Trevone answered, swiftly reviewing the data in front of him. "There was an obstacle at our programmed exit point."

"What kind of obstacle?"

"Wait. I'll see." He adjusted the viewscreen; a ferocious blaze of light flooded the cabin. Automatic filters swiftly reduced the glare to an acceptable level.

"Bad boy!" Clemis admonished, trying not to grin. "You were heading straight for the sun! No wonder the alarms went off."

Trevone looked glum. "I think my process still needs work."

"Good thing you didn't disconnect those safety protocols."

"Credit me with *some* sense." He returned the cabin lighting to normal, then carefully brought the sphere about and re-engaged the thrusters.

"Nice and slow," Clemis teased. He didn't answer, but she saw he was following her suggestion. After a sedate and uneventful two astallen they settled into Earth orbit.

"Right," said Trevone briskly, "let's do what we came to do. Quite a pretty planet, isn't it? I'll run some scans."

"We need to get closer."

31

"Careful now - it's a bit of an obstacle course here too. Lots of space junk."

"Such as?"

"Satellites, more satellites and yet more satellites. And something that appears to be a telescope. And - discord's dreams, there are *people* in that thing!"

"What, the telescope?"

"No, that piece of ironmongery we're just approaching. See it? All cylinders and solar panels." Trevone tapped hastily at the controls.

"What are you doing?"

"Putting some distance between us and that object. I don't want anyone spotting us."

"But what could they possibly do?" Clemis asked.

"Tell whoever put them there," Trevone said ominously. "Well, I think I've gathered enough data to keep Tralvar happy. We'd best be on our way."

"Oh, *no*, Trevone!" wailed Clemis. "Not yet! I want to look at Laura's home."

"I've no co-ordinates. Where do you suggest we look?"

"Can you display an outline of the land masses?" asked Clemis eagerly.

"Certainly. There you are."

Clemis studied the screen intently. "That's it!" she announced, jabbing her finger at a small cluster of islands. "I've seen this image in Laura's memory. The United Isles of Ing. How do I magnify it?"

Trevone showed her. "It's dark there. You won't see much."

"I can see enough," Clemis said confidently. "Now, in the south-east of Ing there's a huge city called London. And that must be it - that lovely blaze of light."

"Waste of energy, you mean."

"When Idenion came here originally he monitored their broadcasts," Clemis went on. "Shouldn't *we* have been doing that?"

"We have. I sampled the radio output when we first arrived. This sphere carries Narvellan tech: we can copy sound to an info-globe and study it later."

"Why didn't you put it on the speaker?"

"Because," Trevone said with exaggerated patience, "I was concentrating. Here, listen. I bet you can't understand a word."

Clemis listened to an incoherent babel of voices and inane music, feeling as dismayed as Idenion had once done. "It doesn't sound much like Ing-lish," she said forlornly.

"Noisy lot," said Trevone, and closed a switch. The cacophony ceased.

"Imagine," Clemis continued reflectively, "how Idenion must have felt when he first heard Laura singing. He'd turned off the radio, engaged the soundsweep, and suddenly there she was. Dena says he fell in love at that very moment."

"Oh, so *that's* your little plan!" Trevone feigned jealousy. "You're looking for some handsome young Earthman to serenade you."

"Aww. You found me out. But seriously, Trevone: when I said I wanted to look, I didn't mean from this distance."

"Go on."

"Laura was born in London and later moved to Cradle of the World. That's only little so we won't find it. But we *could* have a closer peep at London, couldn't we? Please, Trevone?"

"If we hover at low altitude we'll be intercepted by war machines," Trevone stated bluntly. "That's what happened to Jarras. And it isn't going to happened to us."

Clemis' face fell. "You'd better take me home, then."

Trevone relented slightly. "I never said I wouldn't do it. Choose a location - just one - and we'll go in really close for half an astal."

"But that's no time at all!"

"Maybe not, but it's all you're getting. I'm taking us into a lower orbit now. What do I scan for?"

"A large gathering of people in a park or open area," Clemis said after a slight pause.

"And what would they be doing, these people?"

"Having a music festival. Laura's been to lots - she says they go on for days and days - *and* nights - and there's a wonderful sense of togetherness."

"A drugged haze," said Trevone uncharitably. "Oh, chaos, is that a spacecraft? They can't have detected us so soon!"

Clemis studied the bulky, winged vehicle they had just overtaken. "It isn't under propulsion," she observed.

"You're right, of course," Trevone said after a closer inspection. "Sorry I panicked. It's disconcerting, all these humans orbiting about in

34

dangerous contraptions. I wonder what propellant it uses?"

"Rocket fuel is Laura's nickname for resnay," said Clemis helpfully.

"Discord's dreams! Did *we* ever do anything so reckless?"

"Maybe, when we were pioneers."

"Now don't start romanticising this species," Trevone cautioned. "It's just as Tralvar says - if they discovered transposal they'd be all over space like a rash, with their wars and bombs and chaos knows what else." The logic system chimed for his attention. "Well, you're in luck. I've found you a festival."

"You're brilliant!"

"Co-ordinates locked; standing by to record visuals. Descending now."

The sphere plummeted earthward.

Clemis peered hard at the screen. "We're not getting any detail. I can see there's movement, but - "

"Just a moment. I'll have to compensate for those nasty orange streetlights. There, that should do it. I'm sure we're not in soundsweep range but I'll try it anyway....."

Clemis put her hands to her mouth. "Oh, Trevone, look! *Look!*"

"I have to calculate our drift," he objected. But he spared the screen a glance, and was transfixed. "Discord take us! It's not a celebration, it's a riot!"

They continued to watch in silence as uniformed, shieldbearing men struggled to contain a mob armed with bricks and bottles. The crowd heaved and surged like a single entity, and Trevone had difficulty keeping it in focus. Running battles spilled into nearby streets. Plate glass shattered. A flitter craft with whirling vanes overflew the melee and an amplified voice faintly registered on the sphere's instruments: "Disperse now or force will be used." And this, Clemis understood.

"That's it, we're leaving," said Trevone, a little later than he'd intended. He took the sphere to a point well beyond the orbiting hardware, then took the thrusters offline.

Clemis was still staring at the screen as if doubting the evidence of her own eyes.

"Not what you expected, was it?" Trevone asked gently.

"Not quite," she replied wanly. "Laura's always running this place down. Maybe I'd better take more notice of her!"

"Are you ready to go home now?"

"You know I am." Clemis managed a pallid grin. "But by the *normal* method if you don't mind. No more experiments!"

"Agreed," Trevone promised ruefully.

By the time the sphere attained transposal, Clemis had recovered her spirits. "I'd no idea Idenion was so brave!" she said dreamily. "Rescuing Laura from such a dangerous world, fighting a gang of angry men - "

"I thought it was just her husband."

"Always spoiling my stories! Come here, you." She pinched his behind playfully.

"I'm busy, Clemis."

"Can't it wait? While we're in transposal I want us to make love. Here, on this bunk, like Laura and Idenion did after he'd rescued her. It was their first time."

"We've *had* our first time."

"Trevone...!"

"We can do all that later, in comfort," he promised affably. "I want to start compiling my report."

"You can be so exasperating sometimes," Clemis muttered. He didn't hear. She watched him sulkily as he studied the logic displays and made notes. She'd always been fond of him - in fact, she supposed she loved him - but there weren't any exhilarating highs, such as those she'd experienced with Kalyx. Which was annoying, because she didn't even *like* Kalyx. He simply knew how to make the most of an occasion. Trevone had no sense of the romantic nor of the dramatic: he'd inherited Jarras' engineering skills, and something of Tralvar's genius, but no creative talent such as Nefyrra could have given him. Or, thought Clemis unkindly, maybe his shortcomings were due to his boring name. Trevone, literally "of Treva", because he'd been born there. Two towering intellects like Nefyrra and Jarras could surely have come up with something better.

"There's something I have to make clear," Trevone said as they were nearing Celestra.

"And what might that be?" asked Clemis, still piqued.

"Laura's going to know we visited Earth. Tralvar will want to show her our evidence and get

37

her comments. When she questions you about it, it's imperative that you don't mention the improvements to the Drive."

"But that was why we were there in the first place!"

"I know, but you can't mention it."

Clemis frowned. "I think you've just landed me in a lot of trouble, Trevone. If I can't discuss your experiments it's going to look like - "

" - joyriding," said Laura furiously. "How many times have I warned you about that?"

"About a million more times than I've done it."

"Don't be clever with me, young lady. Space travel isn't a flitter ride. It's complex and deadly and full of unknowns. And yet you stand there and tell me you've been gadding around without a flight programme to protect you, eavesdropping on my old home despite all you've heard about it, and generally disregarding all the advice I've ever given. I thought Trevone had more sense. I was even beginning to hope that *you* had!"

The quarrel was taking place in Laura's akron apartment, but Idenion was gloomily sure it could be heard by half the building. He'd decided not to interfere, just as on previous occasions. Later he intended to take Clemis aside and explain (as he'd already explained more than once) that Laura couldn't help being overprotective due to the special circumstances of her daughter's birth; and being English, she tended to forget that Celestrian girls were deemed to be adults as soon as they reached childbearing age.

"Why *should* I take notice of you?" Clemis was shouting. "You don't trust me and you've never trusted me - that's what it amounts to!"

A hand touched Idenion's shoulder. Unnoticed, Tralvar had entered the room. The decline in his health was now very marked; he was frail and emaciated, and the climb from his villa to the akron was almost beyond him. But his gaze was as keen and forensic as ever, and his voice had lost none of its old authority.

"Laura asked me to play for her," he explained. "It's obviously not a good time."

"How long were you listening?"

"Long enough. Now that I'm here I want to speak to them both - separately of course. I must try and rectify some of the harm Laura's doing."

"Harm?" Idenion queried, but just then Clemis came storming out of her room.

"Two of you! Good!" she exclaimed on seeing them. "Did you hear me telling Laura I'm moving out? I'm going to live with Trevone in the students' quarter!"

"Does Trevone know?" asked Idenion.

"We've discussed it."

Idenion frowned. "It sounds like a decision based on impulse. Leave pairbonding until you've finished your education."

"*You* didn't," Tralvar reminded him. "Clemis' suggestion seems quite practical: it would do her good to get away from the akron for a while. Trevone hasn't lived at the Lyricon for the best part of a year and it doesn't seem to have impaired his character or his studies."

39

"Thank you, Tralvar!" Clemis gave him an exuberant hug, which he parried feebly. "I'm so pleased you've taken my side."

"It isn't a question of sides. If you'll allow me a quiet word or two - "

Idenion tactfully returned to his books.

"First of all, Clemis, I must thank you for keeping Trevone's confidence. I realise this put you in a difficult position with Laura - "

"Difficult? It's *always* difficult," said Clemis morosely. "Sometimes I think she hates me."

"You're so wrong," Tralvar said gently. "If you could remember when she first brought you home, if you'd seen how she reverenced your little life, you'd never claim she didn't love you. But she's trying too hard, and that's why I think it would be wise to put some distance between you - some *real* distance. Trevone will be working at Treva for part of the coming year, continuing our ongoing project. He'll be apprenticed to the best space software experts. Once I have Laura's consent - and she'll give it once I've finished talking to her - I propose to send you with him. You'll study spacecraft maintenance at a basic level. Interested?"

Clemis blinked. "It sounds perfect, but why are you doing this?"

Tralvar merely smiled. "Since you find the rest of the galaxy so fascinating I think you should at least know how your conveyance works."

"Laura won't like it if I drop out of school," Clemis ventured.

"Neither did Ninfi when Kalyx dropped out. And now look at him - the Lyricon's most promising young actor. You're not an academic, Clemis, any more than Laura herself is. She may need someone to point that out." And without another word he was gone, leaving Clemis staring after him in a mixture of bewilderment and excitement.

Laura was on her private balcony, gazing across the city. It was early evening; the sun had just set and the plaza was almost deserted. From further off came the sound of laughter and the faintest hint of music.

She was now thirty, or in Earth chronology, forty-nine. And, thought Tralvar as he approached, still a very handsome woman. He wondered how ill he would have to be before his tired old body stopped wanting her. He knew he would never fall out of love with her, which made his present task the more painful. Without announcing himself, he sat down and waited for her to speak.

"So you want to talk about Clemis," she said eventually. "What can you possibly add to what Idenion's been telling me? I can't get through to her and that's all there is to it. She's so intransigent."

"And why do you think that is?"

"She takes after her birth-mother, I suppose."

"No, Laura. You. She takes after *you*."

Laura bridled. "I was never that obstinate."

"I doubt if Nathaniel would agree," Tralvar remarked. "Don't you see what's happened, Laura? When Clemis was small she read your mind incessantly and you were powerless to stop her. She's absorbed all your character traits, good and

41

bad. She's incredibly like you and that's why you fight."

"I was never reckless. I'm sorry, Tralvar - I'm willing to put up with a lot but I'm not letting her go anywhere near Earth again. Ever."

"Not reckless," Tralvar repeated with an odd little smile. "When you were only a fraction older than she is now, you left your cosy little village and got into a spacecraft with a boy you'd only just met - because he was vulnerable and had a nice face."

"That was different. He and Dena were at risk."

"And you thought you weren't? I find that hard to believe. Anyway, a very short time later here you were, exchanging fighting talk with Alendis and giving *me* a hard time. Outspoken, argumentative and self-righteous - just like Clemis."

Laura acknowledged this fact a little grudgingly.

"Then you must also acknowledge, since you know yourself well, that beneath her brash exterior Clemis is insecure. She wants your approval, doesn't get it, and every time you quarrel her confidence takes another knock. Before you undermine her any more I'm going to split the two of you up - because in the days to come, we're going to need her." And he quickly outlined his plans for Clemis' further education.

Laura stared. "You're grooming her, aren't you? To fight the Eldorians?"

"To help others to fight. She can persuade and motivate - even though, as yet, she's only used that ability to twist young men round her little finger. She's a leader. All she lacks is a cause."

"I can't believe you'd do this to me, Tralvar. Not content with interfering in my daughter's future, you're scheming to place her in the front line when the enemy comes!"

Tralvar forced himself to ignore her reproachful eyes and the sense of betrayal emanating from her. "So you do still think the Eldorians will invade? I was beginning to wonder."

"If I didn't believe it I wouldn't be so angry with you."

"Point taken. So may I ask what *your* plans for Clemis are, in the event of an invasion?"

"I haven't made any. I was..." Laura turned away from his sardonic gaze, aware of how weak she sounded. "I was just hoping to keep her out of sight."

Tralvar gave a snort of derision. "And you think she'd *stay* out of sight, do you? She'll be right in the thick of whatever resistance there happens to be. All *I'm* doing is trying to ensure she's prepared."

"How long have you had these plans?"

"A while. I was going to wait until she'd finished her studies. The Earth trip, or rather your reaction to it, obliged me to re-schedule."

"Fine. Go ahead, send her away." Laura's voice was brittle, querulous. "Idenion and I left you in charge of defence work, and if that includes Clemis then so be it. Why should you bother to consult me? I'm a bad mother. My views don't count."

43

"Laura," Tralvar began helplessly. Her back remained resolutely turned.

+Leave her, Tralvar+ advised Idenion from his study. +She never communicates when she's upset+

+I didn't *want* to upset her!+

+I'll talk to her later. Come and see me+

Tralvar went, guiltily.

Idenion's attitude was more balanced. "For what it's worth, I endorse the Treva idea. Clemis seems happy enough with it, anyway. I imagine it all ties in with your frequent visits to Guildmaster Lann and your meetings with Jarras. And with whatever Lydion's doing, although I can't quite see how *he* fits in with your defence project."

"He's a brilliant technician when he puts his mind to it."

"When," Idenion echoed dismissively.

Tralvar didn't debate the issue. "Where's Clemis now?" he asked.

"Keeping out of the way. I think she went to find Trevone."

"Good. There's something I don't want her to hear."

"Oh?" Idenion regarded him suspiciously.

"Nothing to do with strategic matters," Tralvar assured him swiftly. "There's another, more personal reason why I want her out of Alda Mexa. My son, Kalyx. I assume you know they've been lovers?"

"I was aware of it."

"Kalyx is trouble. He's just discovered that his flair for drama can also be an aid to seduction."

"Trying to emulate his uncle, perhaps."

"No, more's the pity. Lydion adores women; Kalyx merely studies them, a trait he derives from me. When I saw him with Clemis I saw myself and Elanir, my first wife. Two sexually compatible people in a mutually destructive relationship. It's the last thing Clemis needs. Trevone, on the other hand, will steady her down."

"So you're playing matchmaker, too, are you?" Idenion's reproof was tempered by amusement.

"I suppose I am," Tralvar admitted. "Laura might even approve. But whereas she wants the best for her daughter, I want what's best for all of us. When the invader comes, Clemis will have to keep her wits about her - and she won't do that if she's emotionally involved with the wrong person. I may not be able to stop that happening but I can hopefully stop it happening with Kalyx. And yet - " he gratefully accepted the drink Idenion was offering him - "sometimes, I wonder if all my careful preparations are just an exercise in futility. There's bound to be something I've overlooked, some miscalculation. Maybe people won't follow my suggestions once I'm not here."

Idenion made an involuntary protest.

"Don't waste time on platitudes," Tralvar said brusquely. "I'm dying and you know it. Drusa says I should be dead already."

"There's no need to sound so negative."

"Just making sure you don't get your hopes up. I've always been a drinker, and after the stun-cannon accident I drank even more to kill the pain. Except that the pain stayed and the drink killed *me*." He gave a throaty chuckle as he refilled his glass. "Since Laura's not in a singing mood, I wonder if I could borrow your music room for a while? My zirid won't hold its tuning these days. I think there's a hairline crack in the frame."

"But that's your favourite instrument. Couldn't you have it repaired?"

Tralvar gave him a surprisingly gentle smile. "It isn't worth it."

Presently the sound of his playing eddied through the apartment and down the galleried stairs. Idenion had no idea of the music's title, but it was achingly beautiful. Putting aside his work, he went to find Laura.

***

"Get up, lazybones!" ordered Tralvar, giving Lydion a shove as he dozed on a spaceport lounger.

"No need to shout." Lydion swung his feet to the floor and stretched. "I've been here for the best part of an ild, waiting for you."

"Well now I *am* here, look lively. I've had the equipment stowed on board my spacecraft, so we can leave right away."

"Your spacecraft? Not that old wreck with a busted Drive? It can hardly get into orbit!"

"It'll serve." Tralvar led the way onto the spacefield; Lydion followed, blinking and yawning.

"Don't get me wrong, Tralvar - I'm pleased you wanted me on this trip, brothers united and so on. But did we have to leave so mindnumbingly early? I've hardly had any sleep."

"You knew what time I wanted to start."

"Yes, but I often work late. The Lyricon, remember?"

"There was no performance last night, so what were you doing? On second thoughts, don't answer that."

"Then answer *my* question. Why are we leaving at the crack of dawn?"

"Because it's already mid-morning in Ilonna and we need all the daylight we can get. As it is, we may have to stay over till tomorrow."

"Camping out? Sounds fun. I've some stories that will make your hair curl."

"Good! That should help keep it out of my eyes," said Tralvar with a rare show of levity. "Why's your hair always so tidy, Lydion?"

"I don't know. Why isn't yours?"

They reached the sphere, its unspaceworthiness blazoned across the hull: a Drive symbol scored through with a warning blue line. Tralvar carefully initialised the control systems while Lydion poured himself some liman.

"Your daughter doesn't like me," he announced.

"Do you mean she doesn't worship the ground you walk on?" inquired Tralvar, looking up briefly from his checklist.

"No, she doesn't like me. I'm just wondering if I tried to seduce her - before I knew we were relatives, I mean. I don't think I did but it's difficult to be certain."

"I think you can safely assume you didn't," said Tralvar, hiding an inappropriate smile. "She'd have told me. I imagine she's just peeved at your cult status. Some of the younger dance students, and a

47

few of the scolia girls, dare one another to walk - or run - past the generator room. And that disrupts rehearsals."

Lydion sighed. "Then please tell Nefyrra I won't compromise her young ladies. I've enough on my plate with the older ones. Ever since Idenion wrote that book I've been besieged by women, all wanting to mend my broken heart."

"And of course, you allow them to try."

"It would be uncivil of me not to," Lydion said reasonably. "But it's not very rewarding. No resistance to overcome."

"How annoying."

"Don't snipe. Those girls aren't in love with *me*, they're in love with Idenion's verse. It's *him* they should be chasing. As for helping me forget Tarly: it's going to take a very special person to do that." He set down his cup. "Now, are we going anywhere or not?"

Tralvar finished his preparations, spoke briefly with the tower, then lifted off.

"And just take it easy," Lydion added. "I know what your flying's like. We don't want to shake up the cargo - or me!"

"Stop complaining," said Tralvar peremptorily. "While we're on our way you can update me on your research. Since I haven't seen you for a while I assume you've perfected the emitters we're carrying?"

"Nothing's ever perfect." Lydion seized the empty cup before it could be catapulted across the cabin. "When you first singled me out for this project I warned you I wasn't the right man for the job. It was an impossible brief, trying to convert weathershield technology into a forcefield."

"It *is* a forcefield."

"Nonsense. It's a glorified repeller, like the flitters carry. Most of its energy goes towards creating the sky effect. Now that *does* have some odd properties - not that I understand them. Anyway, I couldn't experiment on the Lyricon shield without letting everyone know what I was doing - not to mention bringing down Nefyrra's wrath on my head if I'd caused a malfunction. And in any case, you wanted something portable. So I put together some scaled-down projectors, using stuff from the power plant and a few odds and ends from the Corayn shield, now officially defunct. Some components needed to be hand-milled at Treva: Jarras saw to that.

"I took the prototypes to your quarry workshop for testing, but could only generate enough power to run one at a time. When you last saw me I was trying to iron out some recurrent instabilities. Which I did," he concluded defensively.

"And this one project took you seven years?"

"What did you expect? I've a fulltime job, Tralvar! I'd like to think about retiring - Tonor's handling the shield much better lately - but he's still capable of making a kyffu's nest of it if I'm not looking. And yes, I admit I value my leisure. If you'd wanted the work done sooner you should've lent a hand."

"I had other commitments," Tralvar said guardedly.

"Well, there you are. Why expect *me* to be singleminded when you're not?" Lydion folded his arms implacably.

"You have no idea - " began Tralvar, then thought better of it. "You requested an adequate power source to test all four emitters at once. That's why we're going to Ilonna. The Narvellans couldn't repair the solar collectors so they installed generators of their own, powered by an oil-based synthetic."

"Squandering our resources again, eh? Did you know?"

"I authorised it in the short-term. The refinery at Ninka kept them supplied, and I lost a whole year's production of firi because of that. Anyway - the generators are still on-site and still in working order. Jarras and Trevone have positioned one in the theatre complex and run a cable to the arena. The amphitheatre's on a level plain, unlike the Lyricon, which makes it an ideal testing ground."

"You do realise," said Lydion, "that this could be a total waste of time?"

"You always denigrate yourself," Tralvar replied with an unexpected show of warmth. "You're a fine engineer. I've been observing you."

Lydion gave a disconcerted grin. "If that was meant to reassure me, it didn't work. And can you please go steady on the descent? That desert's coming up to meet us extremely - "

The sphere touched down with only a slight bump.

" - fast. Discord's dreams! I think you left half of me in orbit."

"What are you talking about? That was a perfect landfall." Tralvar cut the power with a flourish.

"I'll assume you're joking." Lydion opened the hatch, admitting a hot blast of desert air. Despite his haphazard piloting, Tralvar's landing co-ordinates had been precise: the ruined amphitheatre lay baking in the morning sun. Quite suddenly, Lydion felt despondent. He hadn't thought that, after so many years of separation, he might find a fresh association with Tarlatine; but the sombre, deserted city had been the last home of her people.

"She probably never set foot in the place," Tralvar said quietly.

"I know, but....they planned their colony here, including her role in it. They chose her a husband. Oh, chaos, I'm not even going to think about it. I'm here to work."

"That's the spirit. I'll unpack the crates and you decide where you want to set up."

Lydion ventured outside and stepped onto the stage. +I've found Jarras' cable+ he reported. +Tripped over it actually: it was covered in sand. If we get just a few grains in the emitter lenses we'll know all about it. Chaos, it's hot out here+

+And it's going to get worse, so hurry up and choose a site+

Lydion cogitated, squinting into the brightness. He had thought to use the centre of the stage, which would have made Tralvar's part in the experiment easier, but some recent excavation work was in the way. Instead he chose an area further to the west,

51

not far from the spot where the cable disappeared down a side corridor toward the generator. Nearby, one wall of an apartment block remained standing, which would afford some shade later. He paced out the site, calculating the probable dimension of the forcefield and positioning markers accordingly; then he went back to the sphere, pausing to re-inspect the dig he'd noticed earlier.

"Hey, Tralvar," he called, his voice echoing round the empty terraces, "someone's been stripping off the top layer of tiles. There's a big mosaic underneath - looks like a picture of Ilonna when it was a going concern."

Tralvar vaguely remembered a Narvellan memo alerting him to the find and asking if he'd like it restored. "So they ran out of time," he murmured.

"Yes, but it looks as if they were working on it till the last moment. Just downed their chisels and took off. Anyway, that's why I've moved our project to one side. It'd be a shame to have our ancestors' art pulverised by one of your therite bolts." Lydion donned a tool belt, a gilet with capacious pockets and a soft cap to protect his head. "There, that's me kitted out. Are you going to wear that overall? You'll fry. And don't you have any headgear?"

Tralvar produced a wide-brimmed ylur hat. "Dena made this for me."

Lydion grinned. "Well, you won't win any fashion competitions but it'll keep the sun off. Now shall we commence?"

Tralvar consulted the sphere's chronometer. "We've just under two ilden before noon. And then, finished or not, we'll have to take shelter."

They carried the grey cylindrical emitters across the dusty expanse and planted them carefully next to the markers. The lenses were then removed from their anti-static wrappings and fitted into place.

It soon became obvious to Lydion that he was doing most of the work. The heat and exertion had very quickly sapped Tralvar's limited strength. He struggled on, furiously silent, until Lydion said: "Look, Tralvar, it must be nearly noon by now. Why don't you go and break out some rations and let me finish up?"

"I can't leave you to do this on your own."

"Yes you can. This is just like repairing the power lines for the Narvellans. Out in all weathers, up ladders, down drains....trust me, Tralvar, I'm good at this. If you think it's too early for lunch why not check out the generator? We don't want it stalling on us later."

"Very well." Tralvar's instant acquiescence was both a worry and a relief. Lydion worked on, linking a multitude of tiny connectors with the calm precision Tralvar had noted and admired. Then, with the four instruments aligned and ready, he thankfully retreated to the sphere.

Tralvar had set out the lunch Dena had provided: salad, sweet and savoury breads and a home-made cake. Lydion ate ravenously, leant back in contentment and promptly fell asleep. He woke to find his chair in the reclining position and mellow sunlight streaming through the open hatch. Tralvar was sitting nearby, sipping some medicine.

"I had to turn off the environmental control," he apologised. "The storage cells are half depleted."

"Thanks for letting me sleep." Lydion sat up and scratched. "Was I snoring?"

"No."

"Was I *talking*?"

"No. You sleep like a man with nothing on his conscience."

Lydion sensed an inferred resentment but decided to let it go. "And you? Are you rested?"

"As much as I need to be. I've tested the generator and checked the main cable, so let's see if this thing will fire up."

In less than two astallen they were at their posts: Tralvar minding the generator, Lydion waiting near the array.

+Ready?+ asked Tralvar.

+Ready. Try for ignition+

There was a brief blue spat of electricity from the array, then nothing.

+Misfire+ Lydion reported. +Reset and try again+

+Resetting. Second attempt in five isk...four...three...+

Blue light darted from lens to lens, settling into a pulsing grid not unlike the Lyricon shield in its warming up phase. The pattern flickered and danced, at times almost vanishing.

+Well?+ demanded Tralvar.

+It's not quite in sync. We may have to abort this run...no, it's settling down. Come and see+

54

Slowly the blue grid was fading, leaving a shimmering violet hemisphere above the four emitters. Lydion stared at it nervously. The field should have been almost invisible by day, but the sunlight seemed to pour away from it like liquid. The violet glow intensified as he watched.

"Nice colour," said Tralvar, throwing a stone at it. It bounced off.

"I'd no idea it would *be* that colour," Lydion confessed.

Tralvar threw a small rock. It too was deflected. "So far so good. Time for phase two. I'll take the sphere up, hover directly over the field and fire all the weapons I have at my disposal. You'll observe the results."

"From a safe distance," Lydion confirmed drily.

Tralvar disappeared into the sphere. As the hatch closed, Lydion felt a momentary qualm. If Tralvar took it into his head to fly away, he would be utterly alone in a wasteland that covered half a continent. A primal reaction, completely unfounded but impossible to suppress.

+Laura felt like that too, when I brought her here+ Tralvar commented cheerily.

+When was that?+

+During the Synectic campaign. It was the middle of the low season - skies the colour of slate, weeds everywhere. This place was a mess before the Narvellans prettied it up. But Laura sang, as if to a capacity crowd. She could rise to any challenge in those days+

+And can she now?+ inquired Lydion.

Tralvar was silent. The sphere approached Lydion's position, poised itself above the array - then made a clumsy sideways lurch and almost hit the ground.

+What's going on?+ demanded Lydion in alarm.

+You might well ask+ Tralvar's thoughts bristled with indignation. +That thing's giving out some kind of energy signature and interfering with the thrusters!+

Lydion framed a robustly graphic contradiction. +Blame that beat-up old spacecraft of yours+ he added.

+I'll check the flight log later, but I know I'm not wrong+ Tralvar replied stubbornly. +I'll have to increase height. Take cover further off, unless you want your eyebrows singed+

Lydion obeyed, crouching behind a low wall. The sphere steadied itself, a dark aperture sliding open in its base.

+I'm now in the bomb bay+ Tralvar reported. +Stand by+

+I don't see any sign of mythol vapour+ ventured Lydion.

+There's no mythol left. Too hot for it I suppose. It probably evaporated while you were asleep+

"I wish you hadn't told me that," Lydion muttered. He'd slept in many strange places, but never before next to a payload of live therite.

There was a flash of green light from the sphere as Tralvar fired the first and smallest bolt. It glanced off the forcefield and exploded on the ground, sending a hail of tiny stones in Lydion's direction. The second bolt detonated as it hit the field, causing the merest of ripples to cross its shimmering surface. Then came one of Tralvar's incendiary bombs, already smouldering as it fell. It erupted with such ferocity that Lydion was sure the field hadn't withstood it; but when the residue of green fire had finished writhing and sparkling, the strange umbrella of violet light was unscathed.

Tralvar was non-committal. +Now I'll try the stun-cannon+ he announced. +It isn't a beam weapon in the truest sense but it's all I have+

Lydion, who was becoming quite complacent about his work, was disappointed when the barbed lightning of the stun-blast punched straight through the field canopy and smote the ground. "Wrong again, Lydion!" he sighed to himself. "I really thought I was onto something there. Why *shouldn't* the field have repelled therite? The weathershield withstands gales, hailstorms, freak conditions. But I more than anyone should know that a direct lightning strike *can* get through. Nefyrra takes it as a personal affront whenever the campanile gets hit."

As he emerged from his hiding place the field sputtered and collapsed, apparently confirming his doubts. The distant whine of the generator dwindled into silence. +I'm sorry, Tralvar+ he apologised. +I did my best with it+

But Tralvar was paying no heed. Instead of setting the sphere down he was now hovering over the Narvellan dig. When he eventually landed and emerged, Lydion repeated his apology.

"You didn't fail," Tralvar said obliquely.

"You're not still on about that glitch in the thruster array? I told you, your spacecraft was playing up. Tralvar? Tralvar, are you listening to me?"

Tralvar was once more gazing at the excavation. "We've got to uncover the rest of that mural."

"Why make it sound like a problem? We can send a team down."

"*Now*, Lydion. We have to attend to it now, before we leave."

"What for?" Lydion looked perplexed. "What did you see while you were up there?"

"Something that I believe will have a significant bearing on our work. I'm not sure, not yet: there's still too much top layer. But it's too important not to investigate, and too sensitive to leave to others. Did you say you found some tools?"

"Yes, in a sand-drift. Picks, chisels - "

"Then come on." Tralvar turned and walked rapidly away. Lydion scrambled after him, perturbed at his increasingly odd behaviour.

"Slow down! We still don't know why the emitters stopped working. We should at least check the generator."

"No need: it stopped because the fuel ran out. Jarras only put in the bare minimum. Now let's get to work before we run out of daylight too."

"By 'we' you mean me, don't you?" Lydion inquired. "You're in no shape to wield a pick-axe."

"Then I'll clear away the rubble."

58

Lydion reluctantly followed him to the dig and chose a slender pick from the Narvellans' store. "There's a right way and a wrong way of doing this," he remarked, "and this is bound to be the wrong way. I hope you'll take responsibility when I get a bunch of irate archaeologists on my tail."

"Absolutely not," said Tralvar, deadpan. "It's about time you took responsibility for something."

Lydion shrugged and swung the pick. The tiles were brittle and fairly easy to break up, but the picture beneath covered a vast area. It was exhausting, thirsty work.

"This is the interesting bit," said Tralvar, pointing helpfully. "Concentrate on that. The other half isn't so important."

"I wish you'd tell me what you saw - or thought you saw," Lydion grumbled. "And why are you closed off? You're starting to annoy me, dear brother!"

"I don't want to spoil the surprise," was all that Tralvar would say.

Lydion laboured on, chipping and chiselling, pausing frequently to swig water or mop his brow. "You'd better make this worth my while," he warned. "I'll settle for a case of vintage wine - or an introduction to that pretty little herbalist who visits you."

Tralvar's idea of clearing the site was to scoop up armfuls of debris and throw it to the outer edges. "Something else for the purists to complain about," he remarked with a bland smile.

Eventually Lydion rebelled. "This is doing my back in. I'll have to leave the rest till morning."

Tralvar inspected the results. "Excellent job. I'm impressed."

"So I should think."

"There are only two small areas left to clear," Tralvar went on encouragingly. "That blue line of mosaic over there, and the remainder of this inscription. And Lydion - I'm sorry to keep pushing you. But if we don't get away by noon tomorrow we'll have no food, no water and no power reserve."

"I'll get it finished. And now, since you're saying my experiment *didn't* fail, don't you think it would be a good idea to dismantle the emitters? Dew in the lenses is almost as bad as sand."

"Yes, yes, you're right. I'll help you with them." Tralvar seemed contrite. "And after that I shall ensure you have a restful evening."

They packed the emitters back into their crates, then, while Tralvar prepared supper, Lydion rigged up some solar-powered lighting he'd found near the dig. Two surplus crates, and the sacking which had protected the therite launchers, served as chairs. Tralvar found some music on the radio, just audible via the Alcine satellite, to dispel the silence for an ild or two. They sat outside, eating Dena's vegetable stew and watching the twilight fade: and afterwards they talked late into the night, Tralvar about his hopes for the next generation, Lydion about life after Tarlatine.

Finally they slept. Tralvar fitfully, shivering under a heavy blanket on the sphere's single bunk; Lydion soundly, in the open air with just a groundsheet and coverlet, his face turned toward the stars.

60

***

Lydion woke to the sound of metal on stone. He roused himself reluctantly, disentangled himself from his bed and peered in the direction of the noise. In the relentless glare of the sunrise, Tralvar's distant figure brandished the pick with angry impatience, kicking rubble out of the way as he worked.

Lydion, alarmed, grabbed for his shoes and stood up. +Tralvar, you imbecile. Are you trying to kill yourself? I said I'd finish that!+

+We were wasting the day+ came the terse reply.

Lydion would have hurried over to him but was obliged to answer a call of nature. By the time he reached the dig, Tralvar was standing defiantly beside some newly exposed mosaic.

"There. All done."

"Brilliant. Perfect. Now come and sit down before you fall down." Lydion marched him back to the spacecraft.

"The picture. I can show it to you now." Tralvar attempted to reach the controls but Lydion barred his way.

"Breakfast first."

"But there isn't - "

"Breakfast!"

"That's what I'm trying to tell you. We're out of liman and the bread's stale."

"And I suppose there's no chance of a shower?"

"Not if you want drinking water."

Lydion sighed in exasperation. "Look, why don't we drop over to Alcine and get provisioned up? It's stupid to go without basic necessities. In fact, I know a nice little place where - "

"If we went to Alcine we'd be stuck there until the sphere was recharged."

"Would that be a bad thing?"

"If you'd just stop thinking with your gonads for an instant, you'd *know* it was a bad thing. At the moment only Jarras and Trevone know where we are. If we turned up at Alcine I'd be obliged to call on its fool of a Prefect, who would then tattle our business across all fourteen city states."

Lydion gave up. "All right, we'll stink and we'll starve. Go ahead and show me your precious picture."

"With pleasure." Tralvar closed the hatch, activated the sphere's systems and - with a surprising lightness of touch - guided the elderly craft to a position above the stage. "For optimum effect the mosaic would have been viewed from the south-facing apartment block - which, of course, is no longer here. This is the approximate position. Screen on."

"Oh, chaos!" breathed Lydion.

Through the accretion of sand, stones and tile fragments, the artistry of the unknown craftsman still had the power to impress; but a greater significance lay in the subject matter. From the skyline of the old Ilonna, a slender ray of blue light lanced upward. In the background, almost invisible, other light-beams played.

"I was right," said Tralvar softly.

"Yes, but - right about what? Is it a weapon?"

"I'm not sure yet. Can you read any of this?" He magnified what he'd recently unearthed: concentric ribbons of flowing ancient script.

"*Me*?" said Lydion somewhat indignantly. "I'm the world's worst linguist. Don't *you* have any idea what it says?"

"I think it's a dedication by or to whoever commissioned the mosaic. It begins: 'Tekla, scientist-regent of Ilonna, protector of our city'. I'll scan it to the flight log and let Idenion have a look at it."

"He's your best bet." Lydion glanced briefly at the control systems. "We'd better not stay in hover mode much longer. The power residue's going down and down."

"I need to study the site," Tralvar said irritably. "I know there are more clues here and we're not likely to spot them from the ground. So if you'd just shut up for a moment...ah, of course. I was wondering about that."

"What?"

"This featureless band of purple on the southern edge. Bit of a mess, I'm afraid - I thought it was just a border and threw rubbish all over it - but I think it represents a canopy. Like the weathershield only many times bigger."

"But that means it must have covered the whole city!" exclaimed Lydion.

"Not just the city. Ever hear of other ruins further out? Small ones?"

"Chaos, Tralvar, you surely don't think - "

"No one knew what they were for," Tralvar went on determinedly. "Observatories, someone suggested, or part of an irrigation system. Now we know. They were booster stations, Lydion - for *that*!" He stabbed a finger at the screen. "A huge defensive shield. Anything that got too close would have fallen out of the sky!"

For once, Lydion was lost for words.

"That little field we generated today had just enough of a kick to throw my spacecraft off course," Tralvar added. "The effect of Tekla's shield must have been devastating."

"Tralvar, we have to land!"

"Indeed we must. We've some exploring to do!" With a return to his usual impatience, he set the sphere down and was outside before the ramp had stopped moving. Lydion caught him up halfway across the arena.

"Mind telling me where you're off to?"

"This plain blue line intrigues me. It's obviously an indicator or pathway of sorts, drawing the eye away from the main picture and toward...well, let's find out."

The worn, almost invisible blue trail halted at the entrance to a dark corridor. The Ilonnan theatre had four vaulted passages leading off it, three on the eastern side, following a forgotten symmetry which had once connected the auditorium to other important buildings.

"Is it safe to go down there?" Lydion asked dubiously.

"Probably not. Let's live dangerously," Tralvar replied. "Fetch some light, would you?" He then succumbed to a fit of coughing, his medication having run out along with everything else.

Lydion ambled off to collect a solar lamp, and on an impulse retrieved the pick as well. At least he wouldn't be completely unprepared if the ceiling caved in. Then, at an irascible prompt from Tralvar, he hurriedly retraced his steps. "One light, as instructed. Nice breeze this morning, isn't there? We could have done with that yesterday."

Tralvar directed a withering look at him, seemingly without cause.

The corridor was scarcely twenty paces long. Just beyond the entrance a metal door lay on its side, rusted and useless, allowing the ever-persistent sand to drift in. The far end was blocked by fallen masonry.

Lydion inspected the rubble. "I can see daylight far above," he reported. "It looks as if the upper storey collapsed onto this level, followed by the roof. Do you think this was the shield chamber?"

"Probably just an ordinary shield, dating from the time the city was abandoned. That mosaic's been here far, far longer. Three thousand years, at a guess." Tralvar peered disconsolately into the ruined machine-hall. "I suppose it was futile to hope that anything else had survived."

Lydion was gazing back toward the daylight and the rusting door. Then he examined the wall closest to him. "I wonder..." he mused. He wedged the pick into a small irregularity, pulled, and a whole section of cladding crumbled into dust. Part of a derelict switching array was revealed. "I thought so! This isn't a corridor at all, it's a galley-style control room like the one at Corayn."

The discovery revived Tralvar's hopes, though the dust particles exacerbated his cough. "The other wall," he managed. "Under all the dirt. More tiles."

Lydion investigated. "Marble, no less. And they're not well adhered. Could you bring the light closer?" Again he levered with the pick, and after some initial resistance a whole row of tiles toppled outward, enabling him to prise off the rest with his bare hands. Beneath was a rotted membrane which ripped to shreds as he touched it; and beneath that, on the wall itself, some faded lettering.

"You understand *this*, don't you?" Tralvar asked after a long silence. "Maths hasn't changed much over the centuries."

"It's instructions for the shield operators," Lydion answered slowly. "The emitters were arranged in pairs, eight in all. The energy formed a loop between each pair before being transferred to the grid. The hemisphere must have been fantastically stable." He moved along the wall a little. "This - I think - shows how to direct the field to a specific area. And over here..." He swallowed uneasily.

"Go on."

"Tralvar, you're surely not expecting me to reconstruct this? I'm only a technician!"

"Don't even think of letting me down!" Tralvar began in pent-up fury. Then he blanched, swayed and almost dropped the lamp. Lydion grabbed it from him.

"Let's get you outside. You've gone the weirdest colour."

Tralvar took a step back. "No....stay here. I just need...a moment..." He fled for the exit but sank to his knees just short of it, retching helplessly. +Keep away+ he warned, and repeated the warning with every fresh bout of sickness. Lydion waited obediently until all was quiet, then approached with discretion. Tralvar hastily scooped several fistfuls of sand over something that looked more like blood than vomit.

"How long's that been going on?" Lydion asked accusingly.

"You sound like Drusa." Tralvar's reply was scarcely audible. "Would you...take me back to the sphere, please?"

He was too exhausted to stand, so Lydion gathered him up and carried him. He weighed scarcely more than a child.

While they had been under cover the balmy breeze had increased to a strong westerly wind. Flying sand particles stung Lydion's eyes, and the distance to the spacecraft seemed to have doubled. But at last he was inside, settling Tralvar very carefully on the bunk and bringing him a cup of their precious water.

"I'll soon have you home," he promised, preparing to close the hatch.

"No you don't." Tralvar had raised himself on one elbow, his eyes twin dark pools in his ravaged face.

Lydion turned in surprise.

"Before we go anywhere, you have to copy the information on that wall. There are writing materials in my personal locker."

"Why don't I just come back with a camera?"

"No." Tralvar's voice was faint but adamant. "Look outside, to the western horizon. What do you see?"

Lydion looked. "A pink cloud."

"It's a sandstorm. When it gets here it'll blow straight down that passageway and probably obliterate the text. So go and copy it, now. Take your time, don't miss anything out and don't make any mistakes."

Lydion hesitated. "I don't like leaving you."

"Just go," Tralvar said wearily. "I shan't run away."

Under his scrutiny Lydion collected a scrip of paper and pens, checked that the sphere's hatch was facing away from the prevailing wind, and resignedly stepped outside. He was beginning to hate sand. Once in the derelict corridor he began to transcribe the formulae, trying not to dwell on their meaning and ignoring the tiny streams of dust falling from above. Finally, the task completed, he bundled up his writings and stumbled out into the increasingly murky daylight.

Back at the sphere he retracted the ramp, closed the hatch and flipped on the environmental systems. Tralvar was asleep, or maybe unconscious; a tentative shake failed to rouse him.

"You *would* decide to pass out on me, wouldn't you?" Lydion said to him reproachfully. "Now I've got to persuade this old nail of a spacecraft to fly.

Do you know how long it's been since I've piloted a sphere? At least a decade, and then some." He studied the battered controls at some length. "All right, Lydion, let's get these auxiliaries warmed up. That's the way. And...thrusters on, nice and steady. Oops! I think I'd better strap you in, Tralvar. And as soon as I'm in range I'd better radio the medics. Drusa, preferably. She'll sort you out. Me too, if I ask nicely."

Tralvar stirred and murmured something as he was transferred to the co-pilot's chair.

"Everything's fine," Lydion reassured him. "Just rest."

"Did you...get the specifications?"

"All safe and sound." He tapped his pocket.

"You have to redevelop the shield, Lydion. No one else has your knowledge. Promise me..."

"I'll do it," Lydion said quickly, not wanting him to agitate himself.

Tralvar gave a thankful sigh and drifted back into his stupor.

"Well, there's another commitment I didn't want," Lydion chided himself as the sphere commenced its sub-orbital glide to Alda Mexa. "I've a habit of walking into these things, haven't I? The Synectic campaign, for instance: one single bad experience with a prostitute and suddenly I'm in the middle of a conspiracy." He gazed sadly at Tralvar's huddled, vulnerable form. "Yes, I'll build your shield for you. But this is the last time I get roped into anything like this. The very last time."

Chapter Two

Under cover of darkness, eleven spheres departed from Treva's spaceport. Taking up a pre-arranged position between the orbits of Celestra and Alda Two, they powered down and waited. Eight of the spheres were manned by trainees from the Treva Academy of Space Science. Trevone was among them. Clemis was not. Two of the Academy's course instructors were in charge of spheres nine and ten: the eleventh contained Jarras and Lydion.

"Right, everyone," Jarras addressed the others, "you all have your instructions so let's make this a nice smooth operation. Spheres one through eight, get into formation and prime your field emitters. You've done this before so I don't expect anyone to foul up."

Eight spheres converged on one another to form a cluster. The other three waited at a distance.

"This is a team effort," Jarras added, "so no private conversations. Stay off your transposers. Now, is everyone ready?"

There was a chorus of affirmatives.

"Very well. Contact in three...two...one...activate!"

The eight tiny spacecraft simultaneously projected an energy grid, piercingly blue against the blackness, the bars of light enmeshing to form a globe. Slowly the precisely etched circumference became diffuse, blending and thinning until the spheres were enclosed in a pale violet bubble. The twin emissions from each individual craft were faintly visible through it. A spatter of static was issuing from Jarras' communicator; he fidgeted with the tuning and the noise subsided to a background crackle.

"Report," he ordered.

The crews responded in numerical order.

"Reception's tolerable. We can proceed. I'm putting Lydion on: he has some advice for you."

Lydion had been studying the formation on the viewscreen. He could deduce a great deal from the appearance of the field and had noticed one or two weak areas. "Sphere Three, your emitters are out of phase. Reduce output slightly, watch the polarity. Better...a bit more...hold it there. Sphere Five, you're starting to oscillate. Bring up the power or you'll have the entire grid down. Sphere Eight - Trevone - your output's a little ragged. Watch it."

"Sorry, Lydion!" came the reply.

"He's still annoyed with me for keeping Clemis off the project," observed Jarras.

"That did seem a mite unfair."

"I'm *not* letting them share a spacecraft during these tests," Jarras declared. "She distracts him. And she certainly isn't capable of handling a sphere alone."

"She's been studying spaceflight for the best part of a year," Lydion pointed out. "Tralvar gets the college reports. He says she's doing well."

"Not well enough for precision manoeuvres - she's too erratic. Trevone's with me on that." Jarras was keeping an eye on the chronometer. "Just

71

between ourselves, I don't think they're the best of friends these days."

"Treva City doesn't have much to offer a young girl," Lydion mused. "Maybe she needs some excitement."

"Don't even *think* about it, Lydion!"

"Discord's dreams, I didn't mean *me*. As far as Clemis is concerned, I'm over the hill. She hasn't even flirted with me since she was six. I simply meant that Treva's a bit short on night life."

"That's certainly true," agreed Jarras. "Well, it'll be the Peisistrata soon. That should cheer her up." He again glanced at the time. "The shield wall's been in place for an astal. That's how long we agreed to give it to test its stability, but we can leave it longer if you want."

"No need. If things are going to fall apart they do it straight away."

"You're the expert." Jarras reached up to the communicator. "Zanna, Plinn, we're going for the attack sequence now."

"Standing by," responded the two experienced fliers.

"Zanna, you're first. Start your run when ready."

"And be careful," Lydion put in.

"Oh, I like taking chances," she replied knowingly.

Lydion caught Jarras' look of surmise, and grinned. "Couldn't have all those youngsters thinking I was over the hill. Ah, look, she's away."

"Recording telemetry," Jarras said. "She's nearing the cluster. Chaos! Where did she go?"

"Way off course toward Alda Two," Zanna answered for herself. "That device packs quite a punch."

"Now you, Plinn," ordered Jarras.

Plinn tried, with similar results. "Couldn't get anywhere near them," he shouted through the static. "Coming round for another pass. I'll try a sneaky approach this time."

"Well?" demanded Jarras when nothing else was forthcoming.

"He's drifting," Lydion announced. "Looks like he's stalled. No, wait, he's powering up again."

"What happened, Plinn?" Jarras tried not to sound anxious.

"I'm not sure, to be honest. All the systems went off-line, and they're still impaired. Life support at fifty per cent, auxiliaries thirty per cent."

"Do you want us to continue?" Zanna asked, unperturbed.

"Call it off, Jarras!" urged Lydion. "It's too risky."

"I endorse that," Jarras affirmed. "The Tekla Shield works, and that's what we came to find out. All recruits, stand down. We're finished here."

It was still dark when the expedition made landfall at Treva Control, but dawn was fast approaching and the early shift would arrive for duty in less than half an ild. Jarras and Lydion conferred briefly with Zanna and Plinn, then exchanged friendly goodbyes with the few students who were still about. Most, including Trevone, had disappeared back to their campus and a few more ilden of sleep before lectures began.

The young men were deferential toward Jarras, addressing him as First Scientist. "I can never get used to that," Jarras admitted when they'd gone. "Tralvar foisted the title on me as a wedding gift and I never thought I deserved it. *You're* more of an innovator than I am."

"Rubbish," said Lydion - a more decorous term than those he'd used in Tralvar's company. "Hey, look - the canteen's just opened. How about breakfast? *I'm* having some, anyway; it'll help me sleep."

Jarras followed him across the chilly landing precinct into the welcoming warmth of the catering block. They settled at a corner table and were soon feasting on toasted grain cakes piled high with grilled vegetables.

"I suppose you'll be returning to Alda Mexa?" Jarras inquired.

"Not for a couple of days. I'm going to disconnect the emitters and put them in storage till needed. We don't want the students conducting experiments of their own!"

"But I can let Nefyrra know you'll be back for the Peisistrata?" pursued Jarras.

"Yes, I'll be there," Lydion said wearily. "Not that I enjoy it any more. It reminds me too much of the night they took Tarly away."

Jarras, who had been witness to Lydion's distress, sympathised quietly.

"The only time of year I'd like to get thoroughly plastered," Lydion went on, "and I can't, because of my commitment to the weathershield. Well, I've decided: this will be my last working Peisistrata. After this year, Tonor's on his own."

"I'm sure Nefyrra will understand."

"She'd better. While we're on the subject, I'd like to thank you for interceding with her over that business at Ilonna. She was convinced I'd half-killed Tralvar by luring him on some escapade."

"I hope she apologised for slapping you," Jarras said with a wry grin.

"Grudgingly. I'll never be her favourite person, alas."

"Tralvar's going to be mightily pleased with you though. A successful prototype in less than a year! That's a fine achievement."

Lydion was swift to demur. "Don't forget I'd already done the groundwork. Finding a set of instructions made a bit of a difference too!"

"Ah, yes, the wall." Jarras cradled a cup of warm liman in both hands. "Tralvar made me take him back there, you know, as soon as he was able to travel. He didn't want anything left for the invaders to find."

"*Was* there anything?"

"Very little. The sandstorm had done its work."

"So the knowledge is all in my head and nowhere else." Lydion gazed out of the window toward the sunrise. "That's an odd feeling, Jarras. I don't mind telling you I spent an anxious few days wondering what I should do with the formula. Since Tralvar was still fighting his way back to some semblance of health, I couldn't ask him for advice. I took the decision myself in the end."

Jarras stared. "The sphere conversions were *your* idea?"

"Shh! I thought you knew!" Lydion glanced round surreptitiously; the few other patrons looked disinterested and half asleep. "It was the obvious thing to do after seeing how the Drive was affected. Tralvar would've thought of it himself if he'd been well. Even with unlimited time and resources we couldn't have reconstructed the Ilonna shield - and I didn't see the sense in putting canopies over our cities anyway. But protecting our spacecraft made a *lot* of sense."

"You amaze me, Lydion."

"Oh yes? Who didn't realise the field would cripple the spheres that carried it? Me! And who rigged some ingenious baffles and solved the problem? You. I'm just the handyman, and don't you forget it."

"You're determined not to take any of the credit, aren't you?" Jarras sounded amused.

For once, Lydion could see nothing to smile about. "Listen, Jarras," he said in a low, urgent voice. "I don't know why Tralvar decided to go public with this research, but whatever his reasons I'd like my name kept out of it. Unless these invaders get a hustle on, Tralvar won't be around to greet them - so it's safer to let everyone think the invention's his. Safer for me, that is. Now can we please talk about something else?"

***

76

Three days before the Peisistrata, Tralvar called a meeting of his defence team: Lann, Jarras, Trevone, Lydion and Idenion. Laura's presence was also requested; but Clemis, despite Tralvar's plans for her, was again left out.

"Yes, it *is* strange," Laura agreed as she and Idenion walked from the akron to Tralvar's villa. "But he wants to speak to her separately. There's probably something he doesn't want to say in front of me."

"Now don't get paranoid. You have to admit that the year at Space Tech has done her good, even if she and Trevone don't always hit it off. She's much more positive these days."

Laura squeezed his arm. "All right, my dearest, I'll admit it. Tralvar knew best. He just went about it in a high-handed way. But that's Tralvar all over, isn't it?"

"He says he wants to make an announcement," mused Idenion. "I wonder what?"

"Isn't it obvious? He wants to say goodbye to us all. He's so ill now, poor old love. Dena says he can't eat, except for some concoction Drusa brings him. And he's even given up playing his music. I really do think this is the last time we'll see him."

"I don't know how we'll manage without him," Idenion said gloomily. "He's always been there for us."

"We'll just have to be there for each other," Laura replied philosophically.

They were slightly late. Dena let them in and showed them to the study, where the others were already in conversation. Tralvar, a scolia robe concealing his wasted limbs, greeted them irascibly.

"You two need a change of image. You're supposed to be an alert and vital First Family, not a pair of middle-aged slouches. What's happened to your dress sense, Laura? You look as though you're wearing a salad. Idenion, you're getting round-shouldered. Too much poring over books I suppose. Straighten up and try to look like an authority figure, not some tired academic."

Lydion chuckled; the rest of the gathering looked uncomfortable.

"First impressions are everything," Tralvar concluded. "Oh, sit down, do. You're wasting time that I don't have. Now, as Laura has correctly assumed, this will be my final meeting with you all. No homilies, please: I should be obliged to enter into a dispute and I'd then become too tired to complete our business." He paused to drink from a glass of purple liquid. "Idenion, we'll hear your report next. Did you discover anything about Tekla?"

"So far, very little," Idenion began. "I even went to Atris, after Lydion reminded me that in Ilonna's heyday Atris was the second most important city state. They mentioned Tekla in a disparaging way, calling him conceited, autocratic - even mad. But there's no record of his scientific achievements. Even the inscription on the mosaic is disappointing, being a celebration of Tekla himself rather than what he did.

"So was the shield successfully used to repel invaders, or was it never put to the test? I suspect the latter. Doubtless such a device could foil an aerial attack - but it offers no defence against land-based armies, cannot distinguish between friend and foe, and pre-supposes that the enemy will have a transposal-based fleet."

"This time, of course, they will," Lydion put in.

"The broader assumption," Idenion continued, "is that while exploring the galaxy, our ancestors encountered something they feared greatly. The shield could have been an attempt to make the citizens feel safe. Subsequently, as we know, space travel was virtually given up. The society which followed, with its emphasis on inner harmony and the arts, found Tekla's brazen science in bad taste and covered up the frescoes. If they'd wanted to, they could have destroyed everything. Someone obviously had more sense."

"Did you find any evidence that written history had been tampered with?" asked Tralvar.

"No, nothing like that. Information's scarce, but that's hardly surprising. What will survive of *us*, in another five thousand years?"

Tralvar, suspecting a poem might be on its way, fixed him with a glare. "Keep searching," he ordered tersely, then took another convulsive swallow of the purple fluid. A spasm of coughing ensued.

Dena looked on anxiously. "Should I order a recess?"

"We've hardly started," said Tralvar with an effort. "Guildmaster Lann, perhaps you'd tell our friends about your work with the scolia-tech."

Some puzzled faces turned in Lann's direction.

"The scolia-tech was formed nine years ago by Tralvar and myself, with Nefyrra's co-operation," Lann explained. "It was - still is - Tralvar's belief that when the Eldorians come, they'll either filch our scientists or keep them under strict supervision. Any covert work would therefore be difficult if not impossible. So we decided to form a secret group of scientifically able individuals whose normal profession offered a perfect disguise for their activities. Who would suspect musicians? We have experts in maths, physics, light engineering and chemistry, and everyone has demonstrated a versatile approach to problems and an ability to work under pressure. And we already have one success: the Narvellan stun-cannon has been adapted for individual protection. The pocket version resembles a torch and can be safely held in the hand. It won't stop an army but it's guaranteed to knock out a single assailant. I ... er ... tested it. We've now begun to study encryption..."

Lydion, preoccupied, didn't hear the rest of Lann's speech. There was one issue that Idenion wasn't aware of, and therefore hadn't addressed. Possibly the Ilonna shield *had* only been a precautionary measure - but what about the variations on that technology, as depicted on the all-important wall? Were they purely theoretical or had they been built along with the shield itself? For a whole year Lydion had been unable to air his concerns, nor even refer to the existence of the formulae. Today, if he wasn't mistaken, things would change.

Tralvar was speaking again. "It will come as little surprise to any of you that Trevone and Jarras have been working to improve the stardrive. Necessity dictates that I share this knowledge with you immediately, instead of waiting for the prototype's final test. This, I understand, will be in a few octals' time."

"We have every confidence in it," Jarras confirmed.

"Unlike our other projects, the enhanced Drive can easily be concealed," Tralvar went on. "No one can tell the difference just by looking. But remember, both of you, to treat it as a tactical device and not a luxury item. Don't allow any casual use of converted spheres."

"We won't," they responded.

"Good. Before you leave Alda Mexa I have an additional task for you: to close down my cellar workshop. There are very few materials in there at present so it won't take long. Leave the theridolyte door seal - Dena wants to remain at the villa and she may have need of a secret exit someday. You can retain the quarry facility if you wish, but be sure to clear up behind you."

Again he lifted his glass. Dena had to support him while he drank, but as before he seemed to derive fleeting strength from the mixture. Lydion, hearing his name spoken, looked up guiltily from his reflections.

"Lydion," Tralvar repeated, sounding almost apologetic, "you already know how pleased I was to receive the news of your sphere-shield. You have ably fulfilled my expectations."

"I sense a but," remarked Lydion.

"How well you know me." Tralvar gave a tired smile. "What I'm about to ask of you will probably sound insane, so please bear with me until I've finished explaining. You're wondering why I chose not to keep your invention secret. It's quite simple. When the Eldorians arrive, they must be allowed to appropriate it."

"*What*?"

"They'll know Axmiol warned us," Tralvar pursued, "and they'll expect us to have developed some kind of defence. After all, we've had nine years. We have to let them find something and this will, in my opinion, do the least harm. Deliver the plans to Dena at your convenience. She'll ensure the Eldorians believe them to be my work. That *is* what you wanted, isn't it?"

Lydion didn't argue that particular point. "Does that mean," he ventured, "that there are other things we *don't* tell them about?"

"You don't really want to know, do you?" Tralvar countered. "Just keep sight of what *you* have to do."

"I can talk about that now, can I?" Lydion sounded a little wretched.

"In present company, yes. The city shield, or sphere-shield as it became in your expert hands, is only the first of Tekla's designs. You know what the next is. If you want Celestra to stay one step ahead of the Eldorians, you'll waste no time in constructing it. Jarras is to help you with the testing, as before. Any questions?"

"None that I can think of," said Lydion resignedly.

"Good. As soon as can be arranged, I want you to view Laura's war retrace - the one Alendis took. Laura, would you go with him to Tafret and fill in the background?"

"Of course," she answered, a little surprised.

"It may seem an unusual request, but I believe Lydion will draw inspiration from what he sees." Tralvar dabbed sweat from his forehead and looked about him with a vague air of satisfaction. "That concludes the meeting of the defence committee, although of course you may talk amongst yourselves later. It only remains for me to..."

+Father!+ A youthful, imperious thought cut across their solemn mood. +Always locking your door. Let us in!+

Dena hurried to comply, and very soon returned with Kalyx and Nefyrra. Kalyx, stage make-up glistening on his high cheekbones, strode noisily into the room and deposited his cloak on Tralvar's desk. "I hope this is important, Father - I'm in the middle of a rehearsal. I've been chosen to play Hymorel."

Oh dear, thought Lydion to himself. There'll be a few broken hearts after this year's Peisistrata.

"My son," said Tralvar with dignity, "you are a selfish little upstart. And for that reason I have no cause to worry about your future. Come here, Nefyrra."

She came in a little cautiously, soberly dressed as always, the key to the campanile glinting at her belt.

"Neither have I any fears for you, dearest daughter. You are the strongest of all of us. Our traditions are in the best of hands." Tralvar finished the purple liquid and straightened his frail shoulders. "Now everyone's here, I can proceed with my announcement. Ever since I discovered my origins I've done my best to bring Scapirion back from isolation. They have established a trading alliance with Corayn and Ninka but as yet there has been no personal contact of any kind. I'm pleased to tell you that I've negotiated a reform. They have agreed that, for the brief time left to me, I can return to them. I intend to do so." He raised a hand for silence. "There is one condition. I have to go alone."

"But Tralvar," protested Jarras, "you're in no fit state to go anywhere alone. At least let one of us take you as far as the trading post."

"They said alone," Tralvar repeated. "I've spoken to Drusa and she believes she can get me back on my feet for a day or two. I might even be able to watch the Peisistrata before I leave."

"Do the Scapirians know how ill you are?" Laura asked gently.

"Oh, yes, they know. And perhaps this apparent success is merely an attempt to humour me." He surveyed each of his guests in turn. "If this is the case - if Scapirion's doors remain closed to you - then you must be unstinting in your efforts to win them over. We can no longer afford to be disunited."

As if someone had suddenly thrown a switch, everyone began talking at once. Kalyx fell to his knees beside Tralvar, uttering profuse and probably insincere apologies for his failure to visit. Lann and Idenion conferred urgently. Lydion accosted Jarras. Eventually, Dena swept everyone from the room except Laura and Nefyrra. Nefyrra was trying not to cry.

"We can't halt the inevitable, my child," Tralvar said, briefly taking her hand. "Now, don't you have a Peisistrata to organise? Back to the Lyricon with you, custodian. I'll see you again before I go."

That left Laura, and she immediately seized her opportunity. "Tralvar, about Clemis. Why have you excluded her from this gathering? She'll be so disappointed."

"I thought long and hard about that," Tralvar said, twirling the empty glass between his fingers. "Unlike the rest of my chosen, she still doesn't know I've singled her out - and I've decided she shouldn't know yet. If I leave instinct to take its course she'll react to the invasion in the way I've predicted; but given too much responsibility too soon, she'll become frightened. Look how worried my happy-go-lucky brother is. I hated doing that to him but in his case there was no alternative. With Clemis, there is."

"But you *will* speak to her?"

"I've said I would, and I shall. Later."

Whenever that is, Laura thought dubiously. He'd best hurry up.

He managed a sad smile. "Trust me, First Singer - Clemis will have her moment. And now, before Dena throws you out, I'd like to offer my thanks."

"For what?"

"For our musical partnership. Despite all our differences, accompanying your singing has been one of my greatest pleasures - possibly *the* greatest. I hope Nefyrra will be a worthy successor. Now go, Laura. Send Dena to me. And Laura - "

"Yes, Tralvar?"

"Get rid of that dress."

***

"Who calls on Hymorel?"

Kalyx's confident young voice rang out across Lateral Four. His translucent bodysuit sparkled in the late spring sunshine; his shoulder-length hair, lips and fingernails all gleamed with gold lacquer. He pivoted, lithe and graceful, seeking the girl who had petitioned him. She stepped forward a little nervously. Kalyx lassoed her waist with a length of gold braid and drew her to him, pausing when their bodies were just a hair's-breadth apart.

Laura, with Idenion, watched the erotic pageant with determined cheerfulness. Everything was near-perfect: fine weather, lively crowds, the city festooned with flowers, tomorrow's concert well-rehearsed. But she couldn't shake off a strange feeling of impermanence. She felt as if she were standing on a plateau with time gliding past her, and that all the festivity - indeed, all that her life had become - was moving out of her reach.

"You cannot put aside your fear, even now?" Idenion asked quietly.

"Not fear exactly." Laura sounded puzzled. "Not a sense of foreboding, more like a vision of things changing. It's probably just a form of migraine. Forget it."

Hymorel's music struck up for the final time that day. The masque was now concluded, and many of the bystanders began to wander off in search of refreshments. Laura and Idenion were about to do likewise when Trevone appeared out of the thinning crowd.

"Dwell in harmony, citizens," he said formally.

"Is Clemis not with you?" asked Laura a little anxiously.

"No, she isn't back from Treva yet. She and some of the other students decided to come by barge and got snarled up in the river traffic. She'll be here this afternoon." Trevone shuffled his feet, deliberating. "I thought you should know: Clemis and I haven't been living together for several octals. Zanna provided separate lodgings while she finished her course."

Idenion sounded unsurprised. "Is there someone else?"

"Not that I know of. We just drifted. She made other friends at the Academy and blamed me when she was left out of the sphere-shield tests."

"Now that you're both back in Alda Mexa you can hopefully patch things up," Laura said encouragingly. "Let us know if there's anything we can do."

"I was hoping to call on her at the akron tonight," ventured Trevone.

"You don't need our permission for that. You're family, or as good as."

Trevone thanked her, visibly happier. "I don't suppose either of you have seen Tralvar?"

Laura shook her head. "We haven't seen him or Dena. Or Lydion, for that matter. Tralvar's obviously not well enough to leave the villa."

"But he *has* left it," Trevone said. "I've already looked there."

Idenion frowned. "That doesn't sound good. You don't think he's trying to get to Scapirion, do you? Today of all days?"

Tralvar was, at that moment, sitting in a hospital room while Dena and Drusa talked about him in his presence. At one time he wouldn't have stood for it. Now, he merely endured. Finally, knowing he was in capable hands, Dena departed for a much-needed rest.

"Sorry for tying up one of your emergency flitters," Tralvar said when he had Drusa's full attention. She gave him her usual disapproving stare.

"If there'd *been* any emergencies you'd have found yourself staying at home. Fortunately it's very quiet as yet."

"What is it you're planning to give me? Starfire?"

"Perception-enhancing drugs like starfire and the Breath of Corayn are no use to you. And because of the side-effects, healers are relying on them less and less. We've been trying to perfect a drug which works in a less dramatic way, sustaining our healing energies by borrowing from the body's reserves. Think of an oxygen debt. Of course, the energy boost isn't confined to the user's perception, and this is where I think it will help *you*. After treatment, your senses should be at their optimum. You may even feel slightly inebriated."

"Sounds just like old times."

"Now you must understand, I'm not guaranteeing this will work. If it does you'll get a day at best, and when it wears off you'll almost certainly become comatose."

"Why?"

"I told you, the drug unlocks energy reserves. You don't have any, so it will drain you. Ask yourself: is it worth it just to die at Scapirion's front door?"

"I've decided," Tralvar said calmly.

Drusa sighed. "As you wish. It's unethical, and I'm sure to get a dressing down from the Corayn researchers, but I'll tell them I couldn't refuse your last request. Your name still carries some weight, you'll be glad to hear." She opened a refrigerated cabinet, selected a vial and stirred its contents. "I'll have to keep checking this suspension as it may be unstable. It's fine at the moment, but if the mixture starts to separate I'll have to inject you straight away."

"I thought you *were* going to do that."

"No. First of all I want you to take some intravenous nourishment. Now will you stop hanging onto that chair as if it's about to take off, put that smock on and get into bed?"

Tralvar complied laboriously, refusing her help. "Why are you shielding? I hope you're not thinking of keeping me here."

"I wouldn't dare," Drusa returned levelly. "If you must know, I was admiring your indomitable spirit - your fight to survive."

"Indomitable? Hardly." Tralvar closed his tired eyes. "I'm about to lose this fight, Drusa. But at least I'll lose on my own terms."

***

Clemis paced restlessly about her room, which, after her lengthy absence, seemed to have grown smaller. She'd planned to spend the evening with friends she hadn't seen for a year, but after her exacting and occasionally dangerous work at Treva they had seemed effete and childish. She had left early. The kitchens were nominally off limits while the cooks laboured overnight on the banquet, but she'd managed to smuggle out an adequate supper. As yet, she hadn't touched it.

She was, she admitted to herself, being unfair to Laura and Idenion by pleading tiredness, but they would only have interrogated her about Trevone - whom she'd also been avoiding. She felt persistently guilty over the way she'd treated him, and at the same time resented him for being the cause of the guilt. Why, precisely, *had* she ended their pairbond? She was still fond of him, and he'd been a most reliable and attentive partner - except for that business with the sphere-shield, when he'd allowed his father to exclude her. The problem was of her making, she supposed. She didn't want cosy reliability. She wanted passion and drama.

Earlier on she'd found herself confiding her troubles to old Forlane, whom she'd met in the street after the Zarf Dance. The venerable actor had given careful thought to her dilemma before replying:

"Trevone reminds me very much of Tralvar in his youth - in his extreme youth before Alendis got to work on him. Your relationship needs a healthy input of life experience, my dear. Not *your* life, Trevone's. He's like a blank scroll. Admittedly you're the same age, but girls mature far more quickly than boys. Give him time, Clemis. He'll catch up with you."

But how *much* time, Clemis wondered, gazing at her reflection in a full-length mirror. She looked weary - or should that have been world-weary? Maybe she should just go to bed.

A muffled impact made her jump. Something had thudded against the outside of her window. She went to investigate and saw the end of a sturdy rope swaying to and fro as someone climbed down it. A pair of sandals appeared, then two muscular legs clad in gold net. And finally there was Kalyx, still dressed as Hymorel and balanced precariously on the window-ledge.

+Well let me in then, light of my life+

She obeyed, opening the window very carefully to avoid dislodging him. "You loon! You could've killed yourself!"

"Not I." He swung himself inside and unclipped a small safety harness from his belt.

"What's the other end of the rope attached to?"

"An extremely heavy desk on the second floor. Now enough of questions! Don't I get a proper greeting?"

Away from the heady atmosphere of the pageant he should have looked ridiculous, but he didn't. In the half-light he seemed eerily attractive and very masculine.

"What are you *doing* here, Kalyx?" Clemis asked, trying and failing to sound severe.

"You didn't come to see Hymorel so I decided to bring Hymorel to you. I think you need him."

"Wouldn't it have been easier to use the stairs?"

"Of course. But nowhere near as exciting." He sauntered across to the supper tray, picked up a decanter and sniffed appreciatively. "Fortified wine, if I'm not mistaken. Does Laura know you drink this?"

"I don't have to ask her permission for anything," Clemis said defensively, hastily scanning for signs of parental intrusion.

"Don't frown, sweet girl. You'll get wrinkles." Kalyx's gold-tipped fingers smoothed her forehead. "Laura's having a final costume fitting and Idenion has his nose in a book as usual."

"Your perception must be better than mine."

"Perhaps. Or maybe I spied on them when I went up to fix the rope."

"Oh, you!"

Kalyx smiled conspiratorially. "So, having established we won't be disturbed, we'll take a glass of wine each and you can tell me all about your year with young master Dismal in Drearytown."

Clemis stifled a giggle. "You're always so mean about Trevone."

"And I'm entitled to be. He made my favourite girl unhappy." Kalyx sat her down, drew her close and handed her the wine. "Now, how am I to cheer you up?"

Trevone, ascending from the kitchen entrance half an ild later, sent his thoughts ahead to inquire if he was welcome. The mix of insobriety and uninhibited unity seared both his perception and his pride. Quietly he turned away and was about to leave the building when Idenion caught up with him.

"I'm so sorry about this, Trevone. I've no idea how he got in. Tralvar warned me he was trouble, but I'm afraid I wasn't vigilant enough."

"Opportunism laced with lies," said Trevone bitterly. "He doesn't care about her. He puts on an act and she falls for it."

Idenion concurred. "All I can say is, she'll probably regret it in the morning."

"That won't change how she feels about me. How can I win her back, Idenion? There must be a way."

"I wish I could answer that. You must know her very well by now....the things she cares about, the ideas she cherishes. A carefully considered gesture, based on what you know, could rekindle her interest."

"I hadn't thought of that," mused Trevone. "Thank you, Idenion. I'll have to think it through, but at least you've given me something to work on."

The next morning, day two of the Peisistrata, dawned clear and bright. The sun had scarcely risen when Drusa ferried Tralvar across the still-sleeping laterals to the spaceport. Tralvar's ancient sphere was parked near the communications tower, its hatch open, Jarras in attendance.

Tralvar alighted from the flitter and gazed wonderingly about. He had never seen the grass look so verdant nor the sky so blue. It was almost a pity to shut himself away in that dark little cabin.

"Er...Tralvar," said Jarras awkwardly, "there's someone here to see you. It's Ninfi. She heard about our conference from Kalyx, sneaked a look at the manifest and found out your departure time."

"It's all right, Jarras - I'll see her. Now go. You too, Drusa."

"But - " Jarras began.

"You know the drill. No one comes with me."

"Leave him," said Drusa quietly; and suddenly they were gone, dissolving into the too-brilliant sunlight. In their place stood Ninfi, in white, the picture of radiant health.

"You weren't going to say goodbye to me," she reproached him fondly.

He took her little hand and studied each slender finger and each oval nail as if he'd never seen their like before.

"Tralvar?"

He started. Chaos, this wouldn't do. He had to stay focused or they wouldn't let him fly. "My bold

Ninfi. Make your farewells, then - but please, no tears. I had all that earlier from Dena."

"I shan't cry," said Ninfi steadily. Then she embraced him, gently and lovingly. He clung to her, unexpectedly emotional himself. She was still so young.

"Have a long and happy life," he murmured at last, his lips against her hair. "Be proud of our son."

"I wanted him to be a scientist," she said dolefully.

"That he'll never be. But you must keep faith with him, Ninfi. You won't be sorry." Then he forced himself to step away from her. Turning his back on the sunlit field, he walked swiftly and resolutely into the sphere and closed the hatch. There, it was done. He was alone. He readied the control systems, called the tower for clearance and lifted off.

"We have you on screen," Jarras reported. "You've got the sky to yourself."

"Good. Then I can misbehave," Tralvar said laconically.

His own viewscreen showed Alda Mexa's white walls in graceful symmetry about their central hill, presided over by the Lyricon. As he continued his slow ascent he could see the silvery thread of the monorail leading to Tivenne and Treva, and to the west the glitter of water as the Lisir meandered toward the distant sea. An unfamiliar emotion stole over him: a fierce love for this planet and its people. Laura would have called it patriotism.

"I've done all I can for you," he whispered to the landscape below. "I only hope it's enough."

Was there anything he'd omitted to do? He would dearly have loved to blast the Ilonna mosaic into pieces, but Jarras had been opposed to it and he'd lacked the strength to set the charges himself. Hopefully something so stylised wouldn't mean anything to an invader. That aside, everything was taken care of. Everything save this, his final task.

It was logical for anyone to assume that with his affairs in order, he could have relinquished his tenacious hold on life and faded peacefully away in his sleep. But no, nothing was ever as straightforward as that. Not with him. It was in his nature to hold on, and hold on still longer, in a coma so deep that no healer could reach him. There would just be him and his conscience - and his victims. Tristell, little Tioni, Zenzie, Alendis, Asterion, Strephin, Floren and Quetri. He'd destroyed them all. And they were still with him, waiting to bring anguish to his last moments.

So he reasoned.

He checked the viewscreen: only scrubland beneath. And above, the blackness of space, which he had always feared. He now knew there were worse things.

"Tralvar," came Jarras' worried voice, "you're on the wrong vector. You should be heading due south."

"Just having a last look round," he replied airily. "Celestra's a very beautiful place. Tell Idenion he should write a poem about the view from up here. A *long* poem."

"Are you disoriented? Should I talk you back down?"

"No, that won't be necessary." He turned to the logic system and entered the personal code which would activate the old, damaged Drive circuits. Crimson lights scampered across the diagnostic panel and a warning chime rang out as he touched the transposal keys.

"Tralvar, what are you - "

"Goodbye, Jarras."

The dull boom of the imploding Drive echoed across the somnolent city. A few observers, Jarras included, saw the orange lightning flash which preceded the sound. The rest only saw a lazy plume of smoke, slowly dispersing to the west. No one outside of Communications realised what it was - none except Dena, on her way to the Lyricon. She halted, small fists clenched against her chest, stricken eyes fixed on the distant smoke.

"Oh, my poor love," she whispered. "My poor, brave, dearest love."

She'd known all along, of course. Ever since she'd overheard Drusa telling him that coma was an inevitable part of his illness.

"It's a great pity I lost the formula for Alendis' poison," he'd remarked. Then, after a pause: "I don't suppose you'd consider..."

"No, I would not. You know the healers' code - we can intervene only on the point of death and then only if there's suffering."

Another long pause.

"Will I dream?" he'd asked, suddenly pitiful.

"I don't know," Drusa had replied truthfully.

Shortly after that, Tralvar had begun talking about Scapirion - and insisting that he had to make contact alone. Dena had supported him, even encouraged him, in the full awareness that she was abetting his suicide. And he, intent on finishing his work, had never realised the extent of her devotion.

At the spaceport, while Drusa comforted Ninfi, Jarras called Scapirion on the transposer. There was just the remotest possibility that the explosion was an accident, although commonsense told him this was not the case. This had been a meticulously planned operation, even to the day of his departure - the one day when there would be no other aerial traffic. Much to his surprise, Scapirion answered him at once.

"I am First Tech Tuhallak," said a strong resonant voice. "We regret the passing of our exiled citizen Tralvar. We have indeed been conducting a dialogue with him about the possibility of his return, but were nowhere near a decision. Four octals ago he told us he was now too ill to consider such a journey, but begged us to acknowledge his children and continue the discussion with them. This we are willing to do."

"I...." Jarras was taken aback. "I am his son by marriage."

"Then you are not of the True," Tuhallak said disdainfully. "There is a son of his line, is there not?"

"Yes. Kalyx. But he - "

"Tell him I will hear his petition in due course. Scapirion out."

Nefyrra received the news as soon as she woke. She reacted with characteristic dignity. "Tonight's concert will proceed as planned," she informed the scolia. "I have conferred with Laura and Idenion and we are agreed that no official announcement regarding Tralvar will be made until tomorrow. The few people who saw the explosion have been told it was a failed experiment of his: we don't want an invaders panic while Alda Mexa is so crowded. After the announcement has been broadcast, some of his zirid recordings will be played as a tribute. And finally - let no-one refer to this event as a suicide. It was euthanasia by his own hand."

She did not weep, nor did she neglect her duties as custodian. Nefyrra was her father's daughter.

Lydion, grim-lipped, remained indoors sketching his new shield design. Tralvar's death, though anticipated, had disturbed him, not least because it was a reminder of his own mortality. Having already decided to shun the Peisistrata, he decided there could be no better way to honour his brother than to make a start on the work entrusted to him.

Toward evening there came a light tap at the door. It was Kalyx, and for once he didn't seem arrogant or flamboyant. He looked young, lost and unhappy.

"I don't know why I've taken this so badly," he said without preamble. "We weren't close. But I did admire him."

"As did I."

"I think he was disappointed in me," Kalyx went on. "You heard him call me a selfish upstart."

"That's nothing to some of the things he called *me*," said Lydion wryly. "For what it's worth, I don't believe you were a disappointment to him. He was something of an actor himself."

"He certainly made a grand exit today," Kalyx remarked, then hastily wiped away some fresh tears.

"Come on, now - enough of the drama," Lydion said awkwardly. "Would you like to see what progress I'm making on your father's last project?"

That had the desired effect. "Chaos, yes!"

"I shouldn't even be talking about this, you understand, but I suspect you know most of it already."

"I knew you were working with him," Kalyx said hesitantly. "That fight you had with my sister - "

"Ah, yes. She packs a mean left-hander."

"And the business of having to surrender your work to the enemy? You were emoting halfway down the street when Nefyrra and I arrived for that meeting."

Lydion gave a shamefaced grin. "Was I? I'm really not much use at this covert stuff. Which is why I'm getting this done as fast as I can and handing it all over to Jarras."

"You don't have to, you know." Kalyx looked at him searchingly. "Finish it, I mean. Father won't be any the wiser."

"I *do* have to," Lydion said quietly. "When he was taken ill at Ilonna I carried him in my arms like a baby, across that vast arena with a sandstorm brewing. It was a humbling experience - such total and absolute trust. I promised him, just afterward, that I'd complete his work. And I will."

Kalyx picked up a sheet of paper. "I'm afraid science was never my strong point."

"This is just theory. I'll need to refine it." Lydion cast a critical eye over his own jottings. "This device has to supercede the last. Tralvar suggested that I viewed Laura's retrace of war on Earth, and now I've done so I know exactly what he had in mind. This is, or will be, a set of miniature disruptors to be scattered in the enemy's path."

Kalyx examined another page. "Music notes?"

"Wave harmonics, plus some oddments I picked up from Tyvian. You won't remember him; he invented the retracer, and was something of a physicist. There was little he didn't know about universal resonance and the like. Since the Eldorians will doubtless be using my sphere-shield, I'm making sure the resonance on this little effort is superior. When the two versions meet, their array will just go pfft. At least, that's the general idea."

Kalyx had brightened. "It's wonderful to think Tralvar's work will live on."

As will the lie that it *is* his, Lydion thought with satisfaction. "I knew you'd approve. Now don't forget: if you ever need advice or just someone to listen, you know where to find me."

"Thanks, Uncle Lydion. I didn't think I'd be able to go on stage tonight but now I'm looking forward to it. Will you be running the weathershield?"

"Yes, as usual."

"Then maybe I'll see you later. Thanks again. It's good to know you're here."

101

***

As soon as she felt able, Laura unsealed the letter that Tralvar had left for her. In it was a list of zirid accompaniments he had recorded for her use, plus details of where to find the discs.

"Is that all?" Idenion asked.

"He wrote a very touching apology to Drusa. She let me read it."

She was deliberately misunderstanding him, but Idenion let the matter go. He knew she was as bewildered as he was. Dena had completed her inventory of Tralvar's effects, and her news was unequivocal: there was no message for Clemis, nor even a mention of her name.

Chapter Three

Clemis perched on a stool in the Lyricon canteen and picked disinterestedly at a slice of fruit pie. There were no other diners present. She was about to conclude her solitary meal when Trevone entered via the terrace doors, and after a moment's hesitation came to sit beside her. She gave him a wan smile.

"Hello. Have you been visiting your mother?"

"Yes. She...er...told me you were here. I've been making a few career moves and I was wondering what you intended to do when the Academy reconvenes. I didn't see your name on the roster."

"Checking up on me again?" Clemis asked, but with no edge to her voice. "I thought about going back - I did enjoy myself last year - but hereafter it gets a bit technical, doesn't it? I think I'd find myself left behind. So at the moment I'm helping Dena with the dancers' costumes. It's quite fun - I get to visit the textile houses and choose the firi. What are *you* doing at the moment?"

"Well, I've decided not to pursue astro-engineering fulltime. It would only degenerate into maintenance work."

"So you're not going back to Treva?"

"Only now and again. Father and I get along much better if we're not working together. I'll put in an appearance at the local spaceport if they need me - they're short of people in Communications. The rest of the time I'm going to teach physics to first-year undergraduates."

"Oh!" Clemis looked startled. "Some of them aren't much younger than you. They'll play you up."

"Quite possibly, but I want to give it a try. Physics is vocational so at least they'll be there by choice. I....suppose this job with the dancers means you're seeing a lot of Kalyx?"

"He's on tour," Clemis said a little too quickly. "And for the record, we're not an item. We fight."

"I see." Trevone tried not to show his relief. "Clemis, I'd like to ask you something. It's a kind of invitation really."

She looked up with a flicker of interest. "What?"

"Remember the improvements Jarras and I were making to the stardrive?"

"Yes, of course."

"Well, they're finished. And tested. So I was wondering if you'd like to re-enact our trip to Symerid Three. With one special little difference."

"You mean you wouldn't run us into the sun this time?"

"No. I mean, I wouldn't. But the difference is, I've found the programme for the Cradle of the World. We could go there and take a look."

Her face lit up. "Really?"

"Yes, really. Would you like that?"

"Oh, Trevone, need you ask? I'd love it. When do we go?"

"No time like the present." He stood up, and Clemis looked flustered.

"Hey, slow down! I know I like surprises, but this is a bit *too* sudden. I'm on a late lunch break - Dena's meeting me at the pattern-maker's in an astal."

"Then what about tomorrow, at dawn? I'll bring a flitter to the akron's side entrance. Anyone who hears it will think I'm delivering liman."

"That's perfect! I can sneak out." Clemis's eyes shone with anticipation. "Don't be late!"

"And don't you oversleep. I'm not climbing in any windows to wake you up."

Trevone assumed she wouldn't blush, and was quite pleased with himself when she did. He embraced her swiftly, then quit the Lyricon with a light step. "Move over, Kalyx," he murmured. "Your mastery of the grand gesture is about to be challenged!"

At first light Clemis was waiting at the kitchen entrance, wearing sensible coveralls and carrying a small hamper. "Syrup drizzle cakes," she whispered apologetically as she climbed into the flitter. "I've had no breakfast. I brought some for you too!"

"Fine, but keep them out of sight when we reach the spaceport. This is supposed to be a scientific trip."

"Who's going to see us? Can't we just get into your sphere and go?"

"Not quite. I haven't collected the programme from the data store."

"But that's halfway up the tower!" Clemis was indignant.

"I did *try* yesterday, but Jarras was breathing down my neck the whole time. I won't be long. Just hop on board and sit tight."

"Who's on duty this morning?" asked Clemis, still frowning.

"Nimion. Bit of an anxious type, but harmless. Now don't fret - we're going to Symerid Three and no-one's going to stop us."

He approached the sphere, tapped in the entry sequence and waited until the ramp commenced its rippling descent. Then he headed for the tower at a jog-trot, leaving Clemis to embark. Her attempt at being surreptitious failed almost before it had begun when she paused halfway up the ramp, staring at something: Trevone's name, etched into the hull near the hatch, in letters of bright gold. The sight perturbed her somewhat. No one, not even Tralvar, had ever personalised a sphere. And not just any sphere - not one of the shabby, well-thrashed variety commonly used by the Academy. Trevone's craft looked brand new, from the pristine white panelling to the softly sprung upholstery.

Trevone soon returned, the all-important crystal in his palm. "I was so lucky to find this! Most of the Symerid programmes have been withdrawn, but this one was listed by co-ordinates only and someone missed it. There's a logging-out system attached to the data store, something they must have installed while we were in Treva, but Nimion probably won't check it. He's running some test programme in the control centre." He loaded the crystal and sat back to wait. "You're very quiet."

"I saw your name on the hull. A bit ostentatious, isn't it?"

"I'm pleased you said that! Tralvar told Jarras and me to keep the enhanced spheres out of circulation, and since this is the only one at present, we're fostering the image of the First Scientist's spoilt brat with his own spacecraft. No-one will guess what it really is."

"You could have converted an old one," Clemis said in the same lukewarm tone.

"It's tactical, silly. We can't have it breaking down. You're not still mad at me, are you?"

"No. No, not at all. I was just thinking about Tralvar and how he pulled strings to get me into the Academy. And then, nothing. Did I do as well as he hoped, did I disappoint him? I'll never know."

"Come here." Trevone put an arm round her; she leant her blonde head on his shoulder and watched the diagnostic screen slowly perform its ritual. "I'm sure he intended to give you more good advice. He also tried to stay alive long enough to see what our new Drive could do. On both counts, time simply ran out for him. So we have to make decisions for ourselves now, based on all the wise words he offered." The logic system chimed softly. "Download complete. Well, my special girl, are you ready for this?"

Clemis' face relaxed into a smile. "You know I am."

Trevone, carefully casual, radioed in his departure time. Nimion's reply was somewhat guarded.

"Tower to Trevone. What is your destination?"

Clemis held her breath.

"That's for me to know," Trevone said coolly. "I saw you gawping out of the window at my passenger, Nimion, so I will simply say this: I'm reconciled with Clemis, and this trip is to celebrate the fact. I don't intend spoiling her surprise by telling *you* where we're going. Now do I have clearance or not?"

"You're cleared for take-off," Nimion said peevishly, and cut the transmission.

Trevone grinned at Clemis and engaged the programme, first amending the transposal point data which had caused so much trouble on their previous flight. As before, the rate of acceleration was phenomenal; transposal was achieved within two astallen.

"Now what?" Clemis asked a little doubtfully as the viewscreen went blank.

"We transpose as normal. This part of the journey remains the same."

"Why?"

"Because Jarras and I decided to leave well alone. We don't know enough about transposal to mess with it. We go in, we come out - but as for what happens *during*, it's best not to wonder."

"If you say so." Clemis, understandably perhaps, was still expecting something to go wrong.

Trevone nonchalantly helped himself to some cake. "You'll be pleased to hear," he said muffledly, "that we'll be able to hover for up to three astallen with minimal risk to ourselves. Jarras has made some fantastic improvements to our scanners. And of course we have an excellent getaway speed."

He was so confident that Clemis' doubts began to subside. "I hope it's daylight over Ing this time."

"We'll soon know. Er...you do realise we can't actually land?"

"*Land*?" echoed Clemis. "Who said anything about landing?"

"We could have done if I'd been able to find a remote, but there are only one or two and they're well hidden. I'm sure Idenion has one."

Clemis was so amazed that Trevone had even contemplated landfall that she was temporarily lost for words.

The Drive behaved perfectly, delivering the sphere swiftly and efficiently to a point above the English countryside. It was indeed day, but dull and cheerless; the screen displayed a bleak chilly landscape with a sprinkle of snow on the ground. Naked trees bordered a patchwork of barren fields.

"It must be the low season," remarked Clemis.

"We're a little too far south," Trevone said in the same breath. "Compensating: that's better. Hmm, those woods look a bit depleted."

"I told you, it's the low season."

"I don't mean they're leafless, I mean they're being cut down. See those bonfires? You can follow the line of tree-felling, leading north."

"Where's Cradle of the World?" Clemis asked apprehensively. "They haven't cut *that* down, have they?"

"Overlaying map reference from programme," Trevone replied crisply. "Searching. We must be very near it now....There! A ninety-five percent match."

Clemis studied the screen intently. "Oh, isn't it pretty! Even in winter. The little village and the woods all round. Can you magnify it any more?"

"No, we're at the limit."

"I wonder which was Laura's house? Do you think - hey, what are you doing? I hadn't finished looking at that!"

"The security scan's just detected a large gathering of people to the east. We've just got time to investigate before I have to leave this altitude."

"Not another riot!" Clemis exclaimed.

"No, they seem quite law-abiding," Trevone said slowly as the screen refocused. "It's a procession. A big one. There must be five thousand people at least."

"I know what this is," Clemis said excitedly. "Laura calls it a protest march." She spoke the term in English; Trevone looked at her quizzically.

"If they disagree with something or want to affirm something, they march," Clemis elaborated. "They carry banners, like the ones we're seeing. Can't we go just a little bit lower? Please, Trevone? White sphere, white clouds - who's going to see us?"

"Our time's already up," Trevone objected.

"I can read these instruments now," Clemis reminded him, "and we're in no danger. We aren't even being tracked."

Trevone conceded. "It's not what I was led to expect. Their surveillance must have grown lax. All right, half an astal to look at the marchers. Then

110

we leave. And if anything shows on our scanners before that, we leave very quickly."

The rally came more distinctly into view as the sphere descended. People of all ages, warmly clad, peaceable but determined. Clemis spelled out the letters on one of the banners, murmuring the sounds under her breath.

"Can you decipher any of that?" asked Trevone.

"My father," Clemis said loftily, "is the best linguist on Celestra. He's always translating Earth stuff into our language. Song lyrics mostly. Did you think I'd absorbed *nothing* from him?"

"Well....yes," Trevone admitted, ignoring a glare. "Go on then, tell me what it says."

"Wait...almost got it. The trees. Save the trees."

"Of course. What else?"

"I didn't guess," Clemis insisted, a hint of mischief in her voice. "Use your perception if you think I did."

"Not now, my little language expert. Reading you always leads to other things."

"And what's wrong with other things?"

"Nothing except your usual brilliant timing." Trevone keyed in the auxiliary power; the marchers and the threatened woodland vanished in a swirl of cloud.

Clemis stretched lazily. "Goodbye, Cradle of the World. I wish I could tell Laura how civilised everyone was being!"

"Not a syllable," Trevone warned, "or I'll catch it for stealing that flight crystal. I've still got to sneak it back without being seen."

"I'll distract Nimion for you," Clemis promised with a sly grin. "One last look at Earth before we go?"

"Coming up, as soon as I've negotiated their satellite collection." Trevone gently settled the spacecraft into high orbit and realigned the viewscreen. And it was then, as they looked back at Laura's vital but troubled world, that they saw the other sphere. It was travelling at approximately their speed but in a lower orbital path.

"Who do you suppose that is?" Clemis asked uneasily. "Do you think they're looking for *us*?"

"There hasn't been time for an unmodified spacecraft to get here," said Trevone, scrutinising the newcomer minutely.

"Oh, so they're here illicitly too! Let's give them a call!"

"Don't!" Trevone seized her arm as she moved toward the transposer.

"Why not?"

"It's...not one of ours."

"What do you mean, not ours?"

"That is *not* a Celestrian sphere." Trevone was surprised at his own composure. His engineer's eye had picked out subtle differences in the craft beneath them, both in its design and manner of flight. He wished he was wrong about its origin, but he knew he wasn't. And Clemis, reading him, soon shared the inescapable truth. The Eldorians, still hunting for Celestra, had found Earth.

She pondered this revelation for one instant before alarm kicked in. "Well, don't just sit there! Take us out of orbit before they see us!"

"Oh, they'll have seen us." Trevone increased speed. The other sphere kept pace.

"Discords, Trevone, don't play tag with them! Start the Drive - we can outrun them!" She made a grab at the control panel: he hauled her off it, then held her firmly until she stopped fighting him.

"Clemis, Clemis, listen. We can't run for home. They'd track us."

"Then what do we *do*?"

"Weren't you paying attention in class? There are procedures." Trevone was already busy at the console. "I'm going to lay a false trail. I've kept all my flight logs on the system, so I'll make use of that random transposal marker we found a year ago."

"The one with no stars close by?"

"Exactly."

"And then what?" persisted Clemis.

"Then I'll have bought us some time. Keep watch on the enemy, would you? Let me know if he makes any sudden moves."

"All right, but hurry up!" Clemis stared fixedly at the innocuous little sphere which had so quickly become an object of dread. The enemy, she repeated to herself. An enemy we've never harmed nor even met. How insane that is. As she watched, the other craft began to emit tiny flashes of light from a point near its base. She counted them. One, two, three and a pause; one, two, three.

"Ignore it," said Trevone when she alerted him. "We can't return their signal, even if we knew what it meant."'

Clemis took her eyes off the screen for a moment to see how he was faring. When she looked back, the Eldorian was much closer and the light was winking again. Suddenly her memory - or rather, Laura's - delivered the truth in a burst of terrible clarity. "That's no signal light!" she shouted. "It's a weapon!"

A green flare blanketed the viewscreen and their craft was rocked by a silent explosion. The gyroscopes whined angrily. Two more impacts followed; Clemis was thrown to the floor as the sphere almost de-stabilised.

"Go, Trevone! Now!"

Earth was suddenly lost in the distance.

"They're following," Trevone said shakily. "We're drawing ahead. Almost out of their scanner range. Transposing....."

Utter stillness surrounded them. Clemis picked herself up, decided she wasn't hurt and subsided numbly into her chair. "Now what happens?"

"When we exit transposal we'll take a breather. Even if they're still in pursuit they won't reach our position for an ild or so. I'll re-transpose to a training run I did, way beyond Myrma: there's a radiation belt close by that'll confuse their instruments. After that I think it'll be safe to go home."

"Sounds like it's going to take a while. Shouldn't we call Alda Mexa, warn them?"

"No, we'd better do that in person. Celestra's in no immediate danger. Unless of course you *want* to warn Nimion?"

"Not a good idea," said Clemis with a brave attempt at a grin. "I'm sorry I panicked back there. It was just such a shock, running into them. And you were so calm and collected...!"

"We've Jarras to thank for that. He taught me well."

"I'm really impressed," Clemis was looking at him with new respect. "I must try to follow your example."

The sphere dropped out of transposal and Trevone carefully checked their quadrant. "Ten light years from Symerid," he reported. "So far, so good. You know, this is probably the Eldorians' marker. An inexpert navigator on his way to Earth, undershooting by one stellar unit. Makes sense."

"Terrifying sense," Clemis agreed. "It means they found Earth over a year ago. Maybe they've already made contact."

"If that were so, Clemis, your protest marchers would have more on their minds than saving trees."

"All right, we'll assume there's been no invasion yet. But Earth's definitely being sized up."

"And the findings?" asked Trevone.

"Now you're teasing me."

"No, seriously. You've got Laura's knowledge of Earth. You *think* like Laura. What will the Eldorians do?"

For a moment Clemis stared in surprise. It had never occurred to her that Trevone's expertise didn't extend to all areas of the crisis. Her background gave her the insight he lacked. "Well," she began, "they'll know how heavily armed Earth is, hence the caution. They'll study every conflict, every bit of civil unrest, and plan their next move in the minutest detail. Then they'll act."

"They must be out of their minds."

"No, just very determined. They certainly don't lack courage - we've seen that today."

"They fired on an unarmed spacecraft," Trevone objected. "I call that cowardice."

"They had no proof we were unarmed," Clemis pointed out. "They took a chance. We could've blasted them out of the sky for all they knew. Anyway, now that I've had a moment to think about it, I don't believe they were firing *at* us. The first sequence of shots missed altogether, didn't it? And you didn't see how they closed the distance for the second volley. If they'd had any real intention of hitting us, they'd have done so."

"You sound very sure."

"I *am* sure. They were trying to make us run, and if you hadn't stopped me we *would* have - straight back to Celestra."

"Which was exactly what they wanted, of course." Trevone wearily returned his attention to the logic system. "At least I can ensure they don't find us just yet."

"What will we do when we get home?" Clemis asked, suddenly despondent.

"Good question," Trevone said morosely. "We'd better divert to Treva and find Jarras - although he won't exactly be pleased at having all

116

this dumped on him. I don't think I can face Idenion."

"Nor I," said Clemis. "And I certainly can't face Laura. Do you realise she'll hardly be aware I'm missing?"

***

"Good morning, First Citizens." Nimion, young, blond and ill at ease, gave Laura and Idenion a formal nod each. "Forgive my calling on you so early. But you did say, Laura, that you wanted to be informed if your daughter went joyriding."

"That was before she attended the Academy. She has an astro-science qualification now," Laura replied a little frostily. She disliked telltales.

"I think you'll want to know about this," Nimion persisted. "She and Trevone came to the spaceport at first light. Dawn plus one and a quarter, to be precise. Clemis carried a food basket. Trevone was being unduly secretive so after they'd gone I checked to see which programme he'd taken." He paused, clearing his throat. "I'm afraid one of the Symerid Three programmes was left in the unrestricted section. That's where they're bound."

"Are you sure?" asked Laura sharply.

"Yes, First Citizens. It had no title but I checked the quadrant and co-ordinates." He recited some figures.

"That's Cheveney," said Idenion.

"Hell's teeth!" Laura lapsed into English. "She promised - they *both* promised..."

"This may be my fault," Idenion confessed. "He wanted to impress her and I encouraged him."

"Never mind whose fault it is. We have to go after them!"

"Have you tried to contact them, Nimion?" asked Idenion.

"I can't get through. They're in transposal."

"Did they take a remote enabler?"

"Not unless Trevone brought one from Treva. Ours are still here."

"Even worse!" exclaimed Laura. "I'm serious, Idenion - we have to look for them. Why would Trevone take the Cheveney programme unless he intended to land?"

"Because it was the only one," Idenion said soothingly.

"Maybe. And maybe because he's intent on showing off. I don't *want* to go, Idenion, but we must. Nimion, will you release one of the proscribed flight crystals to us? And a remote?"

"Yes, of course."

"Can't we have something to eat first?" asked Idenion, mildly aggrieved.

"We'll take some food with us. We can't delay - they've already been gone for two ilden."

"I came here as soon as my shift was over," Nimion said fretfully. "Perhaps I should have had a message relayed."

"No. No, you were right to be discreet," Idenion assured him. "I want Symerid Three kept out of the public consciousness."

Nimion looked pleased at having made the correct decision. "Do you require a lift to the spaceport?"

"Yes," said Laura promptly.

"Please, Laura, less haste!" Idenion protested. "What about our clothes? We don't even know what season it is in Britain."

"I could calculate that for you," Nimion offered, "based on the planet's yearly cycle and the date of your last visit."

"Thank you, Nimion," Idenion said with dignity. "You gather the information while Laura and I have breakfast and decide what exactly needs to be done. Come back for us in one ild, or sooner if you're ready."

"I'll instruct the ground crew to have a spacecraft waiting," Nimion promised.

"One more question before you go," said Laura. "Was Trevone using his own sphere - the one with his name on?"

"Yes. What else?"

"Well, that's something in our favour. I was afraid he'd taken one of the top secret ones."

"Don't be silly, Laura," Idenion chided her. "Jarras wouldn't let him cavort around in one of those. So, we can have a quiet meal together and still arrive only three ilden later than they do. They're obviously planning to stay all day."

"Very well." Laura gave a barely perceptible smile. "Nimion: I don't usually approve of spying on one's colleagues but in this instance you did right. Clemis has committed a breach of security."

"Strictly speaking, it was Trevone," Nimion replied soberly. "I will return shortly, citizens."

"Strange boy," Idenion mused when their visitor had gone. "So serious. Well, Laura, what's your motive for wanting to rush after our daughter? You know how furious she'll be."

"We all think we're invincible at that age. And she isn't. Especially not on Earth."

"Trevone's a sensible lad. I really don't think he'll land."

"If Clemis says land, then he will. She manipulates him, Idenion. Remember what Tralvar said - that she's a leader without a cause to focus on? Until she finds a vocation she'll keep making mischief."

"There's not a lot we can do about that," said Idenion unhelpfully.

"Yes there is. We can give her a say, however small, in the running of our planet."

"That doesn't sound very sensible, dearest."

"It makes perfect sense to me. She won't get much job satisfaction making Dena's dresses. But if we involve her in something more responsible - "

"You *want* to revisit Cheveney, don't you?" Idenion interrupted.

She raised a defiant eyebrow. "I don't remember saying that."

"No, because you never said it. You've always claimed you didn't want to go. But that isn't what your thoughts have been saying - not now, nor in the recent past."

"I..." began Laura, aware that she couldn't even hedge round the truth. "Well, yes, I had been toying with the idea ever since we saw Trevone's flight dossier a year or so ago. But that's all it was - an idea. I realised that if I wanted to see England one last time it would have to be soon, or I'd be too set in my ways to make the effort. In fact if *this* hadn't happened, I'd probably never have budged."

"And now?"

"If I weren't so worried about Clemis I'd be looking forward to it."

Idenion smiled down at her. "I believe I would too. Let's prepare, shall we? I'm sure Nimion will be back ahead of schedule."

***

Trevone surveyed the exterior of his spacecraft in a mixture of anger and dismay. The hitherto spotless hull was blistered and blackened in a narrow band around half its circumference. The effect seemed worse in the region where his name had been.

"We'd better have our cover story ready before the maintenance crew arrives," Clemis suggested.

"I'm working on it," he replied irritably. "Chaos, what a mess. Our rotation must have caught the edge of that last energy beam."

Or some sharp-eyed gunner was having a game with us, thought Clemis privately.

"Well, that puts paid to my little show of vanity," Trevone continued. "Come on, let's go inside and wait for Jarras."

"Trevone," said Clemis uneasily, "I think the Eldorians might have seen that inscription."

"Not very likely. We never lost our spin."

"They'll almost certainly have made a visual recording of us," Clemis persisted. "And if they've got Narvellan tech, or anything similar, they'll be able to slow or pause their recordings. And if they can read Celestrian - "

"Which they probably can, since Axmiol could."

" - then they'll have read your name. They'll know who you are, Trevone."

***

"Laura, Laura, wake up!"

She struggled to obey. It was Idenion's voice, and he sounded frantic.

"Laura, please!"

She blinked and looked around, realising she was slumped in the co-pilot's chair. Idenion was crouching beside her, holding her hand.

"Laura, thank harmony you're all right. What happened?"

"I'm not sure. Remind me what led up to it."

"We were talking about Clemis. Then we went into transposal and you said you felt unwell. And suddenly, you were just...not aware. At least, not of me. I couldn't even reach your mind."

"We're not in transposal now." Laura tested each limb cautiously. She had pins and needles.

"No, it's over. We're decelerating."

"I had a bad dream." She sat up and he hugged her, more to reassure himself than anything else.

"What kind of dream?"

"Weird. I saw space, the cosmos, whatever you'd like to call it, as an endless series of curved lines - a bit like a music stave. And it was sounding, like the aldacite crystals."

"The universal resonance," Idenion said in hushed tones. "Tyvian claimed to have heard it on his travels. It's what transposal's all about."

"And...and then it changed," Laura went on unwillingly. "There was this awful noise like something broken, and all the lines were full of holes, like a torn spiders-web. And there were people, although I couldn't see them. Someone was shouting."

"Are you sure it wasn't me?"

"No, it was a woman. We have to do this now, she was saying, or we never will." Laura suddenly paused, abashed. "Oh, Idenion, how silly I'm being. That was *me*! That was what I said about this trip."

"Yes, but - "

"It was just a worry dream. Maybe I'm too old for transposal. I've always hated it."

Idenion wasn't reassured. "I don't think we should dismiss this too lightly. What about that other little episode you had, at the Peisistrata? The one you said was a migraine?"

"I daresay that's what it was," Laura returned. "The Peisistrata can be very taxing. All of this is due to stress, Idenion. Chasing after Clemis without a clue what to say when I find her - and more importantly, wondering if we'll have to land in Cheveney and what we'll run into if we do."

"Will you promise to see a healer when we get home?" Idenion persisted.

"I promise. Now let's drop the subject, shall we?" Laura rose decisively to her feet. "I'm going to freshen up. When we reach Earth, don't forget to watch for all that paraphernalia Trevone told us about."

"I hadn't forgotten. I'll take it very slowly." Idenion returned to the control chair, noting that the programme had less than an astal to run.

When Laura came back, looking more like her normal self, Earth was on the viewscreen. "It's still there, then," she said softly.

"Large as life. Now, Nimion's given me a vector that will safely avoid all that orbiting stuff, but before I engage it we need to confer."

"What about?"

"Procedure. Do you want to go straight to landfall or try to locate Trevone's sphere first?"

"*Can* we locate him?"

"Depends. I can scan for a theridolyte signature but Nimion says it won't work here. Too much metal."

"It still makes sense to try it," Laura said promptly. "Nimion can't always be right."

"Let's find out." Idenion tapped hesitantly at the logic keyplate.

"Is the scan running?" asked Laura after a barely perceptible pause.

"Indeed it is, but now I have to interpret the results. They're a bit chaotic to say the least." He pored over the screen for almost an astal, Laura peering impatiently over his shoulder, until one specific trace caught his eye. "This seems promising. Yes, I'm sure that's a sphere."

124

"What's it doing?"

"Orbiting. I'll try for more details." He magnified the trace and overlaid the template from the search programme. "There. Not a complete match, but it has to be theridolyte."

"Then call them," Laura said peremptorily.

"Are you sure that's how you want to proceed?"

"I'm sure. I realise Clemis will fly off the handle as soon as she hears my voice - which is why I want *you* to do it."

"Very well." Idenion turned resignedly to the transposer. "Trevone, Clemis, this is Idenion. Please respond."

Silence.

He repeated the call three times at Laura's behest, then gave up. "This is pointless. I don't think they're even on the sphere. I never thought Trevone would steal an enabler but he obviously has."

"They're in Cheveney?"

"I assume so."

"Then we'll have to follow. Take us in, would you - and we'd better have our cloaks, boots and warm hats at the ready. It's February, which means it's a bit nippy."

That, thought Idenion a few astallen later, was a slight understatement. They had emerged into the woodland clearing which Laura still called "The Cradle of the World" - the name given to it by her childhood sweetheart Jimmy. The wood itself was known, less romantically, as Wickens Clump. It looked miserable. A gaunt framework of branches encircled the dell, a few persistent leaves still clinging here and there; and at ground level a battalion of tangled bushes stood ready to ensnare passers-by. Dead leaves crunched to brittle fragments under Idenion's boots.

"Can you read Clemis?" asked Laura anxiously.

"No, but most of the village is out of my range." Idenion took a small square device from his pocket, holding it clumsily in his gloved hands. "Time to banish the sphere, I suppose."

Laura gazed suspiciously at the object. "Is that Narvellan?"

"Standard issue to their fleet," Idenion confirmed. "There were one or two left over."

"I hope there aren't any defective crystals in it."

"They were all replaced years ago," said Idenion reassuringly. "Nimion wanted me to have this version - it's better than ours. As well as summoning the sphere to me, I can communicate with its transposer - "

"What use is that when there's no one on board? Hurry up and launch it. The camouflage is pretty thin this time of year."

Idenion still seemed reluctant. "Laura, are you sure about this? I can't believe Clemis would put up with such cold weather."

"She enjoyed going to Ninka with Kalyx," Laura reminded him.

"That probably had more to do with Kalyx than Ninka."

Laura pursed her lips. "If you're thinking we should scurry back into the warm, forget it. I'm not leaving."

Idenion sighed and adjusted the remote. The sphere took off with a barely audible whisper.

"You're getting better at that," Laura observed.

"Actually, I couldn't remember a thing. Nimion took me through the landfall procedure while you were sorting out the clothes."

"What a paragon that boy is," said Laura, and strode out briskly.

Idenion followed her along the frost-hardened track, feeling as if he were wading through glue. He vowed he wouldn't ask her to slow down, but before long he had to. "Why isn't the gravity affecting you?" he asked somewhat reproachfully.

"It is," she confessed, pausing to let him catch up. "I feel twice my normal weight. But I did spend half my life here, so it's bound to be less difficult for me."

They left the thicket and walked slowly down the lane toward Cheveney. Nothing appeared to have changed. When the familiar outlines of Windbourne came into view, Laura had to blink back tears.

"Can you detect who's in there?" she asked Idenion, already knowing what he'd say.

"It isn't Nathaniel," he answered gently. "I'm reading two strangers, a married couple. Just walk past, Laura. You don't belong here anymore."

She endeavoured to comply, then ground to a halt outside the gate. Following her gaze, Idenion saw that the nameplate no longer read "Windbourne".

"That sums up the situation, doesn't it?" Laura remarked sadly. "The Hawthorns. And look -

127

they've got rid of the old conservatory and put that fake-Palladian thing in its place."

Idenion stamped his feet to keep them warm, wishing she'd move on. "Are English winters always so cold?"

"No, just every so often. We seem to have picked a bad one. And there's another problem too." Laura squinted ahead of them, into the west. "I didn't ask Nimion to work out the precise time of day, but maybe I should have. I think it's getting dark."

"Oh." Idenion was disconcerted.

"Either that or it's going to rain. I wish there wasn't so much cloud. We really do need to know the time."

"Well!" said a voice behind her. "Look who's turned up!"

Laura whirled abruptly and found herself face to face with Caitlin Stretton.

"I knew it was you," her ex-neighbour continued in thin disparaging tones. "Laura Gilcoyne and her fancy man."

"Husband," Idenion supplied. She continued to address Laura.

"Oh, so the first one managed to divorce you, did he? If you're looking for your uncle, you're seven years too late. He's dead and gone. Died penniless, so I hear."

Laura reacted predictably. "Penniless? Why?"

"I really couldn't say. Why don't you ask Margaret Moffat? She seemed privy to all his secrets."

"Mrs Moffat? Where is she?"

"In her cottage, where she's always been - her and those mangy cats." Caitlin glanced at her watch. "Just one piece of news before you hear it from anyone else: my son came home a year ago - "

"Jimmy? I'd love to see him!"

" - but don't come knocking on my door because he's not there now. He's with the tree people at Snelsmore Common."

"Tree people?" Laura was mystified.

"Eco-warriors. The Third Battle of Newbury, as they call it. I call it dangerous and stupid."

"It's in a good cause," Idenion said, having read some of her surface thoughts.

"You *would* say that. I know you of old, remember. Always hugging trees and lying on the ground looking at creepy-crawlies." Caitlin's faded blue eyes regarded him disdainfully. "Well, I can't stand here gabbing all afternoon. Sorry you've lost your inheritance, Laura - you should have made more effort to stay in touch." And she turned and walked away with small angry steps.

"Same old Caitlin," sighed Laura. "She still detests me. Now what was that about tree people?"

"First things first. The time's ten to five, and it's a Sunday. I prompted her to inspect her watch."

"Well done." Laura squeezed his arm. "But that means I was right - it *is* getting dark. And we've no money, no shelter, and it's going to get colder. Suggestions?"

"We could call on Mrs Moffat."

"And I'd love to do that, but we'd be there for hours. We have to keep looking for Clemis."

"I wonder," said Idenion, half to himself.

"Wonder what?"

"There's something I should check, but it means using the remote. And for that I need to be somewhere warmer."

"The Green Man, then. Has to be."

"I'll be seen!"

"Not if we're careful. There used to be a payphone in the lobby. If it's still there we can use the remote while pretending to use the phone."

"And if it *isn't* still there?"

"Oh, come on. We'll improvise." Laura headed down the lane toward the pleasant country inn, its lights mellow and enticing in the dull daylight.

The telephone was in its customary place. They crowded into the alcove, Laura lifting the receiver while keeping her other hand on the cradle. Idenion peeled off his gloves and began to programme the enabler, muttering Nimion's instructions under his breath. Laura shielded him while he worked. Everything was mundanely familiar: the odour of beer and cigarettes, the hunting prints on the wall, the murmur of voices from the saloon bar. The sheer ordinariness was disarming. She almost relaxed her vigil, then suddenly and guiltily pulled herself together. *She* mightn't be at risk, but Idenion was - every single moment he was on Earth.

"It's just as I thought," he murmured close to her ear. "Look at these two traces. This one's our sphere, and this is the other trace I was studying. There's a twenty per cent variation when you see them together."

"Meaning?"

"Meaning it's confession time. Laura, I don't think Clemis is here at all. I think I've brought us here for nothing."

"We can't be sure," Laura objected.

"With persistence, we can. I tried to tell you earlier..."

A strident whooping came from the telephone's earpiece and Laura jammed her hand back onto the cradle. "Tell me what?"

"About the Narvellan tech this enabler has. It can access a sphere's instruments, as I've just done. And explorers in trouble can call a default setting via the onboard transposer."

A young couple, deep in conversation, entered the pub and disappeared into the bar. Laura waited until the heavy inner door had swung to, then said: "These embellishments are all very well, but do watch what you're doing with that thing. You've never had much of a rapport with gadgets."

"I know, and I *am* being careful."

"Then why not leave well alone? What other checks could possibly help us?"

"Laura, you still don't see. I'm trying to call Alda Mexa!"

"What?" Laura stared sceptically at the tile-shaped object with its minuscule display screen. "How's it done? Where does the sound come out?"

"I don't know. I've never tried it before. And Nimion says - "

"Don't tell me! It mightn't work here."

"It will, but badly. Too much planetary interference kind of shoves a transposal beam out of line."

"Very scientific," Laura said drily. Another customer strolled past them. "Look, Idenion, we've been in one place too long. Give it one more try and then we'll have to move."

"Move where?" Idenion objected. "I'm finally starting to make sense of this. Can't I have a little more...hello? hello? Nimion?"

"Ask about Clemis!" Laura hissed.

The reply from Celestra was inaudible. Idenion tried various corners of the instrument against his ear before continuing: "Yes, I can hear you. Just. I *can't* speak up! Increase the gain your end. Now listen: we can't find Clemis and Trevone. Did they...discord's dreams, Clemis, what are you doing at Communications?"

Laura grabbed the enabler. "...trying to call you," her daughter's voice said, infinitely fragile and far away.

"Clemis? Clemis, I was so worried!"

"We didn't land," whispered Clemis via the tiny amplifying crystal. "Laura, you must... immediately...danger..."

"Say again," Laura urged.

A raucous burst of laughter from the saloon bar drowned the reply completely. Laura rushed outside, ignoring Idenion's plea for discretion. The renewed cold smote her face and ears.

"...come home," Clemis pleaded.

"Soon, little one. Now I know you're safe, I want to see a friend or two."

"...danger!" Clemis repeated. "...sphere...orbit...Idenion..."

"There's no danger to *me*, dearest. And I'll look after your father."

Nimion took over. "Tell Idenion," he said, his voice carrying better than Clemis' had, "to call Communications before leaving Earth. For all our sakes, he mustn't..."

"Mustn't what?" demanded Laura.

Silence.

"Damn and blast it!" She turned to hurry back indoors and collided with someone on the path.

"Steady on, love!" said a goodhumoured voice. "What's that you've got? One of those new mobile phones?"

"Er...yes," said Laura warily.

"Bit of a funny shape, isn't it?"

"Well, it..." Laura floundered. "It's designed for a woman's handbag. Same size as a compact or mirror..."

But the man wasn't listening. He was staring closely at her in the light from the porch. "Laura? Laura Gilcoyne?"

Laura returned the scrutiny and her frown gave way to a slow smile. "Barney! It is, isn't it? It's really you!"

Barney responded with a bear-hug. "You weren't just rushing off, I hope? Got time for a drink?"

"Yes, of course. But what are you doing in Cheveney?"

"Damn marchers invaded my local. All the regulars stayed away."

"Oh, I see," said Laura, although she didn't. "Let's go inside, shall we? I'd like you to meet my husband...er, second husband, that is."

Idenion was waiting at the entrance, a little anxious, but aware that Laura had things under control.

"Denny," she said when they were all seated at the bar, "this is Barney Cresset, guitarist at the Firelight Jazz Club."

"It's a pleasure to meet you, Mr. Cresset," Idenion said in his flawless English, shaking hands with the affable little man.

"You do still play, I assume?" Laura asked.

Barney grinned. "Old jazzmen never retire. Gus is still there, and Bill. Bill's picking me up in an hour. It's his turn to drive."

Laura made an instant decision. "Could I...could we...come along, do you think?"

"I don't see why not. Gus will be really chuffed."

Idenion, of course, knew what she had in mind. +Singing for your supper?+ he inquired. +Clever girl. Go on, tell a few fibs. I'll back you up+

" - maybe I should ring him," Barney was continuing.

"When you do," Laura said, "would you explain to him that I'm in a spot of bother and need an evening's work? For cash?"

"Why, what's happened?"

"Our hire car was stolen, and we - "

"So that's why you were swearing in the middle of the car park! Don't worry, leave everything to Barney."

In next to no time, the old musician had accosted the publican and secured a double room for the night, explaining that the lady was a professional singer *and* a native of Cheveney, and that she'd need a key to the premises as her engagement would finish late. Then he ordered the three of them a pub meal. Finally he went to ring Gus and came back beaming.

"There, all settled. I've paid Stan here for your room, and you can repay me when you get your wages. There's normally a good crowd on Sundays, so there'll be a few gratuities coming your way. Now, tell me what brought you back to this neck of the woods..."

Laura, after a ploughman's and two vodkas, was more than ready for her impromptu gig. "I'm sorry I don't have any evening wear," she said apologetically.

"No problem - that gym-slip will do nicely. I'm not sure about the boots though!"

"I'll sing barefoot," Laura promised. "I'm used to that."

The conversation turned to general matters. Idenion, with consummate skill, talked freely about everything except where he and Laura had been living. No-one save Laura noticed.

He was not so happy jolting down ill-made roads in Bill the bass-player's Volvo, but managed to hide his discomfort. Later, as he sat in the dimly-lit club watching Laura sing, he knew the awkward journey had been worth it in terms of the fulfilment it gave her. All through the time of his absence she had performed her songs here,

135

dreaming of his return, imagining him in the audience. With a certain amount of awe, he witnessed her celebration of him. For her, he had written the epic poem Clemoridys; this was what *she* had done, expressing her love in the sincerest way she could.

He was less able to appreciate the music itself, although he acknowledged the skill involved. Tralvar, you'd have revelled in this, he thought regretfully. I'll miss you, old friend, in more ways than I can imagine.

It was 1.30 in the morning when Bill dropped them off at the Green Man. Laura, long unused to the effects of Earth alcohol, was unashamedly merry - though drunk on success as much as the liquor. The audience had received her warmly and demanded a second set. Idenion was more sober but, as always during a sojourn on Earth, very tired.

Laura led the way to the back door, where a security light burned. "Quick, Idenion, where's the key? I'm freezing!"

"Wait." He hunted through the folds of his cloak, hampered by the presence of the enabler. "Look after that for a moment, would you?"

She took it from him. "I was wondering," she remarked in the tone of one in search of a mighty truth, "how this thing knows which spacecraft to send for."

"We've only got one," Idenion pointed out.

"No, silly. The Narvellans had *thousands* of spheres and thousands of these little gadgets - so how did the right signal get to the right sphere?"

"Don't know."   Idenion started on another pocket.   "Must be a bit like that remote locking device on Bill's car. It didn't open all the cars in the street, did it?"

Laura considered the notion and began to giggle. Idenion finally persuaded the back door to open and bundled her inside.

"Shh!" he scolded. "Everyone's asleep!"

An inquiring woof came out of the darkness: the pub's Alsatian, a room or two distant.

+Quiet, Buster. Good dog. We're friends+ Idenion responded hastily. Dogs didn't have the same empathy with him as cats, but the command must have sufficed as Buster gave a puzzled whine and settled down.

The landing light had been left on. Laura sailed up the stairs, stumbled near the top and righted herself with a thud of boots. "Hello mister!" she said brightly to someone. "What's new? Hey, that's a song. Want to hear it?" And she trilled a few phrases.

"Shh!"   Idenion, in between hauling Laura toward their bedroom and silencing Buster's renewed challenge, was vaguely aware of a half-open door and a disapproving presence. "I beg your pardon, sir," he intoned gravely.   Laura dissolved into a fresh fit of giggles.

Once in the bedroom, with its oldfashioned mahogany furnishings which reminded her of Windbourne, she became quieter. "I've just realised something."

"What?"

"We've no night clothes, so we'll have to keep eachother warm." She squeezed his groin and he had to suppress a yell.

"Stop it, Laura. I'm too tired."

"No you're not," she insisted. "No you're *not*!"

And much to his surprise, he wasn't.

***

The following day, after a late breakfast, Idenion and a rather subdued Laura made their way to Mrs Moffat's cottage. The door was opened by a freshfaced youth of about twenty.

"Oh...hello," Laura said uncertainly. "We were told Mrs Moffat still lived here."

"She does," affirmed the boy. "I'm her nephew, Jack. And you must be Laura and Denny."

"News still travels fast, I see," Idenion observed.

"It does when Caitlin's involved," muttered Laura.

"Come in," urged Jack. "Aunt's been waiting for you all morning."

Mrs Moffat was hurrying to the door as fast as her arthritic limbs would allow. She hugged Laura fiercely, eyes bright with tears, then embraced Idenion with no less affection. "Bless you, Denny, for bringing her back - even if it *is* only for a little while. But where did you *go*, the pair of you? We tried everything to find you when Nathaniel was terminally ill - even put an SOS on the radio."

"I wanted to ask you about Uncle," Laura said swiftly, evading the question. "Caitlin said he died in poverty. Is that true?"

"Come and sit down." Mrs Moffat led the way into the small living room, headed for a rumpled armchair and subsided into it. A cat promptly leapt onto her lap. "Meet the rest of my family," she continued. "This is Milly, and that one over there is Tilly. They're sisters. Then there's Smudge - he's probably out. And this - " She made a grab under her chair and brought out a struggling ginger tom - "is Rocky, Tib's great great grandson."

Rocky spat and raised a threatening paw.

"That's very bad manners," Mrs Moffat said to him reprovingly. "Well, Denny? Do you think you can work your magic on this delinquent?"

"Watch out. He bites," said Jack laconically.

"He just needs to be understood," Idenion replied, confidently taking charge of the ill-tempered pet.

"Aunt Margaret...about Uncle," Laura pursued anxiously.

"Don't fret, my angel. He had enough to live on, although he did lose most of his savings."

"How?"

"After you left for the second time he made several bad investments. And what was more, he didn't seem to care: said money meant nothing to him any longer."

+That sounds as if it was *my* fault+ Idenion remarked to Laura. She nodded ruefully.

"So he used Windbourne to buy an annuity," Mrs Moffat went on. "That meant it had to be sold on his death. He said - insisted - that you'd never come back to claim it. That isn't why you're back, I hope?"

"No, no. I thought my daughter was here," answered Laura, not knowing what else to say. "Jack, I'm sorry. I'm ignoring you."

"Don't mind me," Jack said amiably. "I'm fascinated. Real human interest stuff."

"Jack wants to be a journalist," Mrs Moffat explained. "He's at college."

"Political studies," Jack elaborated. "I'm doing a thesis: the role of the media in protest issues. And since Auntie lives next door to the most well-organised protest I've ever seen, she has the pleasure of my company while I do some research."

By now, Laura knew all about the proposed Newbury bypass and the unprecedented campaign to save the woodlands. "Have you spoken with the eco-warriors?" she asked.

"With them, and townspeople who want the road - not to mention the local press. I'm hoping to sell them an article or two while I'm on my sabbatical. Denny, are you all right?"

Idenion was carefully prising Rocky's claws from the front of his shirt. "No damage. He's just a little nervous."

"I thought he'd be chewing your arm off by now," Jack said, mildly impressed. "Do you work with animals?"

"No, I'm ....in local government."

Jack grinned. "If you can't beat 'em, join 'em, eh? Aunt Margaret said you used to be a bit of a radical."

140

"In my younger days," Idenion said modestly.

"And now I want to hear more about your daughter," prompted Mrs Moffat. "What's her name? Is she your only child?"

Laura glanced at Idenion.

+You know what works best+ he responded. +As much of the truth as is feasible+

"Clemis isn't mine," began Laura bravely. "I found I couldn't have children, so we made an arrangement with a young woman."

"A surrogate?" asked Jack curiously.

"Yes. She gave birth to Denny's daughter and we adopted her." Despite the intervening years she was unable to keep the emotion out of her voice.

"Jack, love," said Mrs Moffat tactfully, "Why don't you run up to the attic and bring down those things I rescued from Windbourne?"

"Oh, yeah. Will do. I should be typing up this morning's notes anyway. If any of it's repeatable."

"You've already been to the camps?" asked Laura, slightly dismayed.

"Bright and early. Bit of a wasted trip, actually - the evictions were due to start today but the contractors are all on health and safety training. Sneaky, I call it - get everyone geared up to repel boarders and then leave them standing around."

"Did you happen to see Jimmy Stretton while you were there?"

"Not today, but we've met. Why?"

"We have a history." Laura lowered her gaze demurely. "I haven't seen him since I was sixteen."

"You don't say!" Jack was suitably intrigued. "I could re-unite you if everyone's happy with that.

141

He's bound to be at Snelsmore tomorrow, defending the tunnels. Did you know they've buried great concrete blocks in the ground and they're going to handcuff themselves -"

"Jack," said Mrs Moffat patiently.

"Souvenirs. Notes. Right away. " He vanished upstairs, returning a few minutes later with a dusty bundle of music and scrapbooks. "I think that's all of it. Give me a shout when you want some lunch."

"He's a good lad," Mrs Moffat said fondly. "Life's going to be very dull when he leaves."

In the momentary silence, Rocky's purr could be distinctly heard.

"I don't believe it! You certainly do have a way with cats, Denny."

Raucous music suddenly issued from above. Everyone was startled except Rocky, who seemed blissfully unconcerned.

Mrs Moffat sighed. "You'll have to excuse Jack. He doesn't seem able to work without some racket going on."

"What a peculiar song," commented Laura.

"He plays that a lot. It reminds him of his girlfriend, apparently. I dread to think what she's like!"

They chatted on, Laura giving a lively description of Clemis but remaining vague about the missed rendezvous. Idenion supplied some anecdotes about fatherhood before they turned their attention to the pile of memorabilia. Most of it centred around Laura's singing career in the Sixties, but there were one or two school photographs and

142

some wartime sheet music which had belonged to her mother. And, curiously, one 45 rpm record.

"Forever Autumn," Laura mused, picking it up. "I didn't buy this. Look, it says 1978. I wasn't here in '78."

"Nathaniel bought that, the spring after you left," Mrs Moffat informed her softly. "He said it could have been written about you. He really did miss you."

Laura felt a pang of guilt.

"Nathaniel gave us his blessing," Idenion said swiftly. "He knew he wouldn't see her again."

Jack pounded downstairs. "Why the long faces? Something's just occurred to me, Aunt M - a new angle for my thesis - and I'll have to make a quick dash to the reference library."

"Again?" asked Mrs Moffat.

"Soon. So, if anyone wants lunch..."

Laura helped him prepare sandwiches. "What's this new idea of yours?"

"Well, there was this weirdo making a tour of the camps this morning. I've seen him before, going on about his missing friend. This time he was giving out leaflets." He fished a crumpled piece of paper from his jeans pocket. Laura smoothed it out and read: "Have you seen this man? Christopher Edgewood, 48, last known whereabouts Earley, Reading..." And as she gazed at the picture of the missing man, she had a vivid impression of a day in late summer and a cheeky voice remarking: "I like your dress!"

"This...weirdo," she said slowly. "Was he short, bespectacled and called Darren?"

"You *know* him?"

"From long ago. They're UFO hunters, aren't they? He and Chris turned up the day I left my husband - that's why I remember them. Is Chris really missing?"

"Oh yes, that part's true."

"Then why call Darren a weirdo?"

"Because," said Jack, pausing for effect, "he says his friend was abducted by aliens."

"Er....oh."

"The camps tend to attract odd types," Jack went on. "The serious protestors indulge them but don't really want them around. So I was thinking: how much publicity has been given to these airheads, and is it bringing the movement into disrepute - maybe intentionally? I shall have to do some reading."

While they ate, Laura played "Forever Autumn" on Mrs Moffat's ancient radiogram. Idenion fed Rocky tidbits from his sandwich and listened intently to the song's lyrics, already at work on the translation he knew Laura would request.

"You can take the record if you want," Mrs Moffat said.

"I wouldn't be able to play it," answered Laura regretfully.

"Me neither," Jack put in. "Who wants vinyl these days? Now, has anyone seen my library card...?" And, bolting the rest of his lunch, hurtled upstairs again. "All stop looking!" he yelled after a couple of minutes, reappearing with the elusive card and an armful of notebooks. "See you later, Aunt M. I'll stop by Snelsmore on the way home, Laura, and see if Jimmy's back. Oh, nearly forgot - here's the CD you were asking about. Alice Cooper."

The front door slammed and Laura stared mystified at the small square of plastic she was holding. "What on earth?" she began. Then, catching Idenion's warning eye: "Oh, yes. Yes, I see."

"Right, you two," said Mrs Moffat purposefully. "Now that Jack's out of the way I want a word with you both."

"Have we done something wrong?" asked Laura.

Idenion said nothing.

"I don't get around much these days, so I have a lot for time for thinking," Mrs Moffat began. "And I've thought a lot about *you*, Denny. Even so, I very nearly didn't say anything - not until I saw Laura with that CD just now. You'd never seen one before, had you?"

"No," Laura admitted.

"And I'll never forget how sad Denny was when he came back and found Tib so old. He didn't know cats had such short lives - did you, Denny?"

"No," said Idenion quietly.

"And there were other things too, little things. I can't remember them all. But I *do* know that every time you've turned up there's been lost luggage or a stolen car or some other excuse why you've no money and only the clothes you stand up in. And you appear and disappear as if you're part of a conjuring trick."

"Aunt M - " ventured Laura.

145

"Let me finish, love. Even then, the penny wouldn't have dropped if it hadn't been for something Nathaniel said. He could still talk after his stroke, you see, although a lot of it didn't make sense at the time. He said he'd been at peace with himself since you came into his life, Denny. He said it was because you'd shown him Ida. Those were his exact words - *shown* him Ida. Do you know what he meant?"

"Yes," Idenion said even more quietly.

"Then if I asked you - *if*, mind - you could 'show' me my late husband George?"

"I could. If you wished it."

Mrs Moffat was silent for a moment. "But I don't *need* to see him, do I?" she said at last. "I'm not brokenhearted like poor Nathaniel. George and I had a long happy marriage, and he's here in my memory as clear as ever. So, why don't you show me your daughter instead?"

"If you're sure."

"I *am* sure. I don't think I'll have another chance to see her - *or* you."

"It's becoming more and more difficult to get back," Laura said.

"I know, love. I know. Well, Denny my boy, get weaving. Don't keep me waiting now I've decided."

Very carefully, Idenion gave her a smiling image of Clemis: two-dimensional, as in a photograph. The old woman's face lit in wonder.

"She's beautiful," she whispered. "You must be so proud." Then, briskly: "Well, that's done. I'm sorry to have put you on the spot, Idenion - that's your proper name, isn't it - but I wanted my little bit of proof."

"There's so much more we could tell you," Laura said impulsively.

"No, poppet, let it rest. You're with the man you love and that's all that matters." She chuckled suddenly. "I never could look you in the eye, Denny! I'm glad there was such a good reason why."

***

At seven the following morning, Jack picked up Idenion and Laura from the Green Man and drove them through the chilly dawn to nearby Snelsmore Common. He'd succeeded in tracking down Jimmy, who had agreed to meet with Laura but advised an early visit before the bailiffs arrived. But the approach road was cordoned off, and in the distance were vehicle lights, milling figures and silhouetted machinery.

"Bloody hell, they're here already!" muttered Jack.

"Maybe we should just turn around," Idenion said; but the barrier was unattended, and Jack was already half out of the car.

"I'll soon shift those cones," he promised. "Don't go away!"

"Idenion, why did you suggest turning back?" asked Laura reproachfully.

Her partner sighed. "I know how much this meeting means to you, but it does rather look as though Jimmy has his hands full. Added to which,

I'm tired and cold. Some breakfast would have been nice."

"I've run out of money."

"Also, we've been here too long. We should have gone home once we knew Clemis was safe."

"Oh, Idenion, it's only been a day and a half. And weren't you in touch with Alda Mexa last night?"

"No. I couldn't get a signal."

"Well, I'm sure it doesn't matter. They'll cope."

"We're supposed to leave someone in charge - " Idenion began, but just then Jack returned.

"All clear!"

"Won't you get into trouble for taking that down?" Laura asked.

Jack shrugged. "I didn't notice anyone watching. Now let's find your boyfriend - er, ex-boyfriend."

When they reached the edge of the camp they saw a small army of security guards and police holding back a straggle of vociferous spectators. Further on, protestors were being dragged out of holes and down from trees under the ever-brightening skies. Chainsaws whined and cherry picker cranes swooped on fragile tree-houses. The eviction crews worked fast and furiously, with little regard for the occupants.

Confused and slightly alarmed, Idenion and Laura joined the onlookers - mostly protestors arriving from other camps. Jack tried to find Jimmy. Then Laura suddenly noticed a girl clinging to some undersized branches at the top of a tall tree. She had no safety harness. The bailiffs had sawn through every branch beneath her, leaving her no way down. A cherry picker lurched forward; its operator made a grab at the girl, who dodged and almost lost her footing.

Laura, her attention divided between the girl's plight and Jack's search, failed to notice Idenion's horrified expression. Thus she had no idea that he would make a sudden dash for the trees.

"Stop that!" he yelled ineffectually. "Stop that *now*! She'll fall!"

He didn't get far. One of the security guards brought him down in a rugby tackle, and seconds later he was being shoved into a police van with two other protestors who had tried to breach the line. Somehow he managed to re-emerge from the van just long enough to hurl something into the air.

+Laura! Catch!+

It was the enabler. She caught it, more by luck than judgement, just as a gruff voice said:

"That wasn't very clever of him, was it?"

She turned, and at first didn't recognise the gaunt, greyhaired man next to her. Then something about his eyes evoked a tender adolescent memory. "Jimmy?"

"The same."

"Oh, Jimmy, you've got to help me. I have to go after them!"

"Take it easy, Laura." This was Jack. "They're going to Newbury nick, not the Tower of London!"

"You don't understand. Denny's never been arrested before - he'll be completely lost."

"They'll only hold him a few hours."

"Then I'll go in and wait. Or if that's not allowed I'll wait outside."

Jack sighed. "Okay, I'll take you."

"No, I will," said Jimmy. "This is *my* fault; I should have met her somewhere else. Stay and watch awhile, Jack - you'll find plenty to write about."

"I already have. See you later, Laura."

Laura wondered if he would.

Jimmy led the way to a battered Mini and they were soon in pursuit of the police van. "What was your husband so keen to get rid of?"

"Mobile phone." Laura stared ahead at the road, her expression tense and angry. She was desperately worried about Idenion, and at the same time furious with him.

"It's nice to see you too," Jimmy said pointedly.

"Oh, I'm sorry, Jimmy. It *is* nice to see you. I've often wanted to tell you..." She paused, seeking the right words.

"That you got away from Cheveney and became a rock chick? I know that much from Ma." Jimmy grinned appreciatively. "And then you went and blew it by marrying an accountant. Bad move."

"I soon ditched him. And you? What happened to *you*? You look..."

"....ancient. That's what living rough does to you. Don't worry, I'm respectable now. I work for Friends of the Earth."

"So you won't be staying in Cheveney?"

"For another month or two. After that I'll go wherever I'm needed. Ma knows the score: I imagine your uncle did too."

Contrary to Laura's expectations, Idenion, though annoyed with himself, was neither lost nor in a panic. He quickly ascertained from his new companions - veterans of such arrests - what would be expected of him, and was fully prepared by the time they reached their destination. Courteous without being deferential, he gave his name as Nathaniel Gilcoyne and his address care of the Snelsmore protest camp. Ordered to turn out his pockets he discovered two cat biscuits and an apple core, which he solemnly handed over.

...He was aware of Laura's anxious presence outside. +I hope Jimmy can't see you talking to yourself+ he sent warningly.

"He's at the pay and display," she replied obscurely. "I'll stay in your horizon the whole time, darling, so if you want anything - anything at all..."

+Breakfast?+ he suggested.

"I'll ask Jimmy."

A minute or two later, Idenion and a protestor who called himself Dave were escorted to a cell and ostentatiously locked in. Just before the door hatch was slammed shut, Idenion favoured his jailer with a most winning smile. "My friends will soon be bringing some food. Would you see it's delivered to me, please?"

"I'll speak to Room Service," came the laconic reply.

Dave chortled his approval.

The cell seemed unnecessarily hot and stuffy. Idenion soon discovered the reason - a convector heater beneath the wooden bench he was sitting on. "Doesn't this thing turn down?" he asked.

"Nope," said Dave without budging.

"Well, it's better than being cold I suppose." Idenion spread his cape on the bench to make it more comfortable. He hoped the dusty airlessness wouldn't trigger any breathing problems, but decided he'd manage as he wasn't exerting himself. The food duly arrived: sandwiches, biscuits, and soup in a lightweight container. There was more than enough to share with Dave.

After he'd eaten, Idenion wanted nothing more than to doze off; but Dave suddenly waxed garrulous about the iniquities of the British government, the justice system and life in general. Idenion let the unfamiliar phrases wash over him until he abruptly realised an answer was required.

"I said, what's your real name?" Dave was asking. "Where are you from?"

"You could say I'm homeless."

"Yeah? With that cut-glass accent? You've probably got a stately pile somewhere. One thing's certain - you're not Nathaniel Gilcoyne. I did some gardening for him once."

"I'd rather you didn't ask me anything else."

"This isn't a spy movie, you know. There aren't any bugging devices. Just you, me and the walls."

"Look," said Idenion irritably, "I'm not Nathaniel and you're not Dave. Now can we please leave it at that?"

The injured silence which followed was worse than the monologue.

"You wouldn't believe me if I told you," Idenion supplemented.

Dave continued to sulk. "If we can't trust one another then the battle's lost."

Idenion sighed wearily. "All right," he said at last, "you wanted the truth and here it is. I don't *have* to tell you this; I could make something up and you wouldn't be any the wiser. But as you say, this is all about trust." He paused, straightened his shoulders, then continued: "My name is Idenion and I'm the First Citizen of Celestra. That's a planet about three hundred and twenty light years away. I came here looking for my daughter but she'd sensibly gone home again. And now I'm stranded, and I'm also very worried because my people need me and I'm not there to govern them."

There was another long silence, an incredulous one this time. "You really *believe* that, don't you?" breathed Dave at last.

"Of course. It's who I am."

"Yeah. Okay." Dave sounded disillusioned.

"And now I'm going to sleep," Idenion concluded, bunching his cape into a pillow.

"Go ahead. Sweet dreams. Tell you what - I'll introduce you to King Arthur tomorrow."

At 2 pm, Idenion and Dave were photographed, fingerprinted and freed. As soon as Idenion emerged into the daylight Laura hurtled into his arms.

"Steady on," he admonished gently. "Mind my inky fingers."

"Did they charge you with anything?" asked Jimmy.

"No, just told me not to be a bad boy in future."

Laura continued to fuss over him while Dave drew Jimmy to one side. "Jim, your friend is seriously Out There." And he recounted some of what he'd been told.

"Sounds like he was winding you up," Jimmy remarked. "I don't know his surname but his first name's Dennis and he's married to Laura here."

"Are you sure?"

"Course I'm sure. Look at them!"

"No, I mean....oh, never mind." Dave slouched off and Jimmy turned back to the others.

"Come along, First Citizen of Sou'wester. Your chariot awaits."

"What have you been saying, darling?" asked Laura with a tinge of alarm. Jimmy answered for him.

"I don't know, but Dave's really freaked. Serves him right. I know what he's like when he gets on his soapbox."

"My other half. Always into mischief." Laura gave Idenion a meaningful look.

"Right, here we are." Jimmy unlocked the Mini with a flourish. "Afraid it's the back seat for you, Denny. Sorry there isn't much room. Now, where can I drop you both?"

"The Green Man," Laura said promptly. "I still have their back door key."

Idenion endured the short ride in pained silence. How he hated cars, especially noisy little

154

ones with no leg room. Hopefully this was the last time he'd ever have to ride in one.

Back in Cheveney he left Laura and Jimmy saying their farewells, took the key and strolled into the pub. In the aftermath of a hectic lunchtime the staff were busy clearing tables, so he leant on the bar and waited. The saloon was now empty of customers save for two darkhaired men seated at the far end. Idenion recognised one as the guest Laura had woken the night before last, and wondered whether to offer an apology. But his instinct, which had served him so badly that morning, correctly held him back. The man looked round, turning a dark cold gaze in the direction of the bar. Idenion quailed inwardly; a trickle of sweat ran down his back as he strove to maintain his casual stance.

The man was a killer. Not a reluctant one as Tralvar had been, nor one who delighted in murder. He had killed routinely, noncommittally, as part of his profession. He was an agent of the Eldorian Empire.

"Be with you in a moment, sir," trilled the barmaid as she hurried past Idenion with a trayful of glasses.

"Thank you," Idenion managed. Trembling, he forced himself to read the two Eldorians as they resumed their murmured conversation.

" - wasting our time when we've work to do. Control must have got it wrong."

"Control doesn't make mistakes. This *is* the landfall area, and bursts of aldacite activity suggest our target's still nearby."

"And how do we recognise this Celestrian? Nobody tells us that!"

"Leave it to me. He'll give himself away or someone will give him away. And when he does show up, he's to be taken alive. Is that clear? There's to be no sudden direct action from you."

"Such as?"

"Such as your unilateral decision to take out that investigator. He was just an amateur."

"What was I supposed to do? He'd stumbled on one of our ops!"

There were sounds of raised voices from the kitchen. Idenion placed the key on the bar, but stayed rooted to the spot in dread of revealing himself. For the Eldorians were now discussing *him*.

"...the one with the inebriate wife. No wonder he looks drained. I wouldn't mind some of what he was getting!"

"*There* you are, darling!" Laura breezed in, all smiles. "Jimmy's gone now. We had a long talk. I'm glad he's found something to do for the environment - he always wanted to. I knew he'd never marry. He just isn't into...Idenion, are you listening?"

"Yes, dear." He shot a frantic glance at the Eldorians. Why in chaos had she called him Idenion?

"And here, you'd better have this back." She handed him the enabler. "It's been digging in my ribs all morning."

Idenion suddenly found the power of movement. Grasping Laura's elbow he steered her rapidly out of the pub and up the lane.

"Where are you going? We're supposed to be having lunch at Mrs Moffat's!"

"We can't. We have to go, now."

"In daylight? And what about my photographs?"

"Discords, Laura, keep walking!"

Sensibly she obeyed. "Idenion, whatever is it? You look terrified!"

"Once we're round this bend in the lane," he continued as if she hadn't spoken, "we're going to run until we reach the concealed track. Ready?"

"Ready," she replied uncertainly.

"Don't look round," Idenion added. The Eldorians had left the pub and were trailing them at a distance, believing the lane led nowhere.

They ran, Laura the faster as usual. When they were well into Wickens Clump Idenion halted, sobbing for breath. "We've lost them for the moment," he said hoarsely as soon as he'd recovered.

"Lost *who*?"

"The men in the pub. They're Eldorian spies."

Laura paled. "Those two business types from the room next to ours?"

"Yes. Oh, don't look like that, my best girl. You managed to fool them brilliantly until now."

"Eldorians...on Earth...?"

"We can't think about that yet. Come on!"

As they neared the dell, Idenion was already keying in the retrieval sequence. "That will have

157

alerted their surveillance people," he warned as the sphere alighted, "but we still have to contact Alda Mexa before we go anywhere. Once we're in orbit we're exposed to everything they've got, and I'd prefer to take my chances on the ground."

"Now we know what Nimion was so anxious to tell us," said Laura with a shudder.

It was Trevone who answered them. "Idenion, thank harmony you're safe. You've seen the Eldorians? Then you'll know what procedure to follow."

"Lead them away from Celestra?"

"Yes, just as I had to. Jarras and I have worked out some co-ordinates for you; I'll transmit the data direct to your logic system. It'll triple your journey time, but there's no alternative."

"I understand."

"What you must also understand is that it might not be enough. I was flying the prototype: *your* sphere may not be any faster than the Eldorians'. In which case, all the false trails in the galaxy won't shake them off."

"I copy." Idenion answered steadily. "Send your data. I'll do the best I can."

"Oh, Idenion!" Laura crept shivering into his arms as the panel display cascaded and whirled. "They'll find Celestra, I know it. And we'll be responsible!"

Chapter Four

Less than a day after Idenion's sphere had touched down, a lone spacecraft appeared in the sky above Alda Mexa. Its hull was a rich shade of bronze, with yellow markings. It circled the city once, insolently, then made one complete orbit of the planet before leaving at maximum speed. There was no communication, but the message was clear: the Eldorian Empire was on its way.

Laura and Idenion had returned to the spaceport, having called an emergency debriefing. They wanted to pool information, including all recorded material, with Clemis, Trevone and Jarras before deciding what measures were required. Clemis was at her most solicitous and Trevone was calmly forensic, but the normally equable Jarras was seething with anger. When the Eldorian sphere made its fly-by, his temper finally erupted.

"This is all *your* fault, you pair of incompetents!" he snarled at Idenion and Laura. "You brought them here!"

"Father, that's unfair," ventured Trevone. "If it weren't for me the First Citizens wouldn't have been anywhere near Earth."

"And who put it into your head to go there?" Jarras swung back toward Idenion. "*He* did."

"These recriminations will get us nowhere," said Laura irritably.

Idenion, with true diplomacy, stifled his own anger long enough to study Jarras. The younger man looked understandably tired and tense, but there was something beyond that. His shadowed gaze and generally edgy stance made Idenion suspect he hadn't slept properly for some time. "Perhaps if Jarras has a grievance," he said quietly, "we should hear it now. Then we can set it aside and proceed with other matters."

Jarras wasn't expecting kindness. "I...." he began, "I just don't think you fully understand what an impossible position you and Laura put me in. You went careering off without a word to anyone except Nimion, and without deputising anyone to officiate in your absence - so I was in charge by default. I was at my wits' end when Trevone came back with his news. I didn't know whether to inform the people, send someone after you or just keep quiet."

"I apologise, Jarras," said Laura. "We were thoughtless - or rather, I was. My only concern was for Clemis."

"At least *one* decision's been taken out of our hands," Idenion remarked. "Everyone will have seen that sphere."

Clemis spoke up. "The one thing we mustn't do is let the Eldorians get their hands on the enhanced Drive."

"It's vital they don't," Trevone agreed, taking his cue from her. "I've already had some thoughts on that. I'll get a burnt-out sphere from Space Tech, duplicate the scorch patterns on the hull and claim I only achieved high acceleration by wrecking it. And I'll hide the original, of course."

"I had a team ready to convert more spheres," said Jarras, "but we'd better postpone that - at least until we've assessed the risk."

Idenion endorsed this proposal. "The Eldorian presence on Earth changes many of my existing plans," he confessed. "We can't conceal Earth's whereabouts or pretend we don't go there. But we'll have to convince them that my landfall was a one-off, that I only acted out of concern for my daughter."

"We could tell them we study Earth's music," Laura suggested. "From a safe distance."

"That could work," mused Idenion. "But our most difficult task, because it will require the co-operation of every citizen, is to persuade the enemy that Laura is a native of this planet."

There were puzzled stares from Jarras and Clemis.

"Don't you see," pursued Idenion, "that Laura will be in immediate danger if they guess she's from Earth?"

"They might not need to guess." Jarras still seemed intent on scoring points. "It depends what they were able to find out from Axmiol."

"Axmiol told them nothing. If he had, they'd have been here years ago."

"From Cheveney, then."

"Do you honestly think they'll bother with Cheveney now they've found Celestra? Those two agents would have returned to their previous assignment as soon as we were out of the picture."

"Since when were you the expert?"

161

"I was there, Jarras. I read them," Idenion said patiently. "They'd infiltrated somewhere important and were anxious not to lose the advantage."

"Surely the Eldorians will know Laura's different?" asked Clemis.

"The Earth agents didn't. They assumed she was Celestrian too. And something else: although they thought us easy prey, they were still extremely wary. Unless I'm very much mistaken, that attitude will persist."

"Why?"

"They're nonconversants. There can be no covert studies as on Earth - no secrets. As soon as they land they'll be subject to our scrutiny, and they won't like it."

Clemis cheered up. "And they won't know Laura's not telepathic, will they?"

"Oh, I'm not sure about that," Laura said doubtfully.

"No," declared Idenion. "They won't. So my first priority is to organise the relayists - everyone must be warned not to mention Laura's origin. Few people do anymore, but we have to ensure no-one does."

"And will you withdraw all copies of Clemoridys?" Jarras inquired sarcastically.

"What in chaos is wrong with you?" demanded Laura.

"It's a perfectly valid question."

"It isn't," Laura contradicted, "because my homeworld isn't mentioned in the poem. The Narvellans thought Clemoridys was a myth, and I daresay the Eldorians will too."

162

"That's if they bother to read it," said Trevone. "They don't strike me as literary types."

"Some will be," Idenion answered quietly. "And they may well be the most dangerous."

"Have we any other business?" asked Laura.

"No, I don't think so. Not until they make contact." He rose to his feet, ignoring a twinge from the bruises he'd received at Snelsmore. "But we'll have to dispose of a few items that connect you with Symerid Three. Old Lyricon programmes, for a start. And we may even have to doctor the marriage register."

A duty operator looked in. "First Citizens, we're receiving calls from the other city states. They want a statement from you."

"Tell them," Idenion replied testily, "not to use the radio. From now on, all updates regarding the Eldorians will be via transposer and relayist only. You may also add that statements require facts, and as yet I don't have any."

The technician retreated.

"Come on, you," Jarras said to Trevone. "Back to Treva. We've a sphere to customise!"

"May I help?" asked Clemis.

Jarras shrugged. "Suit yourself. Not that you ever do anything else!"

Alone with Idenion, Laura said: "I didn't dare mention this in front of Jarras, but this big cover-up you're planning might be futile. Those agents heard me sing!"

"And they *still* thought you were Celestrian. They obviously know nothing about us."

"They might tell someone who does."

163

"Laura, my love, they had a mission and we were just a hindrance. Their report's going to reflect that." He put an arm about her. "It *is* a worry, but we'll have to proceed as though it never happened. We'll soon know if our deception's worked."

***

The day after the de-briefing, Laura went to see Nefyrra. The custodian, calm and focused, greeted her visitor cordially. She had all but lost the skinny awkwardness that had characterised her younger self; now in full maturity, she carried her imposing height well. Her long brown hair was unbound. As always, the campanile key was her one item of jewellery.

"Is Jarras - " began Laura, looking about.

"He's at Space Tech today. You may speak freely."

"You obviously know why I'm here." Laura tried not to sound embarrassed.

"Of course. You want to know if there's anything wrong between Jarras and me." Nefyrra handed her a beaker of liman and poured another for herself. The drinks cooler was the single concession to luxury in the otherwise ascetic living quarters.

"And *is* there anything wrong?"

"On a personal level, no. By that, I mean he's the same as he's always been - a passionate and devoted partner. Almost *too* passionate, you could say. He always chooses the most inopportune times

164

to make love - usually when I've just called the scolia." She smiled indulgently. "But I manage to keep him happy."

"And what about his recent behaviour toward Idenion and me? Is it simply anger at the way we behaved?"

Nefyrra deliberated before answering. "I think it's partly a career issue," she said at last. "Jarras never intended to spend so much time at Treva, but circumstances demanded it. He knows I don't mind - I've more than enough to occupy me here - but I know he'd rather not have to do it. And he *never* wanted to be First Scientist, with its attendant duties. He keeps saying he'll pass the title on to Trevone as soon as he's mature enough. Not yet, obviously!" She smiled again.

"Thank you for that insight, Nefyrra," Laura said gratefully. "It might be possible to reassign Jarras, but I can't promise anything in the light of this uncertainty. Except..."

"Yes?"

"We'll soon need to bring the scolia-tech into operation. Someone has to co-ordinate them."

"I thought Lann was in charge of that?"

"There's a limit to what he can do from Tivenne. Everyone assumed Jarras would be the overseer."

"In that case," declared Nefyrra, "he *will* be."

"It's extra work."

"Yes, I know. But I can share the responsibility with him, can't I? Jarras has always sided with the resistance and this time will be no different."

If she could have heard Jarras at that moment, she might not have been so sure.

"Are you off your head, Lydion? We can't start testing new inventions now!"

"That was the arrangement," Lydion protested.

"Well, the rules have changed. Sorry."

Lydion bridled. "Aren't you forgetting something? In the very near future, Dena's going to be handing my sphere-shield plans to the invaders. So it's very important to have the next version up and running!"

"And it's equally important that we don't get caught testing it. We'll have to wait."

Lydion conceded with bad grace. "All right, if we must. Here are my calculations. Let me know when you're ready to try them out."

"I'd rather you kept them."

"That wasn't the deal," Lydion argued. "We're pretending this is Tralvar's work, remember? I don't want to be stuck with it."

"Neither do I."

"Discord's dreams, Jarras! You've got the whole of the Academy to hide it in, plus two spaceports and several factories. All I have is one small house and the generator room at the Lyricon!"

"I'm sure you'll think of something."

Lydion glared. "Don't push me, Jarras."

"Then shut up and stop trying to evade your responsibilities."

Lydion finally lost his temper. "Now listen to me, First Scientist. As far as I'm concerned I've fulfilled my duty to Tralvar and my part of the work's over. So you have a choice. Either you take

166

this incriminating stuff off my hands or I go home and make a little bonfire. It's up to you."

For a moment their eyes locked; then Jarras sighed and turned away. "Very well. Leave the paperwork with me."

"With the greatest pleasure." Lydion placed the folder on his desk. "And when you've chosen a hiding place for it, you *could* just forget to tell me where."

"Anything you say."

"Oh, and another thing. Those emitters I put in storage: Tralvar didn't say we had to hand *those* over, did he? At least, not all of them. If you keep a few back, the components will come in handy for the new assembly."

"I'm....not sure."

"Look, *I'll* see to that, if you like." Lydion's good nature quickly reasserted itself. "I'll have a word with Zanna; she can help me shift them."

"Where to?"

"Well, I know she has connections with Ninka. That far enough away for you?"

"Yes, of course. Thanks, Lydion."

"And if I might venture a word..."

"What?"

"I know you're in a front-line position, but we can't have you caving in before the invaders have even arrived. You won't have to face them by yourself. You've got that clever son to help you, and Nefyrra will be like a rock."

"I know that," said Jarras quietly.

"And the kids here at Space Tech are marvellous. They'll be looking out for you too.

You've nothing to worry about, Jarras - not like me. Who's going to watch *my* back?"

"All right, Lydion, you've made your point. I'll keep your work secure until it's needed."

Lydion left, thankful to be emptyhanded. But something still nagged at the back of his mind, no matter how hard he tried to ignore it: the final part of Tekla's formula. It was his negative reaction to it which had brought about Tralvar's seizure. I never promised to build *that*, he told himself. One man couldn't. And it's too late now, anyway. Jarras is worried that two or three people might get caught; how would he feel about the entire resources of Treva? Forget it, Lydion. You'd get no support and no gratitude, just a bunch of thieving aliens at your door. Let the knowledge stay lost in the sand. It's for the best.

***

Celestra waited. And waited. One octal went by, then another, and there was still no sign of the Eldorians.

"It's a psychological ploy," said Laura, but remained just as tense as everyone else.

Then, after twenty days, the deep-space monitor on Alda Six registered the approach of twelve spheres. They moved steadily sunward, in close formation, before settling into a geosynchronous orbit above Alda Mexa. Shortly afterward, Communications received a message which was promptly relayed to the akron.

168

Kyrin, still at the peak of his profession despite his advancing years, acknowledged the contents with his usual aplomb. Then, by prior arrangement, he made his way to the First Citizens' suite. "They want to land a delegation," he reported. "Diplomatic envoys, they said."

Clemis sniffed. "A likely story."

"Your cynicism invites hostility," Idenion said sharply. "Until some ground rules have been established we must try not to provoke these people."

"Fair enough. I'll provoke them later," Clemis said blandly.

"They speak Celestrian, then," Laura observed, trying to keep the peace within her own family.

"Oh yes," Idenion replied. "They've been thorough. We always knew they would be." Then, to Kyrin: "Give them my permission to land, and have the perimeter flares ignited to guide them to the spaceport."

Kyrin relayed these instructions to the Communications operator and waited for the reply. It arrived almost instantly. "They say," he announced with the faintest air of disapproval, "that the flares won't be necessary. They know where the spaceport is. Apparently they have aerial photographs."

"From the sphere that circled the city," Laura surmised.

"Of course. It was to be expected." Idenion straightened up and tried to look positive. "Well, shall we go?"

"I'd better stay here," Laura said with great reluctance. "We don't know how many of them speak Celestrian, and I'll have no means of conversing with the ones that don't. They'll know I'm not telepathic sooner or later, but it doesn't have to be yet. Take Kyrin with you."

"I'll come!" Clemis piped up brightly.

"Oh, now, Clemis, I don't think you should - " Idenion began.

"Yes she should," Laura said firmly. "I was just about to suggest it."

"Really?" Clemis affected surprise.

"Yes. While Idenion is....negotiating, I want you to stand about looking pretty and study the Eldorians' reaction to you. It's very important."

"I presume you have a reason for suggesting this, Laura," Idenion said with a slight frown, his mind already preoccupied with his welcoming address.

"Eldor's a military dictatorship, Idenion. Think! These representatives aren't likely to be civilians. And traditionally, occupying armies have an exploitative attitude toward women."

"Worse than the Narvellans?"

"Hell's teeth." The epithet emerged as a weary sigh. "You've no idea. When did you ever have anything to do with soldiers? Yes, they'll be worse. The Narvellans kept their women under wraps but they still respected them and allowed them to have important careers. The Eldorians, unless I'm very much mistaken, will do neither."

"Three of the spacecraft have landed," Kyrin said. "The others remain in low orbit. The

170

delegates want first contact to take place in the open; we are to send no more than three people."

"You're worrying needlessly, Laura," Idenion declared. "As I said earlier, they fear us. Come along, Kyrin, Clemis: let's see if we can maintain this advantage."

Laura watched them leave. Suddenly thankful to be alone, she leant briefly on the nearest wall before moving like a sleepwalker toward her bedroom. From the moment the Eldorian landfall had been announced, she had again felt disembodied, unreal. There had been no chance to consult a healer as she'd promised. She lay down as a precaution, but there was thankfully no repetition of her transposal-induced blackout. This, instead, was more like the sensation she'd had on day one of the Peisistrata - a feeling that she was out of step with time. For a few moments she seemed to be two people; one resting, one watching herself rest. Two selves, two versions of Celestra. She hazily recalled an Earth poem about a road not taken, believing she truly had come to a divergence of the ways. "I took the one less travelled by..." Then instantly, in a heartbeat, her mind snapped back into focus. There was but one Laura, one road ahead. She felt that a choice had been made. She was equally sure she hadn't made it herself.

She put on a fresh tunic, drank a small glass of wine and went out onto the balcony. It was a typical Celestrian summer's day - sunny but with enough breeze to keep the heat in check. How treacherous of the elements not to provide weather more suited to the occasion.

"First Citizen Laura." The voice at her elbow was subdued, apologetic, and belonged to a small nondescript woman.

"Yes? May I help you?"

"Forgive the intrusion, but Kyrin was concerned about leaving you with no relayist cover. He asked if I could stand in. I'm Alcis, eastern sector. I can send strongly enough to augment the chain from here."

"Alcis! I know your name so well, but I don't believe we've ever met. How thoughtful of Kyrin."

"Kyrin is always thoughtful," said Alcis with a faint blush.

"Are you in touch with him now?" Laura asked eagerly. "Could you tell me what's going on at the spaceport?"

"They're still waiting," Alcis replied after a pause. "Clemis is growing impatient. And Kyrin says there's some kind of disagreement at Communications..."

"What in chaos is wrong *now*, Nimion?"

"Something appeared on the scanner. Something large."

"Well, it isn't there anymore. Not than one can see much with reflected sunlight all over the screen. Are you sure you didn't make a mistake?"

"Positive. And with respect, if you hadn't been so busy craning out of the window you'd have seen it for yourself."

"Show me the readings." Jarras inspected the logic system. "Is *this* the object? Iron, minerals, carbon...probably a meteor. And it's apparently been captured by Alda Five."

172

"It didn't behave like a meteor," Nimion persisted. "It just appeared out of nowhere."

"Sounds like a scanning glitch. Get the array serviced."

"It's just been done."

"Then get it done again. And in the meantime, if you see anything else that isn't Eldorian, isn't theridolyte and isn't anywhere near us: don't bother me with it. Understood?"

"Understood."

"It had better be. Now come and see what's happening outside. That's far more important." Jarras hastened back to the window, and Nimion reluctantly followed.

The bronze sphere was squatting complacently on the spacefield, flanked by two unadorned vessels. Clemis, Idenion and Kyrin stood at a respectful distance as instructed.

"If they don't soon come out I'm using conscious telepathy on them," Clemis muttered ominously. No-one heeded the threat. The truth was, she couldn't have done it. It was the first time she'd tried to read a cluster of nonconversants, and the result was incomprehensible.

At last there was some activity from the trio of spacecraft. All three hatches began to open, the ripple effect slightly less fluid than the Celestrian original. Five men descended the ramps. Superficially they resembled the two Earth-based Eldorians: darkhaired, brown-eyed, lightskinned. All five wore uniforms of bronze and yellow, re-emphasising the colours of the flagship. Their jackets were high-collared and double-breasted, with a multitude of buttons: the breeches, trimmed with yellow braid, were tucked into calf-length boots. Three of the men wore small brimless hats, set back from the hairline; the other two were equipped with helmets and carried side-arms. The two armed men, who were obviously not there to take part in any dialogue, stationed themselves to either side of the three emissaries.

"From the Empire of Eldor, greetings." It was the youngest man who had spoken, in tolerably good Celestrian. His coldly patrician features did their best to smile. "My name is Pervain Ephren-Noveen of House Patieron, and I have been appointed ambassador to your world. You may address me as Pervain. This - " he indicated the plump middle-aged man to his left - "is General Grenthap Nith-Prella, in charge of this expedition."

Grenthap clicked his heels and waved an arm.

"And this - " Pervain pointed to the man on his right, slightly older than himself, "is Escir Drage-Tula, our medical officer."

Escir caught Clemis' eye and gave an apologetic little grin.

"Finally," announced Pervain, "May I present Mror, from the kingdom of Miiyat. Mror's having a little trouble with your sunlight but he doesn't want to miss the entire ceremony."

Idenion drew in his breath sharply. The creature picking its way down the central ramp appeared, to his startled eyes, to be a large grey cat - but a cat the height of a man, walking on its hind legs and wearing battledress. On reaching the foot of the ramp it gave a sudden leap forward and landed near one of the soldiers. At closer quarters Idenion noticed that its feet were unshod, and guessed they would be employed to damaging effect in combat. The forepaws had an elongated central digit, bestowing a limited degree of dexterity. It apparently had no tail.

The paws clenched, then relaxed, the claws sliding from their sheaths for an instant. The broad bewhiskered face, with its down of blue-grey fur, turned suspiciously toward him. The tufted ears flattened involuntarily. Large amber eyes, the pupils contracted to vertical slits, regarded him with insolence.

First Narvella, then Eldor, now these creatures, Idenion thought despairingly. Where will it end? And why didn't I realise the Eldorians had brought another species here?

The answer was obvious as soon as he looked into the cat's mind. The Eldorian mindset consisted, in the main, of wariness, ambition and conceit. Mror's was much the same, although laced with idleness.

The cat's thin mouth opened, displaying pointed teeth. He hissed a brief sibilant phrase in his own language, leaving Idenion even more taken aback. For what Mror had said was, "It will be pleasant to usurp the land of my ancient enemies."

"Would someone kindly translate?" asked Pervain. "We have no interpreter with us."

"He says he's pleased to be here," Kyrin stated impassively.

"Idenion," whispered Clemis, "aren't you meant to be saying something formal?"

175

Idenion recovered himself. "In the name of my people, welcome," he intoned. "I, Idenion, recognise the Empire of Eldor."

"Very nicely put," remarked Pervain. "And now perhaps we can dispense with formalities. I understand your leader is a man called Tralvar."

"Tralvar is dead," Idenion replied. "*I* rule now, together with my wife."

"Your information is somewhat out of date," added Clemis pointedly. "You'd be wise to keep that in mind, ambassador."

Pervain looked her up and down with studied indifference. "You're very young to be his wife," he observed.

"My wife is performing her civic duties," Idenion returned. "This is my daughter, Clemis."

"I stand corrected." Pervain gave an ironic little bow.

"And this," Idenion went on hastily, "is Kyrin, my relayist."

"Who, no doubt, is transmitting news of our conversation to the entire city."

"No doubt," said Kyrin, turning his clear-eyed gaze on Pervain, who after a moment frowned and looked away.

"Perhaps," said Idenion tactfully, "we should consider a change of venue to somewhere more congenial. May I suggest - "

He was interrupted by a long, low wail from Mror. The cat-man had both fore-paws pressed to his head and was rocking to and fro in obvious pain. He rasped something through rigid jaws.

"He says he's in agony, that his head's on fire," Kyrin supplied.

"Tell him," Escir said urgently, "to go back into the sphere and purge the air - "

It was too late. Mror fell to the ground, writhing and slavering. He began to rend and rip at his clothes. Spittle flew in all directions.

"He says he's being flayed alive," Kyrin gasped. "I'm sorry, I must close off this contact..."

Obscene swellings appeared on Mror's face and neck. Trickles of blood ran from his eyes and ears. Escir went to the cat's aid, but stepped back after a moment with a gesture of defeat.

Mror's flesh had begun to suppurate and lose cohesion. Tufts of bloodstained fur littered the ground as the stricken creature thrashed about. The wail became a feral shriek, then a series of coughs. The three Celestrians looked on, shocked and silent, Kyrin's stoic presence sustaining the others.

Eventually Mror's struggles subsided into feeble twitching, then stillness. His strangulated breathing ceased. But even when he was obviously dead, the tissue degeneration went on. Large viscous bubbles formed on his ruined skin; each one broke with a sluggish pop, emitting a spurt of pus and a noxious smell. Everyone windward of the corpse shielded their nostrils and moved hastily aside.

At last the deterioration seemed to have settled. Escir gave discreet instructions over his communicator, requesting a disposal team and a body bag. Then, suddenly, the carcass ballooned to several times its normal size.

"Get back," Escir ordered unnecessarily, just before the stomach burst open in a shower of acid filth. One of the soldiers, not quite quick enough, was spattered with the stinking mess; he turned white and vomited into the grass.

Finally, all was quiet. Then the other soldier, staring wild-eyed at the Celestrians, drew his side-arm. Escir slapped it out of his hand.

"Don't be a damned fool! They had nothing to do with this. Can't you see they're as shaken as we are?"

"Then would you mind telling us what *did* happen?" demanded Grenthap, piqued at having the Empire's dignity sabotaged.

"Obviously, the cat's immune system attacked itself," the medic replied. "I can't be more informative until I've examined the remains. But we all know about the bio-defences this planet has. I think we've just seen them at work."

"The viral strain the Narvellans carried was harmless, according to you."

"It only becomes active *here*. A co-factor. I strongly recommend more tests on our landing party - just to ensure we aren't being killed slowly."

Pervain hadn't turned a hair. "Where were we, Idenion, before this distasteful incident? Ah yes - you had just suggested a change of scene. This seems an appropriate time for me to accept."

"As you wish," Idenion said quietly.

Pervain then addressed his superior officer. "General Grenthap, may I respectfully suggest you stay here to calm the men? I can handle these negotiations alone."

"Very well, Pervain," Grenthap growled a little reluctantly. "Leave your communicator on. We'll be with you at the first sign of trouble."

"There will be none." Pervain gave another of his cold smiles. "You can rely on me, General, and on our hosts."

Idenion led the way toward the base of the tower, where one of the disused passenger lounges had been opened up.

"Well now," Pervain said conversationally as they walked, "I'm beginning to think the Narvellans were wrong about you people. They thought you were weak. You showed little sign of weakness just now."

Idenion merely shrugged.

"And you," Pervain went on, turning to Clemis, "are not quite the delicate flower you appear to be."

"Never judge by appearances," she replied sweetly.

"Yet - and correct me if I'm wrong - Celestra has never raised an army nor fought a war."

"We don't wage war on ourselves, if that's what you mean," Idenion said loftily.

A sphere passed slowly overhead; they paused and looked back as it touched down. Several men in protective clothing disembarked and set about removing what was left of the cat.

"Just between you and me," Pervain said ingratiatingly, "I'm glad the Miiyatans are out of the picture. They're nothing but a liability."

"Then why did you give them transposal?"

Pervain looked affronted. "We've given them nothing - they just invited themselves along. A few

179

lackwits in our Senate thought they'd make good mercenaries. We soon learnt otherwise. The average Miiyatan soldier is lazy, undisciplined and only follows orders if it suits him."

"Then," said Kyrin shrewdly, "your intention was merely to disconcert us."

"Not so; Miiyat insisted on sending a representative. Grenthap knows more about it than I do."

Clemis followed her father and the ambassador into the communications centre, enduringly grateful for Kyrin's quiet company. +I don't know what to make of Pervain+ she confessed. +I didn't expect to *like* the Eldorians, and I don't like *him*. He's sexist and condescending, just as Laura predicted. But there's something underlying all that, something ruthless, and I'm not getting to it+

+He has a superbly disciplined mind+ Kyrin answered. +Thus, there are aspects of his personality that elude us. He's obviously been trained to resist telepathic study+

+Trained by whom? The Narvellan prisoners?+

+Axmiol, probably. Pervain doesn't have any first-hand recollection of him, but I imagine these are his techniques+

Clemis guessed that Kyrin knew more than he was admitting about Axmiol's fate.

+He was a very brave man+ the relayist confirmed sombrely. +He never gave away our location, and his silence cost him his life+

They reached the lounge. Pervain strolled inside, selected the most comfortable chair and unhesitatingly helped himself to fruit and wine. Clemis watched expectantly, hoping to see him spill pilif juice down his immaculate uniform. Disappointingly, he didn't.

"Succulent," he remarked, looking directly at her.

"What exactly do you want from us?" Idenion asked abruptly.

Pervain didn't reply immediately. He picked up another fruit, peeled and ate it, then made elegant use of a fingerbowl. "You're a sensible man, Idenion. You don't waste time. I like that. Basically, the position is as follows..."

A tiny cylindrical craft, only a third the size of a sphere, hurtled through the upper atmosphere toward Alda Mexa. Its projected landing site was somewhere very close to the akron. High in the communications tower, a blip appeared briefly on the scanner along with some figures which scrolled and vanished. Jarras and Nimion, still at the window, failed to notice. The soldier who had drawn his weapon was being marched toward a spacecraft, and a blistering row had erupted between Grenthap and Escir.

The cylinder continued its vertiginous descent until it was level with the akron's top floor. Then it slowed with drastic suddenness, thudding unceremoniously to the ground near the kitchen entrance. An airlock whirred open; a darkhaired young man stumbled out, dizzy and disoriented. He fell to his knees on the flagstones, vaguely aware that his transport had sealed itself and taken off.

His eyes wouldn't focus. He crawled sideways, shaking his head in an attempt to clear it, and bumped into a tub of flowers. Their scent was exquisite and he inhaled deeply, temporarily unmindful of his situation. Then something hard and metallic poked him in the back.

"Get up, Eldorian!" said a woman's voice.

He turned, squinting up at the middle-aged cook and the ladle she held. "I'm not Eldorian," he replied hoarsely.

She stared intently at him, then suddenly put a hand to her mouth. "Oh! Oh, you poor boy!"

Finally he managed to stand. "I'm here to see Laura," he said with as much firmness as he could muster. "Will you take me to her?"

Moments later the courtyard was empty save for the tub of eprys blossoms, one broken stem trailing on the ground.

"We are aware of your recent history and the indignities the Narvellans visited on you," Pervain was proceeding in his slightly irritating drawl. "*Our* terms couldn't be more different. Most of our personnel would be garrisoned in one place, typically a section of the capital. We would possibly maintain a presence in sensitive areas such as this communications facility and centres of industry such as Treva, but the impact on your lifestyle would be minimal. We have no need of anyone to build our spacecraft nor manufacture our crystals."

Idenion was not reassured. "Then let me ask you again: what *do* you need us for?"

182

"As teachers; specifically in the areas of astro-navigation and transposal theory. Our knowledge of these subjects is somewhat tenuous. Eventually, some of you - a select few - will enjoy the privilege of serving on our vessels as fully-fledged crewmen."

"Your tame telepaths," Idenion remarked. Everyone was startled by the bitterness in his voice. "Your mind is beautifully controlled, Ambassador Pervain, but you can't hope to gloss over the truth. Whatever plans the Empire had for Celestra have been shelved because Symerid Three is considered more important. Instead, we will be little more than a way station to give you easy access to that treacherous planet."

"Eldor *is* over twelve hundred light years distant," Pervain said, unruffled. "Please don't feel marginalised. I for one understand Celestra's full potential and I shall do my utmost to see that it's appreciated."

"Exploited," Idenion corrected him cynically.

For the first time, Pervain displayed a little anger. "Think carefully before you reject our offer. Symerid Three will remain on our agenda no matter what you do, so wouldn't it be advantageous to have us on your side once the Earthers are abroad? You've spied on them yourself, so you know what they're like. I doubt if your tiresome pacifism would carry much weight with them." He paused, eyeing his now silent audience. "Of course, no one expects you to decide straight away. Would an octal be long enough for you to confer?"

183

"It will suffice," Idenion replied steadily, though his thoughts were in turmoil.

"Very well, I shall return in an octal. Same time, same place."

"And now," Clemis put in slyly, "hadn't you better go and separate your doctor and your general before they throttle one another?"

Pervain stood up, saluted, then almost ran from the building.

"Well done!" Kyrin murmured to Clemis.

Idenion, at last able to relax, slumped forward in his chair.

Clemis darted forward. "Father!"

"I'm all right, Clemis. Just very relieved they don't know about Laura. Now, with luck, they'll be too distracted to look into one woman's background." He glanced out of the nearest window in the direction Pervain had taken. "Especially as there's so much dissent in the ranks!"

Pervain had reached his two fellow officers. "What in Ebbon's name is going on?" he demanded breathlessly. "Do you want to make us a laughing stock?"

"Freelord Harmost," said Escir, addressing Pervain by his title, "General Grenthap has forbidden me to take the cat's remains to Eldor on the grounds that it might start an epidemic. Would you kindly explain to him that I'm trying to *prevent* such an occurrence?"

"That animal has to be jettisoned," Grenthap blustered.

"An autopsy is essential to protect the health of this expedition," Escir persisted.

"Enough!" Pervain held up a restraining hand. "Escir, what's the name of your House?"

"House Alon. But why - "

"A respected dynasty," Pervain said thoughtfully.

"It was until he disgraced it," Grenthap remarked.

Pervain ignored him. "As you doubtless know, Escir, we have an excellent hospital at Patieron City, with all the quarantine facilities you could wish for. I shall arrange for you to conduct the autopsy and your other tests, with a skilled team to assist you."

Grenthap muttered an objection.

"It will be on my authority," Pervain said calmly. "The Earth vaccines are perfected there. Containment is assured."

"Oh, very well," scowled Grenthap. "But don't think you can invoke your high and mighty family every time you disagree with an order."

"I wasn't aware that an order had been given, General. I was merely trying to resolve a dilemma."

"Now it *is* resolved, hadn't we better leave?" Escir asked wearily.

"Of course," Pervain replied, his urbane mask fully restored. "After you, General. And, Escir..."

"What?"

"You owe me. Keep that in mind, won't you? And by the way, doesn't anyone want to know what I've negotiated...?"

Idenion, Kyrin and Clemis, motionless at the ground floor window, watched as the bronze sphere departed. Then Clemis turned back to Idenion.

"What will you do?"

"There's nothing I *can* do. You were reading him, weren't you? If we don't give our services freely they'll just take what they want."

"So you're going to let them bring in their army? You're not even going to object?"

Idenion wouldn't look her in the eye. "Don't reproach me, child. Perhaps if I were younger - "

"But *I'm* young!" Clemis knelt beside him. "I'll help you. We can outsmart them!"

"No, Clemis. I know you mean well, but I must handle this alone."

"What about Laura? Doesn't she get a say in things either?"

"Laura will agree with me. We must do as the Eldorians wish - for now."

"It's no use saying for now," Clemis argued. "Once they're established here we'll never get rid of them. There must be some way out of this. I can't believe you'd just - "

"Quiet!" interrupted Kyrin. "Alcis has some news. There's something odd going on at the akron." He concentrated; and for the first time ever, Clemis saw him look dismayed.

"What is it?" she demanded. "What's happened?"

"Laura...has a visitor," Kyrin replied slowly. "He's an emissary from an unknown planet - he won't say which. And he wants Celestra to form an alliance."

"An Eldorian trick, surely," said Idenion with a tired frown.

186

"It would appear not. Alcis is in no doubt that he's genuine."

"Popular all of a sudden, aren't we?" remarked Clemis. "Come on - we'd better go home and see what this is all about."

***

Laura was waiting in the lobby. "My guest prevailed on me to intercept you," she explained. "He's very nervous. He didn't want to be the subject of any more relays."

"Should that be my cue to depart?" inquired Kyrin.

"It might be best, until we know what's going on," Idenion said reluctantly.

"Very well. I'll be in my quarters if you need me." Kyrin drifted away, once more the picture of serenity.

"He was absolutely brilliant today," Clemis told Laura effusively. "He's been studying all the delegates. I can't wait to hear what he's uncovered!"

"I haven't said you can attend the next debriefing," Idenion pointed out.

"But - "

"Later, Clemis. Now, Laura, to your visitor. Which audience room is he in?"

Laura looked slightly abashed. "He isn't. He's in our apartment. He begged me to send Alcis away, but Eleen is with him."

"Eleen?"

"The caterer who found him."

Idenion, looking even more perplexed, ushered his family upstairs.

"When did he arrive, Laura?" Clemis asked.

"About half an ild ago."

"The same time as Pervain was laying down the law. Interesting."

"He claims he's nothing to do with Eldor."

"Claims?" Idenion repeated. "I thought Alcis had proof. Is he conversant?"

"No, but - "

"Then why is there such a shortage of facts?"

"Alcis and Eleen both tried to read him. They said they couldn't perceive anything much."

"And what's that supposed to mean?"

Laura gave him a reproachful look. "All I know is what I've been told. You'll have to question him yourself. You too, Clemis - you might stand a better chance of getting through to him."

"Why's that?"

"The age factor. He isn't much older than you."

Clemis displayed a detached sort of interest. "Does this mystery man have a name?"

"Aprival, he calls himself."

"Pretty."

"So's he, my dear daughter. Try not to let his appearance dazzle you. Remember he's probably a spy, and just as hostile as the Eldorians."

"Really, Laura, I'm not that impressionable - " began Clemis, but her mother motioned for silence as she opened the apartment door. Aprival hastened forward as they went in; Idenion, noting Clemis' reaction, considered Laura's warning to be fully justified.

"Why was I left here so long?" Aprival asked, looking anxiously from person to person. "My time is limited. I have none to waste."

He didn't speak the language as fluently as Pervain. He sounds like Laura used to, Idenion thought somewhat irrelevantly. Then, introductions over, he left Clemis smiling brightly at the emissary and went after Eleen, who was attempting to sidle away. He caught up with her on the landing.

"Has anyone else seen this young man?" he asked, more severely than he'd intended.

"N-no, First Citizen. Other than Alcis, that is. I sneaked him up the back stair."

"That was sensible. I don't think I need emphasise to you how essential it is to keep this quiet."

"*He* said that. Over and over." Eleen fidgeted with her apron. "He's terrified of doing something wrong, poor lad. I can't think why anyone would choose him as a spokesman."

"Perhaps to impress my daughter." As soon as he'd uttered the quip, Idenion had a pang of unease. He hastily thanked Eleen and went back inside, convinced he'd subconsciously touched on the truth.

"Can't you tell us more about yourself?" Clemis was asking.

"I'm not important, but my mission is," Aprival replied. "We know you fear the Eldorians and their plans for conquest. Join with us and we can defeat them: independently, we cannot."

Idenion let Clemis continue her gentle questioning while he studied the newcomer more closely. Superficially he seemed normal enough;

earnest, albeit a little too handsome. But then he looked into the boy's mind, and discovered what Alcis and Eleen already knew. Aprival had no past, or none that was readable. What memories he did have were disordered, fragmentary, and recent. His clothes were equally anonymous: a short-sleeved overshirt and trousers, neutrally coloured, with no detail or insignia.

Clemis had fallen silent.

"I need an answer," Aprival said, none too hopefully.

"You can't possibly expect us to trust you," Idenion protested. "You've said nothing about your people. Where do you come from? How did you know the precise moment the Eldorians would arrive here? And who or what has been tampering with your mind?"

"I wish I could remember."

"That won't do. The Eldorians, whom you claim to despise, have been open in their dealings with us. Why can't you be the same?"

"The Eldorians don't have our technique of memory editing," Aprival said candidly. "In conversing with a telepathic race such as yours, they had no option but to be truthful."

"And you, having the choice, prefer to deceive us?" asked Laura frostily.

"It's not a question of deceit!" Aprival, aggrieved, forgot to be deferential. "It was done to protect your species and mine in the event of my capture. Do you think I enjoy being like this?"

Clemis was moved to sympathy. "Can't the process be reversed?"

190

"I don't know."

"But presumably there are others of your kind who have the answers we seek."

"Of course. Once you've rejected the Eldorians you'll be told everything."

"Not until?"

"No. Not until."

"I just don't understand it," Laura said helplessly.

"I *do* understand the need for caution," Idenion supplemented. "But by giving you too little information, your people have hindered their cause. The Eldorian delegate is returning in an octal for our decision; I suggest *you* return within six days with a more persuasive argument, if you wish to be taken seriously."

"Very well." Aprival was visibly disappointed. "May I now call my spacecraft and tell them I'm ready to leave?"

"You may. And, if possible, have your transport sent to the akron roof. That should prevent anyone from seeing your departure."

"I'm much obliged." Aprival touched a button on his shirt collar and recited some Celestrian numerals.

"The channel's secure, so never mind all that." A masculine voice, also speaking Celestrian, crackled from the miniature transceiver. "You got it wrong anyway."

"Thanks for nothing, Nordall." Aprival threw a shamefaced glance at his hosts. "Where's the shuttle?"

"In the shadow of a comsat. Ready to be a human meteor again? The Eldorians have left the system so you won't be shot at."

"In that case you can kill some of that speed," Aprival said crossly. "I made my ambassadorial debut on my hands and knees."

"I wish I'd seen it," said the invisible Nordall. "Where do I set down? Same co-ordinates?"

"No, the top of the akron. If you can manage that."

"Scanning site," Nordall responded amiably, and there was a short pause.

Clemis listened to this display of levity with growing approval. +He's a different person when he's talking to his crewmate+ she observed. +Any species with a sense of humour can't be all bad+

+The jokes would sound better in their own language+ Idenion replied caustically. +It seems they don't deign to use it in front of us+

+Don't be so mistrustful!+ Clemis was at her most disarming. +Language-wise, they're doing nothing the Eldorians haven't already done+

+Mispronunciations apart+ returned Idenion, in no mood to concede.

"There are several small elevations on the roof," Nordall announced at last.

"Solar collectors," Idenion supplied. Aprival forwarded the information.

"Copy. The centre looks clear though: I'll aim for that. Get yourself up there and stand by."

"On my way." Aprival signed off somewhat resignedly. "Er - would someone please escort me?"

"I will," said Clemis promptly, without asking permission. Then she checked the gallery for passers-by before leading him swiftly onto it and up a side stair.

"I take it you weren't impressed?" Laura inquired of her partner.

"Evasiveness isn't becoming in an ambassador," Idenion replied. "Especially one who copes so badly with our language."

"There was something very odd about that," Laura mused. "Did you notice that he and the crewman both made the same mistakes, as if they'd been taught wrongly?"

"They probably had," Idenion said dismissively. "I'll add sloppy preparation to the list of shortcomings."

Clemis opened a sturdy mechanised door and helped Aprival up the last few steps of the escape ladder. His balance was definitely not all it should have been.

"I'm sorry," he panted. "Too many days of shipboard gravity."

It was windy on the bleak expanse of roof. Clemis smoothed her hair ineffectually and took shelter by the open hatchway. "I just wanted to say," she ventured, "that you've won *my* vote at least."

"Why? I made a complete mess of things back there."

"That's just it. If *we* needed help from another world, we wouldn't conduct ourselves with military precision. We'd be like you - ill prepared, making mistakes. I know, because it's happened from time to time. Idenion needs reminding of that, and I'll do it the first chance I get."

"Thank you for your kindness." Aprival was scanning the sky intently.

"Will your government be angry with you?" Clemis asked, not very tactfully.

"Well, let's put it this way: I'm not looking forward to seeing my captain." Aprival smiled ruefully. "I, and everyone else, thought the difficulty would be over once I'd convinced you people I wasn't Eldorian. In fact, that was the *only* thing you believed! And I still don't know what made you accept it."

"I do," Clemis said quietly. "You've suffered loss at the hands of the Eldorians. The memory has gone but it's left a hollow, an echo. Plus, of course, the need to punish those responsible."

A bright point of light appeared in the sky and descended with remarkable swiftness toward them.

"I suspected my loss was personal," Aprival said, half to himself. "Do you think they killed my parents? Why else was I not permitted to remember my childhood?"

Clemis didn't feel qualified to guess. "If we chose to join you, and if between us we saw off the Empire, would we then be released from the pact? We wouldn't be dragged into any more wars?"

"Of course you'd be released. We'd go back whence we came, and leave Celestra free."

Clemis wished he'd told Idenion that. "I still don't see why Celestra's so important to you," she went on. "Unless it's telepaths you want."

The shuttlecraft, the same metal cylinder that had delivered Aprival to the courtyard, touched down on an adjacent part of the roof. A narrow airlock opened, barely large enough to accommodate a man.

"I have to know," persisted Clemis.

"The type of war we envisage," said Aprival after some deliberation, "is fought in space, with the enemy mere dots on a screen. Telepathy's no use under such conditions."

"Then why come to us? We can't even fight our own battles, let alone other people's. We've no weapons to speak of."

"Haven't you?" Aprival inquired softly. Then he stepped into the dark little cylinder without a backward glance.

Clemis was left watching forlornly as the tiny vessel catapulted into the blue. There were still so many unanswered questions! For instance, where was Aprival's home planet? It certainly couldn't be any nearer than Eldor, since an emergent spacefaring species in Celestra's part of the galaxy could hardly have gone unnoticed. And there was a further anomaly. Each time Aprival had mentioned his spacecraft, his mind had given an impression of something vast, a complete world in itself. At Space Tech, Clemis had been taught that nothing larger than a sphere could endure the rigors of transposal and retain its molecular integrity. A ship like Aprival's simply couldn't transpose. Celestrian physics forbade it. Which led her straight back to her first question: where in chaos had Aprival's people come from and how long had the voyage taken?

She went back inside, ruminating. Perhaps Communications had seen something relevant. Trevone, unfortunately, hadn't been there, but she could easily find out who had. And after that there was the small matter of the debriefing. Despite Idenion's reluctance, she knew she had a right to be present; and for once she was sure Laura would side with her.

***

"The purpose of this meeting," said Idenion, "is to examine what we've learnt about the Eldorians. We should *not* let Aprival's proposal distract us." He directed a significant look at Clemis. "Kyrin, we'll start with you. What is your assessment of General Grenthap?"

"He isn't as stupid as his manner suggests," Kyrin began. "He's shrewd, logical, and a good tactician. He has no detailed knowledge of, nor involvement in, the strategic studies of Earth - but it will be his job to make the first push succeed when the time comes. He's aware that it won't be easy, but has confidence in the intelligence teams."

"Nothing there that we didn't anticipate," Laura said resignedly. "They wouldn't risk exposing their plans to us. At least, not until they were sure we wouldn't interfere."

"However," Kyrin went on, "Grenthap had very specific memories of his past campaigns - so specific, in fact, that I was able to piece together a little slice of history. It appears the illustrious Empire isn't the united fighting force he'd have us believe."

Laura tensed. Aprival had said something very similar to her yesterday.

"I'll make this as brief as I can," Kyrin promised. "The Eldorian solar system is fortunate enough to have three habitable planets, which were colonised centuries ago. There are also some outposts on the less hospitable worlds. Recently one of the planets tried to declare independence, and there was an exchange of hostilities. On another occasion one of the outposts was annexed by dissidents. Grenthap distinguished himself in the suppression of both rebellions.

"On the Eldor homeworld, there's a continuing blood feud between two factions: House Patieron, which Pervain belongs to, and House Patierade. Their enmity was the cause of the civil war mentioned by Axmiol, which continues to break out from time to time.

"The planned interaction with Earth is not seen as a matter of conquest, but a calculated risk designed to counter disunity within the Empire. Grenthap knows a war with Earth is the likely outcome once contact has been made."

"All of that ties in with Aprival's summary," Laura said reluctantly.

"I thought you weren't going to mention him?" Clemis queried.

"In fairness, I thought I should make the point that his story wasn't just hot air. His people seem to know a great deal about the Eldorians."

"You sound surprised."

"Well, yes, I am. Just a little."

"Shall we return to the agenda?" asked Idenion.

"Of course. Sorry, darling. You were saying?"

"I don't have Kyrin's talent for reading a person's psyche like a book, but I endorse his opinion of Grenthap. The man lives and breathes military strategy. What did *you* read in him, Clemis?"

"Lust," she replied succinctly.

"Now that *doesn't* surprise me," Laura remarked. "And what was he doing, this general, while you three were garnering all this information?"

"Studying *us*," Kyrin replied, "and wondering if we'd put up any opposition. He'd prefer a peaceful occupation but he's willing to use force if he has to."

"So Pervain wasn't making idle threats," sighed Laura. "All right, let's move on. What do we know about their medical officer?"

"Escir has had his sensibilities blunted by war, but is basically a humane man," Kyrin said. "Moderately disaffected, which is worth bearing in mind; and, of course, he probably saved our lives when that footsoldier panicked. Nevertheless, he has issues. The cat's death prevented me from learning the whole story, but it seems Escir was once the Emperor's physician and was ignominiously sacked through no fault of his own. An Army career was one of the few options left to him, and he is determined to serve well and restore honour to his House."

"With that blot on his copybook, how did he end up here?"

"The young Narvellan, Sijek, was a favourite of the Emperor. Escir had the task of keeping him healthy, and I imagine that over several years he heard a lot about Celestra. That made him an obvious choice for this mission, although he and Grenthap don't often see eye to eye."

"Sijek fared better than Axmiol, then," observed Clemis.

"Initially," answered Kyrin obliquely.

Idenion cleared his throat. "Clemis, your opinion of Escir?"

"I support what Kyrin says. He seems well disposed toward us. He thought me very young and of little interest to him personally, although he was aware of the effect I was having on the others."

Idenion made a scribbled note on the paper in front of him. "Thank you, Clemis. I - er - don't suppose either of you know any more about the strange comment made by the cat, and why his people insisted on his being here?"

Clemis shrugged.

"If Grenthap did know anything," said Kyrin, "it was well down his list of priorities. I saw no reference to it."

"So noted." Idenion wrote accordingly. "Now, to Pervain. I studied him extensively while he was alone with us, but to little effect I'm afraid."

"I can add nothing useful," Kyrin admitted. "His shielding is amazing for a nonconversant."

"And he knew you were trying to read him, so down came the shutters," Clemis said. "But did either of you think to check what the *others* knew about him?"

"No. Did you?"

"Of course." She smiled demurely.

Idenion looked a little rueful. "As Pervain himself might say, how like a female. Devious!"

"Ingenious," she amended. "Anyway, here's what I found. In common with those of his line, Pervain's early life was mapped out for him. He attended the best academic institutions and then entered the Army at officer level. He's already distinguished himself in the field and is a skilled swordsman. Success isn't merely expected of him - it's demanded. He has a reputation for brawling, so that rigid self-discipline isn't always what it should be; and he has some health concerns which he works to overcome."

"He's trouble, then," stated Laura. "I know these must-win types."

Clemis frowned. "You're still assuming he's going to be a permanent fixture. Surely you're going to give Aprival a bit of credence now?"

"I admit his people have done their homework. But that hardly places them on the winning side."

"Then at least let me tell you what I found out at Communications. I had discord's own job persuading Nimion to co-operate."

"He might have been more forthcoming if we'd given you leave to approach him," Laura said pointedly.

"I've *never* asked your leave to approach anyone!"

"Then maybe it's about time you did."

"Can we please refrain from squabbling?" Idenion remonstrated mildly.

"I will if *she* will," Clemis returned. "As I was saying: Nimion was embarrassed because his last indiscretion helped bring the Eldorians here. I told him we were all as much to blame as he was. Kyrin excepted, of course."

The relayist inclined his head graciously.

"Plus," Clemis went on, "Jarras had told him to disregard the readings and he didn't want to contradict his superior."

"Jarras worries me," Laura muttered.

"It seems like a genuine mistake on his part. The object doesn't have theridolyte in its composition. Anyway, Nimion showed me the recorded data and it confirmed what he'd seen. The thing materialised out of nowhere."

"So they *can* transpose," mused Idenion.

"To the middle of our solar system. So much for our safety," remarked Laura.

"Oh, Laura, be fair!" Clemis protested. "They've just challenged the basic premise of transposal theory."

"Maybe. And they're now in orbit round Alda Five?"

"Yes, hiding amongst the small moons."

"And how do we explain their presence when the Eldorians return?" Laura queried icily.

"We needn't consider that now," Idenion said hastily in an attempt to avert an argument.

"Because you're both hoping they won't *be* there!" Clemis shrilled.

201

"Please," said Kyrin, "let's keep our tempers. We should now reassess our findings and wait to see if Aprival brings us more information."

"He will," Clemis said eagerly. "I'm sure he will."

"We'll see." Laura was unconvinced. "And now, if you've finished shouting at us, maybe you could find time to contact Dena. She wants to know if she still has an assistant."

"Oh, chaos!" Clemis looked genuinely ashamed. "I'd better go and see her. Is she at the Lyricon?"

"No, she said she'd be at home today."

"Then I'll go now. I don't think I'll serve any useful purpose by staying." Clemis left the committee room and returned to her parents' apartment, walking rapidly. She knew they'd start discussing Aprival as soon as she was out of the way; she also knew they'd say little as long as she remained there. At least he'll get a hearing of some sort, she told herself. In her room, she exchanged her beaded slippers for flat sandals and put on a thin cloak before descending the akron's spiral stair to the main exit. She overtook several administrators, but no-one ventured to question her.

At the top of the long path leading down to Lateral Three she paused momentarily, remembering the times when, as a small child, she had stood on this very spot and watched Tralvar trudging toward her. "Run ahead and tell Laura I'm here," he'd always said on reaching the top; and she had scampered off obediently, wondering what the rest of the day had in store. Tralvar always brought the unexpected with him.

Now the path stretched emptily before her in the afternoon sun. It would be the first time she'd been to the villa since Tralvar's death seven octals ago, and she wondered why Dena had chosen to stay there on her own instead of moving back to the Lyricon. Perhaps it was still too soon for her to break with the past. Or perhaps she was content there, in the home of the one man who had been able to make her happy.

Dena, when she opened the door, seemed vastly relieved to see her. She also looked a little nervous. "Are you alone? Is Trevone anywhere about?"

"He's at Treva. What's wrong?" Clemis, attempting to read her aunt, was surprised to find the older woman's mind closed against her.

"We'd best stick to speech for the moment," Dena said, closing and bolting the door and leading the way into Tralvar's study. Neatly organised and devoid of clutter, it hardly looked like the same room.

"Are you angry with me?" Clemis asked hesitantly.

"No, child, not at all. If my behaviour seems odd, then I apologise. I'm merely carrying out Tralvar's instructions."

"Oh?"

"In my possession is a sealed package which he insisted should be given to you, and only you, at a specified time. Under no circumstances was I to disclose its existence to your parents. There's a recording which goes with it; I daresay you'll understand things better when you hear what he has to say."

"Have you played it?" Clemis was both intrigued and uneasy.

"No. I honoured his wishes, though I've several times been tempted to listen to his voice again." Dena retrieved two slender packets and laid them in front of Clemis, who made no move to pick them up.

"Haven't you any idea what this is about?"

"Indeed I have," Dena said sombrely. "I desperately wanted him to have a proper retirement, to rest and play his music, and maybe see more of his children and grandson. The message from Axmiol put paid to any such hopes. As soon as he'd stepped down as First Citizen he went back to his weapon-making."

"I know about that," said Clemis. "The sphere-shield project."

"You know nothing about the real project," Dena returned, "and I know very little. Tralvar never spoke of his research to me. But I'm certain he's left you a full account of his work. Why else would he have told me to keep it until the Eldorians came?"

Clemis repressed a shiver. "The alliance hasn't been made yet."

"Alliance!" repeated Dena scornfully. "Tralvar had some definitive views on that subject. When the Eldorians turn up, he said, Idenion will probably try to make some kind of deal with them. Don't wait for the result. If they agree it will only be for as long as it suits them."

"He had all the answers, didn't he?"

"Let's hope so. Take your inheritance, Clemis. It's time."

Clemis hastened home with the packages under her cloak. Laura and Idenion were still in conference, so she resolved to play Tralvar's message there and then. Her bedroom door had no restraint on it, but the main apartment door had a seldom-used lock which, although she didn't know it, had been installed by Tralvar himself when he lived there. The key resisted her, but eventually turned. She then scurried to her room, stumbling over a rug as she went, and fed the record into a slot on the wall.

"All right, Tralvar," she murmured. "Talk to me."

"Belated greetings, dear girl," said the familiar weary voice. "First, an apology for apparently having forgotten you during my last days. You were ever at the centre of my thoughts, as this record will explain.

"It was always my belief that, one day, my preoccupation with weapons would prove vital to our world's future. With the arrival of the Eldorians, that day is surely here. And why did I choose to confide in you, not your parents? That can be explained in a single sentence: you're the only one I can trust. You, Clemis, are like the Laura of the past - the girl who defeated Alendis and helped free the Narvellans. Your mother has endowed you with her ideals, her fearsome honesty, and above all her venturesome spirit. But in Laura herself these qualities have become muted, perhaps by Idenion's pacifist leanings. They'd probably suppress the knowledge you now hold. So, unfortunately, would my brother and son-in-law. They may be good scientists, but they're both weak-willed.

"It occurred to me that if the Eldorians have found Celestra they'll in all likelihood have found Earth as well. And if not they soon will, once they have access to our databases. I've no need to emphasise what a disaster it would be if Earth were given transposal at this point in its history. It must not be allowed to happen. *You* must not allow it to happen.

"And now to my new, and final, invention. Well, perhaps invention is the wrong word. The technology already existed, and it was purely a matter of persistence and experimentation to adapt it to what I wanted: a weapon of war. A means to decimate, even totally destroy, the Eldorian space fleet. At Space Tech they'll have taught you that, whilst in transposal, the Drive generates a protective envelope around your sphere. This is essential, as the region we call transposal-space is intrinsically hostile to this continuum and everything in it. With this in mind I devised a means of compressing a localised transposal field into a narrow beam. When a hostile spacecraft is targeted, it will fall unshielded into t-space and be annihilated instantly. To an observer the target would simply dissolve, and I've therefore named this weapon the Dispersal Engine. You can re-name it if you wish. The function is perhaps too undramatic; there are no pyrotechnics nor explosions involved. But since it would be more demoralising to the enemy if there *were* such effects, they can be added if desired.

"In the accompanying folder are diagrams and instructions for building the device. I've tested it in secrecy and proved its efficiency to my own satisfaction. Take this knowledge, Clemis, and use it wisely. With it our world can be invincible. The only danger lies in the Celestrian people and their reluctance to go to war - and that, my brave girl, is something you must help them overcome. Make them fight back! Your future depends on it."

The recording ended. Clemis, at first elated, began to feel inadequate and irresolute. She examined the folder, handling it as if it were red-hot. To whom could she turn for assistance? Trevone? He wasn't on Tralvar's proscribed list, but she wasn't sure how he'd react. Should she break the news now or later? Who would undertake to build such a weapon without shying away from the task?

"Aprival," she said aloud. He'd somehow known what would happen. He had, it seemed, been waiting for it. But intrigued though she was, Clemis hadn't the slightest intention of handing over Tralvar's plans to a stranger. She'd have to discover a lot more about Aprival and his companions before considering such a step.

After much thought, she decided to keep the information to herself for a while. Taking up her diary, she hid the record in a pocket designed for mementoes and slipped the blueprints between the pages. It was the one place she knew Laura would never look, having suffered the outrage of having her own diary read in her youth.

As if on cue there was a pounding on the outside door. "Clemis!" Laura yelled. "Why's this door locked? Have you got Kalyx in there again?"

Clemis sighed and went to admit her mother, catching a glimpse of herself in a mirror as she did so. She looked understandably stressed. "I just wanted some time alone," she apologised. "I thought the administrators might be round, or Eleen."

"Did you see Dena?"

"Yes. We talked about Tralvar." Clemis poured two glasses of liman and handed one to Laura. "I'll go back to work tomorrow if that's all right. It'll help the next few days pass more quickly."

"I could do with a distraction too," Laura said with a tired smile. "There's nothing I'd like better than to escape into music. But there are serious decisions to be made, and Idenion needs me with him all the way."

***

Clemis did her best to put her life back in order. She worked diligently, socialised at the Lyricon, ignored Kalyx's blandishments and dined quietly with Trevone. But her mood, matching that of the city, was pensive; the sinister package in her room had imposed an ever-present distance between her and her contemporaries.

Two days before Pervain's scheduled return, Laura came back from yet another meeting looking very grave. "It's agreed," she told Clemis. "We ally ourselves with Eldor."

"What? But that's insane!"

"We only have two choices, and both are wrong," Laura replied wearily. "Whichever side we join, we'll gain an enemy. The only sensible course is to favour the more powerful of the two regimes."

"And you think that's Eldor, do you?"

"Don't you?"

"Not necessarily." Clemis tried to stay calm. "We can't make comparisons when we don't know what one side consists of."

"No, but we can use our eyes. Aprival's little spacecraft is strictly short-range. And the mind-wipe, in Idenion's opinion, is a clumsy attempt to conceal inferiority."

"They can't be that backward if they think they can wage war on Eldor. They managed to get here, after all."

Laura frowned. "I don't follow."

"Well they're not exactly local people, are they? Probably just popped across from the next galaxy."

"Now you're being ridiculous. I don't trust Aprival, neither does your father, and neither would you if you had any sense. I've known his type on Earth - handsome, shallow, and downright treacherous."

"But he's not like that!" Clemis's denial was even more vehement than she intended. "His mind's as good as any Celestrian's. You can see how unhappy his memory loss has made him - "

"That's enough," said Laura sharply. "You meet an alien with more than his rightful share of good looks, and you straightaway have to make a tragic character out of him. For the last time, Clemis, he's nothing but a con-man. His people want to liberate themselves and they haven't a hope of succeeding until they're more versatile in space. They're just after our spheres - and they're not having them." Her voice softened somewhat. "Face it, Clemis. Aprival isn't coming back. But if it's any consolation, Idenion and I have agreed not to tell the Eldorians about his visit. His expedition will be free to go."

"Why are you being so unfair to them?" Clemis demanded. "Why won't you give them a chance? I'm sure their motives aren't the same as Eldor's - "

"Clemis, you're an idiot. You're letting personal feelings interfere with your judgement."

"I am *not*!"

"Oh yes you are. You like Aprival, don't you?"

"You know I do."

"And you don't like Pervain."

"No, but - "

"That's all I wanted to hear," said Laura. "The decision rests."

Chapter Five

Pervain returned at the appointed time. He was confident of victory, and listened in noncommittal silence to the news of Celestra's capitulation.

"Well," he said when Idenion had finished speaking, "that would appear to be that. Welcome to the Empire and long may you continue to serve her."

They were alone in the spaceport lounge, though armed men stood guard outside as before. The bronze sphere stood a little further off. Pervain spoke crisply into his communicator, and a middle-aged man - obviously a servant or secretary - came down the ramp, carrying what appeared to be a large canvas scroll. He hurried past the sentries, placed his burden on the table between Idenion and Pervain, and retired without a word. Pervain released the ties which bound the scroll and spread it across the table, using tumblers to anchor the corners.

"I had this readied for your perusal, as our image projectors would have been tedious to set up," he explained.

Idenion found himself looking at a meticulously drawn map of Alda Mexa with an area highlighted in yellow. "You must have been very sure of our decision," he remarked.

"As I said before," smiled Pervain, "you're a sensible man. The outlined region marks the proposed site of our base, as discussed with you on my previous visit. The site has been carefully chosen to minimise the effect of our presence in your city. Due to the existence of high walls, footbridges which can be removed, and so on, it will only be necessary to establish two checkpoints: at the eastern boundary with Lateral Three and to the west adjoining Lateral Four. The area measures approximately four square silmi, extending from intersection twelve east to fourteen west.

"To the best of my knowledge, this area is predominantly residential with a little light industry. If the plan satisfies your criteria, we would be more than happy to assist with clearance procedures. As well as airlifting the populace, we would dismantle and reassemble machinery, remove furniture and prepare inventories. I understand that all property is assigned, not owned, which should obviate any need for compensation."

"That's correct."

"And are there sufficient vacant premises within the city to cope with the resettlement?"

"Just about," Idenion said without going into detail. He didn't feel like discussing Celestra's falling birthrate with Pervain. "How many of your troops will be occupying the base?"

"About five hundred, which will include a team to be based at Communications. Then there'll be another garrison at Treva, of perhaps two hundred. We haven't decided where to put them yet. Also, a few civilian scientists will be arriving to study astro-dynamics."

"Anyone else?" queried Idenion.

"No, I think that's all. The catering requirements will have to be discussed, of course."

"I believe you're forgetting something," Idenion said coolly.

A flicker of hostility crossed Pervain's face." "What?"

"Five hundred *men*, you said. Young, physically fit men with healthy sexual appetites. I trust we're not expected to cater for those particular needs?"

"Ah. Now I see." Pervain relaxed a little. "Grenthap will take care of such arrangements."

"No, *you* will," Idenion said in the same even tone.

"Perhaps you'd like me to send for the wives and families?" Pervain inquired with a sneer. "We'd require a much larger slice of your city if I did. Fortunately for you, that won't happen. Camp-followers are for barbarians. In our society, soldiers expect their families to remain safely at home. In fact, Army rules insist on it."

"Then in that case - " Idenion began.

"Never fear, First Citizen - your demands will be met. Our recreation girls are recruited from the best professions and are often from good backgrounds. Thirty will suffice, I think, and I shall choose each one personally."

Idenion stared. "Your prostitutes are *conscripts*?"

"Why yes. Our Army is vast and its needs cannot always be served by volunteers." Pervain, in authority once more, gave another of his superior smirks. "I see you don't approve. Let me assure you that our girls are content and well paid. Many choose to stay on after the mandatory two years."

"I...see," Idenion replied with an effort. Laura had been absolutely right about the status of women in the Empire.

"Would you like final approval of my selections?" Pervain inquired, still faintly amused.

"Thank you, no." Idenion regained his composure. "I shall bow to your greater expertise. Please ensure the women are brought in at the same time as your troops."

"Of course. Does this infer acceptance of the plan?"

Idenion sighed and returned his attention to the map. "I accept in principle. I know Alda Mexa as well as anyone, and this area does seem best suited to your purpose. How long will it take you to make it viable?"

"The men work speedily. I'd say three, maybe four days to move everyone out, and two more to get the barriers up. The fine tuning can be done later." Pervain deliberated for a moment, then continued: "Since you are unfamiliar with military matters, I think it prudent to warn you that certain restrictions have to be observed. You must regard the territory within the base as Eldorian, and therefore subject to our own laws and customs. Intrusion will not be tolerated: in fact, any Celestrian caught trespassing is likely to be incarcerated or even shot. Those with legitimate business may obtain a day's permit at the checkpoint. Conversely, our men will have to be signed out and be back by roll-call, which is at dusk. I will have leaflets printed to help you apprise your people of these matters. I shall also prepare a

214

list of building materials for immediate delivery to the site."

"You have our compliance." Idenion hoped his growing dismay didn't show.

"Good. I shall return to Eldor for approximately five days while our treaty is ratified. There will be documents for you to sign later."

"I assume my wife is to sign them too?"

Pervain registered slight surprise. "That won't be necessary. While I'm away, and assuming your advisers have no misgivings, I'd be grateful if you could begin assigning new homes to the displaced. You don't have to evict anyone yourself, just decide where they should go. It will make our job much easier. Any variation to the area plan must, of course, be communicated to us at once."

"And how do I notify you of any change?"

"We will remain in transposer contact this time." Pervain seemed satisfied with the outcome of the meeting. "Now before I leave, I've a favour to ask."

"More demands, ambassador?"

"Not at all. I merely wish to borrow some of your writings to study - your *own* writings, First Citizen."

Idenion eyed him quizzically. "Would you mind telling me why?"

"Sheer curiosity. You were a social commentator long before you were a statesman, and your work will help me to know you. Perhaps I might inspect your library...?"

Idenion couldn't very well refuse. Pervain nonchalantly dismissed his retinue and the bronze

215

sphere lifted off, leaving Idenion to suspect that the Eldorian's literary sojourn would be prolonged. Nearing the akron in a flitter he managed to warn Kyrin of the imminent visit, asking him to alert all interested parties. Laura, fortunately, was at the Lyricon. Clemis, who *had* been at home, promptly chose to absent herself. Another time Idenion might have been irritated with her; as it was, he made use of the opportunity and took Pervain to his study rather than the akron's mighty reading rooms. The sudden appearance of an Eldorian would doubtless have sent various academics into a panic.

Pervain, to give him his due, was a good scholar and read Celestrian well. For more than two ilden he studied, commented and drank Idenion's wine - seemingly without impairing his concentration. Finally he chose a political history of the Narvellan occupation and a copy of the Golden Girl sonnets to take with him.

"Golden Girl is only love poetry," Idenion pointed out. "Is that really what you want to read?"

"Absolutely. Apart from yourself and your wife and sister, this Lydion is the only surviving freedom fighter, is he not?"

Idenion mentally totted up the list. "There's Jarras."

"Oh yes, the engineer. Perhaps I can meet him later. In the meantime I'd like to read more about your friend."

Discords, thought Idenion grimly, Lydion *is* going to be pleased. "His part in the resistance was only incidental," he offered ineffectually.

216

"Such happy accidents can win or lose a war," Pervain replied. "I know, I know - your spat with the Narvellans was hardly a war. Conquest by stealth, some might say. It's what you people seem good at. Well, I must be going. I shall enjoy these." He indicated the books under his arm. "I shan't have much time to read once the alliance is up and running, so I'd better make the most of it."

Back on board his spacecraft he sank onto a couch and closed his eyes thankfully.

"Is the officer unwell?" asked his secretary anxiously.

"Just eyestrain. Keep reminding me that their wine plays havoc with my shielding."

"Yes, Freelord."

"And get me a drink of iced water."

"At once, Freelord."

Pervain snatched the proffered cup and drank deeply. "I'd better have some sedation before we hit transposal," he said reluctantly. "That crystal timbre always does my head in. But just before I take the shot, make a note of these names: Idenion, Lydion, Jarras."

"Does the officer want these men disposed of?"

Pervain gave a sour grin. "Unfortunately, they're supposed to be on our side. Let's just say they're ones to watch. There's more than one way to deal with potential trouble, and if the right moment presents itself I'll be ready."

***

Aprival had not returned. Laura hadn't actually said "I told you so", but she'd thought it. Nevertheless, Clemis had refused to give up on the enigmatic stranger. She had a feeling that he, like herself, had been over-ruled. While her father played host to Pervain, she took a flitter and made her way somewhat erratically to the spaceport. Unsurprisingly, Nimion was on duty. He seemed to do nothing but work.

"What do you want *now*?" he asked suspiciously.

"Just checking to see if the big spaceship's still there," Clemis said breezily to cover her anxiety.

"It is," Nimion said in a tone which discouraged further discussion.

"I wish it were possible to send them a message," Clemis continued undeterred.

"It isn't, and you know it," Nimion replied tetchily. "And even if I could, I wouldn't. I don't want to do anything to prevent them from leaving."

"What makes you think they're planning to leave?"

"Well, when their agent didn't come back, I hoped - I mean, I assumed - "

"Then stop assuming. They've made no attempt to leave the system, have they? They're still in orbit round Alda Five?"

"Yes."

"Then until that changes, you've no reason to believe they're deserting us. Would you put them on the screen for me, please?"

Nimion sighed, but didn't argue.

"Er - which trace is theirs? All I can see are moons."

Nimion pointed superciliously.

Clemis stared wistfully at the extraneous blip. "How many people know about them, other than my parents and myself?" she asked.

"No-one's going to give them away, if that's what you mean. Idenion spoke to all the tracking stations."

"But did he speak to all the staff *here*?"

"Yes, all eight of us. And I sincerely wish I wasn't one of them."

Clemis scrutinised him critically. "Why? Can't you keep secrets?"

"I don't want to be involved, that's all. The Narvellans executed my father for conspiring against them. I daresay the Eldorians have similar ways of dealing with traitors."

She regarded him with more interest. "Who was your father?"

"Corython, the astronomer."

Clemis remembered the name. "He was in the resistance, wasn't he?"

"He calculated the impact event that was supposed to take out the Synectic base. Only the Synectics got wise to it and the plot failed." Nimion swallowed noisily. "My mother says he was a hero, that he distracted the Synectics long enough for Quetri to finish them off. But the transcripts of the trial don't say that. He was just a clever but helpless individual caught up in something against his better judgement."

"He was trying to save Celestra," Clemis declared. "That's what matters."

Nimion scarcely heard. "I'm not hero material, though my mother would have it otherwise," he said self-effacingly. "Don't ask me to do anything risky. I'd only let you down."

"It's a case of inaction rather than action," Clemis said encouragingly. "No risk to the individual."

"Explain."

"Firstly, I want you - all of you - to go on keeping quiet about the big spacecraft."

"The Eldorians will be all over this facility. They'll see it for themselves."

"Not if you do as I say. There's bound to be some way to keep it off the screen - some computer trick that you understand and they don't."

"I'm no good at lying."

"You won't *be* lying - the equipment will. Please, Nimion!"

He appeared to consider it. "Whose orders are these? Idenion's, or yours alone?"

"Idenion doesn't want the Eldorians to know they have rivals," Clemis reminded him. "I'm just trying to ensure his wishes are carried out."

"Clemis, I'm positive the ship will leave soon - "

"And *I'm* positive it won't. Look there!"

A smaller blip had detached itself from its parent and was already halfway toward Celestra's capital. The on-screen figures confirmed, even to Clemis' unpractised eye, that the incoming craft was heading for the landing field and not the akron.

"I'll go and meet him," she said eagerly. "Now you *will* reprogramme the surveillance system, won't you? You'll be putting people's lives in danger if you don't."

"Very well," said Nimion resignedly. "And I'll acquaint my colleagues with the new procedure. I'm not sure what Jarras will say, though."

"Refer him to Idenion if you get any trouble." Clemis was halfway to the elevator. "Thanks for your help. You won't be sorry!"

"I wonder if anyone said that to my father?" Nimion inquired of the empty room.

The shuttlecraft had landed near the maintenance block, nestling unobtrusively beside some storage drums and sections of pipe. Aprival had already disembarked and was pacing restlessly back and forth.

"I knew you'd be here," he said warmly as Clemis reached his side. "You don't choose to share your home with Eldorians."

Clemis was again startled by the accuracy of his statements. "*One* Eldorian. Pervain. And as soon as he's finished plundering father's library he'll be back this way."

"There's time enough," Aprival replied calmly. "You seem angry with me, Clemis. Why?"

"Why do you think? You didn't keep to your deadline!"

"Xorian wouldn't give me leave."

"Xorian?"

"My captain. After my poor showing, the alliance with Eldor must have been a foregone conclusion."

221

"So foregone that you didn't bother to turn up for the verdict?" asked Clemis. "That looked very bad to Laura, you know."

"I can well believe it. She never thought much of me anyway," said Aprival with an unexpected smile. "I couldn't even speak the language properly when I met her. Haven't you noticed an improvement since?"

Clemis had indeed noticed. "You've learnt a lot in eight days," she observed. "And the knowledge was implanted while you slept, if I'm reading you correctly."

"You are."

"Then why didn't you have this - treatment - a bit sooner? If you'd expressed yourself properly to begin with - "

"The programme had pronunciation errors. We were able to correct it, but not until we'd heard you speaking."

Clemis thought there was something a little odd about this statement, but let it go in her haste to be the bearer of good news. "Well, if it's any consolation to you, Idenion won't say a word to the Eldorians about your visit. And I've told Communications to keep your ship off our tracking screens."

"I'm very grateful."

"You'll still have to deal with the Eldorians' onboard scanners, of course."

"Of course," Aprival repeated.

"Although that won't be a problem for another octal or so."

"I'll make sure Xorian's aware of it," Aprival said blandly.

Clemis decided to dispense with niceties. "Discord's dreams, you know what I'm trying to say! Now the decision's gone against you, how long do you people plan on staying here?"

"That depends on you," came the swift rejoinder.

She eyed him warily. "What do you mean?"

"It depends how long you keep us waiting for the information."

Frantically she read him again, trying to ignore the disturbing lack of memory and concentrating on his immediate thoughts. To her relief, he knew nothing of Tralvar or the secret she'd inherited.

Aprival waited, knowing she was studying him. "As you can see," he said at last, "I've no idea what this information *is*. But Xorian says you alone have access to it."

"I...have nothing to disclose," Clemis faltered.

"As you wish." Aprival was only slightly put out. "You won't speak yet: that's to be expected. You need to spend some time under Empire rule. When you change your mind, you know where to find us."

"I want what's best for us all," Clemis said impulsively, "but surely you realise what a difficult choice I'm faced with? Your people, Xorian in particular, could be incredibly subtle enemies. They could be using you to plead their cause."

"That isn't what you believe," said Aprival, "so I won't waste time on shocked protests. The truth's much less elaborate. Previously we made

223

assumptions which turned out to be wrong, and we're *still* making them. We thought you'd jump at any chance to keep the Earthers on their planet. We never thought you'd try and elicit the Empire's protection against them."

"That was Pervain's suggestion," Clemis said ruefully. "Idenion fell for it."

"The Empire doesn't protect *anyone*, Clemis!" His hands grasped her shoulders. "Oh, chaos, how can I convince you of something I'm not allowed to remember? Read me again - rediscover that hurt you sensed in me - and then try to imagine what put it there!"

+Are you all right, Clemis?+ asked Nimion from the control tower.

+Yes. Keep out of this+ she answered ungratefully.

+Trevone's just arrived. I'll send him over+

Aprival stepped back apologetically. "I'm sorry. That was impolite."

"Trying to shake the truth into me?" she inquired gently. "I don't mind. You needn't apologise."

"When I'm back on the ship," said Aprival with sudden resolve, "I'll go straight to Xorian. I'll say that if you come to us, you're to be told everything before we start negotiations."

"A generous offer," said Clemis, "but Xorian might not co-operate. Anyway, let me make a promise of my own: if I fly out to Alda Five, I'll have already made up my mind to trust you. Otherwise I'll stay on Celestra."

"Very fairly spoken. Feel free to bring any sympathisers with you."

She smiled wryly. "What makes you think I'll have recruited any?"

"You haven't yet encountered the true Eldorians," Aprival reminded her. "And now I must leave. You do realise this has to be my last landfall? Xorian won't authorise any more once the soldiers arrive."

Clemis regarded him a little guiltily. "You gave up your memory for the sake of two unproductive visits?"

He took her hand briefly. "I don't believe it's been in vain. I'll see you again, Clemis."

"Perhaps," she answered.

"Without a doubt." Aprival gave her a poignantly beautiful smile and disappeared into the shuttle. Moments later, the little craft hurtled skywards in blissful disregard of spaceport protocol.

Trevone strolled across to join her. "So that's your mysterious friend. Nimion's just outlined the new scanning arrangements."

"Then make sure you comply with them on your watch," Clemis replied curtly, annoyed that he'd cut short her reflections.

"Don't worry, I'll do as I'm told. Though I honestly can't see how your Aprival intends to rid us of the Eldorians."

"I can't explain," Clemis began.

"I *know* that. Your mind's in even more of a turmoil than usual. Well, at least I know your hero exists. I was beginning to wonder."

Clemis glared. "Surely you can tell the difference between fantasy and reality?"

"It's sometimes difficult in your case," he remarked. "Only joking."

Clemis didn't smile. "That's just the kind of comment I'd expect from someone with no imagination. Your mind's like a chronometer, Trevone - predictable and monotonous."

"Maybe. But at least it's all in one piece," he retorted. "And at least I don't career around in an antiquated spacecraft, making crazy promises that can't be kept."

Clemis held her anger in check. Trevone was jealous, that was all. He'd said similar things about Kalyx and his lack of reliability. "Have you finished customising your sphere?" she asked, changing the subject.

"Just finished it today. One beaten-up old tub from the Academy, lovingly inscribed with my name and then blasted with a blow-torch."

"And the *real* prototype?"

"Repaired and hidden on Alda Two."

"That's fantastic! The Eldorians will never find it there, and it'll be ready later on when we need it."

"They won't find it," Trevone agreed, "and neither will anyone else. If - chaos forbid - your parents had backed Aprival instead, what makes you think I'd have given the Drive to *him*? I don't know what improbable schemes you're trying to hatch, Clemis, but let me make one thing clear: that sphere stays hidden!"

Clemis felt dejected. If he was so intent on doing nothing with the Drive, how could she risk telling him about Tralvar's plans? He'd take them from her and hide them - or even destroy them. What was it Aprival had said? 'You need to spend some time under Empire rule.' *That* might change Trevone's mind, and Idenion's too, before circumstances forced her to make that trip to Alda Five. She still hoped it wouldn't be necessary. Superweapons were best kept in the family.

***

Six days later the Eldorians returned in force to claim their territory. They swiftly and disinterestedly removed all remaining occupants (most hadn't waited to be thrown out) and set about establishing their presence. A demand was issued - and hastily implemented - that all Celestrian spaceflights be grounded while a continuous stream of personnel and freight was delivered. Idenion granted leave for the spheres to offload near the base, which had rapidly begun to take shape. The Eldorians brought in communications gear, rations, basic medical supplies, clothes - and guns. A great many guns. At the east and west boundaries, fortress-like gates were assembled with rapid efficiency. Armed sentries patrolled them. At intervals along the high perimeter wall, pennants fluttered in the breeze; and in the zone's centre, atop the tallest building, a huge flag billowed. Against a background of the now-familiar yellow and bronze, three letters were blazoned in a flowing purple script.

Pervain eschewed these preparations, instead surveying them from the top floor of the akron with the aid of a pocket telescope. "That denotes the Empire motto," he remarked proudly to Idenion as the flag was unfurled. "Strength, victory, enlightenment."

"It's too high," said Idenion, unimpressed. "It's a hazard to flitters."

"Only ours," replied Pervain amiably. "Did I forget to mention that you're forbidden to overfly our base? Your vessels will be shot at if you do."

"I'll make sure everyone's told," Idenion said resignedly. "You said you had business to discuss. Would you please stop admiring your flag and tell me what you want? I do have other duties!"

"Of course. How thoughtless of me." Pervain gave one of his icy smiles. "I, and some other senior officers, wish to meet the heads of your city states. It would be to our liking if you could assemble them rather than send us on a grand tour. And I also think it's time I met your elusive wife and became reacquainted with your daughter. Lastly, I'd like to meet the young man - Trevone, I believe his name is - who gave our Symerid Three surveillance craft such a runaround."

Idenion had anticipated most of these requests. "Then why don't I organise a reception? A social gathering is preferable to a conference, and gets everything over with in one evening. My cooks will provide food and wine to your taste, and I can arrange for some music if you wish. You..."

Pervain blanched suddenly. Several beads of sweat ran down his face and disappeared under his high collar. "Would you...repeat that last sentence, please?"

"I said, you'd be advised to wait until your acclimatisation is complete."

"What acclimatisation?" Pervain gripped the windowsill to steady himself.

"I though you knew!" Idenion was genuinely concerned. "When the protections adopt newcomers, normally when they've been here about four days, there's always a degree of discomfort. Some people just feel out of sorts, others run a temperature or develop a rash. It's just the same with us if we've been offworld long enough."

"I must inform the medical team about this." Pervain rallied himself with an effort. "Is there an antidote?"

"Only bed rest and plenty of fluids, especially liman. And yes, the onset is always sudden - as you're finding out. I've sent for a flitter: you'd better let me help you downstairs."

"No - I - "

"We can use the back stairs if you wish."

"Thank you." Pervain knuckled the sweat from his eyes and allowed Idenion to take his arm. "I'm glad my malaise has such an innocent cause. I was beginning to think you'd poisoned me."

"We don't - " began Idenion, then stopped.

Pervain laughed hoarsely. "You *do*, First Citizen! At least your predecessor did. Quite an adept, from what I've heard. I really wish I could have met him."

Once they were airborne, Pervain switched on his communicator. Immediately a call came in from

Grenthap. "Pervain, where in Ebbondrear have you been? There's some kind of epidemic breaking out and Escir needs info, fast. He thinks it's those bio-defences again."

"I'm aware of the situation. Tell him to meet me by the east gate." Pervain was now perspiring freely.

Idenion touched down as close to the gate as he dared. There was only one sentry on duty. He allowed Pervain to stumble through but waved Idenion back, side-arm at the ready.

"No Celestrians past this point," he recited in a monotone, obviously having memorised the phrase. Idenion was just about to make a spirited retort in the man's own language when a harassed-looking Escir hurried toward them.

"Stand down, soldier," he ordered, and the guard grudgingly obeyed.

Pervain gasped out his information and collapsed. Escir knelt anxiously beside him.

"Gods! He's burning up."

"It's a particularly bad reaction," said Idenion, worried in spite of himself. "I'm sorry no-one thought to warn you. If you need any medical assistance from us, please don't hesitate to ask."

"Stretcher!" Escir bawled. Then, more quietly: "I may well need that help, First Citizen. I've got a hundred sick men on my hands." He returned his attention to Pervain. Idenion, dismissed, left him to it.

Now that Escir knew what he was dealing with, he was better able to cope. He called Central Command, urgently requesting an embarkation roster, and when it came through he swiftly drew up lists of personnel and when they were likely to be affected. Then he had one of his auxiliaries post the datasheets all over the base. Next he rounded up a squad of new arrivals and set about converting a school building into a temporary infirmary. There was no risk of person-to-person contagion but in the interests of efficiency he wanted all the sufferers under one roof.

While he worked, he wondered what other surprises this planet was going to throw at him. He'd thought he'd have an idle time of it, and thus had requested only two auxiliaries. What would there be to do except deal with the odd minor injury, mop up after fist fights and dispense remedies for hangovers and foot fungus? Given this planet's curative properties he'd even be spared the usual cases of love's disease. And since the rec girls had all undergone tubal ligations, there wouldn't be any accidental pregnancies either. That, he'd been sure, was everything. Wrong, Escir. Wrong, wrong, wrong.

He did his rounds for the tenth time that day, fielding the usual barrage of complaints from the invalids. If they were complaining then they weren't that sick. The girls seemed less badly affected than the men - or maybe they were just more stoic about it. He allowed them to stay in their lodgings, with strict instructions to page him if anyone got worse.

Pervain's condition troubled him, however. He even suggested a transfer to Alda Mexa's hospital, but Pervain would have none of it.

"I won't be beholden to these people," he whispered. "And I can't shield when I'm like this. There are things, personal things, I'd rather they didn't know."

"You've a dangerously high fever," Escir argued. "You need someone with you and I can't spare the staff. I've no option but to hand you over."

"There *is* an option." Pervain's voice was almost inaudible. "One or two of the whores used to be nurses. I saw the profiles. One of them could..." He began to cough, and asked for water. Then he turned his head aside, unable to speak further.

Escir, not wishing to incur the Freelord's subsequent wrath, made his way to Grenthap's office and pulled the files on the rec girls. "Tildy, trainee midwife," he muttered. "That's no use. Teacher....singer.... beautician... Ah. Mallina Vye-Dressel, student nurse, one year's experience at Nova City General. She might do."

The girl wasn't as young as he'd expected. He supposed it was the red hair which had caught the attention of the conscript patrols. Unless she was that rarity, a volunteer. "How long have you been a recreation worker?" he asked.

"Three years," she replied.

"Three?"

"I signed up for seven. My family needed the money." She gave him a bright but artificial smile. "How may I serve the officer?"

"I didn't ask you here for that," Escir said hastily. Then, briefly, he explained what was required.

"Yes, I can look after him," Mallina said confidently.

"And you? Have you had the sickness yet?"

"Yesterday. It was gone this morning."

"You were fortunate. Come with me, then, and I'll show you the patient." Escir gave her a rueful grin. "Be warned: by tomorrow you could be nursing me too!"

Pervain's fever worsened. He became delirious, and had to be moved to a separate room as he was disturbing the other men. Mallina applied cool damp cloths to his forehead and kept him hydrated, and from his constant prattle began to learn something of his past. A picture emerged of an isolated, insecure child with a weak mother and tyrannical father. Mallina wasn't surprised at this; aristos seemed incapable of raising well-adjusted children. But his youthful anxieties were interspersed with something more sinister.

"Make the pain stop," he pleaded over and over, not seeing her. "Make it stop..."

"What's he remembering?" she asked Escir when he came to check on them. "Was he a prisoner? Was he tortured?"

Escir was reluctant to tell her. "Do you know about his psi ability?" he inquired at last. "Our military scientists tried to enhance it. They didn't succeed."

"You mean they experimented on him? That's dreadful!"

233

Their patient gave another moan.

"He wouldn't have shown weakness in their presence," Escir added. "He's Patieron to the core. All the screaming was in his head - till now."

"I'm glad I'm not an aristo," said the girl.

Escir glanced at her narrowly. "Don't ever mention this to him," he advised. "He wouldn't thank you for it. Now, can you be left unsupervised for a while? I have to organise some more pallets. Either that or persuade some of these malingerers that they're fit for duty."

"What about *you*?" Mallina asked. "You look rough."

Escir *felt* rough. He'd seen the first signs of the telltale rash on his upper body, and had buttoned the neckline of his shirt to avoid displaying it. Then he'd taken a couple of stims and hoped for the best. "Just tired," he lied.

For the next day and a half, Mallina nursed Pervain. Escir had food sent to her and twice took her place so she could catch up on her sleep.

"You're doing an excellent job. I'll make sure you're paid for it," he promised.

"Pay my family," she replied.

Around noon on the third day of his illness, Pervain's fever broke. Mallina left him sleeping naturally and went to tell Escir. She found him in his temporary office next to the main ward, writing a bulletin.

"That's a weight off my mind," he said on hearing her news. "I didn't want to alarm you, but there were times when I thought he wouldn't make it."

234

"He's a fighter," Mallina said soberly. "I've washed him and changed the sheets, so he'll feel comfortable when he wakes, but do you think I should give him a shave? He likes to look smart, doesn't he?"

Escir fingered his own stubbled chin. "Nobody thought to order razors. It'll be a day or two before they arrive."

"Can't we get some from the Celestrians?"

"They don't have facial hair," Escir said laconically.

"Oh!" said Mallina, amused and intrigued. "I assumed they were just like us. Wrong, eh?" Then, returning her attention to more immediate matters: "I noticed some of the pallets were empty. Does that mean the epidemic's over?"

"Yes, this is the final stage. I've asked Central to slow all future embarkations to a trickle, so we don't have this situation again." He stood up and stretched. His uniform was creased and sweat-stained.

"You look as if you've slept in that," Mallina remarked.

"I haven't had much chance to sleep," he confessed. "Just dozed a bit. Now everyone's on the mend I suppose I should try to...to - "

She caught him as his knees buckled and eased him back into the chair. Despite mumbled protests she loosened his collar, exposing the blotches he'd been at such pains to conceal.

Just then, Grenthap walked in. "Ebbon's balls! Now *he's* got it!"

"Did have it, General," Mallina corrected him. "See - the rash is almost gone. He stayed on duty the whole time, and he's exhausted."

Escir raised his head with a mighty effort. "I'm sorry, General," he croaked.

A calloused hand briefly gripped his shoulder. "Get some rest," Grenthap said gruffly. Then, to Mallina: "How's Pervain?"

"Recovering," she answered.

"Well done, my dear. Didn't want to lose the heir to the Patieron estates. We need their funding!" He chuckled, and went to inspect the men.

"You heard him," Mallina said to Escir. "Bed."

"But - "

"But nothing. Come on, lean on me."

She helped him, weaving and blinking in the sunlight, across the street to his quarters. Someone yelled a lewd comment. "Catch you later, soldier!" she called back cheerfully.

"He thought I was drunk," Escir muttered, aggrieved.

"Well, aren't you? How many stims have you had?"

"Er..."

"Never mind. We're here." They had reached his front door. "Now let's get you to bed."

"I can manage, thanks. You go."

"And have you sneaking back to the infirmary as soon as I'm out of the way? No, I'm making sure you do as you're told."

Escir, too weary to argue, sighed and allowed her to fuss over him. It was a long time since anyone had.

When he was asleep she went back for one final look at Pervain. She touched his forehead, which was cool, tidied the room a little and filled the water carafe. As she reached down to adjust the covers a hand seized her wrist; startled, she twisted away.

"Where's Escir?" Pervain demanded huskily.

"Off duty," she answered.

"Fetch him."

The arrogance in his tone, weak though it was, infuriated her. "No, damn it, I won't. I've only just persuaded him to rest."

Pervain smiled unpleasantly. "*You've* only just persuaded him? Interesting. What's your name, girl?"

"Mallina."

"Mallina." He repeated the name experimentally, then tried to sit up. His failure brought home to him how enfeebled he still was.

"Please try to sleep," she entreated. "You've been extremely ill."

He subsided unwillingly, a look in his eyes she didn't much like. "My little nurse," he said with an edge of resentment. "I'll see you again, girl - in your other capacity."

***

The akron was a blaze of light and finery, a display not often associated with the austere building. Delicate music issued from within. The principals of the other city states - with the exception of Scapirion - had arrived earlier that afternoon. Now, as the last of the daylight faded, they nervously prepared to meet the Eldorian guests.

Punctually at dusk, a succession of flitters delivered the Empire's dignitaries to the reception. First came a news correspondent, stationing himself next to the main entrance with his recording equipment. The next to alight was Pervain, in full dress uniform of gold and purple, complete with ceremonial sword.

"The only son of Lord Ephren certainly cuts a handsome figure," droned the reporter into his machine. "If you look carefully, viewers, you will see the twin dagger emblem of House Patieron on his left shoulder and again on his belt buckle. And on the sword-hilts is the lurlan rampant, mascot of his regiment - the Ninth Expeditionary Force. It's rumoured that Pervain is recently recovered from an assassination attempt. You certainly wouldn't know it, looking at him today. He is now receiving his official welcome from First Citizen Idenion, the poet dictator."

Clemis, dutifully in line next to her father, smiled politely as Pervain paused in front of her. He took her hand and imprisoned it in both his, holding the pose far longer than etiquette demanded.

"Let go or I'll kick you," she murmured, still smiling. His lips twitched in amusement.

"And now," crooned the commentator, "our very eligible ambassador greets Clemis, Idenion's exquisite little daughter. There have been several attempts, over recent years, to unite Freelord Pervain with the daughters of other aristocratic

Houses - attempts he has always resisted. Could it be that he had his mind on greater things, such as a diplomatic union between House Patieron and the ruling family of this, the Empire's furthest outpost? One would venture to suggest that, for our Freelord Harmost, such a marriage would be a very pleasant duty.

"Now here is General Grenthap and his -ah - lady companion. The illustrious General wears the battle honours of many successful campaigns, but I'm authorised to remind viewers that he is here not as conqueror of Celestra, but to lead our valiant soldiers and our new allies on a top secret mission."

Grenthap's jacket positively creaked under the weight of many medals. The little prostitute on his arm giggled and said: "Remember not to hug me too tight, General, or I'll get stuck on them!"

"Was it really necessary to bring a whore with you?" hissed Pervain as they crossed the threshold.

"Well, why not?" Grenthap replied ebulliently. "Idenion didn't seem worried when I asked permission. You bachelors might not mind turning up alone to a social event, but I'm a married man. I like having a lady in tow."

"Lady," repeated Pervain scornfully.

Escir, dismayed by the presence of the camera, tried to keep Grenthap's bulk between himself and the prying lens. He was not successful.

"And there, if I'm not mistaken, goes Dr. Escir, the despair of House Alon. Escir's fall from grace is too wellknown a story to repeat, but here's some news just out: his lovely ex-wife Droxina has remarried into a very prestigious House, and moreover, her new man has legally adopted her children. So the good doctor will now be able to keep all his Army pay."

The cynical monologue continued as each new arrival hove into range. Technical staff, visiting Army chiefs: all, it seemed, had chequered histories. A catalogue of military blunders and engineering disasters followed them into the akron. At last, his memory chip almost full, the reporter paused for a final shot of the galleried ground floor. He knew better than to try and enter. His place was to comment, not socialise.

Suddenly there came the sound of another flitter landing. He whirled, camera automatically at his shoulder. An elderly man in rumpled civilian dress was being helped to disembark. "Well, what a surprise to round off the evening! Is there anyone watching who doesn't recognise Preceptor Habbon Mol-Varna, renowned anthropologist and expert on lost civilisations? It's truly amazing that at his venerable age, he's opted to travel a thousand light years to see a new species at first hand."

"Hello, Geffin!" Habbon exclaimed - the only guest to acknowledge the newsman. "Still scandalmongering? Well, here's something for the network. My fourth wife has just given birth to triplets."

"Yours, I assume?"

"Indubitably. No-one else's babies could be that ugly. Must go! Goodbye!" And he bustled into the akron, his aides hurrying to keep up.

"Well, what can I say?" murmured Geffin. Lack of recording time spared him from having to think of something.

The reception was centred around the stateroom which had once played host to the Narvellan show trial. A quartet of scolia performers occupied the dais. Discreet flower arrangements had been placed at intervals about the starkly functional room, along with comfortable chairs and dainty tables. Trolleys of food and drink were on hand, along with caterers to provide details to the uninitiated.

To pre-empt any leading questions, Idenion had previously given the Eldorians all visual data from the recent Earth trips: Trevone's recordings, including the London riot, and his own, when he was attempting to hail the orbiting Eldorian vessel. Trevone's material was demonstrably genuine, proving that no landfall had taken place, and there was little doubt that Idenion's subsequent misadventure could be blamed on the Eldorian presence. Grenthap had seemed satisfied. Pervain was not; and, now that the General was a captive audience, wasted no time in pressing the point.

"Do you really believe that the Celestrians go to Earth just to coast around and sample music broadcasts?"

"Why shouldn't I believe it? It's just like them."

"It needs more investigation."

"Why? I've no doubt they were more bold in the distant past when they could impersonate local deities. But now? Credit them with more sense than to tangle unarmed with that bunch!"

241

"Idenion and Laura seemed to think it worth the risk."

"Because they were terrified for their daughter. And what happened? Our agents tracked them down after just one day. I'm surprised the Earthers didn't get to them first."

"It was *two* days," Pervain corrected him. "That report was sketchy. There's too much time unaccounted for."

"They were looking for the girl," Grenthap reiterated irritably. "And here she is, right on cue. I was wondering where she'd got to. Ebbon's balls! Is that her mother? Ve-ry nice!"

Remembering Tralvar's last words to her, Laura had thrown out her patterned dresses and asked Dena to design her a new outfit for the occasion. She was wearing the result: an off-the-shoulder, bias-cut gown of sea green. Her hair was styled in an elegant pleat, from which a few soft tendrils had been allowed to escape.

"If you don't stop drooling, Grenthap, you'll cause a diplomatic incident," Pervain advised.

"Do your homework, Pervain. They can't read you in a crowded room."

"Is that so?" Pervain affected surprise. "I'd prefer not to take the chance. Now where's that stupid girl with our drinks?"

Grenthap squinted across the room to see Neelah, the plump little blonde who should have been his ornament for the evening, deep in conversation with an attentive middle-aged Celestrian. A *very* attentive Celestrian. "Who in Ebbon's name is that?"

"Whoever he is, General, he's out of line." Pervain squared his shoulders purposefully. "I'll deal with him."

"This isn't the time nor place to start a fight," Grenthap warned. "Break them up, but do it politely."

Laura had also noticed the breach of etiquette. "I *knew* Lydion would find a way to be difficult," she lamented to Idenion. "He didn't want to attend, but I insisted. I didn't think there'd be any Eldorian girls here!"

Idenion followed her gaze, moderately amused. "There's just no stopping him, is there?"

"It's not funny! That's General Grenthap's escort. Oh, chaos, Pervain's going over."

"Don't worry. I'm sure everyone will behave sensibly." Idenion took Laura's arm. "Come on - we have to circulate."

Neelah's little squeak of fear alerted Lydion to the approach of authority. He took one look at Pervain's disdainful features and flamboyant attire and made up his mind to detest him. "Ambassador!" he said, trying his best to make it sound like an insult. "Do please sit down. That's if you *can* sit down wearing that thing." He pointed to the sword.

"I can sit down," Pervain said neutrally.

"Show me."

Pervain remained standing. "You have me at a disadvantage. You are....?"

"The name's Lydion. Some call me Lydion of Atris. Others call me worse things."

Pervain inspected him with a degree of curiosity. "So you're the one all the poetry's about!"

"Expecting someone younger?" Lydion inquired acidly.

"Well, since you ask..." began Pervain, then apparently thought better of it. "That needn't concern us at present. I've come to request the return of Neelah, and to respectfully point out that you haven't paid to enjoy her company."

Neelah looked from one to the other uncomprehendingly. Lydion put a reassuring arm around her.

"I can hardly be accused of monopolising her after a mere two astallen. Look on it more as a cultural exchange."

"The General wants her back," Pervain stated bluntly.

"And he shall have her in just a moment." Lydion waylaid Idenion, who was in conversation nearby. "Sorry to interrupt state proceedings, but did you know this girl was a singer? Why don't we put her on the stage briefly? It'll help break the ice."

Pervain looked expectantly at Idenion, assuming he would dismiss both Lydion and the idea. He was swiftly disappointed.

"Lydion may be somewhat over-enthusiastic," Idenion said in a half-apology, "but I believe he has a point. These proceedings are, wouldn't you say, a little too formal. A familiar song in this unfamiliar setting would surely appeal to your people."

"You don't know the type of place she sang in," Pervain retorted.

"Tell me more," suggested Lydion. Pervain ignored him.

"Please," said Idenion, "grant us this favour. We'd welcome the opportunity of hearing a singing voice. We don't hear many of them."

Pervain remembered his role. "Very well," he said reluctantly. "If the General agrees."

"I'll clear it with him." Idenion turned to Neelah and, in excellent Eldorian, explained what was being discussed.

"Excuse me, First Citizen, but I ain't much of a singer," said the girl in a strong regional accent. "I did tell Lydion that. If I sing unaccompanied I'll go out of tune."

"I couldn't make her understand about the scolia," Lydion confessed.

"You won't be unaccompanied," Idenion assured her. "Provided you've an idea of what you want, the scolia will read you and follow you. It's what they do."

Her eyes widened. "Really?"

"Really. So you've nothing to worry about. Let's have a word with Grenthap and then I'll announce you." Idenion ushered Neelah away, but not before she'd directed an impish grin at Lydion.

Left alone, Lydion and Pervain tried to think of something civil to say to one another. Fortunately, Laura was on hand to relieve the situation.

"Ambassador!" she exclaimed in conciliatory tones. "At last. I'm so sorry my duties have kept us apart until now."

"Charmed," intoned Pervain, lifting her hand.

245

+Reptile+ Lydion remarked for her exclusive benefit.

Her smile didn't waver. "I look forward to a fruitful association with the Empire, and a happy working relationship with its subjects. Er, Lydion - someone's been asking for you. Losara, deputy Prefect of Alcine."

"Chaos! What's *she* doing here?"

"The Prefect was indisposed."

"Discords, Laura, why didn't you warn me beforehand? I hate to abandon the party so soon, but I'm afraid I'll have to leave. Rapidly."

"Why?" Laura looked baffled.

"Nothing happened, I swear. Well, just a mild flirtation which she completely misread. Now will you please let me out of here before she spots me?"

Pervain's arm barred his way. "At a more propitious time I'd like to have a talk with you about your brother."

"Yes, yes, later. Send word to the Lyricon. Sorry, Laura!"

They watched him mingle expertly with a group of kitchen staff who were removing empty food carts. "Lydion's intrigues would fill an encyclopaedia," Laura said, laughing.

"You don't say." Pervain didn't seem amused.

"May I have everyone's attention, please?" Idenion's voice floated across from the small stage. "We're privileged this evening to have a singer in our midst, and she has kindly agreed to perform just one song. Here, with the popular Patieron ballad "The Homecoming" is Neelah Jarod-Asra." He repeated the announcement in Eldorian.

Neelah stepped onto the dais. She looked composed now, almost eager. The scolia played the opening chords. And Neelah sang, very touchingly, of a woman awaiting the return of her soldier husband. Her voice was untrained but sweet, with a plaintive edge which suited the song.

The applause which followed was much more than polite.

"See, what did I tell you?" murmured Lydion before he vanished into the city byways.

Pervain did not applaud. Instead, he turned a troubled gaze on the scolia. An alien mind, an alien melody - a precise sequence of note values and sonorities - and those four girls had decoded and read it instantly, performing it without error. It was almost frightening. What else can these people do? he wondered.

Neelah beamed gratefully at everyone before skipping across to Grenthap. "Excellent, my dear," he said with an expression that was almost benign. "You must sing for me again, back at barracks."

There was now a healthy buzz of conversation in the hall. Clemis noticed Escir sitting alone and slid into a vacant chair opposite. "Hello! Remember me?"

He looked up guiltily, caught in the act of dabbing his eyes with his sleeve. "So much for good impressions," he said with a rueful smile. "That song caught me unawares. I suddenly realised I'd never see my kids again." He spoke in Eldorian, as his command of Celestrian was slight. "Can you understand this?"

247

"Yes, if you concentrate only on what you're saying," she replied painstakingly in his own tongue. "How many children do you have?"

"Two. A boy and a girl. I suppose you overheard what that hack said?"

"Most of it."

"It wasn't entirely true. I knew my ex-wife had married into House Ixtis. It wasn't a love-match: she did it for the children. They'll have a secure future now, whatever happens to me."

"Why exactly did the Emperor dismiss you?"

He raised an eyebrow. "You mean you still don't know?"

"There are many opinions on what happened - too many. They obscure the event itself."

"Then allow me to put you straight. First, I should explain that our leading family's health is somewhat fragile. They're very inbred. I happened to be on hand when the Emperor's daughter was brought into hospital with anaphylaxis and breathing difficulties. All the usual treatments had failed, and everyone was too scared to touch her - it would have meant death for them if their procedures hadn't worked. Then she stopped breathing altogether. I took over, all youth and confidence, opened her chest and performed heart massage. It saved her.

"The next thing I knew, I was forcibly retired from my hospital practice to become the Emperor's personal physician. Droxina loved it - the prestige, the social events, and above all the money. I hated it because my real work had been put on indefinite hold. Then one night the Emperor's favourite

248

nephew got high on hallucinogens, decided he could fly and leapt out of an eighth storey window. I was ordered to save him. I couldn't."

"And they ruined your career for *that*?" exclaimed Clemis in outrage.

"You don't understand what was at stake," Escir said with weary patience. "There are no sons of the line, so that young man was heir to the Empire. I should have *been* there, not off socialising. I knew he was on drugs. I should have watched him."

Just then, Preceptor Habbon tapped him on the shoulder. "Hello, my boy. Still in uniform? I was hoping you'd have got yourself back into research by now."

"That's not for me, Master Preceptor."

"Nonsense! I read your early papers on genetics. Very very promising."

"Not in a military context. They'd probably ask me to engineer the perfect soldier and then demote me when I failed. I'm much better off here, believe me."

Habbon's smile didn't falter. "And you've found yourself some delightful company, I see. A very pleasant world, this - a refreshing change from that dreadful Miiyat!"

Clemis was suddenly on the alert. "You've been to Miiyat?"

"Yes, indeed I have. Couldn't pass up the chance to study the Miiyatans thoroughly, irritating creatures though they are."

"In that case my father would like to talk to you," said Clemis carefully, not wishing to say too much in front of Escir. "He also studies alien societies."

"Her father's First Citizen Idenion," Escir put in.

"Is he now? I'd be happy to answer any of his questions, young lady. And perhaps in return he could answer some of mine."

Clemis spied Jarras passing by and managed to hail him amid the profusion of thought strands. +Jarras! Send Idenion over, would you? It's important!+

Escir had followed her gaze, and wasn't at all surprised when Idenion appeared and ushered Habbon away.

"Now," said Clemis, suddenly businesslike, "stop brooding over that drink. Laura wants to meet you. And I believe you've booked a dialogue with the Prefect of Corayn?"

"Yes, with a view to examining your medicines." Escir reluctantly set down his glass. "I'm in your hands, First Daughter. Let's see if I can get through the rest of these introductions without swearing."

"It isn't *that* much of an ordeal, surely?"

Escir grinned - the first time Clemis had seen him smile wholeheartedly. "I'm a bit too free with my language these days. All part of being an enlisted man."

"Just be yourself," Clemis said earnestly. "That's all we ask. And by the way, we've no such designation as First Daughter - but I like it!"

With some difficulty Idenion extricated Habbon from the main gathering and eased him into a side room. The loquacious academic seemed to be personally associated with every Eldorian present, and when he wasn't exchanging greetings he was firing dictation at his aides. Finally, when they were alone, Idenion was able to repeat the question that had plagued him since the Eldorians' first landfall: why had Mror of Miiyat called the Celestrians his ancient enemies?

"I think I may be able to help you there," beamed Habbon. "The Miiyatans told us that several millennia ago, they went spacefaring as the allies of the Draldir - a most aggressive species by all accounts. There are numerous legends about them, each more savage than the last, which pass for entertainment on Miiyat. However, it seems the Draldir's rampage through the galaxy was cut short by some humanoid telepaths, who confined the Draldir to their homeworld by surrounding it with an energy field of some sort. And the Miiyatans, of course, found themselves equally cut off. They never had any technology of their own, you understand; just tagged along, as cats do."

"How true do you think this is?" asked Idenion.

"It sounds improbable, doesn't it? But Miiyat's ancient star charts led us straight to Dral, or what was left of it. The radiation had dispersed long ago, and it would have been safe to land, but the Eldorian Central Command doesn't waste time on dead planets. Much as I'd like them to."

"And these telepaths are assumed to have wiped out the Draldir?"

"Not intentionally. But they must have known a species like that would fight each other to the death rather than endure their own company."

"That could have happened of its own accord." Idenion was determined to be sceptical.

Habbon fixed him with a beady eye. "It happened because they were trapped. We found the orbiting mechanisms that kept them there. I really shouldn't be discussing this, you know."

"You didn't, if anyone asks. I read your mind."

"Er...of course. Quite so." Habbon spluttered a little. "To be frank, I didn't see the need for secrecy when the devices hadn't worked in centuries. Our bright boys tried to make sense of them but they were too badly damaged by cosmic debris."

Idenion refilled the little man's glass. "And you saw these machines before the military took over?"

"Not for long." Habbon's amiable features clouded briefly at a remembered slight. "They were works of art, First Citizen, works of art - even in their ruined state. Ornate, strange, enigmatic."

"So," said Idenion ruminatively, "the cats blame us for this ancient attack on their freedom because we happen to be psi-conversant humans."

"That's what it amounts to, I'm afraid. As soon as they were told about you they decided you must be the perpetrators. And I have to add that the fate of their emissary has done nothing to change their minds."

"But surely, in this saga of theirs, the enemy had a name?"

"Yes, of course. Now what was it...? Forgive me, First Citizen, my memory's not what it was."

252

Habbon frowned in concentration. "Plenty of epithets to describe them, of course, but as to their actual title...ah, I have it. The Nevrii, that was it. The Wizards of Nevri and their warlord Tekla."

Idenion felt the blood drain from his face. "Wizards and warlords? It doesn't sound much like *us*," he managed.

Habbon was too busy with the wine decanter to notice anything amiss. "I don't suppose we'll ever know the truth," he sighed. "We don't even know what the Draldir looked like. If only I'd been able to study that planet..."

Just then an apologetic Laura looked in. "I'm sorry to interrupt, Idenion, but we need you as mediator. The Eldorians want to set up their school for scientists in Treva, which makes sense to me, but Jarras assumed they'd want it in Alda Mexa. He's not best pleased."

"On my way," Idenion answered wearily. He could now hear the dispute through the open door, and thanked Habbon with his customary politeness before following Laura. Seeing the akron's chief administrator nearby, he accosted him briefly and said: "When you arrange Habbon's tour, allow him to visit anywhere he wants except Atris and Ilonna. I'll explain later." Then he set about placating Jarras and his interlocutors, explaining that the First Scientist had hoped to return to Alda Mexa in order to be with his wife. Surprisingly, Pervain backed him up, suggesting that the tuition could be shared between Jarras and his son.

"Don't let Trevone's extreme youth deter you," he advised. "I've just been conversing with him and he's a mature and intelligent young man."

The Eldorians provisionally agreed to this solution.

"You have a career wife, First Scientist?" one of them inquired. "What does she do?"

Jarras, grateful to be off the hook, launched enthusiastically into a description of Nefyrra and her duties. Pervain listened in a mixture of contempt and curiosity. So the fellow was in awe of his wife, was he? That was a weakness, and weaknesses could be exploited.

His communicator sounded discreetly, incurring a glare from Laura. She and Idenion had specifically asked their guests not to bring radio equipment or weapons. Pervain had ignored both requests.

"That was my secretary," he informed them. "I'm afraid I must deprive you of my company for a short time, but I shall return before the evening's out." Then he strode away, proud and confident. Laura watched him resentfully.

Idenion slid an arm round her shoulders. "Since we don't have to contend with *him* for a while, shall we step outside for some air?"

She accepted gratefully. Convincing everyone she was telepathic had been gruelling, to say the least. Fortunately, the Eldorian scientists had been eager to practise their limited Celestrian, and she had been careful not to attach herself to any group unless there was at least one colleague present to bail her out.

"You've been exemplary," Idenion declared. "Just be thankful you didn't run into Habbon. Even I had difficulty keeping up with his output!"

"I'd better learn to speak Eldorian," Laura decided. "Just as soon as I can. Now, aren't you going to tell me what's bothering you?"

"Is it that obvious?"

"Only to your wife, I suspect. Well?"

Idenion told her the story of the Draldir. "Fortunately," he concluded, "Habbon doesn't have any proof that *we* eradicated them."

"And you're sure it was us?"

"Doubly sure. Tekla you know about; but you probably *don't* know that Nevri is the archaic name for this world. The Scapirians still use that name."

"So much for our pristine past!" said Laura with a nervous laugh. "At least it shows Tekla's devices work."

"And that's another thing. At his final conference, Tralvar reminded Lydion that the sphere-shield was only the first of Tekla's designs, and prompted him to get on with the next. That implies there were more than two. I need to know exactly what was on that wall!"

"Oh, darling, don't start going on at Lydion. Not now. He's dreading being interrogated about Tralvar. Once that's out of the way he'll be a lot more receptive."

"I wish we didn't have to rely on him at all."

"Now you're being unfair. He turned in the second lot of work, didn't he? It was Jarras who decided to put it on hold."

"That's true."

255

"Then you've no reason to mistrust him. If he does have more of Tekla's writings he'll keep them safe, believe me."

"I wish I had your faith in him. Look how he behaved tonight, running off to avoid some woman."

"Losara," said Laura with a hint of superiority, "is a charming old lady who wanted to give him a present for repairing the Alcine satellite uplink. He staged that panic flight to make Pervain think he was a harmless fool."

Idenion acknowledged his mistake with good grace. "I really should have a better idea who's running the provinces!"

"Liaison's always been *my* job, hasn't it? Come on, it's time we went back inside. People will start to talk!"

By the time Pervain returned, most of the company had left. Grenthap was still present, canoodling with Neelah, and Trevone and Clemis were trying to calm a drunken group of military engineers. The men kept breaking into raucous song: "We'll rule every (expletive) world in the (expletive) galaxy. We're the Eldorians and the stars are ours!"

They fell guiltily silent as Pervain walked in.

"Don't stop on my account," he said, seemingly amused. "I just wanted to confirm you were still here, First Citizens. I've a surprise guest for you."

He disappeared briefly and returned with a prisoner under armed escort. Idenion stared with growing recognition at the shabby, emaciated captive. Beneath the layer of dirt was gold skin,

256

and a hint of beauty still clung about the bruised face.

"Sijek!"

The shaven head turned vaguely in his direction. "Idenion....?"

"Release him at once!" Laura demanded furiously.

"I'm not at liberty to do so," Pervain replied, coldly distant. "He's only on loan to us from Central Command. He'll be kept at the base indefinitely."

"Then," said Idenion, "I shall insist on visiting him. I want to see him better cared for than he appears to be at the moment."

"He'll receive the best of care," Pervain assured him. "He isn't much use to us like this."

Idenion suddenly became aware that Grenthap and the other Eldorians were watching him closely. "Explain yourself!"

Pervain smiled. "Hitherto, you've enjoyed an unfair advantage over us in terms of perception. Supposing - just supposing - you were planning something unfriendly. Your relayists could co-ordinate a city-wide resistance and we wouldn't know until it was too late. Now that we have our very own conversant to redress the balance, your relayist chain will no longer be secure. Goodnight." With that he turned on his heel and departed, followed by the two soldiers and their prisoner. The remaining guests filed out after them.

"The gloves are off," Laura murmured.

"Whatever that means," Idenion said despondently.

"It means," said Clemis, "no more pretence. From now on we'll be dealing with the *real* Eldorians. Don't say I didn't warn you!"

258

Chapter Six

Two days after the reception, people near the Eldorian base awoke to the sound of demolition work. Those on the lateral above could dimly see, through clouds of dust, that several buildings were being flattened. As usual the work progressed at relentless speed, and by evening an open space had been created. Most of the rubble had been cleared, stone blocks hauled away and roof tiles stacked neatly for future use.

Idenion, naturally enough, had demanded to know what was going on. It was several ilden before Pervain returned his radio message.

"We need a parade ground," he explained casually. "Soldiers require a place to assemble, to march, perform weapons training and suchlike. Incidentally, you're on a restricted frequency. Military use only. And that reminds me - "

"Chaos, Pervain, will you *listen*?"

"My colleagues at Communications," Pervain went on without a pause, "inform me that you used to have a public broadcasting service. You don't seem to require it anymore so maybe we could take it on. Music and pep talks for the troops, something brainless for the girls..."

"We'll discuss it later." Idenion tried to sound authoritative rather than ineffectually angry. "At the moment, I'd like to know when I gave you permission to knock down our houses."

"When you signed the treaty." Pervain was reasonability itself. "To refresh your memory: it

259

says that everything within the zone becomes, to all intents and purposes, part of Eldor. That means we can do anything we want with it. Out of deference to you, we haven't felled any trees. Neither have we touched the houses with the pretty patterns on the roofs. I thought they might have some religious significance."

"Mythological," Idenion said.

"What's the difference? Now, regarding the parade ground, we're going to need some concrete. A lot, actually. Flagstones aren't suitable and neither is gravel."

"You'll have to contact Treva for that. Unless you want me to fetch it for you?"

"Please, Idenion, no sarcasm. I'm trying to maintain efficiency, difficult though that is when you people set such a bad example. Now is there anything else on your mind?"

"You could give me a report on Sijek."

"Why don't you ask your daughter? She's here at this very moment talking to Escir. I noticed they were getting pally at the reception."

Idenion was concerned, but hid it well. "Is that something I should be worried about?"

"You don't have to worry about Escir - he's the respectful sort. But I shouldn't let her hang around the neighbourhood if I were you."

Idenion sensed he was being baited. "I'll talk to her," he promised, and ended the call.

Escir had stepped outside the east gate to speak with Clemis. "I can't sign you in. Orders. Unaccompanied female visitors aren't allowed on the base."

"But you *can* tell me how Sijek is." Her clear grey eyes regarded him intently.

When she looks at me like that, he thought, it's as if she already knows the answer. Maybe she does. But she still doesn't know enough to stay away from our men. If she were a few years older I'd be all over her myself.

"Would you indeed?" she murmured.

He felt himself blush. "You should be just a little cautious. I suppose you think your telepathy protects you. But dressed like that - "

"It's summer. I always dress like this. Now tell me about Sijek."

He sighed. "He's in much better health than I anticipated. I knew the Emperor had grown tired of him and I expected to find he'd been tortured for sport. But of course he's a valuable commodity, so Central kept him more or less safe."

"Then why was he in such a mess?" asked Clemis.

"He'd been loaned to a mining company to dowse for gemstones - an illicit deal on someone's part, which is why he was literally hauled out of a mine and sent straight here. The foreman had roughed him up a bit, but bruises heal."

"How is he mentally?"

"Not so good. In effect, he's the last of his kind. How would that make *you* feel?" He was interrupted by his pager. "It looks as if I'm wanted."

"Then I won't hold you up. Thanks for your time, Escir."

"My pleasure. Sorry it wasn't better news."

Pervain was watching from the radio room adjoining the gatehouse. "Escir seems to have made an impression," he remarked to Grenthap, who had just arrived to send some dispatches. "Maybe he should have *my* job. The little bitch won't speak to me."

"Girls like doctors." Grenthap busied himself with his paperwork.

"General..."

"Something eating you, Pervain?"

"Yes, as it happens. Apart from seeing the look on Idenion's face the other night, I'm not sure it was a wise move to bring back Golden Boy."

"You were the one who wanted extra surveillance."

"I meant security checks and random interrogations, not the likes of him. He's just as likely to spy on us and tell the Celestrians."

"He won't like what will happen if he does."

Pervain brightened. "That's the first encouraging thing you've said since he was brought here. Maybe we should offer him a small demonstration."

"Give it a rest, Pervain."

"Why? If it weren't for that little catamite we'd have found this place a lot sooner. We couldn't break Axmiol because he knew the Emperor would protect his boyfriend."

"So?" Grenthap sounded bored.

"So our charming hosts have had years longer to prepare."

"Prepare what? If the Celestrians had the capacity for resistance they'd have hit us with all they'd got when we first showed up."

"Maybe that isn't their way. Could I at least carry out the procedures I suggested?"

"If you must," Grenthap conceded wearily. "We aren't properly settled in so we can't be blamed for being jumpy. But after this, we'll have to rely on subterfuge."

Pervain made a crudely dismissive remark and Grenthap fixed him with a steely glare.

"Are you questioning my judgement?"

"No, General, but - "

"You're chasing shadows, Pervain. The Celestrians may well have some nuisance value but nothing we need lose any sleep over. Now can I please get on with my work?"

Clemis noted this exchange with a degree of hope. Then, to an accompaniment of razing and levelling, she found an empty flitter and returned to the akron. Idenion was waiting for her, grave of face.

"Now listen, Clemis - and I really mean listen," he began. "I don't want you going near the Eldorians by yourself. Do you understand? Take a responsible male with you, or stay away."

"I was only passing," Clemis said, unrepentant as ever. "I had an errand in the student quarter. And I'm not defenceless. Look!" She hitched up her short flared skirt and, from the decorative holster strapped around her slender thigh, produced what appeared to be a torch. It was angled to fit the hand, and fashioned in lightweight grey metal with

263

fluting around the lens. "It's one of the stun-guns the scolia-tech made. Dena designed the fancy garter. There's also a shoulder sling for use with a cloak."

"How did you acquire all this?"

"Lann brought the guns to the Lyricon. Only six have been completed so far but he wanted me to have one. He offered one to Dena but she said she was too old to need that kind of thing. Nefyrra said she wasn't interested but he left one anyway, in the custodian's suite. Maybe Laura would like it."

"I'll ask her." Idenion inspected the gun closely. "I'm pleased you have this, but remember: always keep it deactivated when you're wearing it and don't point it at anyone unless you intend to use it. Otherwise your foe could disarm you."

"I didn't realise you knew about guns!"

"I learnt a little from Tralvar, and Laura knows even more from her days in Cheveney." Idenion smiled, a rarity in itself since the start of the occupation. "So, my dear daughter, your parents aren't as clueless as you think."

"Glad to hear it!" Clemis gave him a boisterous hug. "Do you know what I'd really like? No, I'm not trying to get round you. I'd like a family dinner - just you, me and Laura."

"We haven't done that in years."

"Which is why I want to do it now. To affirm our solidarity."

"What about Trevone? Is he invited?"

"I'd rather it was just the three of us," Clemis said after a pause.

Idenion didn't question her. "As you wish. I'd certainly welcome an evening to relax and be myself. I don't often get the chance these days."

***

They had just finished eating when Lydion hurtled in, more agitated than Clemis had ever seen him. "Is it true?", he demanded. "Have they brought Sijek back?"

"If you hadn't absconded from the reception you'd have seen him for yourself," Idenion said, mildly irritated. "Where have you been, anyway?"

"Ninka. Business, sort of." Lydion discarded his winter weight cloak and retrieved a fallen mitten.

"Ninka in midwinter? That must have been fun!"

"Just something I had to do. Idenion, I *must* talk to Sijek about Tarlatine. You've got to get me into that base!"

"More easily said than done, since you went all out to aggravate Pervain."

"I know, I know. I shouldn't have. It was just the way he swaggered up and down in that fancy suit, looking as if he owned the whole world."

"We don't like him either," said Laura, "but sometimes you just have to grit your teeth and be polite. He's the intermediary, and seemingly the only Eldorian to speak fluent Celestrian. So you and I need him more than most."

"Don't remind me." Lydion's ineptitude with languages was known to them all. "This is serious,

Idenion. Sijek has information I need. You've seen him, you say. What state was he in? Do you think he'd know me?"

"Lydion," Laura said gently, "Sijek's been a prisoner of the Eldorians for many years. He mightn't even remember Tarlatine."

"He has to remember something. He helped found the colony, and he'd have worked alongside Tarly as a healer. If he recalls one scrap, one grain, one fragment of that time, it will be precious to me. I have to see him, Laura!"

"Do you still love her that much?"

"That much, and more." Lydion helped himself to some wine from the table. "*You've* been separated from your lifebonded. Did you stop loving him, even for one moment? No, of course not."

"Pervain can't dictate who visits Sijek," Clemis offered. "Escir will have the final word, and he's much more amenable."

"Idenion...?" Lydion ventured.

"All right, I'll speak to both of them tomorrow," Idenion said. "And Lydion - don't pre-empt me. Wait for permission."

"Then don't take all day about it." Lydion was still burning with impatience. "Contact me as soon as you get the go-ahead. And don't take no for an answer, otherwise I'll - what in chaos is that noise?"

"It's an auxet," said Clemis.

"A what?"

"Auxet. It's a musical instrument."

"You could have fooled me."

"The Eldorians sound it every morning as a wake-up signal, and every night at roll-call."

Lydion listened as the dismal wail again echoed from the lower laterals. "Sounds like a kyffu having its tail twisted. It can't be heard from the Lyricon, I hope?"

"Nefyrra says not."

"Thank harmony for that. Well, I'd best get some sleep, if I can. Sorry to gatecrash the family party." Lydion gave Laura a swift hug, ruffled Clemis' hair and was gone.

"I'd make that call at sun-up," Clemis said to her father. "He isn't going to wait."

She was right. Less than two astallen after Idenion had tactfully explained the situation to Pervain, and before he could relay the ambassador's suspiciously prompt agreement, Lydion was at the east gate trying to communicate his requirements to a deliberately obtuse sentry.

"I want to see - to be seeing - " Discords, didn't this moron know his own language? "Sijek, the Narvellan. Understand? Narvellan?"

The sentry didn't even look at him.

"Oh, kyffu's piss. Fetch Pervain, then. Ambassador Pervain?"

"The ambassador's off duty," said the soldier, still barring the way.

Lydion's eyes flashed fury. "Now listen, greasebarrel - ah, you understood *that*! - just go through that door, get on that intercom and - "

"Let him enter." Pervain had materialised, unobserved, from the shadow of the palisade. He was wearing a long-sleeved shirt and loose-fitting trousers in matching black, embellished with a broad silver belt. Even to Lydion's jaundiced eye, he looked effortlessly stylish. He strolled into the gatehouse and returned with a slip of paper, which he handed to Lydion.

"Your permit," he explained. "Come with me."

Lydion threw him a puzzled look, but complied. The sentry watched balefully.

Pervain led the way to Escir's surgery, not far from the newly levelled parade ground. "You two have met, haven't you?" he asked, shoving Lydion through the door; and without waiting for a reply, disappeared.

Escir, slightly taken aback, looked up from his desk. He'd seen Lydion at the reception and been quietly amused at the backchat he'd given Pervain, but hadn't actually been introduced. "I'm sorry, I wasn't expecting you yet," he said, rising to his feet politely.

Lydion, while not sensing a kindred spirit, nevertheless responded to his aura of hardworking decency. "Is my fault. Am early." Then, seeing Escir's involuntary frown: "When you speak, I understand. Is more difficult to make answer."

"Sijek's in my examination room," Escir began, remembering to stay focused on his own words. "You might as well talk to him there. I'm not sure how he'll react to having his past raked up - "

"Is already done. Celestra's his past."

"I realise that. But just to be on the safe side I've given him a light tranquilliser. When he gets upset his psi talent goes peculiar and things tend to fly about."

268

"No problem. I always land on my feet." Lydion smiled despite his concerns, and Escir decided that he liked him.

"Go through. I'll be here if he plays up."

The room had, until recently, belonged to a child. Brightly coloured letters and numerals adorned the walls and curtains. Lydion tiptoed inside, still with an image in his mind of Sijek as he had once been: a beautiful youth, Axmiol's beloved. The truth came as less of a shock to him than it had to Idenion, as Sijek was now scrupulously clean and no longer starving. He wore an Eldorian Army shirt and shorts, and white canvas slippers.

"Lydion." Surprisingly, his voice hadn't changed much apart from a drug-induced languor. "They told me to expect you."

"You still speak Celestrian!"

"Oh yes. I've used it a lot - to teach *them*." Sijek stared expressionlessly at the closed door. Lydion sat down on the bunk next to him.

"Sijek - I want to ask you about the colony. About Tarlatine. Do you remember those days?"

"Of course." He smiled dreamily. "My last days of freedom."

"Then talk to me. Tell me anything, whatever comes into your head." Lydion had to fight hard to be patient. He wanted to turn the Narvellan's fragile psyche upside down and shake the memories out. But Sijek was a synaesthete and he'd never been able to read him. Then, as now, the younger man's thoughts were a dancing mass of colours, sounds

269

and tastes - his own particular brand of association, incomprehensible to an ordinary telepath.

"It was a frugal, difficult time," Sijek was saying unhurriedly. "Our first harvest failed and the second one wasn't much better. Then the plague arrived, decimating us. I was one of the first to contract it."

"What about Tarly?" Lydion interrupted.

"Tarlatine was wonderful. She had countless sick people to nurse, but whenever I woke she was there. I'm told she saved many lives. I'm convinced she saved mine. At last there were no new cases and we thought the epidemic was over. But two winters on, the virus returned - an altered strain. No one had any immunity. That was when we decided to move on.

"By then, Tarlatine was expecting her second child and having a wretched time of it. She couldn't keep any food down. When the plague hit, she didn't stand a chance." Sijek paused, unwilling to deliver the words which would sunder a lifebond. "I'm sorry, Lydion. She's dead. She died a long time ago."

Lydion had turned as white as chalk, but his reply was oddly neutral. "She can't be dead. I still sense her."

"You sense the child, perhaps."

"What child?"

"You have a son. He survived both epidemics."

Lydion reacted angrily. "No, Sijek, you're getting it all wrong. Now start again, slowly. Who did Tarlatine marry?"

"She was assigned to Bydlor."

270

This was something tangible to grasp at. "I remember him - he helped supervise the emigration. He seemed a caring sort."

"He was kind to her," Sijek confirmed.

"I'm glad she wasn't married to a wifebeater." Lydion's casual tone had returned.

Some lingering trace of empathy, some vestige of his healing skills, awoke in Sijek despite his poor health and the soporific effect of the tranquilliser. "Lydion, listen to me. You *do* have a son. Let me tell you about him." Because, he wanted to add, the knowledge will support you once you admit your loss.

Perhaps Lydion understood. "Then tell me, if that's what you want," he acquiesced.

"Tarlatine discovered she was pregnant very soon after we made landfall," Sijek began in his slow, deliberate manner. "Everyone, she included, assumed Bydlor was the father. When her time came I assisted with pain relief, so I was one of the first to see the newborn after the women had washed him and dealt with the cord. His skin was pale with just a hint of gold, and he had your grey eyes. His hair was black, like Tarlatine's.

"When we put him into her arms she wept for joy. He's Lydion's! she kept saying, over and over. And straightaway she gave him his name: Tarlion. Everyone rejoiced for her, even Bydlor."

Lydion was dumbfounded. He'd always longed for a child, but had consistently failed to sire one despite his myriad relationships. With his consent Tarlatine had run some fertility tests on him; he knew her conclusions by heart.

"You've a low sperm count. If you'd lived anywhere other than Celestra and had the same number of sexual partners, you might have had offspring. But here, with the bio-restrictions working against you, it's out of the question."

He remembered something else too. He and Tarlatine had made love several times the day she was taken from him. He'd reluctantly left her and gone to work: two ilden later she was off-world.

"The protections don't fail for sixteen days," he said at last. "How could she possibly have conceived?"

"Your protections worked differently on us," Sijek said wryly. "Remember what happened to our birthrate? We didn't *have* a birthrate!"

"Chaos, I'd forgotten all that!"

"But when any of us left your world, the effect was reversed within two days," Sijek concluded triumphantly.

So it was true - all of it. Lydion stared into vacancy, still in retreat from the joy and pain he knew he must soon confront. "How old was Tarlion when you last saw him?" he asked almost conversationally.

"He was four. A happy, lively child, much loved by his peers." Sijek tried unsuccessfully to project an image of the boy. "If you want, I'll draw him for you. I can achieve a good likeness. I used to draw the ladies at the Emperor's court."

Lydion wasn't sure if he dared accept. Perhaps seeing a likeness wouldn't help. "Do you think he knows about me?" he asked.

"Bydlor took your scieshanar. He promised he'd give it to Tarlion when he was old enough to understand."

"Then he'll have it by now." Lydion tried to smile. "And one day he might come looking for me. Imagine that!"

"I *can* imagine it," Sijek replied. "Your son's an adventurer. He followed Axmiol and me onto the sphere when we were leaving for the last time. Bydlor had to grab him."

"He sounds just like my father. Oh, chaos..." Lydion was suddenly overcome. The little anecdote had affected him in a way the greater issues had failed to do. The alphabet pictures on the walls danced before his brimming eyes. He stumbled to his feet, forgetting Sijek, intent only on putting some distance between himself and the base before he completely fell apart.

He yanked open the door, startling Escir, who took one look at him and produced a tall bottle from somewhere in his desk. "Bad news? Drink some of this. It'll take the edge off."

Lydion drank. The Eldorian alcohol tasted vile, but he felt a little more in control.

"Lydion!" called Sijek. "Don't go. Don't be angry with me!"

"I'll see to him," Escir said hastily. "Get yourself home, quickly. Got your pass? Just hand it in at the gate."

The sunlight seemed blindingly bright. He walked, manfully suppressing his tears. He'd never cried, never in his adult life, and he wasn't about to start now in front of the Eldorians. But where in the name of discord was the gate? Everything was so changed, so alien...

"Are you all right?" asked a woman's voice. His vision cleared momentarily to reveal a redhaired girl, and beside her the detested figure of Pervain.

"Where's the gate?" Lydion blurted, trying to keep his voice steady and not quite succeeding.

"Over there." The girl pointed back the way he'd come.

Without another word he turned and shambled toward his objective, relieved it was so close.

"What's the matter with him?" Mallina asked Pervain.

"There are some things he'd have been better off not knowing," Pervain replied with obvious relish.

"Is he the one who wanted to see Sijek?"

"The same."

"Gods, Pervain! You set him up!"

"Merely an educated guess." Pervain still sounded very pleased with himself.

"That's *mean*."

"What's it to you? Shut your mouth, girl. I'm not paying you to criticise me."

"I just felt sorry for him," Mallina said in mitigation.

"Save your pity. These people are losers, Mallina. There's going to be a lot more misery by the time we've finished with them."

Lydion, as he neared the checkpoint, still had presence of mind enough to watch out for the sentry he'd insulted. But a different guard was on duty and he was simply waved through. As soon as he was

274

outside he heard his name being called, and an instant later found himself seized by two pairs of youthful hands.

"Clemis..?" he murmured in bewilderment. "Trevone...?"

"Idenion sent us to find you. He guessed Pervain was up to mischief," Clemis explained.

"Come on. Our flitter's this way," said Trevone.

He let them lead him, grateful for the intervention but too distressed to say so. They did, however, manage to prise most of the news out of him.

When they reached his house he went straight inside and didn't emerge for three days. Tonor, his assistant, dealt efficiently with a plethora of enquiries and personal callers. "Just leave him alone," he ordered. "Interfering won't help. Lydion has his own way of handling personal crises and we have to give him the space he needs."

On the third day Drusa called, and was admitted. At this significant sign of recovery, a relieved Tonor went off to Tivenne on an assignation of his own.

A concert had been scheduled for the evening of the fourth day, and a light rain was falling. Just before the scolia assembled a tight-lipped Lydion was seen to vacate his dwelling and walk swiftly to the weathershield generator room, looking neither to left nor right. The shield had not been in use through midsummer, and no-one was very surprised when it failed halfway through the performance.

Nefyrra, however, berated Lydion as she was wont to do.

"I'm sorry," he said, much to her amazement. "I was inattentive."

Nefyrra reconsidered. "Well..I suppose it was bound to give trouble after being idle for so long."

"Maybe," said Lydion, "or maybe not."

Tonor returned the next day. He was repairing some lights in the stage area when Lydion approached, looking composed but world-weary.

"Tonor...I want to take a few more days off. Can you cover for me?"

"Yes, of course. Take as long as you like."

"Thanks. I just need some time to get my head round things without having Nefyrra on my case. Not to mention half a dozen scolia virgins all eager to compromise me."

"I noticed," said Tonor wistfully.

"You don't want the notoriety, believe me. You're much better off with that nice little archivist in Tivenne. Now, since you've been doing so much of my work lately, I thought this would be a good time to promote you from assistant to Guild partner."

"*Really*?"

"Why not? You can run the shield reasonably well now, even though it did take you decades to learn."

"Due in part to your erratic training methods," Tonor retorted genially.

"That's right, blame me."

"It's true! Don't you remember the first time you left me in charge? You didn't even stick around

276

to help - just said 'it's all yours' and went off grinning."

"You understood the control system well enough. The rest was down to intuition, which couldn't be handed on by me or anyone else. I'm sure you realise that by now."

"Well...yes."

"The shield's like an ancient lady, Tonor. She's temperamental, autocratic, but she'll still respond to tenderness. Cherish and respect her and she won't let you down."

"But assuming there *is* an emergency, where do I find you? Will you be at home?"

Lydion hesitated. "By day, I'll be in the Tyvian Gardens," he said at last.

"A nature cure?"

"You could call it that. Just don't tell the girls, please. I'll let Nefyrra know out of courtesy."

"Understood." Tonor regarded him searchingly. "I hope this works for you, Lydion."

"Given time, I'm hopeful it will. The gardens are special in that way. And when I get back, we can talk about my retirement."

***

The Eldorian base was now fully operational; and the worst thing, everyone decided, was the noise. Not just the braying of the auxet night and morn, but a myriad other sounds associated with military life. Soldiers marching, drumming, exercising, constructing things, taking things apart, performing weapons drill, being yelled at, and yelling in turn at their subordinates. To say nothing of the constant whine of flitters landing and taking off, the clatter of equipment being unloaded and the rumble of small wheeled vehicles over the flagstones. And at night, when the city-grid street lights were extinguished, foot patrols circled the perimeter with flashlights and loudly challenged anything that moved.

By day, outside the base, off-duty soldiers strolled around in groups, monopolised the bakeries and helped themselves to an excess of goods from the markets. In other districts armed contingents carried out security checks - descending on selected households and trashing them. Dena's was one such. They discovered the sphere-shield plans but left without doing too much damage, slightly perturbed by her silent contempt. They didn't need reminding that she was the widow of Tralvar, most feared of all First Citizens.

In Treva, some of the Eldorian science students were causing problems. They were disruptive in class, asking infantile questions and quoting Empire propaganda. And on the way back to their spaceport lodgings they sang "The Stars Are Ours" in the street.

Nevertheless, the presence of the Empire was tolerated. The Eldorians were largely self-sufficient, they weren't herding people into factories or making them build spheres, nor interfering with Celestrian morals or customs. The widely held opinion was that once the inevitable war with Earth began, the occupying forces would be diverted elsewhere and Celestra would be left alone.

Laura wondered if she should disillusion the citizens, but decided against it. At least, if the belief persisted, there wouldn't be any riots. And that was all to the good, because lives were doubtless being preserved.

She sifted through the papers in front of her, deciding which matters could be postponed. With Idenion of necessity doing all the running around, most of the administration had devolved on her. Once she'd learnt some Eldorian they could share their duties once again, but that wouldn't happen just yet. She was making a little headway as it was a sensibly constructed language, but her studies were strictly part-time.

The scolia girls had presented her with a wealth of information after the reception: slang, frequently used words, speech patterns. And those same girls, and others, were busy decrypting the Eldorians' radio codes.

By far the best study resource, however, was the Forces Broadcasting Service. Though banal in content - idiotically fictitious news bulletins, sports reports (presumably genuine) and boring music - it had taught Laura more of the language than all other sources put together. There was even a daily drama, popular with the rec girls, called Teera's Fortune - although misfortune would have been more appropriate.

Everything happened to Teera. She had been ostracised by her House, lost her children to the state, made a second disastrous marriage and was

279

now on the run. And throughout the narrative an unsubtle message was hammered home: women should not decide things for themselves.

"Still at it?" asked Idenion, tiptoeing into the office and embracing her. "How are you getting on?"

She sighed, stretched and turned off the transcription. "Slowly. Very slowly."

"You don't have to be fluent to get by. Think of Lydion."

"I *am* thinking about him. In fact, I went to see Drusa today. She understands him better than anyone."

"And?"

"She confirmed he'd never stopped loving Tarly. He's devastated, naturally - and feels irrationally guilty for not realising she'd died. He sees that as some kind of betrayal on his part. And he still hasn't come to terms with the fact that there's a son of his out there, a son who's now a young man, whom he's never seen nor likely to see. He told Drusa he felt burnt out and alone."

"Alone?" echoed Idenion. "Doesn't he realise how many well-wishers he has?"

"No, I don't think he does. I know what you're going to say, Idenion, and there's no chance of pressuring him about that wretched wall. Why the hurry?"

"Because a situation could develop. At least a dozen people know that Lydion and Tralvar were working at Ilonna. If Habbon or anyone else investigates that mosaic they'll have proof of the Tekla legend - proof that we built the Draldir's global prison. There'll be questions, and they'll assume Lydion has the answers. Did you speak with Jarras?"

"Yes, he was on the transposer this morning with his daily bulletin. He only saw the wall after the sandstorm defaced it, so he can't help with that. But he does remember Lydion claiming to have all the formulae in his head."

Idenion's frown deepened. "And you still say I shouldn't talk to him?"

"Tactfully, darling. Very tactfully, or not at all."

Idenion sighed and changed the subject. "So what's the latest from Treva? Anything I should know about?"

"The Eldorians are building armaments into their flitters, as well as adding to their compliment of spheres. Jarras says, and I quote, they're not bothering with the bronze effect anymore, so we won't know if they're friend or foe until they open fire on us."

"I thought only the flagship was bronze."

"Jarras doesn't understand military hierarchy - or maybe he's being deliberately obtuse. Other than the fleet build-up there was nothing new in his report - just another tale of woe about his unruly class. He says the civilian scientists don't give any trouble - it's the Army engineers. Trevone can handle them much better than *he* can, apparently."

"I can believe it. Nerves of steel, that boy. He takes after his mother."

"Jarras is still very edgy," Laura reflected.

"Aren't we all?" Idenion sat down next to her and she rested her head on his shoulder for a moment, wishing they were both far away from the problems confronting them.

"Well, go on," she said at last. "Tell me what happened at the base. I assume they wouldn't let you see Sijek?"

"They did, but not alone. Escir was busy with a patient and his colleague didn't trust me. But there's no need to worry, my best girl. Sijek will never give you away."

"Are you sure?"

"Absolutely. He may be difficult to read at the higher levels but his hatred of the Eldorians came through clearly enough. He's thoroughly on our side. He was also anxious for me to know that he didn't collude with Pervain in trying to cut Lydion down to size. All the ammunition was in the Golden Girl sonnets, which Pervain borrowed from *me*."

"The sonnets don't say Tarlatine's dead."

"No, but they say she's a healer. Pervain already knew about the plague victims, so I suppose he put two and two together. Anyway, I've told Sijek to co-operate fully with his captors over the relayist chain. Once they discover it isn't a treasure trove of select information but a channel for people's grocery lists, maybe they'll stop leaning on him and turn him over to us. We could do wonders for him at Tafret."

"Not much chance of that," Laura said gloomily.

"We'll see. On a more hopeful note, Trevone's physics class - our own youngsters, I mean - have found a vantage point in the student quarter which looks straight into the base's armoury. They're now fairly sure they could assemble and disassemble the Eldorian guns, maybe even use them in a life or death situation. Of course, it's only a matter of time before the Eldorians block the window...." Idenion paused suddenly, his attention distracted.

Laura waited. "Was that Kyrin?" she asked after a moment.

"Yes; Pervain's on his way up. Get those language lessons out of sight!"

Laura hid her notes and audio material in a drawer. She was only just in time. Pervain entered without announcing himself, his expression even colder than usual.

"Can we help you?" asked Laura haughtily.

"There are one or two serious matters which cannot wait until our next scheduled meeting," Pervain answered, dispensing with his usual oily preliminaries. "Firstly, the interruption to our electricity supply. You're aware, I presume, that the base was without power for two ilden yesterday?"

"So was half the city," said Idenion disinterestedly. "These things happen."

"Not under our regime. I'm instructed to advise you that any subsequent power cuts will be considered an act of aggression."

"That's ridiculous!" exclaimed Laura. "The Lisir's running high this summer, otherwise there would have been regular interruptions."

"I can acquire some stand-by generators if Grenthap insists," Idenion added curtly. "They'll be noisy, but you're apparently used to that."

"The compromise seems acceptable," Pervain conceded. "Kindly expedite delivery, or we shall be obliged to station personnel at the hydro-electric plant."

"I'll deal with it," said Idenion in the same irritable tone. "Now as you can see, we're very busy. What other matter was serious enough to divert you from your routine?"

"The papers we found in the home of Tralvar's widow," Pervain replied.

"We've been through all this before," Laura said heatedly.

"Such a vital development warrants more than a single discussion," said Pervain, completely earnest for once. "You had in your possession a forcefield capable of repulsing our weapons - and yet you failed to tell us."

"There was nothing to tell. The device isn't installed in any of our spheres," Laura stated.

"Anyone would think we were at war," Idenion added.

"And you still maintain," Pervain continued inexorably, "that this cache represents all Tralvar's recent work?"

"Absolutely," said Idenion with the blinding sincerity he was renowned for, unaware that a contradiction lay hidden only two rooms away.

"And how can you be sure no-one's carrying on his researches?" Pervain inquired.

"Very few people have the ability, and they're all accounted for," Idenion said calmly.

Pervain regarded him with a cynical eye. "Your trust in your scientists is laudable. Forgive me if I don't share it. I'd like you both to come with me, if you'd be so kind."

"Where to and what for?" demanded Laura. "We told you we were busy."

"To Communications. I assure you it won't take long. It's an exhibition of sorts, which I insist you must see."

"This is most irregular," Idenion began.

"Now, please. I have a flitter waiting."

They followed him, Idenion alerting Kyrin to the turn of events.

At the tower, all looked normal. Trevone was one of the duty operators: Nimion, fortunately perhaps, was not. Neither Trevone nor his two Eldorian co-workers knew what the secretive Freelord was up to, but they suspected they were about to find out.

"Do we have live feed from the Alcine satellite?" asked Pervain.

"Yes, ambassador, as instructed," answered Trevone. "But the link has disrupted normal contact with Alcine itself."

"It won't be for long," said Pervain impatiently. "On screen."

The wall screen lit, showing a cloudscape.

"Are you receiving me, General?" said Pervain via his personal communicator. "We have a visual from the spotter craft. Ready to commence exercise."

The sphere whose viewpoint they shared plummeted through the wispy cloud and halted just above ground level. Before it lay Ilonna's empty towers and colonnades, silent under the shimmering heat of a late afternoon sky. For a moment nothing moved; and then, out of the sunset, came three dancing silver specks.

Laura understood at once what was happening. She knew a strafing run when she saw it, although she doubted if Idenion did. One after the other the three spheres dove on the ruin, spitting crimson fire. Fractionally later the shriek of the particle beams shattered the desert stillness, followed by the roar of impact and the rumble of falling masonry. The surviving city walls were riddled with fresh damage, the surrounding sand churned up in deep swathes. The spheres, superbly piloted, executed a half roll to deploy their firepower. With all weapons blazing from the rim of their underbellies they appeared to Laura like avenging Catherine wheels.

"It occurred to me that you'd never seen an attack force in action," Pervain said casually. "Efficient, aren't they? Imagine if that were Alda Mexa - "

The boom of an explosion startled him into silence. Roiling black smoke, red flame darting within its depths, burst from Ilonna's catacombs. Idenion watched in disbelief as the one remaining section of colonnade shivered and collapsed across the floor of the amphitheatre in a welter of rubble and stone blocks.

"What *was* that?" demanded Pervain.

Trevone knew. Jarras obviously hadn't got rid of the surplus petroleum left over from Tralvar's experiments. "A fuel dump," he volunteered.

"Interesting," remarked Pervain. "A resource you claim not to use, left in a place you also claim not to use." At this point his communicator went wild, and he was obliged to give the caller - presumably Grenthap - his full attention.

"An own goal!" Laura whispered to Idenion.

+You can explain that to me later+ he returned. +For now, I'll just celebrate quietly. I can't believe they've rid us of that mosaic!+

+Try not to look so pleased+ Trevone advised.

"You don't seem impressed by our fighter display, First Citizen," remarked one of the Eldorian staff.

"On the contrary, I'm *very* impressed," Idenion assured him.

Pervain finished placating the General. "Grenthap doesn't like little surprises," he commented. "And that's what this demonstration's been about: surprises. Despite your personal reputation for truth, Idenion, I believe there are some dissenters out there who don't want our alliance to succeed. You now know the futility of opposing our military machine. Kindly ensure your people know it too."

"May we go now?" asked Laura.

"Of course. Use my flitter if you wish; I have business here."

With great dignity, Idenion took Laura's arm and escorted her from the control centre. Pervain watched impassively. Such a devoted couple, he thought. One without the other would be drastically diminished, privately and politically. He glanced furtively at Trevone, busy reconfiguring the Alcine

287

comsat. Could the boy read him? Could any of them? No, his shields were effective; he'd seen the worry and suspicion in their faces. His psi ability had been a gift from the gods, even though it had been the cause of much pain. He'd triumphed over that, and his less than perfect health, to get here. Let his old man try to belittle that, if he could.

His expression darkened as he remembered the interminable bitter quarrels. He'd come home from the Civil War with honours heaped on him, convinced his father would step aside in his favour. But Ephren, Lord Patieron, was still in his prime and relinquishing nothing - even though his son was almost thirty. Pervain had a title but absolutely no authority. All he could look forward to was an arranged marriage to beget heirs, doing a bit more soldiering and generally wasting his life. By obtaining the post of ambassador he'd escaped this tedium, but not in any permanent way. Once Celestra was subsumed into the Empire, there would be no scope for ambassadors. The governorship, however, should he attain it, would not only represent another star in the family crest but a significant career move for him.

He waited on the unoccupied ground floor until the two Eldorians came off duty, then peremptorily beckoned them over. They were obviously expecting to see him there.

"Did you get the stuff?" asked one.

"All eagerness, aren't you, Klonid? This isn't for your consumption." Pervain handed over a tiny spill of plastic. "There you are: six grains of dreamdust. I assume you agree with my assessment of Jarras?"

"Emphatically. No leadership qualities. I don't know why you think he's a threat, Pervain."

"He played an important role in the guerilla war against Narvella."

"Then I imagine someone else was telling him what to do," Klonid remarked shrewdly.

"He's a bundle of nerves," the other technician put in. "Especially since Chillis and company have been ribbing him."

Pervain stroked his chin. "Hmm, yes, one of my better ideas."

"In short, he's easy meat."

"Good. Now don't forget, you must both talk to him at once. Interrupt one another. He'll be so busy deciphering the language that he won't realise you're lying."

"Got it."

"And be sure to play on his ambiguous relationship with his wife. He feels inferior, she doesn't realise it. And she has this peculiar talent for calling musicians to her, which apparently is much envied. Jarras would love to experience it for himself."

"Do you think dreamsdust will let him do that?" asked Klonid.

"No, stupid, but it'll make him *think* he has. Therefore he'll want a further supply. Betrick, your role comes later."

"I know the drill," Betrick grinned. "Don't worry - your little First Scientist isn't going to give you any trouble. And when we've dealt with the father, maybe you'd like us to tackle the son."

"Enough's enough," Pervain chided him. But he smiled as he said it.

After they had left, Pervain wondered if he should have another talk with Trevone. The boy wasn't very high on his list of priorities. Granted, he had a keen engineering bent - something to be monitored - but he had always displayed a pleasant and co-operative attitude toward Eldor. Unlike Jarras, who exuded resentment from every pore.

"You're in my way, ambassador," said an impudent boyish voice.

Pervain turned abruptly. "I beg your pardon?" he said in tones of ice.

"You're blocking the elevator," said the newcomer. "Are you going up, or not?"

Pervain, irritated, was about to step aside when something about the young Celestrian's appearance - gaunt face, high cheekbones, brown hair - made him pause. "You're not related to Lydion, by any chance?"

"He's my father's brother," replied the youth, meeting Pervain's scrutiny with a bold confident stare. "I'm Kalyx, son of Tralvar. Maybe you've heard of me."

"Should I have?"

"If Idenion hasn't mentioned me I shall be most displeased with him."

"Perhaps he forgot." As always, Pervain was intrigued by the mention of Tralvar's name. "I assume you're a scientist like your father?"

"Sorry to disappoint you, but I'm an actor. Possibly the best of my generation."

"Is that so?"

"It is," said Kalyx smoothly. "I've been on tour, but I'm back now. Expect to see me about town."

"Thanks for the warning."

"Here's another. Don't waste time trying to discover my weaknesses. I don't have any. So you've no chance of taking me down as you did my poor uncle."

"I'll bear that in mind."

"Do so. And now, if you'll excuse me, I've matters to discuss with my nephew."

"Trevone's your nephew?" Pervain was surprised, then amused. "Tralvar must have had a very interesting old age."

Kalyx stepped into the elevator. "Goodbye, ambassador. You know the way out, don't you?"

Pervain gave him a mock salute as the door closed. Despite the altercation, he almost liked this brash young man. Kalyx was scarcely into his majority, but he already had arrogance enough to match Pervain's own - unlike the mischievous but ultimately vulnerable Lydion.

"No prizes for guessing why *you're* here," remarked Trevone as Kalyx strolled into the control centre. "You're going to have another attempt at raising Scapirion. How many does this make?"

"Three," said Kalyx. "And I don't see why you're so disparaging about it. Tralvar wanted us to keep trying, and as his only son I'm best placed to succeed. So will you please do whatever it is you do to call them up?"

"Not much of a technician, are you, Kalyx?"

"I stick to what I'm good at," said the other amiably. "How's Clemis?"

"I've hardly seen her," Trevone admitted reluctantly.

"You're slipping! Maybe I should provide some competition."

"You might be surprised at what you find," Trevone said soberly. "She's changed, Kalyx. Ever since the Eldorians arrived she's been very distant with everyone." He wished he could mention Aprival, although he wasn't sure that Aprival alone was responsible for Clemis' odd mood.

"I'll put the sparkle back in her eyes," Kalyx promised. "Haven't you got that channel open yet?"

Trevone closed a couple of switches. "Ready. Press this key when you want to speak, and release it for their reply. If there is one."

Kalyx cleared his throat and put on his most authoritative voice. "This is Kalyx of the True. I wish to speak with First Tech Tuhallak."

"Forget it, Kalyx," Trevone said after several repetitions had produced only static.

"They *invited* me to negotiate," Kalyx said stubbornly. "This is Kalyx of the True. I wish - "

"Tuhallak here," came a sudden response. "Are you calling us at the behest of the invader?"

"Indeed I am not," replied Kalyx indignantly. "As you well know, my father Tralvar was endeavouring to restore contact between our cities. On the day he died, you intimated that I might continue this process. So far, my attempts have not been acknowledged."

"Your father spoke of you, Kalyx," said Tuhallak unexpectedly. "I understand you're an actor."

"Yes, First Tech."

"A pity. Scapirion has no use for actors. Do not approach us again until you can display some scientific prowess."

Kalyx gave an outraged yell as the channel went dead, and Trevone smothered a chuckle.

"That's told *you*! What did you expect, Kalyx? They're a science-based society - hence First Tech instead of First Citizen or Prefect."

"I don't see what in chaos is so funny. I'm not just doing this for Tralvar's sake. I happen to think it makes good political sense."

"It might if they'd co-operate," Trevone agreed.

Kalyx's jaw set in an obstinate line. "There has to be a way to win them round. And I'll find it."

***

"Pervain really takes the biscuit," Laura declared a couple of days later.

"Pardon?" asked Ideniom.

"Earth expression."

"Better watch those. So what's he done now?"

"Well, after forcing us to watch his fighter aces pulverising Ilonna, he now says that there's to be a remembrance ceremony for their war dead, and we've all got to take the afternoon off while it's in progress!"

"Why?"

"In case we make a noise. I ask you! Oh, and they want permission to march west along Lateral Four."

"Why?" asked Idenion again.

"Because the ceremony involves marching west toward the sunset and they'll run out of base before they've gone far enough. Where's that memo?" She searched her untidy desk.

"I hope they don't expect us to provide a pretty sunset," Idenion remarked.

"That's in the lap of the gods, wouldn't you say?" Laura found the memo and smoothed it out. "Where were you this morning, anyway?"

"Talking with Trevone. He may not be able to read Pervain but he can read the other Eldorians well enough."

"And?"

"They're still nervous of us. Apparently, Pervain had to practically beg Grenthap to allow the air raid. The General wants to keep us sweet. Trevone also says his monitoring team has just been replaced for the second time. It's to ensure he doesn't befriend anyone."

"They *are* nervous, aren't they?" remarked Laura.

"Chaos knows why. Well, I suppose we'll have to let them hold their parade."

"Er - there's more. They want *us* to attend."

"Oh, now, Laura - "

"We'll have to go. I don't know a thing about their religion - to refuse might constitute a terrible affront. We should study their beliefs while we're there."

"We? You mean me, don't you?"

"Afraid so, dearest. I can only study the appurtenances, if any."

Idenion sighed. "And when is this enlightening experience to take place?"

"The day after tomorrow. Just time to find out what we should wear and if there are any taboos to watch out for. We don't want another Myrma on our hands, do we?"

"You promised not to mention that again," Idenion said, aggrieved. "Lydion had no business telling you in the first place."

"Lydion can never resist a funny story. And it *is* funny, admit it."

"I suppose so. Now can we please stop discussing my mis-spent youth and get some work done?"

***

"Come on, you lazy specimens of pond life! Out of there!" yelled Pervain at the bathhouse door.

"There's no frigging hot water again!" someone yelled back.

"No excuses. In fifteen zytl's time that auxet's going to sound the assembly, and like it or not you'll be ready. I want everyone out of there *now*!"

They scuttled past him in various states of undress. Pervain continued to harangue them as they went.

"That's right, keep it moving. Do you want the Celestrians to think we've picked up some of their slipshod habits? Report to the parade ground in

295

fourteen zytl. Anyone found with dirty boots can expect to - " He paused suddenly, staring after one of the recruits who had just hurried by in his vest and breeches. It couldn't be, could it? Central wouldn't dare! With a deepening frown he strode back to the admin block.

Somehow the shambles became order. The auxet wailed and soberly dressed soldiers formed tidy ranks before commencing a slow march out of the west gate. They proceeded along Lateral Four toward intersection fifteen, a broad crossroads with the centre laid to lawn. Here had been set the icons of the ceremony, along with a discreet public address system. Two unarmed Eldorians kept watch. At a respectful distance, a row of seats had been placed for official spectators - although many unofficial ones straggled the route or peered out of windows.

Laura and Idenion founds themselves sitting next to Geffin, the reporter. Idenion suspected this was intentional.

+Watch yourself+ he warned Laura. She nodded imperceptibly.

"Surprised to see me?" Geffin inquired. "I haven't been home, just out of town. I went to have a look round Treva and bam! your bio-defences got me. I was laid up for three days. Then I got word that Ilonna was going to be trashed and decided to check it out."

"Who told you?" Idenion asked.

"Anonymous tip. Anyway, I didn't get my story because the brasshats confiscated my gear. I *saw* everything, though. Old Habbon's hopping mad, going on about wanton destruction and the like." Geffin paused, pursing his thin lips before continuing. "You were stupid not to act pre-emptively while everyone was ill. You'll never get another chance like that."

"I wish no-one any harm," Idenion said blandly.

Drum rolls, increasing in volume, indicated that things were on the move; and presently the vanguard of the procession appeared round the curve of the lateral. To Laura's surprise, the drummer was only a boy. He wore a scaled-down version of the Eldorian dress uniform, and an expression of intense concentration.

"His name's Hyni," Geffin informed her. "He's a Civil War orphan adopted by the Army. There are many kids like him but only a few are taken up. A dubious privilege in my opinion."

Laura managed to understand most of this - probably because Geffin, as a broadcaster, enunciated well. "How old is he?" she asked.

"Twelve summers. In another two he'll be old enough to bear arms, and after that..." The newsman shrugged. "These lads always volunteer for the trouble spots. He'll probably be dead at fifteen."

The soldiers ranged themselves round the crossroads. Various regimental devices were carried aloft, including the company standard - an effigy of the ferocious lurlan. The sun's lengthening rays illuminated the beast's bronze head, teeth bared in a silent snarl. Laura gave an involuntary shiver.

"I'd rather have our zarf," she remarked to Idenion.

Grenthap came forward and stood close to the altar-piece: a simple bronze hoop mounted on a stone slab.

"Plastic, actually," Geffin murmured. "The circle represents infinity - we end as we began, and so on."

"Then there's no belief in an afterlife?" queried Idenion.

"We're not that benighted, First Citizen. We're more concerned with improving our lot in *this* life!"

"Then who's this Ebbon whose name everyone takes in vain?"

Just then, Grenthap began to speak. Somewhat ill at ease, he delivered a brief - very brief - eulogy to the dead, then announced the first hymn, an ode to victory. The troops sang raggedly but enthusiastically, while the two auxet players accompanied them to the best of their ability. Hyni drummed loudly to camouflage the wrong notes.

Pervain spoke next, listing some of the illustrious dead and outlining the high points of their careers. His speech went on long enough for Laura to start fidgeting. Geffin had disappeared briefly during the singing, and now sidled back with a pocket-sized hymnal filched from one of the men.

"Here we are," he announced, opening the book at an illustration. "This is Ebbon, the keeper of the balance. It's not very detailed at this scale but you'll get the idea."

The god, depicted in skilled, powerful brush-strokes, had two faces in profile: one severe, one benign. To the left - the benign aspect - his chin rested on one massive hand: to the right, his adamantine fist was raised.

"He'll always hear your prayers," Geffin added, "but you never know which face he'll turn toward you. In other words, life seldom does us any favours."

Laura couldn't resist a chuckle. "He looks like Pervain. The scowling half of him, anyway!"

Geffin laughed too. "Well, to my knowledge, our Freelord hasn't yet declared himself Ebbon incarnate - but I wouldn't put it past him someday!"

"Shh!" said someone behind him.

From the other side of the green, Pervain glanced across as if aware he was being talked about. Then, his oratory at an end, he announced another musical item.

"Why in Ebbondrear are they singing that?" Geffin muttered as the auxets struck up discordantly.

"Is something wrong?" asked Idenion.

"Oh, just Pervain being partisan as usual. These services are supposed to be non-sectarian, and that's the Fraternity Song of the Patierons. Nobody here to object, I suppose."

For the duration of the event, the base stood virtually empty. At the back of the armoury, a sturdy plank was being positioned against the sill of a slightly open window. The other end of the plank was being manoeuvred by three nervous but determined students - a girl and two boys, leaning out of their own window at the top of a four-storey building. Below was the wooden palisade surrounding the base, its sharpened posts festooned

299

with barbs, nails and other deterrents to the trespasser.

"It looks very shaky, Dessin," said the girl dubiously. "Are you sure it won't slip?"

"We practised, didn't we?"

"Not up here. Maybe we need to rehearse more."

"There won't be another of these parades for a year. Do you want to wait that long? I thought not. So stop fretting, Linni my treasure, and give me an update on personnel."

Linni, the best telepath of the three, scanned the area. "Still no-one, except the guards on the gate and the canteen staff," she reported. "And I still can't read Sijek. He's probably asleep."

"What about the women?"

"In their quarters. Teera's Fortune has just started."

"Good; that'll keep them occupied for a while. Ready with the sling, Raan? Tie it round my waist and make sure the pulley skein doesn't tangle. Now hang onto the plank, both of you. Put your weight into it."

They did so. Dessin crawled across, not looking down, and gave the opposite window a push. It opened readily. +There's a sink here which we didn't know about+ he told his friends. +Can't avoid standing in it. I hope it stays on the wall!+

+If it doesn't they'll know we were in there+ Raan warned.

+Stop agitating+ Dessin advised. +I'm inside; now I have to concentrate+

+Just hurry!+ urged Raan.

Dessin had been mentally rehearsing this part of the operation. He ignored the neat, slender pulse-lances; he'd no idea how long their energy crystals held a charge whilst stored. Instead, he went to an adjacent rack and selected two bulky breech-loading firearms which were reputedly more reliable. The sheer weight of them, however, took him by surprise. Even a single one was probably too heavy for the sling.

+I'm going to dismantle them and send the pieces over separately+ he told the others. +Chaos, they're heavy!+

+Don't forget the ammunition+ Linni responded.

Raan took delivery of the components and sent the empty sling back six times. +Now come out of there+ he pleaded.

+I have to change the inventory+ answered Dessin stubbornly.

+No, Dessin, you don't!+ shrilled Linni. +We agreed not to touch their computers+

+Since when did inventories ever tally?+ put in Raan.

+Theirs might. I should at least try+

+You've already taken longer than we planned+ Linni reminded him. +Come back *now*!+

+In a moment+

+Come back now or you and me are finished!+

Dessin wisely gave in. He rearranged the weapons to obscure the gap he'd left, then made his escape. As he clambered back into his own window, assisted by his friends, the plank slewed sideways and fell with a resounding crash. Fortunately, it fell on their side of the barricade.

"I'll go and get rid of it," said Raan shakily.

Dessin poured himself some fortified wine. He too was trembling, though he tried not to show it.

"What do we do with the guns now we've got them?" asked Linni.

"We hide the components and wait," said Dessin. "I'll report to Trevone, and he'll tell his contacts. When the word comes, we'll be ready. I hope."

At the ceremony, Escir was the last to take the microphone. He uttered a brief but moving tribute to the friends he had lost in the Civil War, then took up two small urns which had been placed next to the circular icon and poured their contents on the grass. "We salute the fallen: with oil, with wine, with reverence for their sacrifice," he concluded, then led the assembled troops in the singing of the Three Worlds Anthem. He had a light, pleasant baritone voice.

"Is he qualified to perform religious duties?" asked Laura.

"Any non-combatant can offer the libation," Geffin replied. "The Army declined to send a minister all the way here."

Idenion was absorbed in thought. "Now I know why Pervain wanted us to see this," he said at last. "There isn't a man here who hasn't lost a relative or loved one in that stupid war. These soldiers would do anything - *anything* - to ensure peace in their homeland, and they think the invasion of Earth will accomplish that. They can't be talked out of it."

Laura was taken aback. "Did Pervain really think we'd try and stir up dissent?"

"It seems my natural eloquence has been the cause of some concern," Idenion replied with a grim little smile.

Geffin's hazel eyes regarded him shrewdly. "So you've got the message, have you? I told them you would."

"That's why you were here, wasn't it?" accused Laura. "To enlighten us if we were slow on the uptake?"

"I always land the dirty jobs," Geffin said wryly. "My advice, for what it's worth, is to let these Earthers take care of themselves and concentrate on preserving what you have here. I like Celestra, First Citizeness. I like it very much."

"I can see why a classless society would appeal to you, Geffin," Laura remarked.

"Ouch!"

"If you're that fond of what you see, make it count," Idenion suggested coolly. "You're in a far better position to sway opinion than I am."

Geffin was startled. "Ebbon's blood! Pervain was right about you. I'm very much afraid, Idenion, that if I were other than my normal scurrilous self I'd be off the air quicker than you could say revolution."

"But there are other ways you could help," pursued Idenion, amazed at his own daring. "You have sources. You observe things. If you're allowed to stay here as correspondent - "

"Oh, I'm sticking around," Geffin assured him. "The uniforms won't like it but it isn't up to them.

303

The network invested a hefty sum in this expedition and they're entitled to some feedback."

"Then share your findings with us," Idenion requested.

"Darling - " began Laura irresolutely.

"It's all right, Laura. Our friend has no love for the military elite. Well, Geffin, what's your answer?"

"Sometimes," the newsman said obliquely, "getting involved is the only way to guarantee a scoop. I'll give careful consideration to what you've said. In confidence, naturally."

"Thank you. And now, we'd best make a move. Everyone's leaving."

***

After roll-call and dinner the men relaxed with drinks, wrote letters home, listened to the sports results or went to acquire a girl. Grenthap had gone to dine with the head of the Treva contingent, but the levity this might have occasioned was dampened by Pervain's surly presence in the bar-room. After downing two measures of spirits he roamed the tables until his eye finally alighted on the recruit he'd been studying that morning.

"You weren't singing, soldier," he accused.

The young man looked up from his conversation. "Pardon?"

"I said, you weren't singing the Fraternity Song this afternoon. Why was that?"

"I'm from the provinces. I don't know the words."

"Your name?"

"Casil Johl-Bretta."

"Then, Casil, perhaps you'd care to tell me *which* province. In fact, why don't you tell everyone the name of your House?"

The men fell silent, sensing trouble.

"Am I on a charge, Freelord, for not singing?"

"I wouldn't go that far."

"In that case, it's none of your damned business what my House is." Casil turned away in an attempt to end the confrontation, but Pervain had other ideas. In a lightning movement which impressed even the veteran onlookers, he flicked a small dagger from his boot and with one swift flourish ripped open Casil's shirt sleeve. Such was his dexterity that the youth wasn't even scratched.

"Interesting tattoo," Pervain remarked. "A star and a flaming torch. Anyone know what that represents? No? Then permit me, one and all, to enlighten you. It's the family crest of House Yaxeth."

An angry murmur followed his announcement. "That nest of traitors!" someone declared, and with good reason: House Yaxeth had changed sides during the Civil War, electing to support the Patierade rebels and causing heavy Patieron losses.

"I had nothing to do with that," Casil said angrily to the protestor. "I was just a child. And the war's over, in case you hadn't heard."

"Oh, we'd heard," drawled Pervain. "But it seems the men aren't willing to serve with you."

"Too bloody right," said the dissenter.

Casil glared at him. "This isn't a Patieron-led expedition, though Pervain does his best to convince you otherwise. I've just as much right to be here as you have."

"We made peace with the Patierades, not with traitors and cowards," retorted the old soldier.

"Now, Gruna, credit where it's due," Pervain purred. "No-one said anything about cowardice. Casil's House gave of itself generously during the conflict. The Widow Yaxeth alone serviced half the Emperor's Own Regiment and most of the Patieron Lancers."

Casil flushed to the roots of his hair. "Don't you dare talk about my mother like that!"

"And afterward," Pervain went on amusedly, "she didn't even get out of bed - just waited for the rebel army with her legs apart!"

Casil flew at him and slapped his face on either cheek. "Take that back, Freelord!"

Pervain smiled unpleasantly. "Are you calling me out, soldier?"

"Yes. Yes, I am!"

"Cas, that isn't a good idea," murmured one of the younger men.

"Name the time and place," Casil went on recklessly.

"Oh, I think we can settle this here and now, don't you?"

"Agreed. And the weapons?"

"The sword," Pervain replied promptly. "And tell me, Casil - where do you want this to end? At first blood, defeat, or death?"

"Defeat," said Casil after slight hesitation. The flicker of contempt in Pervain's eyes showed what he thought of that choice.

They transferred to the gymnasium, accompanied by Gruna and Casil's friend Navin. A few other men followed, but most decided that discretion was the best policy. Each duellist had his own blade, so there was no ostentatious choosing of weapons. After a few experimental moves, the two faced one another and raised their swords in salute.

As was his custom, Pervain attacked before his adversary was quite ready. Casil quickly parried and went on the offensive, and for several zytl there was no sound under the bright artificial lighting save the ring of steel on steel and the rasp of the opponents' breath. The witnesses, expecting Pervain to make short work of the lad, were surprised at how good a swordsman Casil was. Pervain gave ground repeatedly, his defence erratic, then flinched as he took a shoulder wound from Casil's sword-tip.

The pain seemed to focus him. He renewed his attack with cold determination, and at length Casil began to tire. Pervain then drove him into a corner and kept him there.

"Like a lurlan with its prey," whispered Navin. "Yield, Cas. Why don't you yield?"

And suddenly, with one sweeping downstroke, it was over. Casil gave a harsh cry, his sword clattering to the floor. Blood spurted from his right hand.

Pervain threw down his sword and walked away. "Take him to the infirmary," he directed over his shoulder, "and tell Escir to stop by my quarters when he's treated him - no matter how late it is."

"What about *your* injury, Freelord?" inquired Gruna.

"I'll see to it myself," answered Pervain, just before the door thudded shut behind him.

"Doesn't want to face up to his dirty work," muttered Navin. "Come on, Cas. We'll look after you."

Pervain headed straight for the bawdy-house. Mallina's room was upstairs facing the main street; she had seen him approaching and was waiting at her door. "You're very late. I thought you weren't - oh, gods, you've been in a fight. Why didn't you go to Escir?"

"He's busy. You can patch me up, can't you?"

Mallina kept a medical kit in her room. Some of the rec girls preferred to consult her on minor matters, and Escir was grateful for her help. Pervain's wound didn't require surgery, so she pasted on some coagulant and bound it tightly. "It'll seize up overnight," she warned.

He didn't reply, merely sat with furrowed brow. The shadows under his eyes were almost black.

"Headache?" inquired Mallina.

"They're getting worse," he replied despondently. "This one almost got me butchered."

"Oh?"

"The sword-fight was in the gym. The lights were so bright, painfully bright - I could hardly see what I was doing. I just about managed to turn the blow that caused this." He indicated the bandage. "My opponent was aiming for the carotid."

308

Mallina didn't comment. He didn't have the look of a man who'd just killed, which was all that concerned her. "Shall I massage your neck?"

"If you would. It does help, unlike Escir's pills."

"Come here then. Relax your head into my hands. Relax, I said! You're always so tense."

"Just get on with it," he replied ungraciously.

Presently he settled down and grew drowsy, but Mallina remained on her guard. She knew him too well ever to be at ease with him. One wrong word or wrong move on her part, and he'd be awake and slapping her around. She wished he hadn't taken such an interest in her. Above all, she wished he wouldn't confide in her. The more she knew about him, the more at risk she would become.

It was well past nadir when an ill-tempered Escir admitted himself to Pervain's quarters. "Since you don't need your wound dressing, I don't see why I had to drag myself over here at this time of night."

"How's the boy?" Pervain asked mildly.

"He won't lose his hand, if that's what you mean. With microsurgery he'll probably retain seventy per cent use of it. But he'll never be able to use a sword or gun again, so his Army career's over."

"I see." Pervain was his usual non-committal self. "I don't think Grenthap needs to know what really happened, do you? We could say it was sword practice that went wrong."

Escir looked astonished, then furious. "Do you seriously think I'm going to cover this up? Not that it matters. Grenthap will hear the truth from someone."

"Will he? The men won't involve themselves and neither will Geffin if he values me as a news source. So before you go storming off with your self-righteous nose in the air, let me put the case for silence."

Escir sighed and helped himself to some of Pervain's liquor. "Go on."

"The boy, Casil, naively believed he could leave the affairs of his House behind him. Both you and I know how impossible that is. Our Houses inform our actions from day to day. Yes, I disclosed his origin, but only to gauge what ill feeling it would produce. As I surmised, there was a great deal.

"Now consider what our men will shortly have to do. I'm not privy to any of the intel sent back from Earth, but the sheer quantity of it suggests a meticulously planned campaign. Since there won't be that many soldiers taking part in the first wave, their task will probably be to secure key positions. Every man will have to trust the man next to him - trust him implicitly. None of them would have trusted Casil. I've done the fleet a service by getting rid of him."

"That's your reasoned explanation, but I know you of old. You saw that tattoo and went into destruct mode. The most worrying thing is, you probably couldn't help it."

Pervain scowled. "Whatever my motives, consider this. Duels are illegal, and he was the instigator. For defending myself I'd doubtless get a fine and a reprimand. He stands to lose his Army pension."

Escir made no reply.

"I thought that would spike your guns," Pervain remarked. "Have I made you see sense? I do hope so."

"I can't lie about my patients," Escir said stubbornly.

"You're being tiresome, Esc. Regrettably, I'll have to call in the favour you owe me. That business of the cat, remember? And the hospital facilities?"

Escir swore briefly but colourfully.

Pervain raised an eyebrow. "Don't take it so badly. We've much in common, you and I: we both have our reasons for keeping our records clean. But sometimes events get the better of our good intentions."

"Speak for yourself," Escir retorted.

Pervain regaled him with a long cold stare. "We're all creatures of impulse, Escir. Even you."

Chapter Seven

News from the city filtered through the Tyvian Gardens, brought by visitors or circulated on the relayist chain. But to Lydion all such activity seemed diffuse and unreal, like sounds underwater. Slowly, with much daydreaming combined with some painfully honest introspection, he'd begun to heal himself. He'd bidden farewell to Tarlatine, whom he'd lost for a second time, and in so doing had acknowledged that he'd never until now found a way of letting her go. From now on he would not exclude her name from his public reminiscences, nor tell everyone to read Idenion's book if they wanted to know the story. By sequestering his memories he'd kept Tarly alive; now it was time to move on. He wouldn't forget her, but instead would celebrate their affair, speak of her openly and without sorrow.

The matter of his son had been less difficult to resolve. He simply had to switch off his imagination and stop thinking of Tarlion as an individual. Somewhere in the vast unsympathetic universe was a fragment of genetic material in which he and Tarlatine would live on. By sustaining that attitude, impersonal though it was, he could derive some comfort from the situation. In time, he might even learn to be pleased about it.

He'd done some additional thinking too. Time and again, unbidden, his memory had taken him back to Ilonna and the derelict corridor he and Tralvar had found. Again the ancient writings had shone out from the wall as he'd held the lamp high, and again he'd heard his own voice in denial: "You're surely not expecting me to reconstruct this?" And Tralvar's anguished reply: "Don't even think of letting me down!"

He *had* thought about it. Often. He'd burnt the notes he'd made, and tried to expunge the text from his thoughts in the same way as the original had been erased by driven sand. But the formula had remained stubbornly in his head, and he'd finally conceded that the knowledge had to be preserved. And not just by one person, subject to the whims of time and chance. As soon as he was back in circulation he'd share it with someone. He wasn't sure who, not yet; but he'd make the decision a priority.

"Lydion?"

He turned toward the newcomer with a weary smile. "Hello, Drusa."

"Please, Lydion, come home. It's been over an octal."

"I'll be home soon, never fear. One more day should see me right." He gave her an affectionate squeeze. "Thanks for worrying about me."

She drew away, perturbed. "Your tunic's damp. You haven't been sleeping out here, have you?"

"Er...no. A bargee caught me with his woman and threw me in the Lisir."

"But you can't swim!"

"No harm done. He fished me out as soon as he realised."

"Lydion....!"

"Relax - we're all friends again. In fact, my little dalliance helped them think of a name for their new boat. They're calling it Lydion's Pride."

"You're impossible. And you're too old for this nonsense."

"I'm inclined to agree. But don't forget what Tarly said in her note: 'Celebrate our love with more love.' I thought I'd give it a try. Meditate by day, carouse by night."

"Is that where you've been *every* night? The river quarter?"

"Afraid so." Then, seeing her downcast expression: "I haven't been very fair to you, have I, Drusa? Forever running to you when I'm in trouble and then running away again."

"But you always come back. That makes me feel special."

"You *are* special. I'll make it up to you one day, I promise."

"When we're both very old?"

"When I'm ready to settle down."

Drusa gave a wry chuckle. "I won't hold my breath, then."

"I'm serious. You were my first love, dear Drusa, and I want you to be my last. It'll happen, you'll see."

The following day, several of the rec girls made a foray into the city. It wasn't the first time they'd done so, but on previous occasions they'd been in military company. Neelah, however, had wheedled Grenthap into letting them go unescorted.

"Stay in twos," he'd ordered, "and report back one ild before roll call. If anyone misbehaves, you'll all share the blame."

In Mallina's opinion the girls had already misbehaved, seizing garment after garment at the market and throwing them to the ground if they didn't fit. The Celestrians hadn't said anything but she was sure it had gone on record. So, while the rest of the party hurried to acquire more free dresses, Mallina and her friend Tildy headed south to the Tyvian Gardens, which she'd heard about from Sijek. Escir, with customary concern, had given both girls communicators in case they became separated from one another.

When they reached the gardens, which looked as beautiful as they'd been led to expect, Tildy wanted to investigate the picnic area with its little stalls dispensing food, flowers and seeds. "I'll be all right here," she said. "You go and explore. I know you want to."

As a child, Mallina had loved to play in the woods bordering her parents' smallholding. Later she'd retreated there with books, and later still, at the age of fifteen, had shyly surrendered her virginity to the second son of the adjoining estate. They planned to marry when she was seventeen. Then her father, having lost all his money in a corporate fraud, had committed suicide. The state had seized his lands.

Mallina, her mother and infant sister had moved to a small apartment in an unsavoury part of Nova City. There she had taken up nursing, but her pay did nothing to alleviate her family's poverty. So

315

she and Tildy, working at the same hospital, had together visited the rec girls' recruiting office.

Now, whenever she had the chance, Mallina walked in woodland and tried to recapture her carefree past. The Tyvian Gardens lacked the wildness of her native land, but she immediately felt at home beneath the sheltering trees. Enticing little pathways drew her further in. The wood seemed deserted, but she pressed on, and eventually came to an ornamental lake. Mellow sunlight glinted on the tranquil water and dappled the trees opposite. It was all wonderfully peaceful.

The clearing had one other occupant. She recognised Lydion at once, but mindful of his previous distress, was reluctant to make her presence known. Instead, she studied him closely as he sat gazing into the distance.

She decided she liked what she saw. Brown hair, neatly combed; two equally neat patches of grey at either temple. Lean, capable hands, at present clasped pensively about one knee. A pleasant face; not handsome, but goodnatured, with many laughter lines about the eyes.

He wasn't laughing now. Mallina had familiarised herself with his sad story, and her sympathy went out to him afresh. It was a cruel trick of fate, and one she was sure he didn't deserve.

Belatedly he realised he was being watched, and turned to face her. "Hello. Help you, I?"

"You probably don't remember me," she said hesitantly. "You'd just left Sijek. I asked if you were all right."

"Oh. Yes." He looked away briefly. "I was rude. Please forgive."

"There's nothing *to* forgive," Mallina assured him.

He surveyed her with new interest. "You have green eyes!"

She took the compliment awkwardly. "It's usual with red hair."

"Please, stay and talk," said Lydion with simple sincerity. "I listen. Maybe learn language better. Or maybe not," he added with a grin.

Mallina obediently sat down next to him. Introductions seemed unnecessary; she knew his name and he probably knew hers too. "It's nice here, isn't it?" she remarked tritely.

Lydion told her, in laboured error-strewn sentences, about the elite-wives and how the garden came to be built. She in turn explained why she'd become a rec girl. She was a little on the defensive, but Lydion seemed unconcerned. Of course, even without telepathy he'd have realised what she was. Every Eldorian woman on the planet was in the sex trade.

"And your lover, he waits?"

Mallina shook her head. "His parents called off the wedding, of course. Shortly afterward he was conscripted, and killed in action during his first year of service. So you see, I didn't lose a lifetime's happiness - only a season or two."

"Your past, you accept it," Lydion said approvingly. "I try the same with mine. Not succeed too well."

"It *can* be done," Mallina answered softly.

317

Presently the conversation turned to the other thing they had in common: their dislike of Pervain. In Lydion's halting but candid opinion, an aptitude for language in no way compensated for the numerous slights the ambassador had inflicted on his hosts.

"In fairness, he's been through a rough time," Mallina said indiscreetly. "The Army scientists wanted a *real* telepath, not just someone who could shield. They messed with his head, Lydion."

"Chaos!"

"And because he's a soldier he had no choice in the matter," Mallina concluded. "He couldn't refuse an order."

Just then, her communicator sounded. "Where are you, Mal?" Tildy asked anxiously. "How deep is this wood?"

"All paths lead to the lake," Mallina said at a prompting from Lydion. "Come and find me. There's someone I want you to meet."

Presently Tildy appeared, a little suspicious, but swiftly reassured by Lydion's engaging presence. "Sorry to interrupt when you look so comfy, Mal, but we have to head back. If we're late they won't let us out again."

"She's right," Mallina said despondently.

Lydion took her hand. "Then meet me tomorrow. I call for you, if permit I am, at the base. I'll show you the Lyricon, where work I."

"I'd like that very much."

Lydion raised her to her feet, drew her close and dropped a tiny kiss on each eyelid. "I shall call you Greeneyes," he declared. "Thank you for reviving my tired spirits." At least, that was what he intended to say. Confusing two similar-sounding words, what he actually said was, "Thank you for reviving my tired shaft." Mallina and Tildy shrieked with laughter; and Lydion, once he'd realised his mistake, joined in. "Well, that too! Come, ladies, I walk with you to edge of tree."

"He's nice," said Tildy as they took a hired flitter to the base. "And he really likes you. If you worked on him he might even purchase your bond."

"Don't be silly - I've only just met him. Anyway, how could he? These people don't have a currency."

"There's always trade. He might have something we could use. Or," she added shrewdly, "he might *know* something useful."

Mallina allowed herself one brief flight of fancy, then dismissed it. "I wish. But it isn't going to happen. Even if he came up with the goods, can you imagine Pervain letting me go?"

***

"Excuse me, doctor." A youthful head appeared round Escir's office door.

"Oh, it's you, Navin. Whatever it is, make it snappy: I'm due in a meeting with General Grenthap."

Navin shuffled his feet awkwardly. "I just wanted to thank you for, you know, keeping quiet about the duel."

Not my idea, Escir wanted to say. "It seemed the best thing to do," he answered instead. "Casil will need his stipend to pay for the operations on his hand."

"He's very grateful. We both are. But..."

"But what?"

"On his recommendation for discharge, it says he was injured while suppressing a riot."

"Pervain wrote that. We needed something convincing."

"Understood, but...well...it doesn't seem fair to the Celestrians when they haven't given us any trouble."

"Life is seldom fair," Escir said sarcastically. "Seriously, though, I've learnt something of the Celestrians' recent history from Sijek. And believe me, they aren't averse to starting a riot or two."

Navin seemed mollified. "Casil didn't want them to suffer repercussions because of what he did," he explained.

"They won't."

"I'm glad," said the young soldier gravely. "They're good people; kind and clever. We shouldn't be involving them in our wars, Dr. Escir. We shouldn't be here."

"Don't say that to anyone other than me," Escir cautioned him. Then he ushered him out of the office, locked it, and headed for the briefing room.

Grenthap was no fool. He'd have seen through their attempt to whitewash Casil. The fact that he was choosing to ignore it probably meant he hadn't the time nor the patience to conduct a disciplinary hearing. Duelling was a fact of life, especially when soldiers were bored and restless.

Escir guessed that the news from Treva wasn't good. Either the day of the invasion had been put off yet again, or the number of fresh troops had been curtailed. Grenthap kept him apprised of such developments; as well as the usual reports on morale and psychology, he'd been asked to draw up a preliminary list of personnel to be seconded to the fleet. He hadn't yet done so.

"The trouble is, General, they *all* want to go," he said in justification. "And if such a list were made public it would cause resentment amongst those who weren't on it."

"Then we'll have to convince them that maintaining a presence here is equally important," Grenthap declared. "I'll get Pervain involved. It's about time we found a use for his paranoia. Now, you do agree with me that discipline is getting lax?"

"Yes, General. Only minor indications as yet - dress code irregularities, drunkenness, quarrels. But it'll get worse."

"More rapidly than you might think," Grenthap said grimly. "I want you to post a memo."

"What about?" Escir asked blankly.

"Have you heard of Myrma, the so-called pleasure planet?"

"Yes, of course. We located it just after Celestra, didn't we? No intrinsic value and too many endemic diseases."

"But the accommodating nature of the populace was not a myth," Grenthap stated. "We tried to keep the co-ordinates a secret but these things have a habit of getting out. Two officers from Treva thought they'd give it a try and both came down with a virulent dose of swamp fever. They assumed they'd only have to come back here to be cured of whatever ailed them."

"And weren't they?"

"Yes and no. They were symptom-free until they went back to Eldor, where the fever promptly returned. Studies suggest they'll get recurring bouts for the rest of their lives."

"That's what parasitic infections do. At least they won't have started a pandemic."

"I wasn't thinking about that. Come the invasion, our personnel will be at full stretch. What's going to happen if half our lads get sick as soon as they leave here? All those expensive vaccinations against Earth diseases won't count for anything."

"Shit."

"Precisely. So you need to state, here and now, that Myrma is strictly off limits for medical reasons - and that anyone found disobeying will be dismissed with no pay."

"I'll make sure it's on the bulletin board by sunset. But you're right, General - this is going to have a disastrous effect on morale. Can't we do something to counterbalance it?"

"I'm organising some manoeuvres to keep the men occupied," Grenthap said briskly. "Everyone will participate, whether selected for the fleet or not. The Celestrians won't object, not with so many unpopulated areas to choose from, but unfortunately we're going to need more equipment before we can start. So in the meantime -" he paused for effect - "I'm planning an entertainment."

"What kind? Strippers?"

Grenthap wheezed with laughter. "That's your preference, is it? Scrawny ones, knowing you. No, this is something altogether more elaborate.   If Geffin hadn't talked the network into footing the bill, we'd never have been able to consider it."

"Go on," Escir said curiously.

"I've invited Steel and Lace to bring their circus to town."

Escir stared. "Those girls who fight lurlan?"

"Correct."

"But how can lurlan survive here? They'll die like the Miiyatan did!"

"Not so; there are cats and cats, apparently. Someone smuggled a lurlan cub into the Treva barracks.   It survived five days, then died unspectacularly in its sleep. So they'll live long enough to do the show."

"Whose idea was this? Pervain's?"

"He endorsed it, but the initial idea was Geffin's. There was a fullscale brawl while he was at Treva, and he realised before I did that a distraction was needed."

"Do you think it's wise to give his sort the run of our base?" Escir asked pointedly. He detested the reporter. "He's unprincipled, sly - "

"And no longer resident in any of our zones," Grenthap said, stifling the complaint. "I didn't want him hanging around the Treva conference so I sent him to interview Tralvar's widow. There are so many tall stories about the previous First Citizen that I thought it was high time we checked them out. Pervain agreed with me."

"He would."

"Anyway, it seems this woman took a motherly shine to our Geffin and offered him lodgings."

Escir sniffed. "Put him in any situation and he'll end up with his feet under someone's table. But without wishing to sound like Pervain, don't you think she might probe him for information?"

"Geffin doesn't know anything strategic," Grenthap assured him. "Gossip, yes; lots of it. And much good may it do her. Now, about these fleet nominees..."

***

Mallina had been given a two-day pass, so she had no difficulty keeping her date with Lydion. As promised, he had taken her to the Lyricon, and they now stood at the back of the auditorium looking toward the distant stage. The scale of the theatre did not impress her - there were buildings in Nova City many times its size - but she instantly fell in love with its beauty and grace.

There weren't many people about - a few artisans making minor repairs, a handful of dancers discussing their next production - but Mallina detected a strong sense of community, and knew that Lydion was much appreciated within it. No-one seemed surprised to see her there, which possibly meant he'd told them in advance. Or perhaps the sight of Lydion with a new girl was no surprise to anyone.

"Hello, Red!" said someone: a youth with an insolent grin who had approached unobserved. "I'm his nephew, Kalyx. Has he told you how old he is? No? Well, when you've worn him out, come and find me. I'll show you what a real lover can do."

"Scat," said Lydion amiably.

"Anything to oblige. See you later, Red. Oh by the way, uncle, I'd steer clear of my sister if I were you."

"Don't I always?"

"Just thought I'd warn you. She and Jarras are having a falling out."

"Discords, that *is* unusual. Thanks for the tip; I'll leave them alone to settle it."

Kalyx bounded away on some actors' errand and Lydion escorted Mallina down to the basement via the various workshops. "Is a pity you're under curfew, my love. Lyricon not at its best by day. When show there is in evenings, all work together - me also. Everything very different then."

"This place means a lot to you, doesn't it?"

"Yes. A lot. I tell Tonor, my assistant, I retire soon. But leave Lyricon? Not sure anymore."

The generator room was dark and silent. Mallina peered in the door and shivered. "Oooh. Creepy." She couldn't quite see why someone like Lydion would choose such a solitary occupation - except that he was obviously a man of contradictions.

From there it was just a short distance to his house, almost lost under the shadow of the colonnade. Lydion explained that he knew the way in the pitch dark, having walked it so many times after midnight. Mallina somehow knew the interior would be tidy, with minimal furnishings and few possessions.

He warmed some soup, as it had been breezy on the terraces, and turned the room temperature up a few notches. Then, when they had finished eating, he came to sit beside her.

"My Greeneyes, why so shy today?" His gaze was direct but leavened with humour. "My age, it bothers you perhaps?"

She forgot to be bashful. "No, it was Kalyx who bothered me. I wanted to slap his smug little face for saying that. Yes, I know you're twice my age. More, perhaps. I don't mind in the least." She drew a deep steadying breath before continuing. "Kalyx doesn't know about Eldor. There, over fifty per cent of girls marry mature men. Not just for the financial considerations, but because their husbands have done their Army service and aren't about to be shot to bits like my poor Teon."

"Sense, that makes." He stroked her hair lightly. "Go on, my love."

"I can't lie to you," Mallina said, flustered. "Yesterday in the gardens I was so pleased you wanted me. I don't know why I'm being so nervous."

"Then I explain." He put his arm round her. "Lean on me, head on shoulder, relax be. Close beautiful eyes. Close them and listen."

She snuggled up. "Are you going to tell me a story?"

"I'm going to tell you about yourself." His voice seemed changed, more resonant. And, she realised with a start, he was speaking perfect

326

Eldorian. "I'm not speaking at all; you're translating. I'm giving you my thoughts and an illusion of my voice. What I have to say is too important to entrust to my poor language skills."

She knew, then, that his lips weren't moving. That was why he didn't want her to look at him.

"When I first met you," he continued, "I saw a sexually experienced but unfulfilled woman. Your Teon was too young to know how to please you, and those clumsy louts at the base are only intent on their own satisfaction. Permit me, my beautiful girl, to give you the love you deserve. A woman is capable of more pleasure that a mere man will ever know. Let me prove it to you, Mallina."

It was extraordinary, and she should have been unnerved. But he'd communicated so much of his warmth and earnestness that she felt only a sense of privilege.

"Not scared?" he asked aloud.

"Not of you," she answered; and before her resolve deserted her, kissed him.

He returned the kiss many times, each one subtly different until he'd learnt what she liked. Then, without haste, he drew her into the bedroom, stepping easily out of his clothes and unfastening hers with gentle dexterity.

When he came to her breast banding he paused. "Discords, what's this? Wires? Look, it bruises you."

"It's an enhancer," she explained.

"Enhancer is cruel fashion. Not need to please me in that way."

327

As with his kiss, his touch was at first experimental and then assured. But when she tried to reciprocate he took her wrist in a firm preventative grip.

"Don't you like that?" she asked, puzzled.

"I like. But not as, forgive me, part of your routine. Wait, do nothing. When right time, you'll know."

She lay back then, eager and curious. She could almost imagine that she was again in the forest with her long-lost Teon - except that Teon had never been so thorough. For the next two ilden, Lydion applied his redoubtable skill to the task of satisfying her, overcoming her poor self-image and memories of rough treatment. She'd given him her trust, and he didn't intend to disappoint her.

Mallina had guessed her new lover would be special, but was amazed that this apparently unremarkable man, no longer young, whose fractured rendition of her language made her giggle, could bring her to the peak of pleasure over and over. He had the staying power of a youth in his physical prime. At last she lay quiescent in his arms, drowsed and happy, breathing in his unique scent which reminded her of wild honey.

He pushed a few strands of damp hair from her forehead and kissed her eyelids in the manner she now knew well. "More?"

"Please, Lydion, no more. I'm exhausted."

"You're a very sensuous woman, Greeneyes."

"And you're..." She sought for the most appropriate word. "... incredible."

"Just fortunate."

She drew an affectionate hand round his permanently smooth chin. "Do you always mindspeak to your girlfriends?"

"With off-worlders, sometimes necessary is. Or I do picture language, like this."

Mallina convulsed in mirth at what he was showing her. "That's obscene!"

"Or what about this?"

"Stop it, you!" She whacked him with her pillow, and suddenly the room was full of kyffu feathers. They both laughed till they ached.

"Mal," Lydion said in an abrupt change of mood, "I want us to meet many times. Is same for you?"

"Of course it is, you funny lovely man."

"Thank you, my Greeneyes. Together we're good, I think."

"Together we're *very* good. But it might be difficult for me to leave the base when I want."

"Then I come to you. Depend on it. All of Eldorian Army won't stop your Lydion."

***

"I can't understand why you're being so unreasonable, Jarras." Nefyrra moved briskly about the Custodian's apartment, assembling a folio and selecting a cloak from her modest wardrobe. "I'm glad you've calmed down since lunchtime, but you had no business losing your temper at all. You lived through most of the Alendis years - you *knew* him, for discord's sake! So you know how important it is to keep our smallest children away

329

from bad influences. Or maybe you *want* them to absorb how to kill and how to make war on their own kind?"

"Don't lecture me," Jarras said peevishly. "I reacted badly because I didn't expect you to disappear on my day off. I don't get many."

"I've been here most of the day."

"But you *won't* be here tonight."

Nefyrra sighed in exasperation. "I'm sorry you feel neglected but this meeting's too important to cancel."

"So you keep saying," muttered Jarras. "What does Dena have to do with infant schools anyway?"

"Oh, Jarras! Dena's wanted to be involved with children ever since she lost hers. Don't tell me you've forgotten *that*? You were the one who rescued her from Alda Four when she had her miscarriage."

"I hadn't forgotten."

"She would have raised Kalyx if Ninfi had let her. She looked after him every chance she got. Since father died she's kept a close eye on educational matters and she helped relocate a couple of creches that were too close to the Eldorian base."

"And now she wants you to start a school here."

"Not me personally. You don't listen. One of the nursery groups is still a bit too near the Eldorians and Dena thought we could bring it to the Lyricon as a temporary measure. There's nothing much going on during the day at present. But I do need to meet the teachers, get some idea of the numbers, and so on."

"Dena could do that."

330

"I'm Custodian, Jarras! I have to *be* there!"

"Then at least - " he caught at her arms as she made to leave - "come back when the meeting's finished. Don't stay over."

"It could be quite late. We'll be late starting, thanks to you."

"I love you, Nefyrra." He held her so tightly that she struggled. "I want you with me. I want to feel I'm still part of your life."

"You *are*!"

"Am I?"

"Very well, I promise I'll come back tonight. Now can I go?"

He released her, still resentful. "Run along, then."

She paused at the door. "What are *you* going to do?"

"I'll find something. Maybe stop over to Communications and see Trevone."

"He's taking evening classes."

"Then I'll find something else to occupy me. Go on, don't keep Dena waiting."

Nefyrra decided to walk at least part of the way, hoping to calm herself down. But before she even reached Lateral Two, a flitter whined to a halt in front of her and Lydion's voice said:

"Hi! Need a lift anywhere? I'm just taking Mallina back to barracks and then I'm all yours."

Rather than create more tension by refusing, she climbed on board, remaining silent until Lydion had bidden an extremely fond farewell to Mallina at the east gate.

"Sorry about that," he said at length, resuming his seat.

"It would have been quicker to walk," she remarked. "How are you paying for her?"

"What do you take me for?" Lydion expostulated. "We met socially. She's entitled to a private life."

"Is she?" returned Nefyrra cynically.

"Want to talk about Jarras?" asked Lydion, changing the subject.

"Not really."

"I always thought you two were rock solid," Lydion went on regardless.

"Neither of us is seeing anyone else, if that's what you mean. I think he's just overworked. He never wanted to be First Scientist - "

"That's no secret."

" - and to be perfectly honest, I think he's missing Tralvar. All this stressing began at the time of his death."

"You know, I think you may be right," mused Lydion.

"The other day I thought he was getting over it. He was happy and loving, a bit too intense perhaps. And *then* he said he could hear me calling the scolia!"

"That's not possible, surely."

"Of course not. It isn't something you acquire. You don't think he was taking some sort of perception booster, do you?"

"There's only starfire. And if he were using that, you'd know."

"Why would I?"

"For one thing the effects are very temporary, so in order for it to work he'd need to inhale it just before you put out your call. And secondly, it stinks. *Really* stinks."

"Oh. I didn't realise."

"Talk to Dena. She's a scolia-sensitive, isn't she? She might have more insight than me."

"I will. Thanks, Lydion."

"Anytime."

When Nefyrra entered the villa she was surprised to find Clemis still there, as it was well past the end of the working day.

"She's interrogating my lodger," Dena whispered. "And he looks very uncomfortable about it."

"So that's Geffin," observed Nefyrra. "I didn't know he could speak Celestrian."

"He's learnt so fast! When he first came to see me his conversation was hardly intelligible. And *now* listen to him!"

"I'm not omniscient," Geffin was saying. "I can only make assumptions based on what I've seen so far."

"Then please make them," Clemis said with her most beseeching look. "What's likely to become of us as servants of the Empire?"

"Well," Geffin began reluctantly, "the best case scenario is that you'll gradually start losing your national identity, and all those quaint little customs of yours will die out. And you'll be over-run with tourists wanting to see them *before* they die out. Alternatively, once the Earthers discover you've been supplying the Eldorian military with telepaths, they'll treat you like the enemy. That won't be so good. Another alternative is that they'll try to recruit telepaths themselves, by bribery or kidnap. Either way, you'll be stuck in the middle."

Clemis gazed at him reproachfully. "And there's a fourth possibility, isn't there - that Celestra will become the battlefield when Earth and Eldor make war?"

Geffin spread out his hands helplessly. "Sweeting, I don't know. Truly I don't. Maybe you should stop reading my mind. I wasn't going to mention the battlefield option."

"Nor the fact that your people have a computer game based on it," Clemis remarked.

"It means nothing. It's for the gunners to test their reaction time."

"Like they did at Ilonna?"

Nefyrra decided she'd heard enough and stepped forward to introduce herself. "Walk in harmony, Geffin. I'm Nefyrra, custodian of the Lyricon, representing one of those quaint little customs you mentioned."

"Not exactly little," he grinned. She stood head and shoulders above him. "What's this elegant key at your belt? Do you lock your musical instruments away?"

"This opens the door to the bell-tower."

"But there's no bell!"

"One of my predecessors was negligent and let the bell fall. The key reminds me of my responsibilities."

"Do you always carry it?"

"Always," said Nefyrra emphatically. "Your Celestrian is a credit to you. How did you master it so quickly?"

"I knew a little before my assignment. I hoped it would secure me the job. Being multi-lingual means I learnt pretty fast once I was here."

"I thought Eldor only had one language?"

"One *official* language," Geffin explained. "Everyone's required to speak it if they want to make their way in life. But there are numerous others, and in my profession it helps to know as many as I can."

"Why did you want this job so badly?" asked Clemis.

"Sheer curiosity. I didn't expect to find such an appealing world."

The two nursery teachers put in an appearance at this point, and Clemis decided her presence had become superfluous. "I'd better go. I'll see you tomorrow, Dena. Thanks for the glimpses into the future, Geffin."

"Don't take them as certainties," he called after her. She didn't reply.

Dena had prepared a cold supper for her guests. While they discussed the relocation of the school, Geffin waited table as if he'd done it all his life.

"One of my favourite undercover roles," he explained. "The aristos treat waiters as if they're invisible. So while they're feeding their faces I'm soaking up the indiscretions!"

"We'll keep the scandal for another time, then," Dena laughed.

Inevitably, the talk turned to Alendis' fate and their determination to avoid a recurrence. Geffin listened, so fascinated that he needed prompting to remove the dirty plates. Much later, when the transfer of the nursery had been finalised and everyone had gone, he ventured to re-open the subject with Dena.

"So what you're saying is, little kids can't shut off their telepathy and they're always at risk from bad influences. Better keep them away from *me*, then."

"You denigrate yourself," said Dena. "Don't forget, I can see right through your cynicism. You've a good honest spirit."

"Don't tell anyone, please!" begged Geffin in mock horror. "Seriously though: I realise you don't want your little ones exposed to the Eldorian war machine, but don't you think you're being a bit *too* protective?"

"Explain."

"Well, for generations untold your children have only absorbed the thoughts of their elders. When the newborn themselves became elders it's their turn to programme the kids. Correct?"

"Well....yes."

"That's bad. It's making your people stagnate. A society can't stand still, Dena. It has to reach out, adapt, or go under."

"Our species is slowly dying, Geffin."

"That's defeatism. Someone will find a way to turn your birthrate around. There's plenty of time yet."

"We've been trying for centuries."

"That doesn't mean you won't succeed, so try behaving as if you're going to! I told your brother he should take steps to preserve what you people have."

"He wasn't sure what you meant by that."

"I meant, nurture a sense of pride - a belief that your civilisation has just as much right to be here as ours does. You're too self-effacing. You're an ancient race, you have powers. Make sure nobody forgets it."

***

Nefyrra parked her flitter at the charging station nearest the Lyricon, then set out to walk the short but steep path to her home. It was late: not far from nadir, she estimated.

+Jarras+ she called. +Jarras, I'm back+

But there was no response. He was either asleep or ignoring her. Probably the latter.

Her route took her past some theatre-related cottage industries, long since closed for the night. She had almost reached the Lyricon square when, unbelievably, the silence was shattered by singing - crude, raucous singing. It was "the Stars are Ours", its lyrics almost lost amid a variety of expletives. The singers rounded the brow of the hill: two Eldorian soldiers, aggressively drunk, who had missed their rollcall and were now past caring. Nefyrra attempted to sidle past, but they moved to intercept her.

"Hello darling!" exclaimed one. "What's the key for? Husband lock up your virtue, does he?

337

Doesn't he know he's supposed to take the key with him?" He guffawed at his own joke.

"Give us a kiss," suggested his companion. "Come on, love. We won't bite. Yet!" He made a grab at her shoulder. She tried to push him away, but he held on. In mounting panic, she aimed a slap with her free arm; he seized that too.

"Hoity-toity, ain't she? Thinks she's too good for us lads. Well she ain't."

"Varn, maybe we shouldn't - " began the first soldier. Varn backhanded him across the mouth, temporarily releasing Nefyrra. She made a lunge for freedom, but he tripped her and she fell sprawling. The little key tinkled in the gutter. She lay very still then as Varn pressed a knifeblade to her face.

"That's right, bitch. Nice and quiet. Any more tricks and I'll mark you." The blade went away for a moment as he slit open the front of her dress. "Oh, nice. Want some of this, Stibon? Thought so. Get in line, pal."

He paused to fumble with his breeches, awkwardly, with his left hand. Then he suddenly gasped and staggered back, dropping the knife. He uttered one muffled word which could have been "no" or "don't". Then he began to scream - shrill, agonised screams, terrible in the silence.

"Varn!" Stibon laid hold of him, shook him. "Varn, what's wrong with you?"

Varn didn't hear. He fell to his knees, hands beating the air, his screams slowly subsiding into whimpers.

Stibon glanced at Nefyrra. She was huddled against a wall, knees drawn up to her chest. Was *she* doing this? He took two irresolute steps toward her, then hastily turned back to Varn, who was having a convulsion. His eyes were half closed and there was blood on his lips where he'd bitten his tongue. Stibon resisted an urge to run and keep running; instead, he waited helplessly by his friend until the fit had passed. Varn now appeared to be unconscious. His face was set in a rictus of pain, and he had soiled himself.

"Stibon."

The frightened soldier looked up. Nefyrra was standing a little way up the path, tall and forbidding, unmindful of her ruined dress.

"I'm sparing you," she continued, "as someone has to inform your commanders what happened here. Tell them this is the penalty for attempted rape. And tell them my name: Nefyrra, daughter of Tralvar. Make sure you remember it. Now take your companion and go."

She watched dispassionately as Stibon, half dragging and half carrying Varn, stumbled down the path until he was lost to view. A moment or two later came the whine of a flitter taking off.

Nefyrra had just begun a frantic search for her lost key when she was plunged into darkness. It was midnight, and the street lights had been extinguished. Finally, her nerve deserted her. She sank down near the edge of the square, sobbing bitterly, her mind reaching out to the husband who had failed to be present when she needed him.

+Jarras! Jarras! *Jarras*!+

Not long afterward, swift footfalls approached and a lamp was shone in her face. She recoiled instinctively. Someone knelt beside her, took her shoulders and gently turned her around.

"Nefyrra, it's Lydion. Shh, don't cry. It's only me."

"Oh...Lydion..." She collapsed into his arms, limp with relief. There was a faint oily smell on his clothes and hands, redolent of the generator room. Of normality.

"Hush now," he murmured. "You're safe. Let's get you inside."

She expected to be unceremoniously dumped at her front door. Why would he trouble himself further? For years she'd regarded him as an irritating, womanising wastrel - and frequently told him so. But to her wonderment he proceeded to take calm, sympathetic charge of the situation. Knowing she would only fret without the symbol of her office, he searched up and down the path, found the key and restored it to her. Then he took her to his house, sat her in the kitchen and bathed her grazed elbows. He discovered a cut on her chin and bathed that too. Next, with quiet insistence, he eased off the remains of her dress and gave her one of his tunics to wear. And finally, he handed her a beaker of hot liman with a dash of resnay in it.

"Drink it all," he instructed, "and then we'd better have a chat."

While she drank, he hastily changed out of his grimy overall and scrubbed his hands. When he returned, Nefyrra was about to throw her dress in the waste disposal.

340

"Don't," he said hastily. "It's evidence. And so's this." He unfolded a piece of rag to reveal Varn's knife. "I found it near your key. Care to fill in the details?"

"I have to thank you, Lydion," she said unexpectedly.

"What for?"

"If it hadn't been for your stories, I'd never have known what happens when we attempt unity with a nonconversant."

"Chaos! You did that?"

"And saved myself from being raped." Nefyrra briefly described her encounter with the two Eldorians. "I think I'll carry my stun-gun from now on!"

Lydion eyed her with new respect. "Tralvar was right - you *are* the strongest of us all. Not many women would have fought back on those terms."

"I'm not proud of myself. That poor soldier will be on my conscience for a long time."

"He got what he deserved."

"I keep telling myself that, but I'm worried I may have injured him. Permanently, I mean. I couldn't judge when he'd had enough - I was terrified he'd kill me if I stopped too soon. Through it all I kept thinking he wasn't really a *bad* man. Just selfish, stupid and drunk - and angry because his trip to Myrma had been cancelled."

"That's hardly an excuse, Nefyrra."

"He was so frightened," she continued sorrowfully. "He screamed and screamed. Didn't you hear him?"

"I was in the generator room. Street sounds don't carry down there. I didn't realise there was anything going on until you panicked afterwards."

Nefyrra accepted some more liman. "What were you doing in the generator room at this time of night?"

"Working, what else? I was otherwise engaged all day, as you know. And then after I'd dropped you and Mallina off I remembered that Tonor had reported a problem with projector four. Since the masterclass auditions start later today, I thought I'd better fix it."

She sighed deeply. "Oh, the auditions. I'd forgotten."

"You could always postpone them. No one would blame you."

"No. No, I'm not doing that. A lot of young people would be very disappointed."

"Then you should try to get some sleep. I know you don't feel much like it but you may surprise yourself."

"Jarras has some windflower opiate at home," she said. "In fact, that might be why I couldn't raise him. Yes, that's bound to be it."

"Nefyrra, he isn't there," Lydion said gently. "I saw him leave in a flitter."

"I don't understand." Hurt began to creep back into her face. "I was going to stay at Dena's. I only came home because he insisted."

"In that case I'll have a few choice words to say to him when he turns up," Lydion declared. "Come on. We'll go to your suite, find that sleeping

342

draught and get you to bed. I'll sit with you if you don't want to be alone."

He placed a warm cloak round her shoulders and ascended with her to the custodian's apartment. It was cold and dark along the high narrow balcony, and she was glad of his confident presence.

"The year's on the turn," he said softly. "Do you feel it on the night air?"

"I feel it," she answered sombrely, releasing the casement latch. "It makes me wonder what's to become of us all."

"You realise," said Lydion when they were inside, "that all chaos is going to break loose at sun-up? We'll have to let Laura and Idenion know what happened as soon as we can, or the Eldorians will get their version in first. I'll pay an early visit to the akron if you like."

Nefyrra halted halfway through mixing the sedative. "Lydion - when you see them, tell them they have to keep the investigators away from here while the auditions are on. Lann's bringing an update from the scolia tech. I've heard, unofficially, that they've cracked the Eldorians' radio cipher."

"Leave everything to me," Lydion said reassuringly. "No Eldorian will set foot in the Lyricon until you're ready."

She regarded him apologetically over the rim of her cup. "I've been so wrong about you. Can you ever forgive my insults?"

He gave one of his infectious smiles. "Oh, please don't stop fighting with me, Nefyrra! It reminds me so much of your late father. We have to keep the tradition going, you know."

343

She smiled back. "If you insist. But I won't forget how you helped me tonight - and if you need *my* help at any time, I'll be here."

***

When news of the attempted rape reached Grenthap he reacted swiftly and decisively. Security was stepped up and all non-essential passes rescinded. From now on, he declared, no one would be permitted to leave the base for frivolous or spurious reasons - and that included the rec girls. The personnel at the spaceport would be subject to the same curfew as everyone else, and similar restrictions would apply at Treva.

Stibon was interrogated for most of the day. Since he had done nothing other than miss roll-call he was not expelled from Celestra, but demoted and restricted to the base indefinitely. There didn't seem much point in punishing Varn as he would hardly have been aware of it. Escir, baffled, likened his state to a complete nervous collapse and even enlisted Sijek's help in reaching a diagnosis. The fear, it seemed, had not gone away, and no-one knew if it ever would. Much as Escir would have liked to study the case, he simply didn't have the resources, and arrangements were made to send Varn home. One salient fact had emerged: Nefyrra had not acted gratuitously. In order to protect herself she had suffered in her own right, and no blame could be apportioned to her.

344

Pervain thought differently. "Where would we be if *all* the Celestrians did that?" he asked Grenthap.

"It wouldn't get them far because it's too slow to take effect," Grenthap declared. "A bit like that nonsense of Axmiol's when we first caught him. If Stibon had realised the woman could only target one person at a time, we'd be looking at a very different incident."

"Then ask yourself," Pervain persisted, "what we'll discover next. What *else* can they do? I've been reading about Alendis, their home-grown dictator. It seems he could instantly stun people with a mind-bolt, although no-one seems to have followed his example."

"Then we've nothing to worry about, have we?" said Grenthap indulgently. "You read too much. Go and have an early night. And tomorrow, visit Idenion and make a formal apology on behalf of us all. That rigid Patieron morality of yours should help smooth things over."

"We've already apologised once."

"In haste. That will hardly do. If you stopped looking for conspiracies for five zytl you'd realise this business with Nefyrra couldn't have happened at a worse time. I was just about to request a day's use of the Lyricon."

"For the circus?"

"Precisely. There isn't another suitable venue and I'm damned if I'm going to cancel. We'd still have to pay them."

"Have the Celestrians even heard of Steel and Lace?"

"Not that I'm aware."

Pervain sighed. "All right, I get the picture. Let's hope Nefyrra's in a magnanimous mood."

When he returned to his office he found Klonid and Betrick waiting for him. They looked jaded and on edge.

"I thought you two clowns would show up," Pervain remarked, kicking the door shut.

"Look, Freelord - about Jarras," began Klonid.

"He was with *you*, wasn't he? When he should have been rescuing his wife?"

"I'm really, really sorry."

"Don't be. If he'd taken on Varn and Stibon he'd have wound up dead - and then his enterprising young son would have become First Scientist. Hardly what I had in mind."

"Oh," said Klonid, vastly relieved.

"Moreover, Jarras will reproach himself constantly for having been absent, and turn to dreamdust all the more." Pervain smiled with genuine pleasure, and the two technicians relaxed.

"Why did you transfer us to Treva?" asked Betrick. "To see if he'd come looking for us?"

"I had to get you out of Communications, dimwit, before Trevone realised what you were up to," Pervain answered witheringly. "Do you think he'd have calmly stood by while you made a dreamhead out of his father?"

"We told Chillis to stop disrupting the lessons," Klonid reported hastily, "and now Jarras thinks he faced him down unaided. At the moment we're still emphasising dreamdust's stress-busting qualities."

"And psi-enhancing potential," added Betrick.

346

"May I enquire," Pervain asked in a dangerously soft voice, "how you convinced him you knew about the latter?"

"I, well, er, told him I had it on good authority that you used it to boost your psionic shielding."

"And what did he say to that?"

"Oh, he wasn't surprised. He said you couldn't possibly have maintained your shields without a chemical stimulant."

"So when that piece of slander starts going the rounds I'll know who to thank," Pervain remarked sourly.

"You wanted results and you've got them," said Klonid with a trace of defiance. "Innuendo works when lying doesn't. To be frank, I don't believe we *could* have lied to him much longer, even when he was translating in his head. So I warned him dreamdust was addictive."

"You did *what*?"

"He's already addicted," Betrick said positively. "He just doesn't realise it yet. He says he can handle it."

Pervain smirked. "Don't they all. Well, you've an idiosyncratic way of going about things but it seems to work. Did he reveal anything of significance while he was with you?"

"No, just more of the same. He really hates being First Scientist and wants to give it up."

"In favour of his son, I suppose."

"Oh, no, Freelord. It wasn't Trevone he had in mind. It was Lydion."

***

347

"I can't understand it," Lann said helplessly. "As soon as we made a breakthrough with their code, they changed it. How did they know?"

"I think I can answer that," said Idenion. "They were importing a ground-based particle cannon - in pieces, obviously - which when assembled could have obliterated anything which flew over their base and put paid to any mass attempt to storm the gate. A burst water main ruined many of the electrical components while they were awaiting shipment from the spaceport."

"I see. And you don't think it was an accident?"

"The Eldorians can't prove it wasn't, so there hasn't been any formal protest. But they obviously revised their code as a precaution. I want you to question your people thoroughly, Lann, and make absolutely sure no-one's been talking to dissidents or taking unilateral action. The point of the decryption exercise is simply to monitor the Eldorians, not try to sabotage them in small ways. If we persist, and they're forced to change their code again, we may miss something of vital importance. Be prepared for periodic changes anyway. It's what *I'd* do."

"Guildmaster Lann." Nefyrra entered the room, looking pallid but poised. "The finalists are ready to play."

Lann bowed his head in acknowledgement and went out.

"Sorry I left you and Laura to cope with Pervain this morning," Nefyrra said, refilling Idenion's wine glass.

"You'd already made it clear you wouldn't see him, and I think for once he understood. For what it's worth, he's genuinely contrite."

"I suppose he asked you about staging this circus of theirs?" Nefyrra inquired.

"You *know* about that?"

"Geffin told Dena."

"You're under no obligation to agree," Idenion said staunchly. "The Lyricon's a centre for culture, not a killing ground."

"We can hardly preach at them for killing animals when they know we slaughtered all of ours," Nefyrra pointed out.

"Not for sport."

"Whatever the reason, they're just as dead. And the lurlan will be just as dead too, wherever the circus ends up."

"So you're going to give permission?" Idenion asked with an air of disapproval.

"My decision goes beyond the personal. This display, entertainment, whatever you like to call it, is to keep the soldiers out of mischief until Grenthap can put together his mock battles. If I don't let the performance go ahead, discontentment will still be rife and other women might be attacked."

Idenion sighed. "I take your point."

"And I won't be involved in any way," Nefyrra added. "I needn't even be present. Geffin says Steel and Lace are well used to touring, and their back-up crew will see to all the preparations."

"And clear up afterwards?"

"They guarantee it, apparently. So, would you mind passing on the good news to Pervain?"

"Very well." Idenion still looked far from happy. "I hope we're not going to regret this."

Chapter Eight

Three days later, the Steel and Lace roadshow duly descended on the Lyricon and proceeded to customise the stage. Spotlights were set up, plus a sound system and what looked like a massive metal climbing frame. In the generator room Lydion could hear various clangs and clatters as the equipment was assembled, and wondered what in chaos was taking shape overhead. He had more important concerns, however: projector four lay in pieces round him. Two new components had recently been milled at Treva, and as usual they didn't quite fit. Calmly methodical as ever, he proceeded to file them down.

"Lydion."

He turned, surprised and not altogether pleased to see Pervain standing in the doorway. "You'd better not come in, ambassador. You'll get your nice uniform all dirty."

"Let's forego the sparring on this occasion, if we can," Pervain suggested. "I want information and I believe there's something you want in return."

"Maybe," said Lydion guardedly. "We never did have that talk about Tralvar, did we?"

"At the moment I'm more concerned with *you*," Pervain replied urbanely.

"I can't think why."

"Tell me, if you will, why Jarras claims you'd make a better First Scientist than him."

"No idea."

"You don't agree with him, then?"

351

"It's a bit late in the day for a career move, even if I did," Lydion returned, inwardly furious at Jarras for sounding off when there were Eldorians around.

"Be serious." Pervain wasn't about to let the matter drop.

"If you want my serious opinion, Jarras needs his head examining. I've no formal scientific training, never served an apprenticeship, don't know a thing about chemistry or the stardrive..."

"But you do have certain skills. With forcefields, for instance."

"*One* forcefield. This one."

"And how did you discover your special talent?"

"By accident, when I was helping Tralvar out." Lydion had begun to look harassed. "Look, I can't go into all that now. I'm up to my ears. You want the shield operational for tomorrow night, don't you?"

"Please don't consider yourself under pressure," Pervain said suavely. "When you've finished here - or tomorrow morning, whatever suits you best - go and see Tovo, my secretary. He'll arrange for you to dictate your recollections and I'll review the recording later." He held up a pass which already displayed his signature. "I've brought you this. It'll get you into and out of the base on two occasions. In return for your co-operation, you'll be permitted to see Mallina."

"How often?"

"Twice, of course. Anything beyond that is subject to renegotiation."

Lydion hesitated. To win more time with Mallina he'd been all set to use stealth, diplomacy, argument and any other means at his disposal - and now he was being handed permission on a plate. Commonsense told him to look very carefully at Pervain's offer, particularly in the light of what Jarras had said; but, incautious as ever, he decided to put his doubts aside. One small objection remained.

"I wouldn't like Mallina to think I was bartering for her company," he ventured. "I'm not one of her recreationers."

Pervain bridled slightly. "Did I say you were? Just do yourself a favour and accept the deal before I change my mind."

"No more dirty tricks?"

Pervain sighed in exasperation. "I shan't even *be* there. I'm needed here to keep the peace between your stonemasons and the Steel and Lace construction crew. And that, considering the proprietorial nature of your workers, won't be easy." He brandished the pass impatiently. "Do you want this or not?"

Lydion almost snatched it from him. "All right, I'll speak to your secretary. Now clear out and let me get on with my work."

Pervain strolled to the door, then turned back briefly. "Don't forget, we know all about Tralvar the man and Tralvar the musician from his widow. We want to hear about Tralvar the scientist. His inventions, his poisons - "

"Tralvar never made any poisons. That was Alendis."

"There you are, that's something we didn't know." Pervain tried to give an encouraging smile: it didn't quite succeed. "We'll meet again soon."

"Not if I can help it," Lydion muttered. He stowed the pass carefully in an inside pocket, then returned to the damaged projector. Presently he began to smile.

***

"No, Laura," Clemis said firmly. "I'm not going."

"You've never accepted any of their invitations," Laura complained.

"And I don't intend to." Clemis searched her wardrobe for a waterproof cape and boots. Outside a drizzly rain was falling, bringing a premature dusk.

"What happened to all that solidarity you were going on about?" Laura persisted. "You always leave us to endure these functions on our own."

"I'm not a First Citizen and I'm not a diplomat," Clemis pointed out unnecessarily. "It isn't my job to fraternise. Anyway, I need to see Trevone."

"I thought he was at Communications tonight?"

"He is, but he'll be by himself. All the Eldorian staff will be at the show, so it's a perfect opportunity to talk to him without being overheard."

"*And* a chance to check on Aprival's ship?" Laura inquired gently.

"Among other things."

"I suppose..." Laura hesitated. "I suppose there's no chance of you and Trevone getting back together?"

"Not while he's co-operating with the Eldorians."

"His co-operation's only superficial, and you know it. He's always been part of the resistance."

"And what has the resistance done? Stolen a few guns, deciphered a few messages? That isn't going to win back our freedom!"

Laura refused to be drawn into an argument. "Well, you need to do something to improve your private life. You've been moping around all summer."

"I'm sorry, Laura. I know I've been in poor spirits, but there's something I need to resolve."

"That much is obvious." Laura sat down on the edge of the bed. "Clemis - I know we've had our quarrels in the past, but I like to think we've been getting on better lately. Whatever your problem is, I promise I won't be judgmental if you decide to share it with me. Maybe not yet, but when you feel able."

"Thanks, Laura." Clemis looked genuinely grateful. "If things don't work out I might be glad of a sympathetic ear. Now, shouldn't you be getting dressed up?"

"I'm not going to dress up. Nefyrra warned me that the temperature in the theatre will be kept down for the performers' sake, so I shall put comfort before fashion and wear something cosy. I only hope the food doesn't disagree with me."

"I didn't realise there was food involved."

355

"Oh, yes, they're all going to gorge themselves while they watch. But they're only being allowed one flagon of wine each, and after that they'll have to make do with water. We don't want any more drunkenness."

"A wise precaution." Clemis pulled on her boots. "Well, it's time I wasn't here. Pervain's picking you up, isn't he, and he has an annoying habit of being early. I don't think I could force myself to be civil."

"Have a good evening then," Laura said a little wistfully. "Have you got your stun-gun?"

"I never go anywhere without it these days," Clemis assured her. "See you later. Oh, and you'd better tell Idenion to get a move on. He's still reading."

Pervain, resplendent in his dress uniform but minus the sword, duly arrived to escort Laura and Idenion to the Lyricon. Most of the troops were already present, having marched uphill - and complained vociferously about it - earlier in the evening. Roll-call had been waived for the one occasion. The officers, including some unfamiliar faces from Treva, had appropriated flitters for themselves and the rec girls.

Since the Lyricon could seat two thousand, it still seemed relatively empty. The soldiers and most of the women were ranged around the lower terraces, and Eldorian caterers were handing round baskets of food. The officers were seated at a series of tables at the edge of the stage, thus assuring themselves of the best view - although the massive closed-circuit viewscreen, high on an adjacent hoarding, would ensure that no-one missed anything. The sound system was already pounding out martial music to heighten anticipation.

Laura found herself seated between Idenion and Pervain. Grenthap and Neelah were close by, with Escir a little further off. There seemed to be no-one else she knew, although if Geffin were present he would hardly have been allowed a place at the officers' table. There was no sign of Habbon, either.

"As you may have noticed," Pervain said to her, "we have adhered strictly to your wishes and left all our weapons at the base."

"Thank you," said Laura, somewhat inadequately.

"Would you like me to describe the entertainments?" Pervain went on. "I should at least give you some idea of what you'll be seeing."

Laura tried to look interested.

"First we have a contest between two girls who will fight using the lirrt, or pain-disc. The contestants wear mesh gloves, with the lirrt situated in the palm of the right hand. The girls themselves can choose the level of pain to be inflicted. Five consecutive strikes are needed for a win. I happen to know that these particular girls, Zoza and Ritax, hate one another - so the lirrt will probably be set to maximum."

Laura finally spied Geffin. He was weaving along the terraces, pausing frequently to talk with the soldiers.

"He's taking bets," Pervain said, following her gaze. "Zoza would normally be the favourite as

Ritax is carrying more weight, but Celestra's light gravity has to be taken into account. The odds are calculated using past performances on the Three Worlds, and Zoza fights better where there's a strong g-force."

The contest began. To brazen fanfares, the girls bounded onto the stage and acknowledged cheers from their respective factions. Lithe and muscular, they were ankle boots, tiny metallised skirts and light body armour to protect their breasts. Their hair was cropped short. In a series of acrobatic moves they pivoted, whirled and grappled, using the metal frame as a launch platform or means of escape.

Once again, noise seemed paramount. The glaring spotlights and the driving music would by themselves have been enough to give Laura a headache; but in addition there was the clangour of the girls' boots on the frame, shouts of encouragement from the audience, and whoops and shrieks from the girls themselves. Despite the din, the Lyricon acoustics magnified even the smallest sound they uttered, from grunts and gasps to muttered curses. When Zoza landed a strike on Ritax's bare midriff, her stifled cry of pain was heard by all.

Idenion was examining one of the food baskets. The little parcels of roast meat, still warm from the ovens, had a sharp, distinctive odour which reminded him of the venison he'd eaten at Cheveney. He tried a piece and pronounced it not bad, but Laura wasn't tempted. She did, however, eat a couple of the vegetable wedges that accompanied the meat.

"It's a bit rich if you ain't used to it," Neelah said understandingly. "But there's cake to follow - you're bound to like that. Want a napkin? I brought some with me. Men always forget the essentials."

A series of yells from the stage indicated that the bout was at an end. Ritax had pinned Zoza to the ground, her gloved hand slapping repeatedly at her opponent's neck.

"Three, four, five - OUT!" roared the crowd. Ritax and a somewhat dazed Zoza acknowledged the applause and retired.

"That was just a warm-up," Pervain told Laura. "To start the real proceedings we have a contest with sword and shield, male versus female. To equalise their strength, the man wears a helmet which limits what he sees."

"Will they be trying to kill each other?" asked Laura apprehensively.

"Fatalities are rare because trained fighters are expensive to replace," Pervain announced with a touch of cynicism. "But yes, sometimes people die. I'm sure Geffin knows what the odds are."

"I don't think I'm going to like this," Laura muttered.

"There's little cause for concern, Citizeness," Pervain assured her. "The event will be refereed throughout, and will almost certainly end in a submission or minor injury."

"I suppose you've placed a bet?"

"Not this time. I saw them in practice earlier and there's little to choose between them."

The contestants appeared, to the usual uproar. The woman was at least a decade older than the pain-disc girls, very tall, with black hair pinned in a circlet. The man was of equal height, lean and wiry. They wore gold tunics, and very little armour other than greaves and gauntlets. The man's headgear, made of animal hide and held in place with buckles, obscured his peripheral vision.

"Those shields don't look very effective," Laura remarked. "They're so small!"

"In skilled hands they're enough to turn a sword blade," Pervain replied knowledgeably.

A blast on an auxet brought the couple to a crouching stance, and a second blast launched them into action. The audience weighed in with shouts and boos, although the fighters scarcely seemed aware of it. Their concentration was absolute, their moves precise and potentially deadly. The clash of their weapons sounded and resounded throughout the theatre. In terms of skill they were, as Pervain had observed, equally matched; it would be a long, arduous contest. Laura knotted her shawl and tried to make herself more comfortable, wishing she'd been able to turn her back on the proceedings as Clemis had done.

At that moment Clemis was pacing about the control centre, recounting Geffin's predictions to an increasingly distracted Trevone. At last, out of verbal ammunition, she stationed herself in front of the console where he sat. "Well, say something!"

"Such as?"

"That you're taking this seriously, for a start. Geffin does know what he's talking about."

"I just can't imagine it happening," Trevone confessed.

Clemis stifled an angry reply. She'd already had one quarrel with Trevone over his imagination, or lack of it, and it would do her no good to criticise him further.

Fortunately, Trevone went on to qualify his statement. "What I mean is, I can't imagine being bombed out of existence. Tourists, yes. Conscription, possibly - though I doubt it." He returned his attention to the logic system.

"What is it you're doing?" Clemis asked impatiently. "Will you be much longer?"

"Finished!" said Trevone thankfully, removing the data crystal. "This is a download of every Eldorian communication over the past octal, including their messages home."

"I thought the transposal wave was impermeable."

"It is. But the Eldorians encrypt everything first, and that can be read before it even gets near a transposer - thanks to a little subroutine I've set up. I'll take this update to the scolia-tech as soon as possible."

"Didn't the Eldorians change the code?"

"Yes, but the scolia girls are on top of it. Now they know the principle, they'll have cracked this version in a few more days." He smiled reassuringly. "And that's why I'm not too worried about the future according to Geffin. The Eldorian Senate hasn't allocated enough men, spheres and equipment to the invasion effort. At least, that's what Grenthap's been saying hitherto. Everything's on hold."

"But they'll order him to invade anyway, and then the Earthers will win!" Clemis did her best not to shout. "You're getting all this intel, Trevone, but you never let me put my interpretation on it these days."

"I thought you just did," said Trevone innocuously.

She resisted an urge to hit him. "Does Jarras know about your, er, subroutine?"

"Not yet," Trevone admitted. "We've agreed that he should concentrate on Treva for the moment. The attack on Nefyrra really shook him up."

"It shook *her* up too, but you don't see her going to pieces," Clemis said caustically. "Now if the computer's free, can you please run a status check on Aprival's spacecraft?"

"That's all you came here for, isn't it? To see if he's run out on you?"

"No," she said firmly. "It was *you* I wanted to see."

"Then why are you closed off?"

"I'll tell you later. Please, Trevone, I have to know if those people are still out there."

With bad grace he overrode the stealth programme, and Clemis looked for the trace Nimion had shown her. It wasn't there.

"I don't see anything," she quavered.

"They've moved into Alda Five's shadow. This, on screen, is the feed from Alda Six. You can just about see there's a geostationary foreign body." He reinstated the programme. "To be honest, I don't

362

know why they're still here. We're committed now. Surely they realise that?"

Clemis said nothing. What was she supposed to say - that they were waiting for *her*? How pretentious that would sound. Oh, Trevone, she thought wretchedly. Did Geffin's warnings have no impact on you at all? I want to trust you, I really do. But you're making it so difficult...

"Er - Clemis."

"What?"

"I know you were hoping for a quiet evening together, but I think I should pay a visit to my students - the ones who live next to the base. They had another raid planned for tonight, and I've been trying to put them off. It's too soon after the last time."

"At least they're showing some initiative," Clemis remarked. "May I meet them?"

"Yes, as long as you promise not to meddle. I have enough trouble getting them to do as they're told without an input of your strange ideas." He de-activated the tracking screen, leaving it on stand-by.

"Are you just going to walk out of here?" Clemis' voice held surprise and approval.

"For once, yes. If the Eldorians can give themselves the evening off, so can I. Nothing's due in, and Treva can take over the watch until Nimion gets here." He sent a brief radio message to that effect, switched off most of the lights and summoned the elevator.

Clemis took one more look at the idling equipment and the not quite inert viewscreen.

Suddenly she felt a strong sense of foreboding, in which Aprival figured very strongly. A pale beautiful face, a strangely imperfect mind...

"Come on, then," Trevone said impatiently, and she followed with an apologetic smile.

The students were lively and enthusiastic. "Trevone's always fussing over us, " said their ringleader, Dessin. "Yes, we'd intended to do another raid, but we found we lacked one important item."

"And what was that?" inquired Clemis.

"Daylight. The base was in total darkness, the foot patrols were out, and we couldn't even see the armoury window. So we very quickly changed our minds."

"But we're not just fooling around," said Linni. "There are other resistance cells besides ours, each with a specific job to do when the time comes. We don't know anything about the other groups, so if we're caught we can't betray them."

"And what *is* your job?"

"To take back the base, of course. Firemaster Wemm is making us some smoke bombs. Once we reach the armoury we'll have all the weapons we need."

Clemis admired their dedication but tried not to show how hopeless she thought the scheme to be. Insurrection was commonplace on the Three Worlds; she'd known that from day one of the occupation. The Eldorians would deal with a minor uprising as easily as swatting a fly. There was only one way it could work, and that was as part of a planetwide coup with powerful weapons to back it up. Stolen guns and a handful of paralysers would be no use on their own.

Trevone hauled her out of the lodging house before she could air her misgivings. "Guildmaster Lann's trying to create some kind of deterrent," he explained hastily. "They don't need to know that yet."

"He hasn't succeeded, then."

"No, but he's an excellent physicist. He'll come up with something."

Clemis doubted whether a gentle aesthete like Lann would have the mindset for such a task. "Do *you* know about the other resistance cells?" she asked.

"No."

"Then someone must. Who is it? Who, Trevone?"

He was silent.

"Not Jarras. Tell me it isn't Jarras!"

"Hello, you two!" said a new voice. "Squabbling again?"

"Lydion!" Clemis exclaimed. "Where did you spring from?"

He pointed to the gate-house.

"Oh, of course! You've been seeing your new girl. Kalyx told me about her."

"You certainly seem a lot happier than the last time we saw you here," commented Trevone. "Can we give you a lift back to the Lyricon?"

"Thanks, kids, but I'm not going near the place until that circus has made itself scarce. Those caged beasts give out the weirdest thought impulses. They don't smell too fragrant either!"

"Where will you go?"

"Oh, don't worry. I'll find somewhere. I always do."

They watched as he strode jauntily downhill. "I'm so glad he's back to his old self," Clemis said fondly. "Every time I've seen him recently he's either been moping or tearing around in a panic. Whatever this girl's like, she's obviously doing him some good."

Trevone was less positive. "Maybe, but it complicates things. He should've stuck with Zanna. Every time he sets foot in that base he's a security risk."

"Not while his cover story holds - and he's very good at maintaining it. It's Jarras we have to worry about."

"I agree, but what do you want me to do?"

It wasn't quite the moment she'd been waiting for, but it would have to suffice. If she didn't speak out, she'd be risking the lives of the students, the scolia-tech and other nameless campaigners for freedom. She let her shields fall away; his quietly affectionate thoughts lent strength to her resolve, as she hoped they would. "Trevone," she began, "I've been given - " Then abruptly, she halted. Her mind resounded with consternation and dread.

"Clemis?" ventured Trevone. "What in chaos is wrong?"

"Idenion!" she cried. "My father..." Then she sprinted across to the waiting flitter, leapt on board and took off.

"Hey!" Trevone yelled.

366

The craft described a crazy arc, narrowly missing a rooftop, before heading for the Lyricon at maximum speed.

***

The theatre was in tumult, the contest having come to a sudden end when the woman sustained a deep wound to her sword-arm. The solicitude displayed by her opponent had left no-one in any doubt that there was some love interest between them.

"I knew it!" Pervain declared. "There was something wrong with that bout from the start. She had several opportunities to score, and didn't."

The soldiers who had lost bets demanded their money back. Geffin stood his ground and refused to declare the betting invalid. A furious row ensued, with Geffin cursing fluently in five different dialects.

"Peasant," Pervain muttered irritably.

In the midst of the uproar Laura noticed that the officers from Treva were sharing out some white pills and swallowing them with water. Concerned, she left her seat and went to confer with Escir.

"Yes, I'd noticed," he replied wearily. "It's a recreational drug called khin, which induces euphoria. I agree this isn't the time nor place to use it, but as it's designated legal I can't stop them."

"But can they be trusted to behave?"

"Khin sometimes causes sleepiness and disorientation, but nothing too anti-social. I'll keep an eye on them."

The amplified auxets blared out again, bringing everyone's attention back to the stage. "And now," proclaimed the master of ceremonies, "the highlight of the evening. Our fearless girls will attempt to subdue the lurlan, the most ferocious beast in the Empire. In answer to a frequently asked question: our animals are not reared in captivity but in the wild, where only the strongest survive. And as is usual in our contests, we feature only the female of the species."

"The female is the most aggressive," Pervain added for his guests' edification.

To another loud fanfare, a large rectangular cage was wheeled out. The interior was divided into two halves, the section to the left containing the lurlan - a magnificent feline with sleek black fur and a luxuriant tail. Its head was massive yet elegant, with a prominent jaw and small neat ears. Sullen yellow eyes glowered at the crowd.

Two gaudily clad attendants, one carrying a goad and the other a pole, climbed into the empty half of the cage and proceeded to torment the animal. Its hackles rose and it emitted a bloodcurdling roar, displaying the most vicious array of teeth that Laura had ever seen. The enraged beast was soon throwing itself at the bars separating it from the men. The partition wobbled dangerously. At this point the attendants decided that the lurlan was sufficiently prepared, and withdrew in short order. The audience sniggered.

"And now," bellowed the announcer, "I give you - Prahina the Undefeated!"

Cheers greeted the small, slim girl who skipped onto the stage. She wore the ubiquitous short skirt and boots, a padded gilet and reinforced gloves. Her only other concession to safety was a pair of eye-goggles. She picked up the goad and entered the cage. The attendants, at her signal, slid aside the partition. The sound system commenced a muted drum-roll.

"It'll kill her!" Laura whispered.

"Watch and learn," Pervain replied. "My money's on the girl!"

Of course, it was less dangerous than it appeared. Prahina had been in the circus all her life and had spent years in practice, initially with elderly animals whose spirit had been broken. All performing lurlan were well fed and had been trained in stimulus-response. Prahina's gloves had a metallised inner layer which rendered them virtually bite-proof, and in addition she had bathed in a solution which masked her natural scent.

All this Idenion perceived as he gazed thoughtfully at the stage. He found the animal mentality intriguing: the intensity of purpose, the survival instinct. He wondered if the creature and others like it had ever been offered kindness instead of abuse.

Throughout her lengthy presentation Prahina exhibited flair, agility and a complete knowledge of the lurlan and its ways. With judicious use of goad and glove she systematically beat her foe into submission and, to conclude, briefly placed her foot on its neck. Then she left the cage, to thunderous applause.

The next lurlan was brought on, snarling and spitting. Its opponent, relatively inexperienced, fared badly: her moves lacked assurance and her control was tenuous at best. Before long the goad was knocked from her hand and she received several cuffs from a huge forepaw. But she kept her nerve, curling into a tight ball and rolling to retrieve the weapon. She was then able to drive the creature back and escape from the cage. The soldiers applauded generously and she took a bow, bleeding from many deep scratches.

"Why didn't anyone help her?" asked Laura indignantly.

"Oh, come now," drawled Pervain, "it wouldn't be much of an entertainment if everyone rushed in at the first sign of trouble. From the moment a girl enters the cage, she's on her own."

The final bout had just commenced when one of the khin-eaters announced that he felt unwell.

"I warned you to go easy on those things," Escir said testily. "There's no antidote so you'll just have to ride it out. Sit quietly and drink plenty of water." He intercepted the nearest pitcher, which was half full. "Drink all this, *slowly*. Keep it by you. And you others, watch him."

At the end of the finale - Prahina versus a beast so intractable that not even the star performer would risk her dainty foot near its jaws - most people assumed the evening was over. But the attendants came on once again, bringing the animal which had fought first. As the cages drew parallel the two occupants began a display of mutual hostility.

370

Grenthap called Geffin over. "I take it the event's been agreed?"

"Indeed it has. The impresario said that since the animals were going to die anyway they might as well be set against one another."

"How do you know they'll fight?" asked Idenion.

"Two lurlan in a confined space will *always* fight," Pervain answered laconically.

"Geffin," said Grenthap, "I'll put all my previous winnings on the matriarch. The young one won't last five zytl against her."

The cages were bolted together and the central divisions withdrawn for maximum floor space. The weathershield projection faded to indigo and the stage lighting was dimmed, leaving a group of spotlights centred on the action. The lurlan circled their prison warily.

Idenion again noted the powerful grace of their movements, the ripple of muscles beneath the smooth fur. "It's a pity they're so opposed to their own kind. Has no-one ever tried to tame them?"

"Tame them?" snorted Grenthap. "Can't wait to see some fool try. He'd have to be very tired of life - "

He was interrupted by a sudden commotion from the stage. The battle of the generations had begun. The younger animal had a surfeit of energy and for a while it seemed that Grenthap would lose his bet. But the old lurlan was merely biding her time. Suddenly she pounced, sinking her fangs into her opponent's foreleg. The injured beast fought valiantly on, but eventually slumped panting to the floor and awaited the deathblow to the throat.

The action of the winner was swift and sure. Then, after crouching over the limp form of her enemy and licking the blood, she raised her head and roared defiance at the world. The Eldorians responded with cheers and yells.

Idenion murmured something which almost went unheard in the din. Pervain, however, turned sharply to face him. "*What* did you say?"

"The lurlan has a rudimentary intelligence, a simple reasoning power. I could communicate with it."

"That wasn't what you just said," objected Pervain.

The applause diminished and their conversation became audible. Heads turned curiously in their direction.

"What did you just tell me?" repeated Pervain.

"I said I thought it was possible to tame the creature," Idenion answered reluctantly.

"You said *you* could do it."

"In theory, yes, but - "

Pervain didn't wait to hear any more. "Friends," he exclaimed, leaping onto the stage, "the fun is not yet over. Idenion will now tame the lurlan - telepathically."

There were jeers and shouts of "impossible."

"She's tasted blood," called someone. "She'll be wanting more."

Idenion glanced at the cages. The dividing bars were back in place; attendants were removing the

372

carcass and scattering sawdust. The survivor again roared out her challenge.

"Still think you can do it?" asked Pervain slyly. "We'll all be very disappointed if you refuse."

"Idenion, don't listen to him!" begged Laura. "You can't reason with a wild animal." Then, under her breath: "Read me, dammit!"

+I have to go through with it, Laura+ he responded to show she had his attention.

No, you don't! she thought as emphatically as she could. You're thinking of Rocky, aren't you? There's a big difference between an illtempered domestic cat and a savage great brute like that lurlan. Tell them you've changed your mind!

+I can't, dearest+ His grey eyes were as loving as always. +Look around you. The whole of the Eldorian regiment is here. Yes, I was tricked into making that remark - but if I try to back out I'll have lost everyone's respect. For the sake of my future credibility I have to do this+

Pervain eyed them, smirking. The rest of the Eldorians were silent, quizzical.

"I'm willing to make the attempt," said Idenion at last.

"You'll go inside the cage?" asked Pervain.

Idenion bowed his head. "Whatever you wish."'

There was a chorus of approval which drowned Laura's cry of protest. Eager hands seized her life-partner and pushed him onto the stage, while the officers cheered and pounded the tables.

Laura watched helplessly. She saw the attendants proffer the goad and pole: Idenion would not take them. She heard his request for absolute silence, saw him approach the cage and enter.

"You don't appear to have much faith in your husband," whispered Pervain.

"*Your* faith seems unprecedented," Laura hissed back. "You forced him into this, and if he's injured I shall hold you responsible."

"On the Three Worlds," said Pervain, "a man seldom makes reckless boasts. Should he do so, he's always called upon to prove his claims."

"Are the odds worth betting on?" someone asked Geffin.

"The book's closed," he answered sombrely.

Idenion's mind reached out questingly to the predatory intelligence before him. On no account must he communicate his nervousness to the animal. Also, he could not be subtle; the lurlan would only understand the simplest commands. +Rest+ he instructed, +lie down and rest. You are tired. There is no threat. I will not harm you+

Once more the partition was removed. The lurlan padded forward, uttering a low growl, but paused as the calming influence reached her. Bewildered, she crouched down and regarded Idenion with deep suspicion. He moved closer, repeating his gently persuasive message. Peace ... sleep... contentment...

The soldier who had overdosed on khin suddenly sprawled across his table. The water-jug slid from his grasp and smashed on the floor.

The noise startled Idenion and broke his concentration. Instantly the lurlan sprang, vengefully flinging herself upon the intruder who had practised such deceit. Idenion screamed once as the vicious claws tore a bloody swathe across his upper body: then, mercifully, he fainted. Laura froze in shock. The other onlookers, in accordance with the rules, made no move to intervene. The lurlan toyed with her victim for a while, rolling him to and fro, but soon becoming bored when he didn't struggle. Casually she opened her murderous jaws to dispatch her prey.

Then a slender bolt of white lightning sizzled across the arena. The lurlan, struck on its right flank, gave a sudden howl and collapsed. The Eldorians turned in amazement toward the source of the light; and there, just inside the performers' entrance, was Clemis, grasping her stun-gun very firmly in both hands.

***

"Interesting little gadget, that," said Pervain.

"I don't see why it should interest *you*," Clemis retorted. "It's defensive only, and doesn't kill."

"Indeed. And I suppose your Tralvar had a hand in its development?"

"No, he didn't," Clemis replied truthfully. "It's Narvellan tech. And in view of what happened to Nefyrra I feel entirely justified in carrying it."

Pervain scrutinised her with a frown. "I warned my colleagues that you Celestrians might have a surprise or two in store. You wouldn't happen to know about anything like that, would you?"

"Of course not," said Clemis in what she hoped was an innocent voice.

"I'm serious, little girl. Don't try and play the heroine with me. Your people are up to something, and if I thought for one moment that you were involved - "

"You're drawing attention to yourself," Clemis said primly.

A few soldiers had paused to stare. Pervain glared at them, and they moved on. The Lyricon was almost deserted now, although the spotlights still blazed. The Steel and Lace crew, accustomed to speedy departures, were removing the last of their equipment. Grenthap had ordered the troops back to barracks at the double; they had filed out smartly, apart from those awaiting transport to the monorail. Geffin was nowhere to be seen.

Idenion had been rushed away by the circus medics. Laura was with him, along with several Celestrians who had belatedly arrived in response to his distress call - the involuntary cry of fear and pain which had shivered across half the city's perception and brought Clemis hurtling to his rescue. She still had no idea how badly injured her father was, since Pervain had confronted her as she was about to follow the others.

He seemed in no hurry to leave. "You know," he was saying, "I really wish we could be friends. You have spirit and courage. The Empire needs girls like you, to act as role models and inspire loyalty in the young."

"Forget it, Pervain. It isn't going to happen." Clemis shifted the stun-gun uneasily from hand to hand. It was still uncomfortably hot after firing, but she wasn't about to holster it with him watching.

Pervain seemed aware of her problem. A tiny smile appeared at the corners of his mouth. "My dear, you must forgive me. How remiss of me to start on politics when you're so concerned about Idenion. We'll talk later." He bowed somewhat mockingly and strode away.

Clemis made a second attempt to reach the dressing rooms but was once again intercepted, this time by Kalyx. "*There* you are! Was Pervain importuning my best girl? Sorry I wasn't in time to see him off."

"I'm not your best girl."

"But you're not Trevone's either, which holds promise. Well, let's go. People are waiting for you."

"What people?"

"You're news! A team from the Forces Broadcasting Service wants to interview you. If you hadn't been so determinedly closed off you'd have known before now."

"There's so much mental hubbub I don't see how anyone could know anything," Clemis said irritably. "And with respect to the Eldorian listening public, my place is with my father."

"Idenion has at least seven healers buzzing round him. Not even Laura can get a look in. He's awake and talking, apparently, so you needn't fret."

"Was this broadcast Geffin's idea?" asked Clemis, beginning to walk.

"No, the presenters used their own initiative. Geffin's inspecting the tele-recording before Steel and Lace take it away. The camera roved the crowd on several occasions and he wants to see if anything incriminating shows up."

"Such as?"

"No idea - that's *his* department. But if it *was* an assassination attempt, someone's going to be thoroughly displeased. All the soldiers are hailing Idenion as a fearless leader. His popularity's quadrupled in little more than an ild. Now will you please get a move on?"

***

Nordall tapped lightly on the door to the communications room. "Xorian?"

"Enter."

"Captain, I don't know what you've been doing, but our residual power level's down by fifty per cent. If we lose any more the solar arrays won't be able to replenish it."

"Hopefully we won't need to lose more. Listen!" Xorian turned back to the waveform receiver. The closing phrases of a newscast, scarcely audible above solar static, whispered into the cabin.

"What am I listening to?"

"An on-the-spot report from Alda Mexa - subject to the usual time-lag, of course. This interview took place just after Idenion was mauled by the lurlan. That's Clemis speaking."

"I'm sorry, I didn't catch what she said."

"She only did what anyone else would have done," Xorian interpreted. "She saved his life,

Nordall. But she doesn't yet realise what a unique opportunity she was given."

Nordall's gaze registered enlightenment. "And when she does, do you think you'll have won her loyalty?"

"Aprival thinks so."

Nordall smirked. "And he's an authority, is he, just because he's met her? With respect, Captain, we've spent far too much time waiting for this girl to see sense. If what she has is so important, why don't we go down there and grab her?"

"Because then we'd have the girl and not the artifact. Moreover, we'd have both the Eldorians *and* the Celestrians against us, and our mission would fail. Laura and Idenion don't know what we are, but they know *where* we are. If we kidnapped their daughter, we'd be over-run before the day was out."

"I never opted for the waiting game," muttered Nordall.

"Possibly not: but we debated long and hard over the right way to do this, and I don't regret having chosen this course. Right or wrong, we can't deviate from it now."

***

"Laura, I wish you'd reconsider," said Drusa. "Idenion should be in hospital."

"He wants to come home," Laura repeated.

"Patients don't always know what's best for them," Drusa pointed out gently.

"The circus people didn't think his injuries were that serious. Their chief medic said he'd seen far worse amongst the girls."

"They're used to it - and they're a lot younger than Idenion," Drusa said bluntly. "It's difficult for me to study him in this environment, but those lacerations could give trouble. Chaos only know what filth that creature had under its claws."

"You talk as if I'm planning to neglect him," Laura accused. "I'd be with him at night and there wouldn't be any shortage of help by day. I want to be near him, Drusa - I'd worry constantly if I weren't - but I also have a planet to run. If I keep him at home I can achieve both aims."

Seeing she was not to be moved, Drusa gave in. "I'll visit as often as I can," she promised. "Stay vigilant, and feel free to send for me at any time."

And so, bandaged and dosed with painkillers, Idenion was carefully airlifted to the akron. Once he was safely in his own room, Drusa administered a sedative which he accepted under protest. "Haven't I been punctured enough already?"

"I want to make sure you sleep. This first night is very important to your healing process."

Laura offered thanks to her and the medical team, then sent them away and thankfully stationed herself beside Idenion's bed. "I thought they'd never go. Sorry it took so long to throw them out!"

Idenion, drowsy but coherent, smiled at her. "Thanks for keeping me out of hospital. I don't know which was worse - the lurlan or Drusa and her needles!"

"You won't be entirely free of her," Laura warned. "She'll be back to change your dressings. But now we're alone, I believe you had something crucial to say to me?"

"Thank harmony. I didn't think I'd got the message across."

"Well, you did. So whatever it is, you'd better say it quickly before that injection takes effect!"

"Pain sharpens the mind wonderfully," Idenion began. "It made me face up to the way things are heading. Once Earth's been invaded we'll be at the mercy of all comers. Pervain promised us protection against the Earthers, but we won't get it because the Empire has neither the inclination nor the resources. We made a bad decision, Laura."

She started to speak, but he held up a weary hand to forestall her.

"Pervain wants to be rid of me. I'm not saying tonight was premeditated but he certainly used the opportunity. He'll try again if he gets the chance. Clemis was right - we should have trusted Aprival."

"What should I do?"

"Talk to her. She knows more than she's telling." Idenion's voice began to slur. "Sorry, Laura. I'm falling asleep."

"Sleep, then," Laura said gently. "I'll speak to Clemis."

"Everything's up to you now," he murmured. "I'm so fortunate to have you. You'll put things right...."

Laura remained at his side, deep in thought. She couldn't in all conscience endorse his sudden belief in Aprival, but she was prepared to give her daughter a hearing - when she turned up. She'd reportedly left the theatre with Kalyx, so the likelihood was she wouldn't be back till morning. But no: here she was, bursting in like a hurricane, seemingly oblivious to Idenion's sleeping presence.

"Laura, I - "

"Shh!" Laura hissed wrathfully.

Clemis made a visible effort to calm down. "So many people, so many questions," she continued in a whisper. "I came home as soon as I could. How is he?"

"Sedated." Laura stood back reluctantly. "Quietly now. Don't disturb him."

Clemis gazed minutely at her father, trying for Laura's sake to mask her concern. She was no healer, but to her unpractised eye Idenion didn't seem to be in a recuperative state. He simply looked tired, infinitely tired.

Presently Laura drew her out of the room. Briefly, and with some reservation, she outlined Idenion's change of heart.

Clemis was overwhelmed with relief. "Oh, Laura, at last! That's such a weight off my mind!"

"It's true, then? You've been holding out on us?"

"Not in the way Idenion meant." Clemis sat down in her favourite recliner and composed herself. A rushed explanation would be worse than none. "Tonight, Trevone took me to meet the resistance workers - the students who've been pilfering weapons from the base. They talked of an uprising, and I was upset because I knew it would fail." She paused, swallowed, then carried on:

"What if I told you there was a way to prevent their deaths and save our people? A new and devastating weapon to use against Eldor?"

"Are you saying that Aprival has one?"

"Not Aprival. Me."

Her mother looked baffled, and Clemis quietly told her of the secret plans and Dena's complicity. As she talked, Laura's expression softened into something approaching reverence.

"Dear faithful Tralvar," she murmured. "So he didn't leave us defenceless after all. But what a burden to place on a young girl! Why didn't he leave his work with Idenion and me, or Lann, or Jarras, or even Trevone?"

"I'll let him tell you that himself," said Clemis, seldom without a sense of the dramatic. She sped to her room and retrieved the two concealed items; then, watched by a quizzical Laura, presented the disc to the nearest player unit and resumed her seat expectantly.

Laura listened, smiling ruefully on being told why she'd forfeited Tralvar's confidence. "Well," she said when the record was over, "what a revelation! My adoptive world's about to be despoiled, my partner's life's under threat - and suddenly my daughter brings me plans for a superweapon. Dare I unleash it? Or do I suppress it and let everything I cherish be torn apart?"

"I think you've just answered your own question," said Clemis.

"Before today, I'd have shied away from this," Laura went on. "Tralvar was absolutely right. As it

383

is, I'm not sure what you expect me to do. Haven't you told Trevone? He'd be far more use than me!"

"I *tried* to tell him," Clemis said bitterly. "But he made it clear what he thought of my improbable schemes - his words - as soon as I started dropping hints."

"It isn't like you to give up so easily."

"No, it isn't, but what if he'd spirited the plans away as he did the new stardrive? I couldn't take the risk. Funnily enough I was going to try again this evening, just after we left the student house. He was worried, and he might well have listened for a change, but I never had the chance to find out. First we ran into Lydion leaving the base, and then Idenion's scream hit me between the eyes. I don't think I've ever moved so fast in my life!"

"Oh, Clemis, you couldn't possibly have been on Lateral Four when the lurlan attacked. You'd never have reached the Lyricon in time."

"I admit it was close. I took Trevone's flitter and left him standing in the street. He's going to be really mad at me!"

Laura frowned. "How long were you airborne?"

"An astal, maybe a little more. I know I was flying dangerously but it *was* an emergency."

"And once you'd landed you had to run down the corridor past the generator room, and up to the stage."

"That's right. It stank down there. Sweat, animal droppings - "

"Clemis, listen. That entire sequence of events - the attack, the scream, your arrival - was over in less than half an astal. I was there! *And* it's on film."

"If it really matters, I can prove I was on Lateral Four," Clemis said with a trace of irritation. "Ask Trevone."

"No, *you* ask. Ask him now."

"Laura...where are you going with this?"

"Just ask. Please."

Clemis sighed. "He's probably gone back to Communications, and that will involve up to three relayists. Are you sure that's what you want?"

"Yes," Laura said adamantly.

Clemis contacted Kyrin, who put out the inquiry. After a short interval he reported back, neutral as always: +Trevone says you left suddenly and inexplicably. He, and everyone else, didn't perceive Idenion's cry until much later+

Thoroughly disconcerted, Clemis passed the findings to Laura. "How could I have been forewarned? And how did you *know*?"

"About your premonition? I didn't. All I knew was, you couldn't have made that journey across town in time to save your father."

Clemis huddled deeper into the cushions in an attempt to hide an involuntary shiver. The stun-gun dug in her leg; she unclipped the holster and sat frowning. "Premonition's the wrong word. It was *actual* - his mental autograph, his pain. But when I was running toward the stage I did have the oddest feeling that I was two people - two different versions of me. One who got there in time and one who didn't."

Laura had turned pale. "Hell's teeth!"

385

"You know exactly what I mean, don't you?" Clemis said almost accusingly. "It's happened to you as well!"

"A feeling of being twinned. Yes, just as you described it. It was just before...."

"Go on."

"Just before Aprival's shuttle landed." Laura leant on the back of Clemis' chair. "So let's think very carefully, shall we? He arrived on a ship which broke all the known laws of transposal to get here. He and the crew are anxious to win our trust, and therefore had a motive for saving Idenion's life. On the face of it they don't seem very advanced, but they know a great deal about us and can seemingly manipulate events."

"They've certainly made a study of *me*," Clemis remarked. "They knew I was concealing something vital."

"Then go to them," Laura said calmly. "It's Idenion's wish, and your story has convinced me he's right. Aprival said his people couldn't fight Eldor on their own. Well, neither can we. Not even with *that* thrown into the equation." She pointed at the envelope containing the plans. "Tralvar believed Jarras and Lydion couldn't take this on, and I have to second his opinion. Jarras would panic and Lydion would pretend the task was beyond him. If there were no Aprival, no ship-dwellers, I might demand co-operation from my scientists, but I'm disinclined to do that now. The weapon belongs with you."

"I'm to take it to Aprival?" Clemis asked breathlessly.

386

"Yes, on my authority." Laura unfolded the plans and examined them. "Let's hope he doesn't ask you to explain how it works. I don't understand a word of this and I don't suppose you do either."

"Why would I need to explain it?"

"He won't be able to read a technical paper, will he? Not when he can hardly speak Celestrian!"

"He can speak it perfectly now," said Clemis with insufficient forethought. "He's had some kind of sleep-hypnosis."

"You mean - he's been back here?"

"Er....yes. I met him on the landing field."

"And you didn't tell me." Laura looked resigned. "Well, I can't really blame you. There wouldn't have seemed much point at the time."

"Hadn't I better go?" Clemis asked, trying not to sound reluctant. She'd campaigned stoically to win recognition for Aprival; now that she'd been successful, her energy reserves had suddenly plummeted. The journey to Alda Five had never seemed so daunting, nor her surroundings so comfortable.

"You're not going anywhere tonight," Laura said, saving her. "It's late and you must be exhausted. Aprival's waited a long time for you, and one more day won't hurt him. Get a good night's sleep, have a talk with Idenion in the morning, and then we'll see about sneaking you through the spaceport."

***

The following morning Clemis tiptoed into Idenion's room to find Drusa already there, gently soaking off his bandages. Disregarding the nurse's admonitions he beckoned Clemis forward.

"Laura says I should thank you," he said feebly. "You're a good girl."

She gave him a fond smile. "I'll try to be even better."

He gazed quizzically at her attire: a close-fitting grey worksuit with the stun-gun strapped brazenly to her hip. "Shouldn't you be keeping that hidden?"

"The Eldorians know about it now, so there's no reason to," she replied. "It's easier to manage like this."

"Well, remember what I said about not pointing it at people." Idenion smiled vacuously. "I'm not much use with guns. The first shot missed completely."

"Pardon?"

"Tralvar told me to shoot out the glass. From the prill tank. Laura was in danger."

Drusa motioned her away. Clemis, worried, went in search of Laura and found her in the office.

"Ah, there you are, sleepyhead. You're missing all the excitement. Kyrin's been fending off enquiries since sun-up, and I've had to station half a dozen administrators down the corridor with orders to admit family and close friends only!"

Clemis helped herself to hot liman from a flask on the desk. "Idenion seems very wandered. Is that normal under the circumstances?"

"It's the drugs I expect. He isn't used to them. I haven't told him about the weapon yet: he needs to be a lot more focused before I can discuss anything sensitive."

A knock at the door interrupted them. It was Geffin, unabashed as always. Laura greeted him with a resigned smile.

"Trust you to get through my security!"

"It's what I do," grinned the little reporter. "Dena says she'll be along shortly - she had to stop off at the Lyricon. Meanwhile, I'm sorry to inform you that we don't have anything on Pervain."

"The film didn't incriminate him?"

"Afraid not. He was nowhere near the airhead who broke the jug. I think it's as you said - he didn't believe Idenion could control the animal and thought he was sending him to his death."

"We'll never prove it, though."

"No, unfortunately. But here's some gossip to cheer you up: Grenthap and his cronies want to send a delegation to Tafret, with a view to recruiting superior telepaths from the relayists' training village. Just a preliminary survey, you understand. Anyway, it doesn't look as if it's going to happen because everyone, and I mean everyone, is refusing to go. Even Pervain. He's terrified someone will break through his psychic defences. They're a superstitious lot, our soldiery; they're calling your relayists freaks, sorcerers and Ebbon knows what else. They think it'll be like Nefyrra many times over if they dare set foot in the place."

Clemis chuckled, and Laura suddenly looked inspired. "Thank you, Geffin. That's very good news indeed."

"Planning a little jaunt, are we?" Geffin inspected Clemis appraisingly.

"We decided a short tour was in order, following my father's accident," she said carelessly.

"Drumming up support?"

"Something like that."

Geffin leaned forward conspiratorially. "Excellent timing, if you don't mind my saying so. The paging system at the base has broken down, and seems to be resisting repair. They've pulled the technicians out of Communications to see if they can help."

"So if I go now..."

" - you can avoid any awkward questions. There won't be any Eldorians at the spaceport."

"That's useful to know," said Laura with another polite smile. Her trust in the reporter didn't quite match Idenion's. Disaffected he might be, but he was still Eldorian. "It looks as though I'll be running things for a bit, so any arrangement you had with Idenion will now revert to me. I assume you're happy with that?"

"Of course, Citizeness. Eyes and ears, as they say."

"Eyes and ears," she repeated. Then, when Geffin had left: "Come along, young lady. Breakfast. And while you're eating we'll go over the arrangements."

Action at last, thought Clemis. I might decide to be nervous later, but for now I'm almost enjoying this.

Laura proceeded to outline her recent idea. "We'll say you're making a courtesy trip to Tafret - something long overdue, as it happens."

"I'll be deputising for you, of course."

"Of course. I'll slot the details into our agenda retrospectively so it'll look as if it was proposed octals ago, and I'll get word to Nohal at the Academy explaining what I've done. If the Eldorians' aversion to Tafret is as widespread as Geffin believes, it'll be quite a while before they discover you're not there."

"Sounds good."

"Now, about the spaceport. You'll need a sphere that no-one's going to miss, and a programme to take you to Alda Five. Thank goodness you did that year at Space Tech, otherwise you couldn't have gone on your own. But you'll still need the connivance of someone on the ground."

"Mother," Clemis began hesitantly. Laura gave her a suspicious glance. It never boded well when Clemis called her that. "I don't think it would be a good idea to involve Trevone at this stage."

"Why not?"

"Because he's jealous of Aprival. You should've heard him that day on the landing field. That was when we had the row about the new stardrive."

"I see. And you don't think my presence would force his co-operation?"

"It probably would, but he'd still make a fuss."

Laura gazed at her shrewdly. "Is that why you've been keeping him at a distance?"

"I've had to keep both him *and* Kalyx at a distance because of the weapon," Clemis explained. "Either one of them could have found out about it through unity. It's been a lonely time."

Laura, naturally enough, hadn't taken this aspect into account. For the first time she observed a maturity in her daughter which she was sure hadn't been there a few octals ago. Any doubts that she had about her suitability for the mission were rapidly being dispelled. She remembered the bitter argument she'd had with Tralvar over his plans for Clemis, and finally admitted to herself that he'd acted correctly. I should be terrified for her, she mused. My little one, about to fly the nest. But what would I gain by holding her back? I can't protect her. There's just as much danger here as out there.

Clemis gave no hint that she'd sensed these reflections. She finished the savoury bread she'd been eating and started on a generous helping of cereal.

"So Trevone blames Aprival for your estrangement," Laura prompted gently.

"Some of the time. When he's not blaming Kalyx."

"Right," said Laura decisively. "I'd better have a chat with Communications. If Trevone's there I want advance warning."

"You don't have to chaperone me, you know."

"Oh yes I do - at least, as far as the spaceport. Trevone isn't the only obstacle. Supposing you ran into Jarras or Nimion? I'd need to pull rank before they'd let you go anywhere!"

Clemis only half agreed with this. Jarras, if he were present, wouldn't offer much of a challenge. Not having seen Aprival, he didn't have the same reality on the situation. Besides which, he was so preoccupied with his marriage he couldn't see what was going on under his nose. Nimion, however, was another matter. She hadn't forgotten how swiftly he'd uncovered Trevone's theft of the Symerid programme. "About Nimion," she began.

"What about him?"

"We'll have to involve him. I know it complicates things but we'll be in trouble if we don't do it. He knows the data store like the back of his hand, and it won't take him long to realise we've taken an Alda Five crystal. He'll then put two and two together and start asking questions."

"Oh dear. I didn't want to drag him into it."

"It's not *that* bad. He responds to trust. He'll go on and on about having a guilty face and not being able to keep secrets, and then he'll do it admirably. He can't even complain about having to keep things from his girlfriend, because he doesn't have one." She giggled. "I wonder if he asks his mother to lock him in a cellar during sciesha?"

"Don't make fun, Clemis. Someday we may need to rely on him for more than secrecy." Laura looked somewhat sad. "I didn't want him involved because history has a habit of repeating itself. I still blame myself for the death of his father."

"Corython? I thought Tralvar recruited him?"

"Tralvar chose him but I talked him into helping us. He was a lot like Nimion. More worldly, but with the same passion for his work." Laura smoothed her hair with a quick nervous gesture. "Anyway, enough of this. I'm going to make that call. And remember: whoever's there, we simply say I've had second thoughts about Aprival and you're going to negotiate with him. Not a word about the weapon."

"I'm not stupid."

"Have you decided how you're going to carry the blueprints?" Laura went on without pausing. "You can't walk around with them in your fist!"

"I've made myself a body belt," said Clemis lightly.

"And where did you get the inspiration for that? My memories?"

"No. Geffin's."

Laura managed a brief smile. "Clever girl. Get yourself ready, then. We're leaving as soon as Dena arrives."

The news from the spaceport was promising. A sphere could be readied for use immediately, as the service bay was free. Most of the Eldorian fleet was away collecting equipment for the planned manoeuvres. Jarras was in Treva and Trevone wasn't due in until afternoon. That left Nimion.

"I'll talk to him," Clemis promised. "I'll make him do as he's told."

Laura looked doubtful. "Just ensure the effect lingers, otherwise he'll be reading me the instant you've gone."

394

"Oh, Laura!" Clemis gave an exasperated sigh. "You don't still believe people are reading your thoughts all the time? Believe me, they aren't. Outside of the family I doubt if anyone's tried it in years."

"Because it's disrespectful?"

"Partly. But mostly because you're so difficult to read."

"That doesn't seem to have stopped *you*."

"I've had lots of practice. Others haven't. You might speak Celestrian like a native, mother mine, but you still have the typically splintered mindset of a nonconversant."

"Thanks," said Laura drily.

"It's true! And it's working in your favour now, so don't complain."

During the flitter ride to the spaceport, and after their arrival, Clemis was wonderfully calm. She spoke so sensibly to Nimion that there was very little left for Laura to add, other than a plea for his co-operation.

"Since she has your sanction, First Citizeness, I have no choice but to assist," Nimion responded unhappily. His slightly stilted manner, often the subject of amusement, seemed perfectly suited to the occasion. "Have you truly thought this through, Clemis? I know you like Aprival, but what of his companions? One little stun-gun won't be much protection."

I do believe he's sweet on her, thought Laura.

"They're not soldiers," Clemis replied earnestly. "I didn't learn much from Aprival but I do know that. They're just people."

"We have additional intelligence to support our decision," Laura volunteered. "But we won't impose that knowledge on you, Nimion."

He looked grateful. "Then if you'd come with me I'll find you a programme for Alda Five."

They followed him down one level to the data store, which was unattended.

"Now don't forget," Clemis emphasised, "everyone, even the ground crew, thinks I'm going to Tafret. I'll switch programmes once I'm in orbit. Then it'll be your job to see I'm not tracked."

"Understood." Nimion placed an aldacite crystal in a pouch and handed it to her. "This will take you as far as Alda Five's outermost moons. You'll then have to scan for the alien ship."

"I can't miss it, can I? It's big enough. Many thanks for this, Nimion: you're a treasure." She hugged him and he blushed. "Oh, and can you try to stop Trevone storming up to the akron in a jealous rage? It won't do any good if I'm not there."

"He won't do that. He'll get in a huff and take it out on me. He's very fond of you, Clemis."

"I know." She averted her gaze for a moment. "Tell him I'll try and get word to him."

"Come along, Clemis," Laura said briskly. "Time you were away."

In bright but chilly sunlight they walked to the maintenance block. There they were welcomed by Daphos, a contemporary of Clemis' from Space Tech, now working as a junior engineer.

"Laura said you'd prefer a sphere that wasn't earmarked for other duties. No sense in having to rush back, is there? This one was decommissioned

396

a year ago, but my friends and I have been restoring it and it's as good as new. We were going to use it ourselves, but now that you're having to carry out Laura's state visits your need's greater than ours. We'd like you to have it."

Clemis was surprised and grateful. "Oh, Daphos, that's wonderful of you!"

"And between trips we'll make sure no-one uses it," he added.

"I...er...might be away for a while."

"Doesn't matter! Do what you have to do. It's yours now." Daphos ushered them into the service bay. "We debated putting your name on the hull but decided it might be bad luck after what happened to Trevone's lovely new machine. He never did get it fixed, did he?"

"Er...no," replied Clemis, wondering how to change the subject without seeming impolite.

"Young man," said Laura, suddenly at her most imperious, "perhaps you'd organise some transport home for me. I don't want to be away from Idenion longer than I can help."

"I'll fly you there myself," Daphos said amiably.

Laura favoured him with a lofty smile. "I'm much obliged. I'll be with you as soon as I've given Clemis a final briefing."

Daphos took the hint and stepped outside.

"One last piece of advice?" Clemis inquired.

"Yes, though I find this difficult to say. Sooner or later you could be called on to use the dispersal engine in a battle situation. If and when that time comes I want you to act as decisively as you did yesterday. Mercy, pity and compassion are all very well, but the Eldorians would regard any such display as weakness. Therefore, be merciless. Try to think like an Eldorian. And good luck, Clemis."

"Thanks. I always knew you were still an Earther at heart."

Laura made a wry face. "I presume that's meant to be a compliment."

"Of course it is. Hasn't your mentality saved us twice already?"

"So people say. Well, let's hope your girlhood studies of my psyche are about to pay off."

Clemis looked slightly abashed. "Did I read you *that* much?"

"You did. Don't you remember how you followed me around when you were little? I'd come out of a daydream and there you'd be, staring and staring. If you'd paid Idenion half the attention you paid me, your personality would be vastly different today!"

Clemis laughed. "Poetry and philosophy were rather dull fare for a lively child. I preferred excitement, romance, adventure."

"It looks as if you've found your adventure." Laura was suddenly serious.

Clemis embraced her lovingly. "I'll be all right - I'm sure of it."

"You'll do your best for us." It was a statement, not a question.

"I promise." Clemis turned, hurried purposefully up the ramp and vanished into the sphere.

This story concludes in "The Stars Are Ours"
Part Two: Powerplay.

GLOSSARY

CAST OF CHARACTERS

<u>Celestrians:</u>

    Clemis - daughter of Idenion, adopted daughter of Laura
    Daphos - young technician
    Dena - Idenion's twin sister, wife to Tralvar
    Dessin - student activist
    Drusa - a healer
    Eleen - a cook
    Idenion - First Poet/First Citizen, married to Laura
    Jarras - a scientist, Tralvar's son in law
    Kalyx - Tralvar's son, an actor
    Kyrin - senior relayist
    Lann - Guildmaster of music at Tivenne
    Linni - a student, friend of Dessin
    Lydion - weathershield operator
    Nefyrra - Tralvar's daughter, custodian of the Lyricon
    Nimion - communications technician
    Ninfi - mother of Kalyx
    Plinn - tutor at Treva Academy of Space Science
    Raan - student, friend of Dessin and Linni
    Tonor - trainee weathershield operator
    Tralvar - genius inventor, ex First Citizen
    Trevone - son of Nefyrra and Jarras, enamoured of Clemis
    Tuhallak - First Tech of Scapirion

Zanna - tutor at Treva Academy of Space Science

Other Species:

Eldorians:

Betrick - communications technician
Casil - hot-headed recruit
Escir - Army doctor, ex-physician to the Emperor
Geffin - investigative reporter
Grenthap - general in charge of the Symerid campaign
Gruna - old soldier
Habbon - elderly professor
Heggs - thuggish soldier, ex-prizefighter
Hyni - drummer boy
Klonid - communications technician
Mallina - a prostitute, loved by Lydion
Navin - young soldier, Casil's friend
Neelah - prostitute/singer
Pervain - devious ambassador to Celestra
Prahina - circus performer, lurlan-tamer
Ritax - circus performer
Stibon - soldier, friend of Varn
Tildy - Mallina's friend, another prostitute
Tovo - Pervain's secretary
Varn - soldier
Ymer - communications technician
Zoza - circus performer

Narvellans:
Axmiol tyl Thuuvin - Narvellan leader in exile
Sijek tyl Thuuvin neph-khet - Axmiol's
beloved, a synaesthete, captive of the Eldorians

Earthers:
Barney Cresset - guitarist at the Firelight Club
Dave - an eco-warrior
Laura Meredith, nee Gilcoyne - a singer, now
First Citizeness of Celestra
Jack (Moffat) - a student, Mrs. Moffat's nephew
Margaret Moffat - Nathaniel Gilcoyne's ex-
housekeeper
Caitlin Stretton - Jimmy's mother
Jimmy Stretton - eco-warrior, Laura's ex-
boyfriend

Unknown Origin:
Aprival - amnesiac messenger

Empire of Miiyat:
Mror - emissary

Draldir:
extinct race, enemies of Celestra

PLACE NAMES

Akron - administration centre and ruler's home

Alda - Celestra's sun

Alda Mexa - Celestra's capital, City of the Sun

Atris - city to the north

Corayn - centre for herbs and medicines

Dral - dead planet: was once home to the Draldir

Eldor - home planet to the Eldorian Empire, 1200 light years from Celestra

Ilonna - a ghost town

Lake Holpen - beauty spot near Alda Mexa

Lisir - river which runs through Alda Mexa

Lyricon - cherished theatre, situated in Alda Mexa

Miiyat - planetary empire of cat-like creatures

Myrma - humid planet near Celestra

Nevri - the Scapirians' name for Celestra – "mother"

Nova City - a province of Eldor

Patieron City - a province of Eldor

Scapirion - town on the south polar continent with reclusive inhabitants

Symerid - Sol

Symerid Three - Earth

Tafret - town where young relayists are sent for training

Tivenne - village near Alda Mexa

Treva - town to north-east of Alda Mexa, industrial heart of Celestra

Virda - fishing village, home to Kyrin

Earth:

Cheveney - Laura's village
Wickens Clump - wood where UFO's have been sighted
Windbourne - Nathaniel's house

ALIEN TERMS

Aldacite - versatile crystal used in logic systems etc.
Astal/Astallen - unit of time, equivalent to six minutes
Auxet - Eldorian bugle
Dispersal Engine - superweapon created by Tralvar
Dreamdust - Eldorian hallucinogenic drug
Firi - filmy material worn by dancers, etc.
Ild/Ilden - unit of time equivalent to just under 50 minutes - (eight astallen): there are 30 ilden in one day
Isk - unit of time equivalent to a second. Used only in stellar navigation and music
Khin - Eldorian recreational drug
Kyffu - waterfowl
Liman - milky drink native to Celestra
Lirrt - Eldorian "pain disc" employed by circus performers
Lurlan - ferocious Eldorian beast used in arena sports
Octal - a period of eight days

Patierades - rival faction in Eldor's civil war

Patierons - the most powerful ruling family on Eldor

Peisistrata - Celestrian festival

Pilif - small succulent yellow fruit

Relayists - telepaths who circulate news and conduct commerce

Resnay - strong alcoholic drink

Retracer - a device for recording peoples' memories

Scolia - Celestrian orchestra

Sciesha - mating fever

Scieshanar - medallion, Celestrian, denoting one's ancestry

Silmos/Silmi - a measurement of distance, equal to one-third of a mile

Span - Celestrian month

Sphere - Celestrian spacecraft

Starfire - powerful stimulant (proscribed substance)

Strelsis - stringed instrument in various sizes

Theridolyte - a strengthened and stabilised version of therite, used in the construction of spheres

Therite - a mineral, unstable when processed, used for quarrying and later for weapons

Total Unity - the telepathic element of the sex act

Transposal - the Celestrian hyperdrive

Transposer - hyperspace transmitter/receiver

Ylur - coarse material from which overalls are made

Ytil - material normally used for garments

Zarf - a mythical Celestrian beast with a voracious sexual appetite

Zirid - keyboard instrument

Zytl - Eldorian measurement of time equivalent to one minute